A DANCE OF BLADES

SHADOWDANCE: BOOK 2

DAVID DALGLISH

orbit

www.orbitbooks.net

Orbit
Hachette Book Group
237 Park Avenue, New York, NY 10017
HachetteBookGroup.com

First Edition: November 2013

Orbit is an imprint of Hachette Book Group, Inc. The Orbit name and logo are trademarks of Little, Brown Book Group Limited.

The Hachette Speakers Bureau provides a wide range of authors for speaking events. To find out more, go to www.hachettespeakersbureau.com or call (866) 376-6591.

The publisher is not responsible for websites (or their content) that are not owned by the publisher.

The characters and events in this book are fictitious. Any similarity to real persons, living or dead, is coincidental and not intended by the author.

Library of Congress Cataloging-in-Publication Data
Dalglish, David.
  A Dance of Blades / David Dalglish. — First edition.
    pages cm. — (Shadowdance ; Book 2)
  ISBN 978-0-316-24249-3 (hardcover) — ISBN 978-1-4789-7909-8 (audio download) — ISBN 978-0-316-24248-6 (ebook) 1. Fantasy fiction. 2. War stories. I. Title.
  PS3604.A376D36 2013
  813'.6—dc23
                            2013019019

10 9 8 7 6 5 4 3 2 1

RRD-C

Printed in the United States of America

*For Dad, for insisting Haern
had more to his story than I first told.*

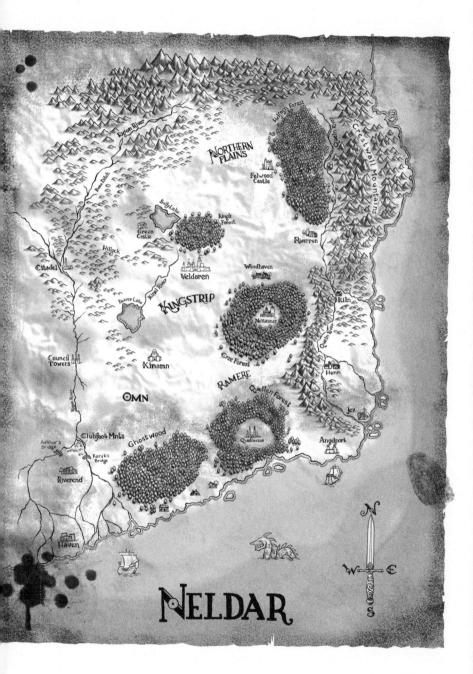

NELDAR

CHAPTER

1

Haern watched the ropes fly over the wall, heavy weights on their ends. They clacked against the stone, then settled on the street. The ropes looked like brown snakes in the pale moonlight, appropriately enough given the Serpent Guild controlled them.

For several minutes, nothing. Haern shifted under his well-worn cloaks, his exposed hand shivering in the cold while holding an empty bottle. He kept his hood low, and he bobbed his head as if sleeping. When the first Serpent entered the alley from the street, Haern spotted him with ease. The man looked young for such a task, but then two older men arrived, their hands and faces scarred from the brutal life they led. Deep green cloaks fluttered behind them as they rushed past the houses and to the wall where the ropes hung like vines. They tugged each rope twice, giving their signal. Then the older ones grabbed a rope while the younger looped them about a carved inset in the aged stone wall, then tied the weighted ends together.

"Quick and quiet," he heard one of the elder whisper to the younger. "Don't let the crate make a sound when it lands, and the gods help you if you drop it."

Haern let his head bob lower. The three were to his right, little more than twenty feet away. Already he knew their skill was laughable if they had not yet noticed his presence. His right eye peeked from under his hood, his neck twisting slightly to give him a better view. Another Serpent appeared from outside the city, climbing atop the wall and motioning down to the others. Their arm muscles bulging, the older two began pulling on the ropes. Meanwhile the younger steadily took in the slack so it wouldn't get in their way.

Haern coughed as the crate reached the top of the wall. This time the younger heard, and he tensed as if expecting to be shot with an arrow.

"Someone's watching," he whispered to the others.

Haern leaned back, the cloaks hiding his grin. About damn time. He let the bottle roll from his limp hand, the sound of glass on stone grating in the silence.

"Just a drunk," said one of them. "Go chase him off."

Haern heard the soft sound of a blade scraping against leather, most likely the young one's belt.

"Get out of here," said the Serpent.

Haern let out a loud, obnoxious snore. A boot kicked his side, but it was weak, hesitant. He shuddered as if waking from a dream.

"Why...why you kick me?" he asked, his hood still low. He had to time it just right, at the exact moment the crate touched ground.

"Beat it!" hissed the young thief. "Now, or I'll gut you!"

Haern looked up into his eyes. He knew shadows danced

across his face, but his eyes...the man clearly saw his eyes. His dagger dipped in his hand, and he took a step back. Haern's drunken persona had vanished as if it had never been. No defeat, no inherent feeling of lowliness or shame. Only a calm stare that promised death. As the crate softly thumped to the ground, Haern stood, his intricate gray cloaks falling aside to reveal the two swords sheathed at his hips.

"Shit, it's him!" the thief screamed, turning to run.

Haern felt contempt ripple through him. Such poor training...did the guilds let anyone in now? He took the young man down, making sure no hit was lethal. He needed a message delivered.

"Who?" asked one, turning at the cry.

Haern cut his throat before he could draw his blade. The other yelped and stepped back. His dagger parried the first of Haern's stabs, but he had no concept of positioning. Haern smacked the dagger twice to the right, then slipped his left sword into his belly and twisted. As the thief bled out, Haern looked to the Serpent atop the wall.

"Care to join the fun?" he asked, yanking out his blade and letting the blood drip to the street. "I'm out of players."

Two daggers whirled down at him. He sidestepped one and smacked away the other. Hoping to provoke the man further, Haern kicked the crate. With no other option, the thief turned and fled back down the wall on the other side. Disappointed, Haern sheathed a sword and used the other to pry open the crate. With a loud creak the top came off, revealing three burlap sacks within. He dipped a hand in one, and it came out dripping with gold coins, each one clearly marked with the sigil of the Gemcroft family.

Interesting.

"Please," he heard the young thief beg. He bled from cuts

on his arms and legs, most certainly painful, but nothing life-threatening. The worst Haern had done was hamstring him to prevent him from fleeing. "Please, don't kill me. I can't, I can't..."

Haern slung all three bags over his shoulder. With his free hand he pressed the tip of his sword against the young man's throat.

"They'll want to know why you lived," he said.

The man had no response to that, only a pathetic sniffle. Haern shook his head. How far the Serpent Guild had fallen... but all the guilds had fallen since that bloody night five years ago. Thren Felhorn, the legend, had failed in his coup, bringing doom upon the underworld. Thren... his father...

"Tell them you have a message," Haern said. "Tell them I'm watching."

"Who?"

In response Haern took his sword and dipped it in the man's blood.

"They'll know who," he said before vanishing, leaving only a single eye drawn in the dirt as his message, blood for its ink, a sword its quill.

He didn't go far. He had to lug the bags to the rooftops one at a time, but once he was up high his urgency dwindled. The rooftops were his home, had been for years. Following the main road west, he reached the inner markets, still silent and empty. Plunking down the bags, he lay with his eyes closed and waited.

He woke to the sounds of trade. Hunger stirred in his belly, but he ignored it. Hunger, like loneliness and pain, had become a constant companion. He wouldn't call it friend, though.

"May you go to better hands," Haern said to the first sack of gold before stabbing its side. Coins spilled, and he hurled them like rain to the packed streets. Without pause he cut the second and third, flinging them to the suddenly ravenous crowd. They dove and fought as the gold rolled along, bouncing off bodies and plinking into various wooden stalls. Only a few bothered to look up, those who were lame or old and dared not fight the crowd.

"The Watcher!" someone cried. "The Watcher is here!"

The cry put a smile on his lips as Haern fled south, having not kept a single coin.

It had taken five years, but at last Alyssa Gemcroft understood her late father's paranoia. The meal placed before her smelled delicious, spiced pork intermixed with baked apples, but her appetite remained dormant.

"I can have one of the servants taste it, if you'd like," said her closest family advisor, a man named Bertram who had loyally served her father. "I'll even do so myself."

"No," she said, brushing errant strands of her red hair back and tucking them behind her left ear. "That's not necessary. I can afford to skip a meal."

Bertram frowned, and she hated the way he looked at her— like a doting grandfather, or a worried teacher. Just the night before, two servants had died eating their daily rations. Though she'd replaced much of the mansion's food, as well as executed those she thought responsible, the memory lingered in Alyssa's mind. The way the two had retched, their faces turning a horrific shade of purple...

She snapped her fingers, and the many waiting servants rushed to clear the trays away. Despite the rumble in her belly, she felt better with the food gone. At least now she could think without fear of convulsing to death because of some strange toxin. Bertram motioned to a chair beside her, and she gave him permission to sit.

"I know these are not peaceful times," he said, "but we cannot allow fear to control our lives. That is a victory you know the thief guilds have longed for."

"We're approaching the fifth anniversary of the Bloody Kensgold," Alyssa said, referring to a gathering of the Trifect, the three wealthiest families of merchants, nobles, and power brokers in all of Dezrel. On that night Thren Felhorn had led an uprising of thief guilds against the Trifect, burning down one of their mansions and attempting to annihilate their leaders. He'd failed, and his guild had broken down to a fraction of its former size. On that night Alyssa had assumed control after the death of her father, victim to an arrow as they'd fought to protect their home.

"I know," Bertram said. "Is that what distracts you so? Leon and Laurie have both agreed to delay another Kensgold until this dangerous business is over with."

"And when will that be?" she asked as another servant arrived with a silver cup of wine. "I hide here in my mansion, fearful of my food and scared of every shadow in my bedroom. We cannot defeat the guilds, Bertram. We've broken them, fractured many to pieces, but it's like smashing a puddle with a club. They all come back together, under new names, new leaders."

"The end is approaching," Bertram said. "This is Thren's war, and he champions it with the last of his strength. But he is not so strong, not so young. His Spider Guild is far from the force it used to be. In time the other guilds will see reason and turn against him. Until then, we have only one choice left before us, and that is to endure."

Alyssa closed her eyes and inhaled the scent of the wine. For a moment she wondered if it was poisoned, but she fought the paranoia down. She would not sacrifice such a simple pleasure. She couldn't give the rogues that much of a victory.

Still, when she drank, it was a small sip.

"You told me much the same after the Kensgold," she said, setting down the cup. "As you have every year for the past five. The mercenaries have bled us dry. Our mines to the north no longer produce the yields they were renowned for. The king is too frightened to help us. How long until we eat in rags, without coin for servants and wood for fires?"

"We are on the defensive," Bertram said, accepting his own cup of wine. "Such is our fate for being a large target. But the bloodshed has slowed, you know that as well as I. Be patient. Let us bleed them as they bleed us. The last thing we want is to inflame their passions while we still appear weak and leaderless."

Alyssa felt anger flare in her chest, not only at the insult, but also at its damning familiarity.

"Leaderless?" she asked. "I have protected the Gemcroft name for five years of shadow wars. I've brokered trade agreements, organized mercenaries, bribed nobles, and done everything as well as my father ever did, yet we are *leaderless*? Why is that, Bertram?"

Bertram endured the rant without a shred of emotion on his face, and that only infuriated Alyssa further. Again she felt like a schoolchild before her teacher, and part of her wondered if that was exactly how her advisor viewed her.

"I say this only because the rest of Dezrel believes it," he said when she was finished. "You have no husband, and the only heir to the Gemcroft name is a bastard of unknown heritage."

"Don't talk about Nathaniel that way," she said, her voice turning cold. "Don't you dare speak ill of my son."

Bertram raised his hands and spread his palms.

"I meant no offense, milady. Nathaniel is a good child, smart too. But a lady of your station should be partnered with someone equally influential. You've had many suitors; surely you've taken a liking to one of them?"

Alyssa took another sip of wine, her eyes glancing up at the shadowy corners of the dining hall.

"Leave me," she said. "All of you. We'll speak of this another time."

Bertram stood, bowed, and followed the servants out.

"Come down, Zusa," she told the ceiling. "You know you're always welcome at my table. There's no need for you to skulk and hide."

Clinging like a spider to the wall, Zusa smiled down at her. With deceptive ease she let go, falling headfirst toward the carpet. A deft twist of her arms, a tuck of her knees, and she landed gracefully on her feet, her long cloak billowing behind her. Instead of any normal outfit she wore long strips of cloth wrapped around her body, hiding every inch of skin. Except for above her neck, Alyssa was still pleased to see. Zusa had once belonged to a strict order of Karak, the dark god. Upon her willful exile Zusa had cast aside the cloth from her face, revealing her stunning looks and her beautiful black hair, which she kept cropped short around her neck. Two daggers hung from her belt, wickedly sharp.

"Let me be the one in the shadows," Zusa said, smiling. "That way you are safe, for no assassin can hide beside me."

Alyssa gestured for her friend to sit. Zusa refused, but Alyssa took no offense. It was just one of the skilled lady's many quirks. The woman had rescued her years before from an attempt by a former lover to take over her family line, and then helped protect her estate from Thren's plans. She owed her life to Zusa, so if Zusa wanted to stand instead of sit, she was more than welcome.

"Did you hear everything?" Alyssa asked.

"Everything of worth. The old man is scared. He tries to be the rock in a storm, to survive by doing nothing until it passes."

"Sometimes a sound strategy."

Zusa smirked. "This storm will not pass, not without action. Not with *his* cowardly action. You know what Bertram wants. He wants you bedded and yoked to another man. Then your womanly passions may be safely ignored, and he can rule through your husband."

"Bertram has no desire for power."

Zusa lifted an eyebrow. "Can you know for sure? He is old, but not dead."

Alyssa sighed and drained her cup.

"What should I do?" she asked. She felt tired, lost. She badly missed her son. She'd sent Nathaniel north to Felwood Castle, to be fostered by Lord John Gandrem. John was a good man, and a good friend of the family. More important, he was far away from Veldaren and its guilds of thieves. At least there Nathaniel was safe, and the training he received would help him later in life.

"Bertram's question... are there any you have taken a fancy to?" Zusa asked.

Alyssa shrugged.

"Mark Tullen was attractive, though his station is probably lower than Bertram would prefer. At least he was willing to talk to me instead of staring down my blouse. Also, that noble who runs our mines, Arthur something..."

"Hadfield," Zusa said.

"That's right. He's pleasant enough, and not ugly... little distant, though. Guess that's just a product of being older."

"The older, the less likely to cavort with other women."

"He's more than welcome to," Alyssa said. She stood and turned away, trying to voice a silent fear she'd held on to for years, a fear that had strangled her relationships and kept her unmarried. "But any child we have... that is who will become the Gemcroft heir. Too many will shove Nathaniel aside, deem him unfit, unworthy. I can't do that to him, Zusa. I can't deny him his right. He's my firstborn."

She felt Zusa's arms slip around her. Startled by the uncommon display of emotion, she accepted the hug.

"If your son is strong, he will claim what is his, no matter what the world tries," she said. "Do not be afraid."

"Thank you," Alyssa said, pulling back and smiling. "What would I do without you?"

"May we never find out," Zusa said, bowing low.

Alyssa waved her off, then retreated to her private chambers. She stared out the thick glass window, beyond her mansion's great walls, to the city of Veldaren. She found herself hating the city, hating every dark corner and crevice. Always it conspired against her, waiting with poison and dagger to...

No. She had to stop thinking like that. She had to stop letting the thief guilds control every aspect of her life through force and fear. So she sat at her desk, pulled out an inkwell and a piece of parchment, and paused. She'd sent Nathaniel away to protect him, to be fostered with a good family. Not so long ago her father had done the same with her, and she remembered her anger, her loneliness, and her feelings of betrayal. Gods help her, she'd even sent Nathaniel to the same person she'd been sent to. Once more she understood her father in a way she never had before. He'd hidden her because he loved her, not to get her out of the way as she'd once thought.

Still, how angry she'd been when she returned...

No, she would not let history repeat itself. Her decision made, she dipped the quill in the ink and began writing.

My dear Lord Tullen, she began. *I have a request for you involving my son, Nathaniel...*

CHAPTER

2

Biggs kept watch at the door while the rest of the Hawk Guild cleared away the bodies.

"How many will be coming?" asked one as he wrapped a body in its dark gray cloak.

"Depends," said Biggs.

"On what?"

Biggs rolled his eyes. "On who is coming. If it's Veliana, only a handful. If it's Garrick, though...maybe twenty."

The other thief's face twitched at that. There were only ten of them weaving through the empty tables and quiet furnaces of the smith's workplace.

"So what do we do if it's him?"

Biggs turned, grabbed his shirt, and yanked him close.

"I didn't betray my guild and execute my friends so you can turn tail and run," he said. His knife was in his hand, and he pressed it against the shaking thief's belly. "We hide, and we kill. You know how to do that, right?"

Biggs shoved him away and turned back to the door. They still had ten minutes until the expected rendezvous, but it wouldn't surprise him if either Garrick or Veliana showed up early. He'd worked the deal himself, the supposed purchasing of a large amount of illegal leaf from a nonexistent merchant from the south. The leaf was known as the Violet, and many nobles had taken a fancy to it down south in Angelport. Reselling it would bring in an absurd amount of money, meaning Biggs's deal would have been the best score for the ailing Ash Guild in over a year. And now his former guildmates lay dead, and once their leaders fell, Biggs knew he would take control. The Hawks' guildleader, Kadish Vel, had promised it.

"Into position," said the highest-ranking member of the Hawks present, a thin man named Kenny, whose nasal voice annoyed Biggs to no end. "And for the love of the gods, keep it quiet."

Kenny slid beside Biggs and glanced up and down the dark streets.

"You sure they're coming?" he asked.

"I know what I'm doing," Biggs said, glaring. "A deal this big needs one of the two leaders to show. I hope it's Garrick, but it'll probably be Veliana. Not a bad thing, though. She's the scary one, could kill Garrick in a clean fight, and even easier in a dirty one. Not sure why she hasn't taken control yet, but I ain't giving her time to change her mind. If she's the one, you make sure you get her first."

Kenny lifted his small custom crossbow and winked.

"I've shot the nipple off a whore at twenty yards," he said.

"Bastard. What'd she do to you?"

Kenny laughed. "After that? Everything I asked."

Biggs chuckled despite himself and their need for quiet.

"Remind me to never—"

He stopped, for he heard a scream from the other side of the building.

"What the fuck?" asked Kenny, spinning about. "The Ash send more scouts?"

"Doubt it," said Biggs. "Watch the door. I'll take care of this."

He tightened his grip on his dagger and ran through a maze of anvils and fire pits. While the full moon kept the streets bright, the smithy was dark and confusing, with only a fraction of the pale light streaming in through windows smeared with dirt and soot. Briggs heard a second scream, and when he turned toward it he smacked his knee into the edge of an anvil. He sucked his breath in through his teeth and tried to ignore the pain.

"What's going on?" he asked, deciding stealth and silence were pointless with the Hawks howling bloody murder. He heard the sound of scuffling, then the rattling of weaponry. When he reached the place where the shop opened up into various displays of blades, hilts, and machinery, he stopped. There was another door in the back, and it was open. Moonlight shone through, falling upon bodies that lay crumpled about. At first Biggs thought them Ash guildmembers, but then he saw their brown cloaks and knew otherwise. Standing over them was a man.

"Who the fuck are you?" asked Biggs.

The man looked up and smiled. His skin was dark, and his long hair darker. He wore the red robes of a wizard, though he held a dagger in his hand instead of a staff. Blood dripped from its blade. Covering his features was a mask of gray cloth pulled tightly across his face, with two large slits to allow sight. His brown eyes sparkled with amusement.

"I have no name," said the intruder with blood on his hands. "But if Karak asks who sent you to his Abyss, tell him the Council's reaper, the outcast, or the dark man in red."

He was chuckling, and the sound raised the hairs on the back of Biggs's neck.

"You're crazy," he said. "You know who you just killed? You'll have the fury of the Hawk Guild come down on you."

He was blustering, of course. He'd made a quick count of the bodies, and knew that only two remained alive in the smithy besides him and Kenny. Still, he couldn't act weak. It took all his concentration to keep the dagger from shaking in his hand.

The stranger made a flicking motion, flinging tiny globs of blood. Biggs swore as they flecked across his shirt and pants.

"They have to know I exist first," he said, snapping his fingers.

The blood caught fire, burning as if it were lamp oil. The heat came sudden and intense. Biggs fought an impulse to drop and roll. Magic fire would not be snuffed out so easily. As he felt his flesh burn he lunged, his dagger aiming for the stranger's chest. Before he could reach it the man fled, still laughing, still mocking. Instead of chasing, Biggs turned and ran for the other entrance.

"Kenny!" he shouted. "Get your ass back…"

It seemed his own shadow tripped him. There was no other way to describe the strange sight and sensation. His head cracked against an anvil on the way down, and the sudden pain disoriented him beyond all measure. His stomach heaved, and he thought he would vomit. When he got to his feet he bolted, not knowing if he was going the right way. He didn't care. He had to move; he had to escape that terrible man who could burn blood with a snap of his fingers.

"Gods!" cried Kenny as Biggs plowed right into him. Biggs clutched him to remain standing, and this time he did vomit. The mess splattered across Kenny's shoes, but to Kenny's credit he didn't bat an eye.

"Kill him," Biggs said, turning and pointing.

The stranger approached, his dagger still in hand.

"You have but a few left," he said as the blood upon his blade burned like embers fresh from a hearth. The light danced across his masked face, casting an orange haze over the gray. Biggs stepped back, doing his best to ignore the pain of his burns and the throbbing of his head.

"Think we need numbers to kill you?" asked Kenny. "All we need is me."

He lifted his crossbow and fired. The bolt bounced off the stranger's skin as if it were made of stone.

"A spellcaster?" said Kenny. "Damn it, Biggs, what shit did you get us into?"

The man's grin spread, but he didn't laugh. It seemed the time for laughter was over. A gleam was in his eye, like that of a predator ready to pounce upon its prey. From either side a thief rushed from his hiding place. Kenny laughed, and Biggs realized it had been a trap for the intruder, prepared while he ran headlong like a fool to see the reason for the commotion. The two thieves stabbed, but their daggers struck only cloth. The stranger twisted and fell, avoiding both blows. When he hit the ground, his hands became a blur of strange motions. An explosion of fire blinded Biggs in the darkness, and then he heard the screams.

"Don't worry," Kenny said as Biggs took a step forward, doing his best to ignore the charred corpses before him. "I keep this baby for special occasions like this."

Biggs saw him pull a bolt from one of his many pockets, its

tip glistening with silver. The stranger rolled along the floor until safely hidden behind a giant hearth. Kenny took a wide step around, trying to get a clear shot.

"What are they paying you for?" Kenny asked. "Wizards aren't supposed to get involved with normal people, and they sure as shit aren't supposed to hire out as assassins. What's your game?"

"No game." Biggs kept close to Kenny, standing opposite his trigger arm and keeping his dagger ready in case the stranger charged. "And I am no wizard."

"Bullshit you're not," Kenny said. "What's this to you?"

Another sidestep, slow and careful. Just as Kenny prepared his crossbow, so too could the stranger be preparing a spell.

"This is a game, an amusement, a moment of enjoyment, a time of laughter..."

"Cut the shit. What's your name, and your price?"

"Out of everything, you ask name and price?" the stranger asked, suddenly stepping from the shadows and into their line of sight.

The bow fired. Biggs saw Kenny shift it to the side just the slightest amount, as if anticipating a dodge. None came. The stranger let the bolt hit him, and it pierced his shoulder just below his collarbone. He gasped at the pain, leaned forward, and then to Biggs's horror steadied himself and stood erect.

"Name? Price? I have neither."

"Reload!" Biggs shouted, stepping between them and holding his dagger out. Fire danced in the stranger's eyes, then to his hands. Knowing he had to buy his ally time, Biggs let out a curse and dashed in, swinging for the man's neck. He never made it. The fire consumed his clothes, its heat beyond anything he'd ever felt. His legs refused to obey. As he collapsed he looked back, hoping Kenny would at least kill the bastard who'd done him in, but of course the rogue was long gone, running like the intelligent coward he was.

"You died for nothing," he heard the stranger say as the pain vanished amid a wave of darkness. His voice echoed in the chambers of Biggs's mind, slowly fading, slowly dying.

"Nothing..."

Veliana led them down the alleyway, her daggers sheathed at her hips. Her hands never strayed far from their handles. Something about this meeting felt worrisome. Perhaps it was the great amount of coin about to change hands. Ever since James Beren's death, things had gone poorly for the Ash Guild. James had been more than their leader: he'd been a sign of stability during the chaos and bloodshed. He'd died defying Thren Felhorn, and while in a nobler world that might have meant something, in theirs it had nearly brought about the guild's dissolution.

"Hurry," she whispered, ushering the rest of her guildmates along. They were at the very edge of their pitifully small territory. The last thing she needed was an ambush. Even if they fought it off, the delay might be enough to disrupt their sale. They were supposed to meet a wealthy, and eccentric, merchant from Angelport. All it'd take was a few minutes of fret and worry before he took his things and left.

Assuming the men she'd sent in advance let the merchant leave.

They curved through the streets, which narrowed because of the stalls that sprang up along the sides. They were passing many tanneries and smithies, and their furnaces seemed to coat the stone street with a thin, ever-present layer of ash. Almost there. She stopped at an intersection with a main road leading toward the castle, looked about for patrols, and continued when she saw none. The sky was clear and bright, but still the chill seeped through her clothes and into her skin. She hated winter. It made her hurry, made her spend only four seconds checking a turn when she should have spent five. If there was anything she was certain of, it was that when she was buried, the ground would be cold and hard. Assuming she was buried at all. Given her life, even that was far from a given.

"We're here," she said. A quick set of instructions sent two around to the other side, and then the remaining six followed her through the main door. She let one of her guildmembers, Pryor, go first, just in case there was a trap. When she heard him gasp, she thought he'd found one, and she drew her daggers. But instead she heard her name.

"Vel?"

She followed Pryor in and surveyed the area.

A man waited for them. He sat atop a large crate, presumably the leaf for the deal. His body was bent over as if greatly burdened. He wore red robes stained with ash and blood. His skin was dark, and his hair darker. His shoulder was bleeding, but only a little. In one hand he held a dagger, in the other a long piece of gray cloth. At his feet was a bloody crossbow bolt. When he lifted his head, she stared into his brown eyes and saw a combination of fury and hopelessness that frightened her. He was handsome, but she felt no attraction. How could she, seeing a gaze like that?

All around him, burned to ash and bone, were bodies.

"What is going on?" she asked, stunned by the sight.

"You were betrayed," said the strange man. "One of your own helped kill the others so they might prepare an ambush."

"Who?" Veliana asked.

The man slowly shook his head.

"This is my time to speak," he said. "Ask your questions

when I am done, for I need your ears listening and your mind open. I do not know who prepared your betrayal, but I am sure they are one of the dead at my feet. They are ash now, a fitting end given the name of your guild. Think now on what you see. I handled what seven men of yours could not. Whereas they died, betrayed, I came and killed the betrayers. I am alone, woman. Now ask yourself, what use might I be to you? Surely I am worth the seven that died."

"He's lying," said Pryor. "He killed them all! Greg, Biggs, Brendan...he killed them!"

The man shook his head, and his shoulders sagged further.

"Don't make a fool of yourself. Fools have a way of dying around me."

Veliana cried out for Pryor to stop, but it was too late. He flung a dagger at the stranger, who avoided the hasty throw by a simple tilt of his head. His retaliation came swiftly as he hurled his own dagger. It pierced a lung as it embedded itself in Pryor's chest. The rest of the Ash Guild prepared to attack, but Veliana snapped at them to remain back.

"Who are you?" she asked. "What is your name?"

For a moment his look shifted, and she saw an incredible sadness lurking behind those eyes. He lifted the gray cloth and let it unfurl from his hand, revealing the eyeholes.

"My real name is lost," he said. "For it was banished from me by a power I cannot challenge. I have only the name they left me. I am Death, and this is my mask."

And then he smiled, and she decided that just maybe she could find him attractive.

"You'd start as the lowest rank," she told him. "You'd receive no special treatment, no favors, and this is only if Garrick accepts you in the first place. That acceptable?"

He nodded. A quick word from her, and the Ash members

hurried forward to grab the crate. "Death" stepped aside, and he laughed when he saw what they were to do.

"The leaf inside is fake," he said. "Did you really think the Hawks would bring a real crate of Violet to an ambush?"

Veliana had to see for herself, and she held back glaring at the stranger. After they'd pried open the crate, she reached inside, grabbed a single leaf, and popped it into her mouth. She bit down, then spit it right back out.

"Damn it," she said, having received little more than the bland taste of a normal leaf. "Gods damn it all. Garrick's going to be pissed."

The stranger shrugged. "Then he'll be pissed. At least it confirms the ambush, yes?"

Veliana chewed her lip as she thought of what exactly she would tell Garrick Lowe, their new guildmaster. He wouldn't be too thrilled with the loss of men, and even more so about the faked merchandise. As for this Death and his mask…

She slipped closer. She wanted to understand him, his motives. He might be part of a trap, or a disaster she was blindly bringing into their guild. The blame would all fall on her.

"Don't betray me," she whispered to him as the rest hauled off the crate. "I don't care how strong you think you are, I've fought stronger, I've survived better. You walk into this willingly, but the only way you walk out is dead. Do you understand me?"

He tied the cloth over his face, and through the holes in the mask winked at her.

"The only way I leave will be as your guildmaster," he said.

Because of the mask she could not see if he smiled, or search his features for tells. In the end she decided it didn't matter.

"Come with me," she said. "You're bound to make waves,

so I think it best Garrick meet with you now...assuming he trusts you enough to be in the same room."

He moved, faster than she'd thought possible. His left hand wrapped around her waist. His right grabbed her wrist, and he pulled her close. She tried to draw her dagger, but he held her tight. Their eyes locked on one another's.

"You were brave enough to come this close," he said, his voice nearly a whisper. "And even in my arms you do not tremble. I will remember that. Tell me, woman, what is *your* name?"

"Veliana," she said.

He let her go. She slapped him, and he straightened his mask.

"Deserved, and well worth it," he said. "Lead on, Veliana. I wish to see your guildmaster."

The Ash Guild had moved many times because of their weak status and constant war with the rest of the guilds. Only recently had they made peace with most, though the Hawk Guild still preyed heavily upon them. If not for this...Death... Veliana knew there was a good chance she'd be a corpse.

Assuming he wasn't part of a trap.

Their current base was in the confines of a small merchant guild, one desperate enough for coin that they'd accepted Garrick's bribes. As lairs went it wasn't the most secretive, but at least it was warm in the winter months, and moderately well furnished. Veliana led her men through a side door. Four steps down they stopped at a basement door with a small lamp burning at either side. She frowned at the lack of guards. No doubt they were on the inside. Garrick liked having his protectors there with him at all times, even if it wasn't safer. They should have been out in the cold, keeping watch so they could lock and bar the door should they notice trouble coming.

But of course the door was locked and barred anyway when she tried to open it. Rolling her eyes, she knocked twice, then once. She heard the scraping of metal, and then a slit opened to reveal a bloodshot pair of eyes.

"Say the pass," said the guard.

"Veliana. Now open the damn door."

There was a password, of course. Three, even, in case she needed to alert those inside to a hidden threat. But she was in no mood, and she knew the guard on the other side was too spineless to refuse her entrance. The slit closed, and as they heard a loud thumping, Death chuckled behind her.

"Your professionalism is astounding," he said. "I know I came with few expectations, but I still feel them failing to be met."

"Quiet," she said. "And stay here. I'll need to introduce you to Garrick first."

She paused and gave him a glance. The mask hid his face, but she couldn't fight off the feeling he was smirking at her.

"Just how should I introduce you, anyway?" she asked.

"I told you, I have no name."

"That makes for a poor introduction. Should I call you Death? It's a little over the top, but I've heard worse."

"Death might be too great a mantle for me to wear," said the man. "But I can bear no name for the curse given me. All I have is my mask. Perhaps you can call me that."

The door opened and she stepped inside. A guard stood at either side, dagger drawn. The room was well lit with many lanterns. At one end were tables covered with maps and documents, and a locked chest underneath for guild funds. At the other were blankets, pillows, and illegal means of comfort. Amid the meager luxury sat Garrick, his eyes glazed from the substance he smoked through a short pipe. Several other men lay scattered about him, their senses just as dull from the smoke and liquor.

"Veliana!" Garrick said, standing. "Did the trade go through as…"

He stopped as Veliana's guest shoved his way inside, so fast that he was beside her before the guards could react. He made no threatening motion, only stayed at her side. With an elaborate bow he greeted the guildmaster.

"Mighty Garrick, how the shadows tremble when I mention your name," he said, and Veliana felt anger burn inside her at the obvious sarcasm. Garrick, however, seemed oblivious to it. Instead he appeared worried by the newcomer's strange attire and sudden entrance. He stepped back and ran a hand through his long brown hair, a sign Veliana knew meant he was nervous.

"And who are you?" he asked. "A friend of Veliana's?"

"This is…Death's Mask," she said. "He helped us tonight, perhaps saved many lives. We've been betrayed, Garrick. When we…"

"Do you still have the leaf?" Garrick interrupted.

"I…yes, we do."

"Good, good," said Garrick. He sat back down on the cushions, drew his dagger, and held it while he listened. "Now what is this betrayal you speak of? And tell me again"—he made a sound like a cross between a laugh and a cough—"who this Death…Deathmask is?"

"One of your men betrayed you, killed the rest, and hoped to have the Hawks destroy your guild as you came to make the trade," said Deathmask, accepting the name without pause. "I killed them as a way of showing you my worth. I wished to join your Ash Guild, and Veliana has accepted me."

Veliana opened her mouth to correct him, then shut it. It was pointless to argue now, and Garrick's eyes flared at what he'd heard. He set his pipe aside and gently touched the tip of his dagger.

"And how did you know this ambush was to take place?" he asked.

Deathmask smiled but did not answer.

"No matter," Garrick said. "I take it our betrayer was killed?"

"Painfully," said Deathmask.

"Good. The more pressing question, then, is why the Hawks are so eager to crush us. I must think about this."

"Think?" asked Veliana. "We need to counter, and quickly, before they know their ambush failed. Surely there's a few of theirs still scouting our streets. If we can mark our borders with their blood, we can send a message."

"We will do no such thing," Garrick said. He winced as he pierced his skin with the dagger's tip, but instead of cleaning it, he watched the blood trickle down the blade. "I will handle this in my own manner. Kadish Vel is no real threat to us."

"With all due respect," said Deathmask, "he'd have killed either of you today if it weren't for me."

The room turned silent, and the rest of the thieves lounging about watched as if awaiting an execution.

"Is that so?" asked Garrick. Veliana tensed, wondering what he would do. "Then it is a good thing we have you now, isn't it? Patrick, take him upstairs and get him fitted for a cloak. Wouldn't want him showing the wrong colors, would we?"

Deathmask bowed, shot Veliana a wink, and then followed his escort out of the basement. Garrick stood and looked to the others.

"Out," he told them. "You've smoked enough of my wealth. Get out!"

They all jumped to leave, all but Veliana. She could see the way he stared at her, a wordless command to remain. As the last shut the door, Garrick strode over and grabbed her by the throat.

"Have you lost your damn mind?" he asked.

She kept her breathing calm as his fingers tightened. He wouldn't leave a bruise, not yet, but if he did...

"And have you lost yours?" she asked. He raised an eyebrow. The veins in his eyes pulsed, their edges yellow. In answer to his question, she drew one of her daggers and pressed its edge against his wrists.

"Tighter," she said. "I dare you."

He let her go and stepped back. Blood dripped from his finger, and he glared at the stains on the floor.

"I am your guildmaster," he said, as if that meant something. "I could replace you in a heartbeat."

"But they'll never follow you," Garrick said, gesturing toward the door. "Them out there...they're savages. They're pigs, and you're damaged beauty. If they thought the only thing standing between them and ruling this guild was...was a *woman*, they'd strip you naked and take turns."

"They'd die if they tried," Veliana said. She knew Garrick thought himself worth far more than he really was, but this was the most brazen he'd ever been. Something had changed, given him confidence...but what?

"Some, yes," said Garrick, and a gleam shone in his drug-maddened eyes. "But not all. You need me, Vel. They listen to me. They trust me. I kept this guild together after James's death. I kept our dealings going. I kept our coffers from emptying and our territory from becoming nothing more than a single penniless street."

"That was *me*," Veliana shouted, not caring if others might hear from behind the door. "I'm the one who bloodied her hands. I'm the one who gave them stability."

"But do they know that?" he asked. He stepped closer to her, a smile growing on his face. It was the drugs, she thought. It had to be the drugs. Ignoring the daggers, he gently ran a hand along the wicked scar across her beautiful face, cutting from forehead to chin, discoloring her right eye from a dazzling violet to a red orb of blood.

"They won't follow you," he said again. "You're dangerous, and they respect that, but they won't submit to it. They listen now only because the specter of my authority hangs over you. Just as James's hovered over you when he was alive. You need me, just as I need you. More, even. Never forget that."

She bit her tongue and fought down a thousand fantasies of plunging her daggers deep into his throat. Garrick walked back to his cushion, retrieved his pipe, and began the laborious process of filling it anew.

"I don't care how powerful that Deathmask freak is," he said. "I want him killed by tomorrow night, no matter how you do it. He's clearly trouble, and in someone's pocket. Cut his throat before he can accomplish whatever task he was sent here for. Deathmask? What a stupid name."

"If you say so," she said, nodding her head. "I'll be in my quarters. I trust you'll handle the matter of the Hawk Guild in an appropriate manner?"

Garrick smiled as she headed for the door.

"Dear Veliana, there are a thousand promises and lies between us all. You aren't aware of half of them. Trust me. We'll be fine."

She left without giving him the dignity of a response.

CHAPTER

3

Haern slept beside the shop of a baker he'd befriended. Besides gaining an occasional scrap of bread, he could take in the warm smells while he slept. He kept himself wrapped in blankets, never bothering to hide his face. His blond hair was matted to the sides of his head, much of his skin covered with dirt. He'd always been a clean, meticulous child. More than anything since his self-imposed exile from the Spider Guild, the filth bothered him most. He knew there were ways he could wash up, obtain cleaner clothes, but it'd never work. What homeless, coinless man lived on the side of the street, yet kept a clean face and hands? A rich man from the northern parts of Veldaren might not notice, but those who'd grown up in the lower portions of the city could sense those things as surely as Haern could smell the bread that baked in the shop every morning.

He had a small bowl before him, not expecting any alms but

feeling his heart warm when he did receive them. It was mainly there for looks. Every guild in the city of Veldaren wanted him dead, and he wouldn't draw needless attention to himself by neglecting the minor details.

Just before nightfall he stirred. The baker had gone home for the day, so he picked the familiar lock and slipped inside. He stole two slices of bread, dumped his bowl's coins across the counter to pay for the meal, and then left. He ate as he walked south along the main road, turning off after half a mile and heading directly into the territory of the Serpent Guild. He added a limp and ran through his persona for dealing with the Serpents. He let his lower jaw hang a little and muttered a few random words, practicing his lisp. His name was Berg. He was often drunk. Like all his personae, Berg worked odd jobs, whatever paid him coin, and that gave him an excuse to know things he shouldn't know.

Like how the Watcher had intercepted a shipment of gold from the Serpent Guild bearing the Gemcroft sigil.

His contact was a one-eyed ruffian originally from the far west nation of Mordan. He leaned beside the entrance of an inn, smoking a long pipe. His name was Mensk.

"What you want, Berg?" asked Mensk. He looked him over with his one eye, and he didn't hide his shudder at Haern's stink.

"I overheard something," Haern said with a lisp. "Something worth at least a silver."

Mensk's eyes narrowed.

"Nothing you could have heard is worth that much. Five coppers if I decide it's useful, one otherwise, and none if I've heard it already."

"Six coppers," Haern said, knowing he wouldn't get it but also knowing his persona would at least make the attempt.

"Five," Mensk said, frowning. "Now spit it out before it gets lower."

"I was drinking by the east wall last night, and I saw something, something strange. There were some of your guild, you Serpents, by the wall. They were lifting something over...a crate, valuable, yes?"

By now he had Mensk's attention. The thief had drawn his dagger and held it behind his back. So on edge...clearly the shipment's secrecy was beyond important.

"It might be," Mensk said. "That all you saw?"

Haern shook his head.

"No, oh no. I wouldn't have come here for just that. Why tell you your own business? No, what I saw was the Watcher. He killed them, all but a few!"

"We know who killed them," Mensk said. He shifted a little, placing his right foot a few inches back. He was preparing for a stab. Haern kept his breathing steady, not letting a shred of fear show in his eyes. Oblivious...he had to act oblivious...

"But did you know the one who killed them was a Hawk?" he asked.

There. He saw the momentary pause in Mensk's eyes and knew he had him.

"What?" he asked.

"Oh no," Haern said, stepping out of stabbing range. He exaggerated his lisp further to pretend excitement. "This gets me seven coppers, or I go to someone else who'll pay."

"Here's six," Mensk said, tossing them to the dirt. "Now tell me what you know!"

Haern flung himself to the ground and began scooping up the coins, all the while rambling.

"I saw him skulking along the rooftop. I wanted to shout warning, I did, but it was too fast, you know? One moment I see him, and I'm wondering what some damn fool is doing on the roof, and then he's whirling and cutting. Gods, never seen so much blood."

"The Hawks?" Mensk asked, prodding him along.

"Oh, well, I saw him pull out a pendant just before he attacked. Now it was dark and far away, but I swear the moon was bright enough. It had a feather on it, just one feather, plus I think an eye. That's their new symbol, right, symbol for the Hawks? Thanks for the coppers, Mensk!"

He stood and stepped back. With the added distance, he knew Mensk wouldn't come after him, not when he could just turn and run. A bit of disappointment came over the thief's face, which pleased him immensely. He'd told such lies before to the various guilds. With the distance and the dark, his proof was meager, but that was the point. A thousand tiny lies and misdirections would add up to a far greater proof than a single disprovable accusation. He wanted the guilds at each other's throats, always convinced the Watcher was one of their own. Mensk would pass along what he'd heard, storing it away with all the other tales Haern had whispered over the years.

"Get out of here," Mensk said. "And I should only pay you three for something that worthless."

"If I'm right, you know I should get a hundred silver," Haern said as he limped along. "But I like you Serpents. Always treated me fair, helped rebind roofs to put over my head. I sure hope that Watcher didn't disrupt anything important. Would hate for him to put you in a bad bind..."

"I said get out," Mensk said, revealing his dagger. "Those shipments'll continue no matter what that bastard does. Now get your ass out of my sight before I decide to take back my coin."

Haern fled, and once he reached the main merchant road he

abandoned the limp and started trudging north. In the light of the stars he pondered over what he'd learned. When he sold information he often managed to sneak out with a little bit more in return. That shipment of gold hadn't been a one-time deal. Obviously the shipments were important, and the Serpent Guild wanted them to continue. Originally he'd thought the Serpents just lucky robbers of the Gemcroft mines, but now...

Now he was intrigued.

Haern didn't always give away the gold he stole. Sometimes he kept a little, with the promise to never spend it on himself but instead his personal war against the guilds. There were many men who responded to gold far better than threats, and it was to one of them Haern hurried next. He was in a quiet section of Veldaren, far to the north and away from the poorer districts and the strongholds of the thief guilds. Here there were rows of homes, most fenced, and Haern climbed over one fence and softly landed on the grass beyond.

Two dogs immediately rushed from around the side of the house, large hounds with black fur and impressive jaws. Haern knelt, not panicking, instead offering his hands. One of the two licked away at it, while the other nearly bowled him over leaping against him for attention. Haern smiled as he petted both the animals. The house's owner, a man named Dashel, had bought the two animals for protection. When Haern decided to make the man one of his contacts, he'd spent weeks visiting the home while the owner was gone, bringing food and treats for the dogs, petting them, letting them get used to his smell and appreciate his presence. Now they hardly barked upon his arrival, and if they did it was out of excitement.

"Easy now," Haern whispered as he finally pushed them back. "I still have work to do."

One whined, the other barking a single time. Haern shot them a wink.

"I'll bring a few bones next time, I promise."

Dashel's bedroom was on the second floor, and in the moonlight Haern climbed up to the rooftop, then hung upside down before the elegant window. It was unlocked. Pushing it open, Haern then rotated about and landed on the sill, crouching down. His shadow splayed out across the fine bed upon which slept Dashel and his wife. Taking a rock out of his pocket, he flung it, striking Dashel across the nose.

The man let out a snort, then groggily looked about. Upon seeing Haern lurking in his window, he froze. Haern tossed him something else, this time a coin that glinted yellow when it caught the light. Dashel pushed the sheets aside, caught the coin, and then staggered out of his bed.

"Outside," the older man hissed before shutting the window in Haern's face. Laughing, Haern dropped back to the two waiting dogs and accepted another round of licks.

A few minutes later Dashel stepped out from his door, a thick white robe wrapped around his rotund form. His hair and beard were gray, his face wrinkled. Haern kept his hood pulled low and his face turned away from the moonlight, hiding his own features.

"Stupid dogs," Dashel said, glaring at them. "Man who sold them to me swore they were as vicious as a wounded orc."

"They have smart noses," Haern said. "They know I'm not here to hurt you."

Dashel rolled his eyes and waved a hand.

"What is it, Watcher? It's cold out here, and I'd much rather be sleeping in my warm bed."

"The Serpent Guild has a new source of gold," Haern said. "What do you know about it?"

The old man frowned at him, then tightened his robe. Dashel was the master of the mint for the kingdom of Neldar, and because of this he had access to resources many people prized. For years he'd worked as a fence, accepting from the various guilds any gold that might be marked or distinguishable and replacing it, for a price, with fresh coin from the mint. Haern had briefly thought of taking him out, but decided the information he might learn from the man was more valuable.

"It's been going on for months," Dashel said. "Though I suspect it is new to you?"

"I'd have been here sooner if I discovered it sooner."

"Of course you would have." Dashel shook his head. "They've come to me regularly, with amounts high enough I've considered several times declining for fear of having my...side activities discovered. As for the source, all I can tell you is that they always have the same mint and mark."

"Which one?"

"The Gemcroft mines up north. My guess is from Tyneham."

Haern frowned. Massive shipments of gold coming in from the Gemcroft mines, delivered in secret to the Serpent Guild? What did it mean?

"Have they discovered a way to rob Alyssa's caravans?" Haern wondered aloud.

"Been happening too long for that to be the case," Dashel said. "I don't know Alyssa well, but her reputation alone suggests if she knew she was being robbed, she'd have swarmed the northern roads with guards until it stopped. So whatever's happening, it's happening underneath her nose."

Dashel gestured to his door.

"Can I go to bed now? This is hardly worth one lousy coin."

Haern pulled out two more gold coins, tucked one into the collar of each dog, and bid Dashel farewell. Before the man was even inside, Haern had already vaulted over the fence and headed south. His mind raced over the possibilities, and every time he came up empty. Everything seemed too large, too far beyond the reach of the Serpent Guild's leader, William Ket. If he wanted to find out more, or put a stop to it, he'd most likely need to leave the comfort and familiarity of his city for the wilds of the north.

Pushing such thoughts aside, Haern focused on his original task: spreading misinformation. He'd already claimed the Watcher was working for the Hawks, so now it was time to inform the Hawks of the Serpents' shipments, adding one more layer to the deception. Perhaps the rival guild might even aid Haern in putting an end to the sudden influx of gold. Wending his way into the Hawks' territory, he put a scowl over his face and adopted a new persona, that of just another hardworking peasant hoping to eke out enough copper for a few extra drinks. He went to their headquarters, a tavern where their leader, Kadish Vel, no doubt played cards in a private room in the back. Again his contact waited by the door, a big man whose name he didn't know, only his nickname: Fists. In working his way into the man's trust, Haern had had to endure a few beatings that showed exactly where that nickname came from.

"It's late for someone weak as you," said Fists as Haern approached.

"Never too late for a good drink," he said.

Fists smirked at that. "Good drink? You won't find that here. What you have to tell me?"

"I saw a shipment coming in over the wall, and I think the Serpents were..."

He sensed the attack coming long before Fists did. Haern dove to the side as arrows thudded into the tavern. He heard Fists groan, and a glance back showed two arrows in his belly.

Haern raced around the building, out of reach of the tavern's torchlight. As he turned the corner he slammed into a cloaked man with daggers at the ready. Haern rolled along, separating their bodies. He leaped to his feet, his swords in hand. With the greater reach, he had the advantage, and his opponent knew it. The man lunged in, hoping for a strike before Haern could prepare.

But the lunge was too slow. Haern twisted so the dagger brushed his side without drawing blood, then slashed around with his swords. One cut deep into his opponent's extended arm, the second kept the other dagger out of position. As the man cried out in pain, Haern pulled his swords back and then stabbed. The man tried to block, but he was unbalanced, his arms poorly placed. Haern yanked out his blades and kicked the body. He frowned at the color of the cloak. He'd first thought the Serpents had followed him for knowing about the gold, but instead this man wore the gray of the Spider Guild.

He heard the sound of a bowstring being drawn tight, and he dove on instinct. The arrow plinked the stone beside him, poking a hole in his cloaks but doing no damage. His attacker was on the roof, readying another arrow. Haern spun, flinging his cloaks into a confusing display, and then leaped in the opposite direction. Again the arrow missed. By now he'd raced around the corner, cursing his bad luck. Why had the Spider Guild come now? What reason did they have to war with the Hawks?

His flight took him back to the front of the tavern. Several Serpents had come out to fight, but nearly all bore crimson stains on their green cloaks. The Spiders moved in, outnumbering them two to one. Haern took in the combat as quickly as he could, searching for an escape route. Underneath the awning over the tavern entrance he was safe from the archer, but in plain view of the rest of the thieves. They'd set up a perimeter, but he trusted himself to break through. He was the Spider Guild's champion, after all, their greatest creation and most disappointing failure. That, and they all thought he was dead, a belief he didn't want to change. He'd grown much over the past five years, but still, someone might recognize him underneath the dirt...

One of the Spiders saw him there, saw the blood on his swords. When he started to attack, Haern met his charge with a vicious assault of his own, surprising his opponent with sudden, overwhelming fury. He batted away a pair of daggers, cut open the man's throat, and then bolted to the street. Two more moved to stop him but Haern slide-kicked between them, scraping his leg along the hard ground. He cut the thigh of one and curled his sword around to hamstring the other. As they fell screaming, he ran, hoping they would not chase. None did, but he didn't go far.

Knowing he was being stupid didn't stop Haern from doing it. He hurried back to the Hawk headquarters. The perimeter had closed in, and it seemed most of the fighting had stopped. Various members of the Spider Guild stood near the entrance, keeping watch while a few rifled the bodies.

And then he saw him: Thren Felhorn, leader of the Spider Guild. His father.

"Why?" Haern asked as he watched him walk into the tavern as if it were his own, accompanied by four of his men. "What did they do to you?"

He resolved to find out, but not now. He turned and headed back toward the city's center, realizing for the first time he was limping. After stealing a bottle from a man lying facedown in the ditch (whether dead or unconscious, he didn't know), he took a momentary reprieve to clean his scraped leg and splash some alcohol across it. After the pain subsided he continued.

He had two possible avenues to pursue. He could discover the reason for the Hawks' and Spiders' squabble, or he could look into the mystery of the Serpents' gold. Doing his best to convince himself it had nothing to do with any fear of his father, he resolved to look into the gold. Guilds fought all the time; he had no proof this was any different. Shipments from the Gemcroft mines, however...

After breaking into another shop and stealing a few supplies, he found one of the quieter stretches along the great wall surrounding the city of Veldaren, went up the steps, and then climbed down the wall with a rope he tied at the top. Once out he trekked northeast, following the main road around the King's Forest toward Felwood Castle many miles farther along. Beyond that were the Crestwall Mountains and the many villages around the Gemcroft mines. It'd take him weeks to arrive, but he held hope it would be worth it. Out there he might find some information. When it all boiled down, the war between the guilds and the Trifect was about pride and money. Both sides had suffered too many losses to endure on pride alone. It was coin that mattered now, and if the Serpent Guild had suddenly discovered a new source of gold, they might endure for years. Even worse, they might score a significant victory against the Trifect, further emboldening the underworld. Haern had to stop it. He had to find some way to crush the guilds and end the war.

He laughed as he walked. End the war. It seemed nothing would. It had continued for ten years and seemed ready for another ten. But at least he might make things uncomfortable for a while. He'd done his part to weaken and bleed the guilds, to punish them for the bloodshed he'd witnessed firsthand. Randith, his own brother, Senke, his friend, Robert Haern, his mentor, Kayla, his first crush. And then there was Delysia...

His father had shot her with an arrow for daring to love him. He still relived that moment in his nightmares, sitting on a rooftop with her bleeding over his hands. He'd thought her dead, but Kayla had later told him she lived with the priests of Ashhur. And then Thren had killed Kayla. As for Senke, Haern had heard he'd died in the fire at Connington's estate during the Bloody Kensgold.

"Maybe I'm afraid," he whispered to the stars as he pulled his cloaks tighter about him to keep in his warmth. "Gods forgive me, maybe I really am afraid."

Amid it all, amid the death and loss and pain that haunted him come his restless daytime sleep, there stood his father. It seemed appropriate. It was a terrible web his father wove, and he was the spider in the center of it all. A spider that Haern was not sure he'd ever have the courage to face.

He continued along the road, part of him hoping he might be ambushed along the way. The bloodshed and excitement would have felt a thousand times better than the dread the memories of his childhood brought.

CHAPTER

4

Mark Tullen rode toward the gates of Felwood Castle, as always in awe of the fortress made of dark stone and covered with ivy. Along with the provisions stashed in his pack was Alyssa's letter requesting him to retrieve her son and bring him back to Veldaren. Mark had been in Riverrun when the letter arrived, not far south of Felwood. He'd written his affirmation in a hurry, for he could sense Alyssa's unease. Whatever the reason, he didn't want to lose any favor in her eyes by tarrying.

"I seek audience with Lord Gandrem," he called at the gate. "I am Mark Tullen, lord of Riverrun, and I come at Lady Gemcroft's request!"

The gates opened and guards escorted him in. After he cleaned his boots, he followed them along the emerald carpet to the throne, the seat of power for all the Northern Plains. John Gandrem stood as they entered, a smile on his wrinkled face. He wore robes of green and gold, and a thin crown of silver atop his gray hair.

"Welcome," said John, clasping hands with Mark. "It's been too long since you visited. The distance from here to Riverrun is not so great that you should visit only once a year."

"I was here in spring," Mark said. "Do not tell me you forgot?"

"I wouldn't be surprised if I did," John said, sitting back down and trying to laugh off the error.

"Sadly, I cannot count this as much of a visit," Mark continued. "I've come for Alyssa's boy, Nathaniel. I'm to give him safe passage back to Veldaren."

A shadow passed over John's face, and he took a sip from a goblet beside him before responding.

"Nathaniel is not here," he said, setting the goblet down. "Lord Arthur Hadfield came a few months back and brought him north to Tyneham. I assumed this was at Alyssa's request, and he certainly implied as much."

Mark felt his gut tighten.

"I'm sure Arthur's done the boy no harm," the old man continued. "Said he wanted to show him the ways of the business, if you know what I mean. If he's to take over the Gemcroft fortune, a bit of experience with their mines would do him much good."

"Thank you," Mark said, bowing.

"Will you not stay?" John asked.

"My apologies," Mark said, glancing over his shoulder. "But Alyssa seemed eager to see her son, and this delay will add many days to our travel. I dare not spend even a single night here when I might be riding instead."

"Very well," said John. "Safe travels."

"And pleasant nights," said Mark.

He left Felwood and immediately followed the road north. Thankfully he'd packed enough rations for both him and the boy, so he'd have enough to make it to Tyneham alone. There he'd need to supply himself with at least enough to get them back to Felwood Castle. He let his mind wander as he rode. It'd take several days to arrive, so he had more than enough time to think.

Mark knew he and Arthur were rivals for Alyssa's affection. In their rare times together, Mark sensed Alyssa found him more interesting, more handsome. But Arthur had wealth and influence, which Mark did not, and something which Alyssa could not ignore. Nearly every town along the mountainside belonged to Arthur in one way or another, while Mark controlled just Riverrun, and even that only recently due to Theo Kull's execution, at Alyssa's hand no less. From the whispers he heard, and the cold stares from Alyssa's advisor, Bertram, he knew he was not the favorite in the rest of Veldaren's eyes.

But he wouldn't let that stop him. He'd been told the same about challenging Theo Kull, who had his fingers in everything. But Theo had died, and amusingly enough it had been because his son Yoren had tried for Alyssa's hand. Alyssa had kept an eye on Mark's takeover of Riverrun in the wake of the Kulls' demise, and that was how he had first met her.

"Ride on," Mark whispered to his horse. "I know you're tired, but give me just a few more miles."

Nathaniel alone with Arthur...the idea greatly disturbed him. Arthur was an older man, calm in all things, always calculating every potential outcome of a choice. It was as if the two of them played a game, moving pieces and exchanging tokens, all for the sake of Alyssa's heart. So far Mark was losing, and now Arthur held a potential game ender. If the boy favored Arthur, his mother's heart might easily follow.

Mark slept close to the path, keeping his sword beside him as he tucked himself into his bedroll. His hard rations were bland and salty, but they kept him going. Several hours into the next morning's ride he found a stream to fill both his water-skins as well as give his horse a well-deserved rest. He kept up his pace, though not to such an extent that it might endanger his mount. The whole while he pondered Arthur's coming reaction. Clearly he wouldn't know of Alyssa's request to have her son returned. Would he refuse? Come with? Ask for proof? Mark had Alyssa's letter, of course, but what if Arthur challenged its authenticity?

Mark pushed the thoughts aside. It wouldn't matter. Trying to outthink Arthur would be pointless. Many would have to make the best decision available at the time, without fear or doubt. That was how he'd risen to his stature. That was how he planned on rising even higher.

On the fifth day out from Felwood, he arrived at the mining village of Tyneham. The lone inn was small, with only two rooms and a post out back to tie his horse. Much of its white paint had long since peeled away. Mark had a bite to eat, drank a cup of the awful ale, and then asked for Arthur Hadfield's location.

"He don't come to town often," said the innkeeper, a portly old woman. "But when he does, you can find him overlooking the mines. He keeps an eye on things, and he's caught quite a few thieves who thought themselves bright."

Mark smiled at her obvious hint.

"I come in the right," he told her. "But if I were a thief, I'd share at least a token of my haul with you, if only for your beauty."

She laughed and waved him off.

He received a few odd stares as he worked his way toward

the mountains. He'd seen the Crestwall Mountains only once before, and he stopped beside a well to take in the view. They rose toward the sky like bony fingers, cracked and weather-beaten. He wondered how vicious the storms might get so far north, something he hoped not to find out. Still the mountains possessed a majestic beauty, towering above him, reaching into the clouds until their tips turned white with snow. Winter was halfway over, but he wondered if it ever ended there. The past several days he'd ridden through snow, and he thanked Ashhur there were an abundance of trees for firewood.

Realizing he was stalling, Mark forced himself onward. As he neared the bustle of activity at the mines, a foreman spotted his approach and yelled for him to halt.

"Not from around here," said the foreman as he neared. He wore furs that were hopelessly dirty, and giant calluses covered his hands. "You dress too well and too lightly."

"I'm warm enough," said Mark. He offered a hand. "Mark Tullen, lord of Riverrun. I'm here to speak with your lord."

The foreman grunted.

"You're in luck. Arthur and the boy are further in. We might have hit a new vein, and he wants to take a look."

Mark tried to hide his reaction at hearing about "the boy," but felt he did a miserable job. The foreman raised an eyebrow but refused to comment. Mark mentally cursed himself. If he couldn't hide his emotions from a lowly foreman, what hope did he have with someone as observant as Arthur?

"Please," he said, deciding to get it over with. "Can you take me to him? I come with urgent business from Alyssa Gemcroft."

The foreman snapped to attention. If there was anyone more powerful than Arthur in the village, it was Alyssa. Her mines gave them work, wealth, and the means to survive on the harsh land. Without them Tyneham would become a ghost town.

"Follow me," said the foreman.

They walked along a path pounded flat by half a century of carts, feet, and wheelbarrows. A few of the men glanced up, but most ignored them, or did their best to look busy. Mark saw several women wandering about with food and water for the men. A few carried needles and cloth to wrap, stitch, and bandage the day's toll of blisters and cuts. He saw at least four main entrances to the lower slopes of the mountain. The foreman took him to the largest, where a crowd had gathered.

The two stopped and listened, for a man had come from inside the mine. A young boy stood at his side, his red hair covered with dirt. Mark knew them both.

"I've looked it over," said Arthur as he pulled off a pair of gloves and tossed them aside. "It's a new vein, all right, the richest we've found in ten years. We'll shift men from mines three and four to help drain the rest of the water, and I'll send word for more oxen. Hard work is ahead, but tonight we'll share a glass to celebrate!"

The crowd cheered and smiled, even the foreman beside Mark clapping in excitement. Mark kept his arms crossed and watched Nathaniel. He stood beside Arthur, his face passive and his eyes to the ground. Such good behavior from someone barely five...it struck Mark as worrisome. Even when the cheering began, Nathaniel only looked around once, and after a few seconds' delay clapped twice.

Mark waited as the rest of the men resumed their duties, cheerfully delving back into the mines or pushing their carts for the smelters and their mills. Arthur saw Mark through the crowd, nodded once, and then approached.

"Lord Tullen, I was not expecting such a pleasant surprise," he said, but the tone of his voice didn't match the honeyed words.

Mark withdrew the letter and handed it over.

"I've come for Nathaniel," he said. "Alyssa wishes his safe return, for she misses him terribly. I must say, I was surprised to find him here instead of with Lord Gandrem."

A smile pulled at the sides of Arthur's lips. He had a long, oval face, and gray hair trimmed extremely short. Mark had never seen a more smug, self-satisfied grin.

"I often talked with Alyssa about bringing Nathaniel here to learn the duties involved in running the mines," he said. "At my last visit I mentioned doing so should the weather break."

"Her letter doesn't say that."

"Given how great her duties are, I am not surprised such a casual comment by myself went unremembered."

Mark didn't believe it for a second, but he tried to act like he did.

"Either way, she wishes him back," he insisted. "So come, Nathaniel. Let us return to your mother."

"You can't take him," said Arthur. When Mark's eyes flared, the grin on Arthur's face only grew. "Not by yourself. You would bring a son of the Trifect along the northern road unprotected? He is far too precious a target for ransom. Let me send some of my men with you as escort."

Mark looked away and muttered. Arthur was testing him, testing his reactions, and he'd given away his thoughts plain as day. As he looked about, he saw two wagons loading up not far to the south.

"Where are they headed?" he asked.

"They?" asked Arthur. He followed his gaze, and then answered far too quickly, "I'm not sure, but they are of no matter to you. Let me get my men."

"Veldaren," said Nathaniel before Arthur could leave. "Every week they bring gold for Veldaren."

Mark shot the boy a wink, not caring that Arthur saw.

"Then I will ride with them," he said. "Surely we will be safe amid a well-guarded caravan."

Arthur's grin faded.

"Very well. They will slow you down, so make sure Alyssa knows the reason for your delay falls upon you, and not myself. I'll tell the men you'll be joining them. Nathaniel, go to the castle and pack your things. Hurry now! Do not keep Lord Tullen waiting."

Nathaniel bowed to both and then ran off. Mark watched him go.

"Not a smart child, but at least he is obedient," Arthur said, walking away.

Nathaniel rode in one of the two wagons while Mark trotted beside them on his horse. He'd purchased supplies from the tavern, not wishing to be a burden on the caravan. Though he'd stayed out of their way as best he could, he made sure to sneak a glance at the cargo—crates of newly minted gold coins, all stamped with the symbol of the Gemcroft family. Each wagon had a single crate.

"Why just one crate per wagon?" he asked the leader of the caravan, a fat man named Dave. "Seems wasteful."

"Each wagon has its own driver, own guards, own cargo," Dave answered. "Makes it harder for someone to get to plotting. That, and we'll fill both wagons on the way back with supplies. You should see how many tools we run through. I swear, for every pound of gold we dig we break two pounds of iron."

Come nightfall they set up camp. Several of the guards had slept during their day ride, and so they wandered about, eating, drinking, and watching the roads. Mark took the time to find Nathaniel. The boy ate by himself, huddled in a blanket with his back to a fire.

"Cold?" Mark asked as he sat down beside him.

Nathaniel shook his head.

"I can't be cold," he said. "Arthur says that makes me look weak."

Mark chuckled. "Even the greatest of leaders needs to wear boots in the snow. You're allowed to be human, Nathaniel."

The boy pulled the blanket tighter about him. He looked so similar to his mother, the same soft features, stubby nose, and startling red hair. He glanced back at Mark, and then a smile crept across his trembling lips.

"Maybe... maybe I'm a little cold."

Mark laughed.

"Take this then," he said, wrapping his own blanket around the boy. "This should help. From here on out, anything Arthur told you, you check with me, all right?"

"Why?" Nathaniel asked, suddenly looking worried. "Does Arthur lie?"

"No, no," Mark said, quicker than he meant to. "He just... has a peculiar way of looking at the world. He doesn't think people get cold, remember? I'd love to see him wander in his skivvies during a snowstorm. I bet he'd look like a blue ogre when he came back inside. What do you think? Or maybe a blue orc. Nah. He's too skinny to be an orc."

He yammered on, telling jokes both humorous and terrible. It didn't matter. He watched Nathaniel slowly warm to him, and it relieved Mark tremendously. He'd been worried that Arthur's words had wrapped a spell about the boy, turning him into some mindless stooge believing his every word. But Nathaniel was still a five-year-old boy, and given the chance he wanted to laugh and joke as much as any other kid his age. Mark knew he might not be the most charming dinner guest, but at least he knew how to make a kid laugh.

Mark let Nathaniel keep his blanket, instead borrowing another from the wagons. They slept beside the fire.

Come the next morning Mark awoke with a chill having seeped deep into his bones. When he stirred he saw a thin layer of snow atop the world, including his blanket.

"About time," said Dave, who was busy untethering their oxen. "You sleep like the dead, Mark."

"Better to sleep like them than to be them," he said, shaking off his blanket and looking for a fire.

"No fire," said Dave. "We need to save the wood in case the snow picks up. Move about. Help us pack. You'll warm up soon enough."

He found Nathaniel sitting in one of the wagons, half-buried in blankets.

"I hate winter," he said when he saw Mark.

"I hear you," Mark said, slapping him on the shoulder. "Just try to endure. We'll be home with your mother soon enough."

The snowflakes were light as they traveled, just a slight nuisance that wetted their skin and occasionally stung their eyes. By midday the snow had thickened, and at last Dave called a halt.

"The wagons might get stuck if it continues," Mark told him.

"Better stuck on the road than in a ditch," Dave shot back.

They used the wagons to block the wind, shoveled snow until they found cold, dry ground, and then built a fire. They gathered around it, their own bodies sheltering the fire from the wind that sneaked in.

"Come morning we'll dig out and then continue," Dave said as they huddled there. "Run this route plenty of times, and I have a feeling for how the weather works. We'll have clear sky tomorrow. Assuming we don't break a wheel, we should reach Felwood in a—"

He stopped, for amid the howling of the wind he heard something strange.

"Horses," said Dave.

"Who would ride in this weather?" asked one of the guards.

Mark drew his sword and stood, and the rest did likewise. There were only four guards per wagon, and the eight hurried to the opening between them.

"It might be a messenger meant to reach us," said Dave, just before a crossbow bolt pierced his arm.

"Shit," he cried, snapping the shaft in half and tossing it. "Stay down, all of you!"

Horses thundered by on either side, and as they passed the gap, many of the riders fired crossbows. Mark dove into one of the wagons as the bolts flew, dragging Nathaniel with him. The horses turned around, and at their return charge he heard the sound of steel hitting steel.

"Stay down," Mark said to Nathaniel. The boy sat huddled in blankets beside the crate of gold. His eyes were wide, rimmed with tears that refused to fall in the chill air.

"I'm scared," Nathaniel said, and his whole body shook.

"I am too," Mark said as bolts tore through the fabric of the covering, thankfully missing them. He kept his sword facing the back of the wagon and listened. He heard screams, plus Dave hollering like a madman. From where he crouched he could only see a small portion of the combat. The guards had cut down two of the riders, but the rest continued their charge, hacking as they passed or firing more crossbow bolts.

Then he heard Dave cry something that made no sense, but at the same time was certain to be true.

"Lord Hadfield? But why?"

He died soon after, or at least his orders stopped. The cries of pain lessened. Swords struck rarely, then stopped altogether. Mark pushed Nathaniel farther into the wagon and tried to shrink down. He might be able to surprise one or two of them if they didn't realize he was inside...

A man rode up behind the wagon, a crossbow in hand. Mark lunged at him, extending his arm as far as it could go. His sword pierced the man's breast, punching through his leather armor. As he bled out, the crossbow fired harmlessly into the air. Mark retreated into the wagon, his blood running cold. He recognized the symbol on that armor. They were Arthur's men, all right. But why? Why would he ambush his own wagons?

He glanced back at Nathaniel and decided he already knew the reason.

"Mark?" he heard Arthur call out. "Is that you in there, Mark?"

"Just keeping warm," Mark shouted back. "What'd your men do to deserve this?"

"Deserve? Nothing. They died in my service, as all men should for their masters. Where is the child? I don't want him to witness your execution."

Mark clutched his sword tighter. Behind him he heard Nathaniel whimper.

"You'll protect him?" Mark asked.

"As if he were my own son."

Or at least until you have a son of your own, thought Mark. *At least until you've consummated your marriage to Alyssa, you heartless bastard.*

"Listen to me," he whispered to Nathaniel. "He's lying, I know it. You need to run, you understand? I know you don't want to, but you have to try. He's cruel. I've always known it, now just..."

"Mark!" Arthur shouted. "Come out and face this with honor!"

"That way," Mark said, pointing to the exit beside the driver's seat.

Nathaniel nodded. Despite his fear he was holding together. Though they lacked any blood connection, Mark felt proud of the boy. A child worthy to raise, to claim the Gemcroft wealth. A child who'd probably freeze to death in the next twelve hours. He almost thought to change his mind, to carry Nathaniel out and discover what Arthur would do. But he couldn't. If Nathaniel was somehow part of Arthur's plans, Mark wanted to ruin them. It was petty, perhaps, but by the gods, he had to do something to avenge his own death.

He stepped out from the wagon, his sword still drawn.

CHAPTER 5

Haern kept his cloaks wrapped tightly about himself as he trudged along the road. He felt foolish for not preparing for such weather. His feet were numb from the cold, and he'd have given anything for a thick coat. He'd dressed like a thief when he should have dressed like a bear.

He lacked the proper tools to build a fire, which was especially problematic given how heavily the snow came down. Moving kept him warm, so that's what he did. It'd been two days since he saw houses in the distance, farms both large and small. Before that he'd stayed a night in the comforts of Felwood Castle, stocking up on food and, like a fool, refusing to steal anything warmer to wear before continuing toward the mines along the Crestwall Mountains. That was before the snow, before he realized just how pathetic he was compared to nature's forces. His hood pulled low, he stared at the white ground and kept his feet moving. Night was approaching, and he pondered what to do. Surely he could find a tree for shelter, and should probably start looking. But he didn't want to stop just yet. He didn't want to admit it, but part of him feared that the moment he stopped moving he would curl up, fall asleep, and never wake again.

The first time he heard the noise he thought it a hallucination. Then it came again, and many times after. It was the sound of steel hitting steel, coupled with the neighs of horses. He felt some of his drowsiness leave him. He'd headed north in hopes of discovering the source of the Serpents' gold, prepared to travel all the way to Tyneham if he must, to where the gold was minted. But could the source be something as simple as raiding the caravans as they traveled south? Dashel had insisted against it, and Haern had agreed with his argument. Then what?

He urged himself on, and despite the snow that blew in his face, he forced himself to stare straight ahead. The snow was thick, and it seemed as if a white fog had enclosed the land so many yards away from where he stood. When he saw the first rider, it was if he emerged from another world. Haern dove for the cover of trees, then glanced back to see if he'd been spotted. He hadn't. The rider turned back and charged into the unseen combat.

Not willing to risk such foolishness again, Haern weaved through the trees, making sure to stay close to the road. If the weather remained foul, it might be days before he found the path again. He was no woodsman. The city streets were his home. Out among the trees, in the snow, he felt like a bumbling idiot.

The sound of combat faded not long after. After a few moments of silence he heard someone yelling. His numb ears at first refused to make words out of the noise. As he followed the sound, he started to understand.

"Where is the child?" he heard a man ask. "I don't want him to witness your execution."

Finally reaching the area of combat, Haern leaned against the thick trunk of a tree and surveyed the situation. Two wagons were pulled close together, the oxen tethered behind them. Eight men on horses milled about, all with swords or crossbows. The speaker seemed older than the rest, and he wore no armor, just a thick coat of bearskin that Haern felt ready to kill for. All around them lay bodies, their warm blood melting the snow beneath them.

It didn't make sense. All the horsed ambushers wore the same insignia, a sickle held before a mountain. This wasn't the Serpent Guild. They didn't wear green cloaks. What then? Should he interfere?

Meanwhile the older man continued talking, evidently with someone inside a wagon given the direction he faced and the command he gave.

"Mark!" cried the older man. "Come out and face this with honor."

And then it seemed Mark obeyed, stepping from the back of one of the wagons. He looked young, his armor dark and expensive. The riders circled about him as the older man smiled.

"Hiding during a battle," he said. "Such shameful behavior."

"Perhaps," Mark said. He lunged at the nearest rider, but never got close enough to swing. Two crossbow bolts pierced his back, and he stumbled, his weapon falling from his hand. Haern winced. At least the man had died bravely, even if he hadn't accomplished...

But then he saw the child leap from the wagon's front and dash for the forest. Haern's eyes flared wide. The kid was heading straight for him.

"Get him!" the riders shouted. One took off, dismounted at the forest's edge, and then rushed on, his sword drawn. Haern flung his back against the tree. Should he interfere? Would they kill the boy, or merely keep him captive? Was this for ransom? Too much he didn't know. Too much!

The boy rushed by, followed by the soldier. Haern stared, paralyzed by indecision. If he acted now he'd reveal himself. Eight riders...what chance would he have? He'd be throwing his life away, and why? For all he knew, the boy belonged to the ambushers.

The soldier quickly gained ground, for he could make longer strides. He kept his sword drawn, and Haern recognized the way he held the blade in preparation for a thrust. This was no capture. This was no attempt at ransom. He ran after the two, feeling slow and clumsy in the snow. The boy glanced behind, saw his pursuer, and then stumbled. Haern wanted to cry out but didn't dare reveal his location. The soldier reached the boy, and his sword thrust. Blood spilled across the snow.

Haern slammed into the soldier with his shoulder, flinging him onto his back. Before he could stand, Haern drew a sword, slapped aside a weak defense, and buried it in the soldier's throat. The man gargled blood, quivered, and then lay still.

"You get him?" a man shouted from the road.

Haern ignored him and instead looked to the boy. He lay on his back, his whole body shaking. The thrust had cut deep into his arm, right to the bone. The blade had continued, piercing his chest. He still breathed, and it didn't sound wet. The tip hadn't gone deep enough to pierce anything vital. With proper care he might live, but at the moment he was wide-eyed with shock. He'd need time, which at the moment Haern sorely lacked. He sliced off a strip of one of his cloaks and tied it around the wounded arm, then took the boy's hands and pressed them firmly against the wound on his chest.

"Stay still and quiet," Haern whispered, propping him against the nearest tree. "I'll come back for you, I promise. No matter what you do, don't let go."

He stood, drew his swords, and looked to the road. Through the forest he saw the faintest glimpse of the riders. Amid the trees and snow the horses would be useless. So long as they didn't know he was there, he had a chance.

He stepped gingerly across the snow, crouched low and hidden behind the trunks. The forest was quiet, and he heard their discussions with ease as they grew steadily heated.

"Terry!" one shouted. "Where are you? Did the brat lose you somehow?"

"Jerek, Thomas, go look for him, and hurry. I don't want to be out in this weather any longer than I have to."

Haern smiled at the lucky break. He stayed to the side and watched two more men walk right past him. He started creeping after them, but they stopped halfway.

"See that, Jerek?" asked Thomas as he pointed. "Something ain't right."

They drew their swords and looked about as Haern realized what he pointed at: the footprints he'd left in the snow when chasing after the soldier and the boy.

Damn wilderness, thought Haern. *Give me a city any day.*

They followed the footprints, but they were no longer hurrying. His surprise advantage was nearly blown. He continued following, using the trees to hide in case they glanced back, but they were getting too close to where the soldier's body lay.

"Found them," said Jerek. "Shit, his throat's cut!"

Haern gave up stealth, knowing he couldn't muffle his running. The crunching of the snow turned them about, but he was too close, too fast. He gutted Thomas, ducked under a dying slash, and then turned to Jerek. Instead of the desperate lunge he expected, Jerek pulled back and held his sword with both hands in a defensive position. Haern felt respect for the man, as well as agitation. He didn't need a drawn-out duel against a worthy opponent. He needed the man killed before any others arrived.

"Ambush!" Jerek screamed. "It's a fucking ambush!"

"One against five," Haern said. "Some ambush."

"There's six of us," said Jerek.

Haern shrugged.

"You'll be dead soon enough."

He feinted, stepped to the left, and then lunged for real. Jerek bit on the feint, but not enough. He parried both blades aside, but he extended to do so. Haern closed the distance between them, slamming an elbow into the man's chest while they shoved their weapons together. Jerek tried to separate, but Haern shifted again, positioning his right foot in the way. When Jerek stepped back he tripped, and that was all the opening Haern needed.

"Jerek? Thomas?" asked another soldier as he approached the bloody mess. Haern watched, doing his best to keep his breathing calm. Only three had come, not five, which meant one had stayed behind to protect the older man, presumably their leader. They were only a handful of paces from where the boy lay, but they stopped at the bodies of their comrades. Two held swords, while the third held a crossbow. They looked about the area, searching. They never looked up, and that was enough.

Haern fell upon them from his perch in a nearby tree, leaving one bleeding from a gash in the neck and another holding a crossbow with a broken string. Haern kicked him in the

chest to force him back, needing the space. The last swords-
man hacked at him, but Haern spun his cloaks, using them to
appear farther to the right than he was. The strike hit nothing
but air and cloth. Haern continued his spin, slashed his foe's
arm, reversed the spin, and buried his sword in the henchman's
stomach, just below his armor.

Pain spiked up his arm. He struck on reflex, ending up cutting the crossbowman across the mouth. The man dropped the
dagger he'd drawn and clutched his jaw as blood ran across his
hands. He tried to say something, but it came out as an unin-
telligible sob. Haern glanced at his arm. The cut would scar,
but assuming it didn't get infected he'd be fine. Frustrated at
his mistake, he leaped at the lone survivor, who turned to flee.
A kick took out his knee, and he fell. Haern's swords pierced
his lungs, and then he sobbed no more.

Cursing at the pain, Haern approached the road. He kept
the blood on his blades, wanting the fear it would bring. The
red contrasted with the snow, made the swords seem all the
more deadly. When he stepped from between the trees, he saw
both riders on the far side. The younger raised his crossbow
and fired. It tore a hole in Haern's cloaks as he flung himself to
the side. He spun around a tree and emerged, but the soldier
had not even begun to reload.

"Who are you, stranger?" asked the older man. "What are
you hoping for? Is it coin you want?"

"Too many questions," Haern said, watching the last soldier.
His hand kept inching toward his hip, but for what?

"Then answer me just one: is the boy alive?"

"I don't know, nor care. He was a distraction. If he lives he'll
freeze by morning."

Their leader seemed pleased by the answer. Haern made sure
he didn't blink, didn't twitch, didn't reveal the lie.

"Good," said the older man. "Then what is it you want now? You cannot kill us, and you cannot make off with my gold. You'd need to tether the oxen and drive it many days to town. So please, accept my offer. Leave us be, and I will allow you take as much gold as you can carry."

"You'd buy your safety with what I can freely take?" Haern asked.

"Freely? Nothing is free, thief. Everything is bought with sweat and blood. Come spill it if you'd dare."

Haern chuckled. Whoever the man was, he reminded him of his father. Not a good comparison.

"Leave," he said. "I have no use..."

He rolled behind the tree as the throwing dagger pierced the bark, hurled with frightening precision from the soldier's hip. From behind the tree he laughed.

"Ride off!" Haern shouted to them. "Even if you have a hundred of those daggers to throw, it won't matter. Flee or die!"

He listened and waited. The men muttered quietly, and when done they rode north. Haern sighed and looked to his arm. Still bleeding, and its pain was now a deep ache. It'd have to wait. He trudged off for the boy, who looked horribly pale.

"I'm sorry I couldn't bandage these sooner," he said as he knelt before him. He pulled the boy's hands away and looked at the stab. "You can thank Ashhur this wasn't an inch deeper, or you'd be like the rest of them."

He used more cloth from his cloaks to tie a bandage around the boy's chest, then turned his attention to the arm. So far the boy hadn't spoken a word, only watched with a glazed look in his eyes. Fearing he might pass out at any moment, Haern slapped him a couple times across the face.

"Stay with me," he said. "I bled for you. Least you could do is survive."

The earlier bandage he'd applied had soaked through, so he removed it, cut another strip, and tied it. Given the depth and severity of the cut, he wondered if the whole arm would need to go, but knew someone wiser in healing arts should decide that. So long as it didn't turn green and rot off, he figured the boy had a chance of regaining its use.

"What's your name?" Haern asked him as he tore the shirt off the dead soldier beside them. When the boy didn't answer, Haern snapped his fingers in front of his eyes a few times. Still nothing. Sighing, he cut up the shirt and used it to form himself a sling.

"Come on, what's your name? We're friends, blood brothers, fellow travelers in the snow. You're not too cold to speak, are you?"

After a few seconds the boy shook his head. Good. At least he was somewhat alert. Haern tore free the cloak of another dead soldier, wrapped it around the boy, and then lifted him into his arms. His wounded arm shrieked in protest, so he shifted a bit of the weight onto his shoulder.

"Name," he said. "I'd really love a name."

But the boy slumped and passed out. Haern sighed again. He returned to the road and surveyed the carnage, laying the boy beside the fire while he searched. It didn't make any sense. The attackers were well armed and well equipped, and they bore the symbol of a lord. When he looked into the wagons, the exact same symbol was stamped upon the crates. The oxen's harnesses had the same as well, a sickle raised before a mountain.

If he'd had time he might have hidden the gold so it couldn't be taken by the first passerby. But he didn't. Furious at his confusion and helplessness, he used his sword to draw an eye in the dirt beside the fire, where no snow lay. Beneath it he scrawled his mark, "The Watcher." At least he might accomplish something out of all this. Let the thieves know that even outside Veldaren they were not safe from him.

"Well, boy," he said, returning to the fire. "I'm sure it's nice and warm, but we have to move. I can't remember the last farm I passed, but it's our only chance. Can you walk?"

No response. Haern bandaged his own arm, tore open one of the crates, and grabbed a handful of coins. They bore a symbol he easily recognized, that of the Gemcroft family.

"What do you have to do with the Serpents?" he wondered aloud. A shame he had no one to interrogate, no time to investigate. He pocketed the coins, hauled the boy into his arms, and started walking south.

There was another reason he needed to hurry. The two who'd fled would certainly return, and he had a feeling it'd be with far more than their initial eight. Step after step he cursed the snow, the wind, the cold, and his clumsy mistake that had cost him a cut. All the while the boy slept in his arms. By nightfall Haern felt ready to collapse. He walked off the road, kicked aside the snow before a tree, and set the boy down. He wrapped him tighter in his cloaks and did his best to keep hope. The boy's lips were blue, his skin a deathly white. He'd lost so much blood, right when he needed its warmth the most.

Still standing, Haern pulled an emblem hanging by a silver chain from beneath his shirt. It was of a golden mountain, and as he held it he prayed over the boy.

"Just keep him warm and alive, Ashhur. And don't forget me, too. I could use the damn help."

He put away the emblem, sat down beside his nameless boy, and pulled him close so they could share their warmth.

"It'll get better," he said, not sure if the boy could hear him or not. He was so thoroughly wrapped Haern couldn't see his eyes. "Don't worry about any pain. As my father once said, pain is a tool that should always be under our control. It teaches us when we err. It distracts and weakens our opponents. And for you, it'll help you for the rest of your life. Who cares about a silly scratch from a sword when you've been struck to the bone, yeah?"

He felt like a moron yammering on, but he did so anyway. At last he heard the boy snore, and he leaned his head back against the bark. His eyes looked to the clouded heavens.

"Couldn't you at least stop the snow?" he asked Ashhur.

Ashhur didn't bother to respond.

Haern slept through the night, waking only once at the sound of hoofbeats. He curled his body tighter against the tree and kept perfectly still. From the corner of his eye he saw the light of torches. Unable to see his tracks veer off the road because of the fresh snow, the horsemen rode right on by.

"Never mind," Haern whispered once they were gone. "Go ahead and let it snow."

He closed his eyes, leaned his head against the boy's, and slept until morning.

Haern had little food and water, certainly not enough for two. He ate the food, deciding he needed the strength for carrying the boy. He did his best to get the child to drink, though. Other than a few quick sips, he was unsuccessful. His back ached, and his arm throbbed, but he forced the pain far away, as he'd been trained to do by his many mentors. He carried the boy, stopping every hour to rest and catch his breath. Any time he let him go, the boy collapsed to the ground.

So much for making the brat walk, Haern thought.

He shook his head and immediately felt guilty. Of course the boy couldn't walk. He was sitting at the Reaper's door. That he even had his eyes open was a miracle.

They walked along the road, encountering no others. Evidently no one else was dumb enough to travel in such weather. The snow had stopped in the morning, and as he followed the road he observed the chaos of hoofprints. They all appeared to be headed south, with no hint of them returning. Haern knew he'd have to stay alert for their eventual trip back north. He was in no shape to fight a group of horsemen.

Keep walking, he told himself. *Keep walking. Keep going.* The son of Thren Felhorn would not die unknown in the wilderness. He couldn't. He wouldn't.

Near the end of the second day he finally found a farm. He crossed the fields, every bone in his body aching. The boy hadn't had a drink the entire day, and his skin was hot with fever. Part of Haern wondered if the cold was the only thing keeping him from burning alive. At the door to the home he stopped, hid his swords with his cloaks, and knocked.

"I come in time of need," he shouted, surprised by how hoarse his voice sounded. "Please, I have a wounded child with me."

The door crept open. In the yellow light of lamps he saw the glint of an old short sword. A man looked through the crack, saw him holding the boy.

"Winter's nearing its end," said the man. "We have little to spare."

"I'll pay," Haern said. "Please, I've walked without rest for days."

The man glanced inside, whispered something, and then nodded.

"Come on in," said the farmer. "And by Ashhur's grace, I pray you mean no trouble."

Haern found what appeared to be the entire family gathered in the front room, under blankets and around a stove whose heat felt glorious on Haern's skin. He saw two girls huddled beside each other, their hair a pretty brown. The farmer had two boys, one of them of age, and they held knives as if to help their father should it come to bloodshed. His wife sat beside the fire, tending it.

"He has a fever," Haern said, setting the boy down beside the stove. "And he hasn't had food or drink for days."

"I'll get some water," the wife said as she stood. She cast a worried glance at her husband, then vanished into the next room.

"My name is Matthew Pensfield," said the farmer, extending his hand. Haern accepted it, and was shocked at how much his own hand shook. He hadn't eaten much, he knew, but had it really affected him so greatly?

"Haern," he said as he pulled his cloaks tight about him and surveyed the house. It seemed cozy enough, and not a hint of draft. The man had done well in building it.

"I know some of the Haerns," said Matthew as his wife returned. He had a hard look, his square jaw covered with stubble, but he spoke plainly and seemed more at ease now that Haern showed no inclination to violence. "Good men, own several fields west of here. What's your full name? I might have heard them speak of you."

"Just Haern," he replied, nodding to the boy. "And I have no name for him. I found him wounded; why does not concern you. That room beyond there, is that your kitchen? Might we speak in private?"

Some of the farmer's worry returned, but he nodded anyway.

"I reckon we can."

Once in the other room, Haern dropped his voice to a whisper.

"I have a difficult request for you," he said. "I need you to take care of that boy until he's regained his health. I cannot stay."

"We don't have enough food to..."

He stopped as Haern drew out a handful of coins and dropped them upon the table. His eyes stretched wide. The gold shone in the dim light.

"People will be hunting for him," Haern said. "No matter what, you treat him like your own child. When he regains his health, he'll tell you his name and where his family might be, assuming they're still alive. Until then, give him up to no one."

"What if they threaten violence?" Matthew asked, his eyes lingering on the gold.

"Would you give up one of your daughters?"

The farmer shook his head. "No. I wouldn't."

Haern let the cloaks fall away from his left side, exposing one of his swords.

"I hope you understand," he said. "I'll return, and if I find him abused, or dead, I will repay you tenfold in blood."

"He's sick and wounded. What if he dies of fever?"

Haern smiled, and he let the coldness he felt in his bones creep into his eyes.

"How well do you trust your children, your wife, to tell the truth? I will know one way or the other what happened to him. Do not give me cause to wonder."

Matthew swallowed. "I understand. This land is harsh, and we've taken in children before. Once he heals up, and the weather breaks, I'll take him where he needs to go. If he doesn't know, well, there's always a need for more hands on a farm."

Haern slapped him on the shoulder, nearly laughed at his terrified jump.

"Good man," he said. "Now how about a warm meal?"

He ate some soup while he watched the wife tend to the boy. She put a wet cloth across his forehead, dressed his wounds far better than Haern had, and then used a spoon to slowly get him to drink. Haern was impressed. Seemed these Pensfields knew how to take care of themselves. Whoever the boy was, he could do far worse for a temporary home.

The soup did wonders for his mood. Its warmth seeped deep into his chest and then spread to the rest of his limbs. With that and the heat of the wood stove, he felt warmed within and without. He could feel his muscles tightening from lack of motion after so much exertion, and he did his best to stretch in the cramped quarters.

"You can spend the night here if you wish," Matthew said as the day neared its end. "I'd be a sad man to banish a guest just as the sun sets."

"Thank you," Haern said. He shifted farther away from the fire so the children could take a turn. He wrapped his blankets around his body and closed his eyes. For the first time in his entire life he found himself in a true home, with a real family. The children bickered, but there was a harmless familiarity to it. He thought of his own childhood, never spent with someone his own age, only the parade of tutors and mentors, training him to read, to write, to move, to kill. Had he ever curled up on the floor beside a fire, surrounded by a family that would never wish him harm? Had he ever been inside a house that felt at peace? Had he ever...

He slept, and his dreams were dull and calm, and he did not remember them when he woke.

CHAPTER

6

It was Veliana's third attempt at killing Deathmask, and the first she'd been personally involved with. She lay atop the roof of their headquarters, a crossbow in hand. The pale sun shone down on her, and she found herself thankful for the winter. In any other season she'd have been sweating like mad on the roof's shadeless wood slats.

"What if you miss?" asked Garrick, who stood behind her so he couldn't be seen from the street.

"Then Rick will take him down," Veliana said. She pointed to the building on the opposite side of the street. A man in gray lay atop it, a crossbow beside him.

"I can't believe he's not dead yet," said Garrick as he took a chunk of crimleaf from his pocket and began chewing. "Are our men truly so incompetent?"

Veliana rolled her eyes. The first attempt to kill Deathmask had been a simple stabbing in the night. She'd selected one of their lower-ranking thugs for the deed. They'd found the thug's body rotting beside Deathmask's bed in the morning. How he'd died, no one knew. Deathmask hadn't shown the slightest irritation at the attempt, either. Veliana held in a chuckle. Shit, the guy had tossed her a wink on the way to breakfast.

The second attempt had actually been three separate instances of poisoning his food. He hadn't eaten any of it. The third time, Veliana caught him waving his hand over his meal. That same day both their cooks died vomiting blood. Garrick ranted and assumed they had mishandled the poison. Veliana knew differently.

"We've given him a simple task," Veliana said, sighting the crossbow on their door. "He's to collect protection money from a handful of vendors a few blocks over. When he exits the door, he should see Rick preparing to fire. In fact, I'm counting on it. He's too damn clever not to notice. Maybe he'll run, or cast a spell, or pretend he doesn't see. It won't matter. That's when I put an arrow through his back."

"So confident," Garrick said. "Remember, if this fails, I make the next plan. This was your last chance to get things done safe and clean."

"I figured you'd like things safe," she muttered.

"What?" he asked.

"I said we should reconsider. He's clearly skilled. What if he isn't here on someone else's payroll? What if he really wants a position in our guild?"

Garrick chuckled. "If he's that good, why choose ours? We're far from the most powerful. Others would have made more sense. Or why not become a mercenary? The pay would be better, and then he could kill our kind all he wants. I'm sure the Trifect would love to have him on their…"

"Quiet," Veliana hissed.

The door opened, and out stepped Deathmask. He wore

his red robes and the dark gray cloak of their guild. As always when he went out in public, he'd tied a gray cloth around his face, hiding all but his eyes and hair. His back was to her. She glanced at Rick, who shot her a thumbs-up. When she looked back down, Deathmask was staring up at her. Slowly he shook his head, as if berating a child.

"Fuck," Veliana whispered. She pulled back from the ledge as Garrick asked her what was going on. "He's spotted me."

"Then Rick should..."

He stopped as they both watched Rick tumble over the edge of the building, blood gushing from his mouth and ears. When his body hit the ground, Veliana let out an involuntary gasp. Rick hadn't even fired, his crossbow lying useless atop the flat roof. Deathmask laughed, and he called out from the quiet street.

"I'm disappointed, Vel! Only the one?"

He walked west, and both remained silent as they watched him. Veliana hadn't seen what he'd done to Rick, but hadn't needed to. Deathmask was no normal thief or trickster. Only a spell could have done what she'd just seen, a dark and powerful one. She was playing a game against an opponent she knew nothing about. Such was a sure path toward losing.

"That son of a bitch," Garrick said. "He's toying with us. He knows we want him dead, and he doesn't care! If we don't do something soon, I'll be a mockery to the rest of the guild."

"Of course you will be," Veliana said as she stood. "You're trying to kill someone you accepted into our guild, all without any proof or reason. *That* is what will upset the rest of our guildmembers, not that you can't kill him. So far you've been lucky enough to have Deathmask kill off everyone who's ever been involved in the attempts, but word will get out in time."

She thought Garrick would explode, but instead he gave her an amused grin.

"You failed, Vel, so now I choose the attempt. Enough of poison and cowardly arrows. It's time you bloodied your hands."

"So long as you don't have to bloody yours," she said, offering him a mock bow. Her sarcasm hid her fear. She couldn't back down, not when Garrick was starting to develop a spine. But did she really want to mess with Deathmask?

She hung from the edge of the roof, dropped down to a windowsill, and then used it to fall to the street. A closer look confirmed what she'd already realized: Deathmask was equal to her in skill, if not superior. She found a thin razor embedded deep in Rick's neck. No doubt Deathmask's spell had required some sort of physical contact, and he'd thrown the razor as a way of carrying that spell. A simple but foolproof ambush, but it was her man who lay dead, not her target.

Laughter floated down. She flipped Garrick a rude gesture, knowing he stood at the roof's edge watching her. So be it. No matter what Garrick thought, the Ash Guild was hers, and she would remind him of that fact. No doubt he viewed her coming attempt as a win-win, for either she or Deathmask would die. There had to be another way. More important, she had to think of a replacement for him, and soon.

"Bury Rick somewhere," she said to her guards at the door as she marched inside to think.

Any deviation from Deathmask's normal routine would immediately alert him, so Veliana played it patient. Two days after the third failed attempt she had one of her lower-ranking members tell him he was to stay up late working as a guard. She hoped the tedium might dull his senses for when she struck. Despite his spotting her before, she took to the rooftop and waited. Four hours before dawn, when her own eyes started to droop, she decided it was time. She drank a mixture she'd prepared earlier in the day, a combination of strong tea and herbs. A few minutes later she felt the mixture kick in. Her head ached, but her drowsiness was gone.

She drew her daggers and crept to the rooftop's edge. No arrows or crossbows this time. If he really was a skilled spell-caster, her only chance was at close range, where she could disrupt the intricate movements needed to cast. She looked down and saw him standing several feet away from the building, keeping watch outside their safe house as instructed.

Damn it, she thought. *Won't be a straight drop. He can't possibly know I'm coming, can he?*

But of course he could. He might be able to read her mind for all she knew. Now was the time. He was mortal. He was fallible. She was the better. She had to prove that, not just to Garrick, but to herself.

She leaped from the roof, silent as a ghost, her daggers aimed for his neck, her knees bent and ready to absorb the impact of their collision. She felt exhilaration soar through her, the wind blowing her hair as she fell. In that half-second she saw him turn, saw him step aside. She twisted, suddenly panicking. He'd known. Somehow he'd known.

Rolling with the landing helped reduce the pain, but not by much. Scraping along the ground, one of her hands flooded with pain, jarred backward before suddenly going numb. The dagger fell from her limp fingers. She tumbled along, then forced herself out of the roll. Turning around, she expected her death, some sort of spell to sap her breath or explode her blood from her nostrils. Instead Deathmask stood there, shaking his head.

"Not good enough," he said. "I need you stronger, faster. Otherwise you are useless to me."

She clutched her numb hand to her chest and glared.

"No matter what it is, I won't help you," she said. "I've worked too hard to let you destroy everything."

"Destroy?" Deathmask said as he looped his arms in a circle. "I've come to perfect, not destroy."

She lunged at him as shadows pooled around his feet, bursting upward to form a wall that her dagger could not penetrate. She stabbed again, then spun about looking for an opening. There was none. Unsure, she closed her eyes and focused. She'd be vulnerable, but so long as the shadow wall remained, she might have the time. Power was focused through her, channeled into her dagger. Purple fire surrounded the blade, and with a cry she thrust it forward. It broke through the wall, which shattered and vanished as if it were made of fine glass. She had the briefest moment to enjoy the look of panic on Deathmask's face before her dagger cut flesh.

It wasn't fatal, and she cursed her foul luck. She'd guessed wrong where he stood, and her dagger only slashed his side and cut his robe. Warm blood spilled across her hand. They were so close it seemed time froze as they eyed one another, preparing the next moves for their dance. He drew a blade as he shifted away from her. Her kick sent it flying, and she stabbed again, wishing she had her other dagger. Deathmask fell back, his palms open. A light flashed from them, except it was black instead of white. It dazed her all the same, and her next two swings cut only air.

"What is wrong?" she asked as she took two steps and jumped. Her heel smashed into his stomach, and he gasped as he crumpled to the ground. "Where is the brutal killer who bested all my plans?"

Veliana dropped to one knee and thrust for his throat, not caring for his answer. He caught her wrist just as the tip of the dagger entered his flesh. A single drop of blood ran down his neck as they struggled. By the gods he was strong!

"Still here," he said, all trace of amusement gone. His voice was cold, merciless. She felt a shiver run up her spine. She jerked her arm back, but still he held her. His brown eyes met hers. If only she could tear off that damn mask of his. If only she could see his face, remind herself he was human, for his strength was unreal.

She swept her left leg around, taking out his feet. He didn't let go even as he fell. Together they hit the ground. The collision bumped her injured hand, and her fingers throbbed in agony. They had to be dislocated, if not broken. Still her dagger hovered inches from his flesh, unable to either attack or pull away. He landed on his back, and instead of rolling over he reached up and held her good arm with both hands.

"I could burn your flesh until I clung to bone," he said. His tone told her he spoke truth. "Are you ready to listen, or must I find another?"

"No others," she said as she prepared. "You won't have the chance."

She dropped the dagger. Her legs kicked, pushing her into the air. Not high, just enough for her to drive her knees into his chest, blasting the air from his lungs. He still clutched her, but she rammed an elbow into his throat, denying him his next few words. She pressed her body against his, keeping the elbow tight. Their foreheads touched. Still he held her other hand.

"What do you want? What is your game? Who are you?"

She released the pressure on his throat just enough for him to speak. Her nerves remained on edge. The second he flinched, or said a syllable that sounded remotely like a spell, she'd crush his larynx and leave him gagging on the street.

"I told you before, I have no name." He stared at her, unafraid.

"Bullshit. Everyone has a name."

"And mine was taken from me!"

The anger seemed to warm his very body. Her arm flared with white-hot pain where he held it.

"By who?" she asked, her voice low. She wanted him calm. She wanted answers before she ended his life.

"The Council of Mages. They banished me, and stole my name away."

"Banished for what?"

She heard him chuckle.

"Everyone has their secrets, and I must have mine. What will you do, Veliana? Will you kill me? Or will you listen? I am your last hope. Your guild is crumbling, and you've lost control of Garrick, haven't you?"

Her hesitation was answer enough, so she didn't bother to lie.

"How do you know that?" she asked.

He shook his head.

"I will answer nothing with an elbow on my throat. Let me up. I promise no harm will come to you tonight."

Her mind whirled as she thought. He was clever, and dangerous. She could kill him, but what would that gain her? Garrick would get what he wanted, his paranoia fed. Clearly this Deathmask had a plan, but whose? Could it be the Council's? Did he lie about the banishment? No, his anger was too sincere. Despite the mask, she felt he spoke truth. Then what? What should she do?

She thought of Garrick's mockery, of his telling her how she needed him.

"Stand then," she said, letting him go as he released her wrist. "And let me hear you speak."

"I will not tell you everything," he said as he stood and rubbed his throat. "Not until I can trust you, and perhaps not even afterward. For now, just know that my assignment from the Council was to...watch over the guilds. I know of your true skill and control, Veliana. I know that Garrick was but a puppet, and you were pulling the strings. But that isn't the case anymore, is it? Something's changed."

He retrieved one of her daggers and tossed it to her. She caught it in her good hand and sheathed the blade. Instead of continuing, he walked over and eyed her other hand.

"If I wanted to hurt you, I'd have done so already," he said when she tensed.

His fingers brushed hers, feeling along the bone.

"Dislocated," he said. "Bite the hilt of your dagger if you must."

"Just do it."

One after the other he yanked the fingers back into place. The pain was immense, and after the third she leaned against him, unable to stand. He held her steady, and when he finished he removed his mask and tied it around her hand as a bandage. Through the tears in her eyes she looked upon his face. The anger was gone. It had never been directed at her, just those who had banished him. She felt her curiosity grow. Just what did he plan for her guild?

"Listen to me," he whispered, as if suddenly worried others were listening. He leaned close, his cheek almost touching hers. "I cannot do this alone. I desire to create something special, something Veldaren has never before seen. You won't be the new guildmaster, I won't lie about that, but you will always be there as my right hand."

"Why would I trade Garrick for you if my position shall stay the same?"

He smiled, a bit of his amusement returning to twinkle in his eye.

"Because I respect you. Garrick only knows fear. Which would you prefer? And I will not replace Garrick, not entirely. My aim is greater. We will be legends in the underworld, Vel. All you must do is accept my wisdom."

She looked to her bandaged hand, then to his eyes.

"I must think on it."

"Time is against me right now, but you may have a day and a night to decide. Garrick will soon stop his tricks and poisons and midnight arrows. A time will come when he publicly orders me to be executed by the rest of the guild, regardless of the fallout. I must have you at my side when that happens."

She pulled away.

"Resume your post," she said.

"Of course, milady."

Before she could go, he put an arm in her way.

"That trick with your dagger," he said. "The violet flame... where did you learn to do something like that?"

This time it was her turn to smile.

"Everyone has their secrets."

He seemed amused, and he stepped aside so she could pass. She went into the headquarters, found her bunk, and lay down, not to sleep but to think. She felt lost and confused. There wasn't anyone within the Ash Guild she could trust for advice, but there was one woman outside the guild who would die to protect her secrets. Someone who had saved her from a horrible death at the hands of a disgusting man who'd gone by the moniker of the Worm.

Veliana left her bed, changed into a darker outfit, and donned her gray cloak. She used a different door from the one Deathmask guarded, and then took to the rooftops. Once she was in the open night air, she removed the cloak signifying her allegiance to the Ash Guild and then set out to meet Zusa behind the Gemcroft mansion.

CHAPTER

7

It was past midnight when Arthur Hadfield arrived at the gates of the Gemcroft mansion, escorted by nine of his soldiers. One of the guards immediately recognized him and opened the gate.

"Our lady sleeps," said the guard, "but we would not turn away such an esteemed visitor in the cold of night. I pray no ill news brings you here at such an hour?"

"Pray all you want," Arthur said. "But it won't change the news I bring."

Inside the main foyer they stopped and forfeited their weapons, even Arthur. He gave the guard a stern look as he handed over his beautiful long sword, a family heirloom of five generations.

"A lash for every scratch," he said. "Unless you think Alyssa would not listen to me."

"Understood, sir," said the guard. "Please, wait here. Our

lady will be down shortly; we have already sent a servant to wake her."

"Warm some food for my men," Arthur said. "And find me something stiff to drink. I'd rather not meet Alyssa looking pale as a corpse fresh from the grave."

"Right away."

Several servants rushed from one room to the next, haggard-eyed and clothes unkempt. Most of the guards looked a little better, but they were probably used to odd hours and the constant threat of thieves sneaking in at night. An elderly lady appeared and gestured to the soldiers to follow her.

"Coming?" one asked Arthur.

He shook his head.

"I'll wait here. All I need is a drink. Enjoy yourselves, and don't forget"—he glanced at the servant—"to find yourselves lodging for the night. We won't go traipsing for an inn at this hour."

It seemed the servant got the message, and even if she didn't, he knew his men would hammer the point home. Standing in the foyer, he removed his bearskin coat and set it aside. A large fireplace burned before him, so he stood beside it and let its heat sink into his skin. When a servant arrived with a glass, he took it and gave it a taste.

"Thank you," he said, doing his best to hold in a denigrating remark. The lady had brought him a recent vintage, no doubt the cheapest bottle in the mansion other than what was reserved for the hired help. Probably thought they were keeping Alyssa's interests in mind since she had not ordered it for him, but they should have known better. He swallowed the rest of it anyway. It might look like brown water and taste like piss, but at least it'd still warm his bones.

He watched the fire burn as he waited, his thoughts racing through the recent events. Alyssa needed to marry soon, and with Mark Tullen dead, Arthur had removed all serious competition. Only two wrinkles remained. One was Alyssa's child, heir to the Gemcroft wealth, as well as a potential danger should he describe the ambush accurately enough to blame Arthur. The other was that strange man who had attacked them. He'd been dressed like a thief, yet none of his colors had marked him as a member of any guild. Plus there was that symbol carved in blood beside the fire. The Watcher. Arthur didn't visit Veldaren often, but it seemed things had gotten far stranger in his absence. Not for the first time he felt thankful he lived in the north, where men had to survive by the plow, the sword, or the pick, and not by the deftness of their sticky fingers.

"Lord Hadfield," Alyssa said, pulling him from his thoughts. He turned to her and smiled as she approached through the doorway. Her hair was immaculate, her cheeks warmed with rouge. The dark circles under her eyes were hidden with powder. Now he knew why she'd taken so long to come down. At least her clothing was appropriate for the late hour, a crimson robe tied with a yellow sash. She wrapped her arms in his and gave him a chaste kiss on the cheek.

"Forgive me for ruining your sleep," he said. "It's a cruelty, waking someone at this hour, but I feared it'd be crueler risking someone other than myself bringing you the news."

"Enough," Alyssa said, holding her arms against her chest as if she were cold. "Good news rarely comes after midnight. Whatever it is, tell me, or my mind will assume the worst."

Arthur frowned and looked away for a moment, just long enough for her to believe he was in doubt.

"You could assume nothing worse than the truth," he said at last. "I'm sorry, Alyssa. Your son is dead."

She'd been preparing herself for terrible news, he could tell, but it didn't matter. She took a step back as if he'd slapped her. Her mouth dropped open, and her hands quivered as she pressed them to her lips.

"No," she whispered. Tears swelled in her eyes, then fell, smearing the powder. "No, no, please, you're wrong, you have to be wrong…"

He shook his head. This was by far the easiest part. None of it was a lie.

"Mark Tullen came and took Nathaniel from Tyneham, where I'd brought him for tutoring. They joined one of my caravans traveling to the city. I thought they'd be safe, but someone ambushed them several days ago, stealing the shipment of gold."

"Mark?" Alyssa asked as she tried in vain to compose herself. "Was he…?"

Arthur wrapped his arms around her waist and pulled her close.

"There were no survivors," he whispered. "They piled the bodies together and burned them."

She fell against him and sobbed. A bit of rouge rubbed onto his vest, and he wondered whether it would come off. As her cries escalated he tightened his grip, holding her against him. He gently rocked her from side to side, his cheek resting on the top of her head. He felt unprepared for her grief, and he mentally delayed his plans of marriage. She'd need time to get over this, at least three months. Perhaps if he could bring her closure he could make things progress faster, but how?

She asked a question, but it was muffled against his chest.

"What, my love?" he asked, tilting her face up by her chin. It was the first time he'd called her that, and he knew it would carry far more impact now given the circumstances.

"Who?" she asked. She sniffed and pulled free of his grip. "I want to know who."

"I told you, someone wishing for our gold. Ruffians, most likely, come from only the gods know where."

Alyssa shook her head. It seemed as if her skin were darkening to red, her whole body suddenly given over to rage. When she spoke again, her voice was held together by such fierce concentration he worried she had pierced his lies.

"That's not good enough," she said. "There has to be something, some clue, some mistake they made. They can't make off with that much gold without others noticing. No one is that perfect, that calculated. If you know something, tell me!"

Arthur felt his opening, and it took all his willpower to keep from smiling.

"There was a...symbol," he said, as if hesitant. "I didn't wish to bother you with it, not when you should be grieving."

"I have the rest of my life to grieve," she said, wiping her makeup with her hands. "What was the symbol?"

"It was an open eye, drawn in blood. Below it was written a name, a strange name. The Watcher. I believe he is tied to the local thief guilds in some manner, though I cannot say more, for it has been years since I lived in Veldaren. Perhaps someone in your employ will better know who he is than I."

By the way she startled, he knew he'd hit his mark.

"How dare he?" she said. "He kills my son, and my...and Mark, and then dares leave his name? I'll see him flayed before me, that heartless bastard."

"Allow me to help in the search," Arthur offered.

"No," she said, shaking her head. "This is my loss, and my fault. I sent Mark for him when I should have left him in safety."

"It was *my* caravan, don't forget."

She looked at him, and he forced a mask of anger across his face. He had to seem regretful, not eager. He had to seem furious at the loss of his men, not pleased with Mark's death. He did his best, and it seemed like she bought it.

"Very well," she said. "Kill him if you must, though I'd prefer him alive."

"Torture and vengeance shouldn't belong to a woman so beautiful as you."

"Then blame the world for giving me this sorrow. If the gods are kind, I'll be the one to cut this Watcher's throat and feel the blood spill across my hands."

After a long pause she asked, "Did you bring...the body?"

"No," Arthur said, shaking his head. "As I said, it was a great pyre, and we left it alone."

"So my son will spend eternity in some common grave, his ashes trodden on by horses and oxen? For all your attempts at kindness, you failed me terribly, Arthur. You should have brought me his bones."

She walked to the fireplace and retrieved a bell from its mantel. When she shook it, two servants came running.

"Please find quarters for Lord Hadfield," she told them, then turned to Arthur. "I need time to rest, and I feel I would be poor company for you. Good night."

He bowed and followed the servants. They showed him to his room, a nice enough place: large bed, soft mattress, and thick curtains he pulled back from the windows to let in the starlight. Given such haste, there were no logs or coals in the fireplace, and the room felt only marginally warmer than the outside. He put his coat back on and sat atop the bed. His joints creaked, and he lay upon the mattress trying to will his muscles to relax. Mere minutes later he heard a knock on his door.

"Come in," Arthur said, wishing he still had his sword.

Bertram, the old advisor who had worked for the Gemcroft family for at least fifty years, stepped inside.

"I've yet to speak with Alyssa about these matters," the man said, "but I know her well enough to anticipate her response. She will put me in charge of the boy's funeral. Did you bring Nathaniel's body with you?"

The question stung, just as deeply as when Alyssa had first asked. He had no body . . .

"Burned," he said. "Back with the caravan. Alyssa didn't take too kindly to that when I told her."

Bertram frowned. "I do not blame her. It would be greatly distressing if we didn't have something to bury for the funeral. Not that it matters, in my opinion. Bones are bones after a fire reaches them, yes?"

Arthur stared at the old man, trying to understand what was going on. Was he helping him, or fishing for information?

"I doubt Alyssa would agree," he said, erring on the side of caution.

"She cannot judge what she does not know." Bertram turned for the door, put his hand on the handle, and then stopped. "I will be very busy over the next few days, and will have no time to venture into the wild. Perhaps you, or some of your men, might retrieve the body for me? I would greatly appreciate it."

"Anything I can do to help."

Bertram glanced back and smiled.

"Claim her hand, and you'll have done all that I could ask. Good night, Lord Hadfield."

Arthur waited a few minutes, then called for a servant.

"Bring me one of my soldiers," he ordered. "A man named Oric."

"Yes, milord," the servant said, bowing quickly before vanishing. Trying to keep his mood from souring too much,

Arthur paced and waited. When the knock on his door finally came, he had no chance to answer it before Oric barged inside.

"You needed something?" Oric asked. He was an ugly man: thick cheeks, round jaw, and flat nose that made him look like his mother had mated with a pig. He was skilled with a blade, though, and meaner than any soldier he'd ever employed. Not a brilliant man, but he could follow events as they happened, and every now and then he'd have an insight that left Arthur pleased.

"Who did you work for before coming to me?" Arthur asked.

"Mostly for the Conningtons. Past year or so they got shy when it came to killing thieves, so I went looking for more enjoyable work." He grinned. "Everyone told me to talk to you. I think you have yourself a reputation, and not a good one."

"Hard times require hard men," Arthur said. "Do you have any friends that might still be here in Veldaren?"

"A mercenary never has friends, not if he wants to live long enough to get his pay. And sure, I have some contacts that should still be around. What you thinking?"

"That man in gray who attacked us at the caravan, the one calling himself the Watcher...we need to bring his corpse to Alyssa so she might move on from her son's death. That, and who knows where his loyalties lie? He could do me great harm by telling the right pair of ears what actually happened."

"It won't be easy," Oric said. "I never met him when working for Leon, but we all heard about him. The thieves can't stand him, but they can't find him either. Everyone's always pointing fingers, convinced he's a member of this or that guild. My thinking? He belongs to none, just wants them all dead."

"I don't care," Arthur said. "Whoever you hire, make sure they're good enough to handle the job. Cost is no object."

Oric nodded. "What about the boy?"

"I must stay here with Alyssa in her time of need. Take half my soldiers and ride north. We must make sure he did not survive."

Oric's grin was ear-to-ear.

"If he ain't frozen in the woods somewhere, we'll find him. Don't worry, Arthur. Might not be how we wanted it, but when it all boils down, you're in control. Just keep whispering them sweet words in that pretty ear of hers. I'll take care of any blood-spilling."

"One more thing," Arthur said. "Alyssa wants Nathaniel's body."

Oric raised an eyebrow. "That's an interesting request to fill, given the circumstances."

"And I expect you, and you alone, to handle it. Remember, I told them the body was burned."

"Consider the problem solved," Oric said, heading for the door. "We never talked, and you know nothing of this. Watch your tongue. We're sleeping in the den of lions now."

"We're the lions in this den," Arthur said, flashing Oric a grin. He followed Oric out the door, but whereas the mercenary headed for his crowded quarters with the rest of the guards, Arthur headed to the eastern half of the complex, to where Alyssa no doubt lay alone, tired, and in desperate need of his comfort.

Alyssa waited until her servants escorted Arthur Hadfield to his room before she fled to her own. She was only halfway there when she stumbled and fell sobbing in the carpeted hallway. In the quiet of the night she felt alone, and if any servants or guards were nearby, they allowed her privacy for her grief. She thought of Nathaniel, her son, her wonderful, handsome son. A thousand memories flashed through her mind, all of them tainted with sorrow. His smile she'd never see again. His laugh she'd never hear again. The way he'd cried at night, the way he'd nuzzled her breast when only a newborn, the way he... the way he...

More sobs. She felt close to breaking, as if her sanity would pour out with her tears. She'd lost many over the years, friends, her father, but why Nathaniel? Why him? Why now? How could she have made such a foolish mistake?

Over and over she slammed a fist against the floor. Not her fault. Not her fault, damn it all, not her fault! It was them, the thieves and their greed and lust. It was this whole conflict, a decade of paranoia and bloodshed and poisoning. Most of all it was that Watcher, a monster unleashed against her by the thieves. Whoever he was, whatever he was, he'd pay. All of them, they would pay.

"I'm sorry," she heard Zusa say. She looked up, wiped her nose with her robe, and then nodded at the woman. Zusa sat opposite her in the hall, her knees pulled up to her chest. She still wore the strange wrappings of her former sect.

"He was supposed to be safe," Alyssa said, trying to regain control. Her voice quivered but a little. "Safe, and now he's dead. Did you talk to any of Arthur's soldiers?"

"They all say the same. They came with Arthur along the road and found the caravan attacked, with the bodies gathered together in a great pyre. Their only clue was a symbol of an eye, that of the Watcher."

"Who is he?" Alyssa asked. "What is he?"

"I don't know."

"Then find out, Zusa. Whatever it costs, whatever it takes, find him. I have never ached for something like I do for this. I want Nathaniel's killer brought to me. I want him to die by my hand. Can you do this? Can you find him?"

Zusa stood and then bowed low.

"The dark of the streets has always been my home," she said. "Nothing can hide from me. I will find him, I swear it."

Alyssa accepted her offered hand and stood. She kissed Zusa's fingers, then bowed herself.

"Thank you. Send Bertram to my room after a few minutes. Wake him if he isn't already."

Alyssa hurried to her room, wishing to wash her face of the garish rouge and powder she'd put on for Arthur. Once there she dipped a cloth into a basin of cold water, left there from when she first went to bed. Off came her painted face. She was still washing when she heard the knock at the door.

"Come in," she said.

Bertram entered, and he looked about half as bad as she felt. Dark circles rimmed his eyes, and his face was covered with uneven gray stubble.

"My dear child," he said, taking her into his arms. She set the cloth down and leaned against him. She felt so tired, so lost.

"It's like a terrible dream," she said softly. "One I can't seem to wake from. What did I do to deserve this, Bertram?"

"Nothing," he said. "No woman should endure this, but endure you must. The Gemcroft legacy must survive, no matter the hardships. And we shall, Alyssa, we shall. Whatever help you need, I am here for you."

"Thank you," she said. "It would help me greatly if you would prepare the . . . the services."

He nodded. "He will have a fine funeral, one worthy of his bloodline."

She bit back a bitter comment. While her son was alive he'd

been displeased with Nathaniel's bloodline. Now Nathaniel was dead, and his threat of succession was ended, Bertram seemed ready to forget all that. No, she scolded herself. She was overreacting. Bertram had never said a harsh word about Nathaniel, at least not an undeserved one.

"There is something else," she said, dipping her cloth in the basin and wiping underneath her eyes. "Call in every loan we have. Whatever stored grain, minerals, property, I want it all sold. We need gold, lots of it. Find every mercenary who needs work, no matter how expensive. Hire them, outfit them if need be."

"You wish to declare war against the guilds?" asked Bertram, allowing a tiny bit of doubt to creep into his voice.

"We're *already* at war, or have you forgotten? Come the night of Nathaniel's funeral, I want the streets to run red with the blood of thieves. I don't care what cloak they wear; I want them dead."

"You'll only reignite their anger, and ruin whatever progress we've made in the last…"

She spun on him, furious.

"I don't care! We've suffered and played the coward. No more peace. No more hope. Red, Bertram. I want the streets of this city red."

Bertram muttered and waved his hands, as if he could not decide what to say. Despite her grim mood she took pleasure in his distress. At last the old man regained his composure.

"But what will the king think when we flood his streets with chaos?"

"The king is a coward. He won't dare refuse me, and neither will you."

"So be it," he said. "We'll have the funeral three days from now. Come that night, you will have your folly. You run the risk of bankrupting a century of wealth, Alyssa. Is your vengeance truly worth so much?"

"That and more," she said. "Go. You have work to do."

He bowed and left, looking far from pleased. Both matters settled, her revenge in motion, she finished washing and collapsed onto her bed. She tried, but sleep remained a distant hope and nothing more. After half an hour she heard another knock on her door, just one, but it was firm. She ignored it. Thirty seconds later she heard it again.

"Come in," she said, removing her arm from over her eyes.

In stepped Arthur, and he paused at the door.

"I don't mean to intrude," he started, but she shook her head. He crossed the room and climbed into the bed beside her. His clothes were on, and for that she was thankful. His arms wrapped around her, and in their comfort she broke down once more. He was something steady, dependable amid the chaos overwhelming her. He said nothing as she cried, only gently stroked her hair and held her against him. His body was warm, and it felt pleasant. After a while he spoke.

"If there is anything you need, I am here. It doesn't matter the hour, nor the reason. I want you to know that."

She clutched his hand in hers and squeezed. Her whole body ached, and her temples throbbed. Her tears still ran down her face, but they were silent. She closed her eyes, pressing her face against his chest and focusing on the sound of his breathing. As long as she thought about that, only that, maybe she could fall asleep. Maybe she could forget the whole damned night, and come the morning the nightmare would be over. Maybe, just maybe...

She slept.

CHAPTER

8

In searching for the Watcher, there was one person Zusa knew would be best to meet with first. Behind the fenced Gemcroft estate was a small empty building. For years it had been nothing more than a shed for tools to be used by the servants tending the gardens and lawn, but Alyssa had turned it into a gift for Zusa. Within were a bedroom and a training room, the floor soft and padded, the walls lined with paintings of distant places. Zusa intended to gather a few things for her task of hunting down the Watcher, but when she stepped inside she was instead surprised to find Veliana waiting for her.

"I know I'm a day early," Veliana said. She'd taken off her cloak, and wore only skin-tight clothing of blacks and grays. "I've come not just for training, but for advice."

Zusa removed her own cloak and set it atop her bed. Veliana's boots lay beside the door, and she padded barefoot to the center of the room.

"Tell me while we spar," Zusa said. "I still feel sleep's allure, so I need the awakening."

They both drew a pair of daggers. No training weaponry for them; Zusa had insisted on real blades. She trusted her skill to make sure she caused no serious injury, as well as to prevent Veliana from doing the same. Over the past five years Veliana had closed much of the gap between them, so now if either scored a hit she counted it a well-earned rarity.

"Have you heard of a sorcerer named Deathmask, or perhaps Death's Mask?" she asked as she stretched. Zusa shook her head. Veliana didn't seem surprised. "Thought I'd ask anyway. He appeared about a week ago, a dangerous man. He has plans to kill Garrick, though I don't know how. I think he has a chance."

"Will you kill him?"

Veliana feinted, then slashed low, fully expecting Zusa to block. Their daggers connected, and as the steel rang out they thrust and parried, resuming a skilled dance they had perfected over the years, a perfect give-and-take of cuts and dodges, parries and thrusts. They talked as they fought, though they were a little out of breath.

"I'm not sure if I still can, nor if I want to. Garrick has turned against me, thinks he can survive without me. He may be right, though he was a lying coward when I first thrust him into his role."

Zusa upped the pace, forcing Veliana on the defensive as she spun and slashed.

"Men change over time, as do women."

"But not like this. It's too sudden. I feel like I'm missing something obvious."

"Perhaps you are, and that is why you miss it. What is it you wish from me?"

Veliana leaped away, but instead of her gaining a moment's breather, Zusa rushed in, her daggers leading. After she parried both, Veliana struck Zusa in the chest with an elbow and then pushed her back.

"I must make a choice, but I don't know which is the right one. You know me best, Zusa. What should I do?"

Zusa pulled back from her attack and rubbed her chest. Veliana must have been terribly distracted to have thrown so much strength into the elbow.

"I see many choices," she said. "Find what suddenly gave Garrick testicles and then cut them off. Join this Deathmask and solidify your position as second-in-command. Weave your own plans to remove Garrick. Accept your diminished role, and wait for the inevitable dagger to remove you completely. It's all yours to decide."

"I'm tired of the games," Veliana said. "I have no time to investigate Garrick. He'll move against me soon, I know it. I promised Deathmask an answer by tomorrow night."

"Will he kill you if you say no?"

Veliana laughed. "He might. I know nothing of him."

"Then how can you trust him?"

"Because I've fought him. He didn't kill me when he had the chance. He never showed fear, even when I had the chance to end his life. He's brutal, terrible, and driven. Whatever his goal is, he'll succeed . . . I guess I'm scared I'll be in his way."

Zusa twirled her daggers and motioned for another spar. "Then join him, and do so without pause or regret. Garrick has turned against you, inviting this betrayal. Hear Deathmask's plan, but always watch and listen. Every plan can be turned to your favor."

It was Veliana's turn to be on the offensive, and she took to it with a wild fury that worried Zusa. Normally the woman was more controlled. This Deathmask must have upset her greatly.

Did she feel guilt for betraying Garrick? Or was she too proud to agree to anything that left her second in the Ash Guild? Whatever the reason, Vel's daggers lacked their normal grace, and Zusa had to leap away several times to prevent blood from staining the floor.

"Restrain yourself, girl," Zusa said at last, after a desperate thrust nearly opened her throat. "If this choice disturbs you so much, I will choose for you, so you can concentrate and not kill me through your carelessness."

"I'm sorry," Veliana said, sheathing her daggers and leaning against the wall. She sounded terribly out of breath. "I should go."

"No," Zusa said. "I have a question for you as well. Someone murdered Alyssa's child. I must discover who."

"Someone killed Nathaniel?" Veliana asked. "I thought you'd persuaded her to move him up north and out of the city."

"I had. She called him back. He died on the northern road."

"It wasn't the Ash Guild, I promise," Veliana said, just in case the thought had crossed Zusa's mind. "I'd never let Garrick do something that low, and he's not yet reached a point where he can plan something so large behind my back."

"Are you sure?"

She paused a moment, thinking, and then sighed.

"No, I'm not. His control might be greater than I've realized. My opinion of him was far too low, and it's blinded me to his ambitions. He's not content to be a puppet. Still, I can't think of a reason why he'd have killed Nathaniel, nor how he'd have known the boy was on his way back. Is there anything else?"

Zusa took her dagger and scrawled the symbol found at the caravan exactly as the soldiers had shown her.

"That," Zusa said. "Tell me all you know of him, this... Watcher."

"We first heard of him about three years ago, but honestly, he might have been killing us for longer. Given the amount of infighting, and the Trifect's war against us, we probably blamed others for his early murders. But then we started finding these runes, an eye here, or the letter *W*. Perhaps he thought us dense, or his confidence hadn't grown yet. Either way he started killing more, and leaving his marker larger, clearer, and often in blood. He kills thieves of all guilds, with seemingly no preference. Every guild has accused the others of secretly harboring him, but we've never had an ounce of proof. Whoever he is, I believe he has a profound hatred of all thief guilds, and he's also incredibly good. Far too many have died by his hand, and those who survive can only speak of a face shrouded in shadow and hidden by a hood and many cloaks."

"Has he ever attacked the Trifect?" Zusa asked.

Veliana shrugged. "If he has, we don't know about it. Not that any of those rich bastards would tell *us*."

Zusa frowned, for she had never heard of the man interfering with Gemcroft activities. What could Alyssa have done to spur this strange killer of thieves into attacking her son?

"I must find him," Zusa said. "Is there anything you know that can help me?"

"Find him? What for?"

"He killed Nathaniel. I must give my lady her vengeance."

Veliana crossed her arms and shook her head, looking all the more upset.

"If the Watcher killed him, something else is going on. Perhaps he thinks you've secretly colluded with one of the thief guilds. Maybe he was confused. Or maybe he's just insane and out for blood. We know nothing of him other than that he is a skillful killer."

"Regardless of the difficulty, he is my prey, and must be found. My honor is sworn upon it."

"Then I wish you luck," Veliana said as she sheathed her daggers and swung her cloak over her shoulders. "Many have tried, and no lead we've ever found has panned out. He might as well be a ghost. If you wish to find him, your best bet is to scour the streets at night and listen for the sound of combat. If you don't catch him in the act, I doubt you ever will."

"Will you not stay?" Zusa asked when Veliana opened the door to leave. "Your daggerwork is excellent, but you still neglect practice of your spells."

"I should be going. Deathmask seeks his answer, and I must prepare until then."

"Good luck," Zusa said, bowing. "May you make the right decision, and in time find peace with my lady and her family."

Veliana pushed open the door, and as the chill wind blew in she sadly shook her head.

"Long as Thren Felhorn lives, this war will continue. Too many fear him, and many more live in the palm of his hand without even knowing. He's a bitter, angry man. Sometimes I think all of Veldaren will burn before the end."

"Perhaps it is not Garrick you should plot against, but Thren," Zusa said.

Veliana's smile turned bitter.

"We did, once," she said. "And the Ash Guild lost its best leader in decades because of it. I'll see you soon. Safe travels."

"To you as well."

Zusa had hoped talking to Veliana would illuminate matters, but instead it had made things worse. An assassin had been killing thieves for several years, yet not once had any of the guilds discovered his real identity. Who could be that skilled? And what had drawn that skill against her lady? What would happen if she did find him? Did she have the ability to take him down?

Only one way to find out, of course. Dawn was fast approaching, less than an hour away. Still, in that last twilight moment, perhaps she might find word of the Watcher.

She scoured the rooftops, an eye always kept on the streets. She saw several deals, a whore earning her pay, and two men dying so their killers might make off with their gold. No Watcher. Up on the rooftops she was alone.

"You must have left people alive," Zusa whispered to herself as she watched the sun rise. "You've hurt many opponents, though none will work together. But I am not one of them. I will piece it together. I will discover who you are. Perhaps, in time, I will be the one leaving my mark for you."

She returned to the Gemcroft mansion, and in her room she slept through the day. Come nightfall she had an underworld to interrogate.

Haern woke to the sound of the door banging open against the snow. A sliver of light lanced across his eyes. Dawn was fast approaching, but the snow magnified what little light crept over the horizon. He rubbed his eyes, then looked again. Matthew was dressed in many layers of coats and furs, and his two older sons were dressed similarly. A glance around showed the daughters still slept.

"Need to break the ice so our cattle can drink," Matthew explained, keeping his voice low so as to not wake the others. "Forgive me, but it's an early morning here on the farm."

"Forgiven," Haern said, rising. He pulled his cloaks tight

about himself. He needed to piss, and he wasn't looking forward to the excursion in what little clothing he had.

"Here," said Matthew, tossing him a coat. "It's an extra, and with what you paid me, you certainly deserve it. I have a feeling you won't be staying around much longer."

"Your feeling is right," Haern said, inspecting the coat. It was old and gray, the fur too faded for him to accurately guess what animal it had been made from. Still, the lining remained intact and well cared for. He slipped it on and nodded his thanks.

"Come on," Matthew said to his boys. "Let's go. My wife's in the kitchen cooking if you'd like a bite to eat, Haern."

"I would, but let me take care of other things first."

When he came back inside after finishing his business, he passed through the curtain into the kitchen. Sure enough, the lady had cooked him a bowl of oatmeal and flavored it with honey.

"Thank you," Haern said, accepting the bowl and using his fingers to scoop the oatmeal into his mouth. "What is your name?"

She kept busy scrubbing and tending to the rest of breakfast, all so she could avoid looking him in the eye when she talked.

"Evelyn," she said.

"Thank you for the meal, Evelyn. How fares the boy?"

"I looked in on him while you slept. His fever still burns, and I don't think he'll get to keep that right arm. Don't worry, though, if it comes to that. I've done it before, and not just on animals. For most of my neighbors, I'm the closest to a healer we got."

"Your husband explained my request?" Haern asked.

She finally looked at him, and he liked the strength he saw in her.

"He told me enough, and I have a brain to figure out the

rest. We'd have taken him in if you'd only asked. Didn't need the coin, or the threats. I pity the life you've led if you thought either was necessary."

The comment stung, far more deeply than she'd probably meant it to.

"Thank you for your hospitality," he said. "I must be going. Take care of the boy."

"We will. Safe travels to you, Haern. That bag on the table is yours. It should last you until you reach Felwood, assuming that's the direction you're headed."

Inside was a small selection of salted meats. He took it and left without checking on the boy, fully trusting Evelyn and her husband to know what was best. He wanted to get back to Veldaren, to the world he understood. He'd watched the farmer talk to his boys. Matthew was raising them to be like him, just as his own father had. But there was no malice, no underlying threat of violence to ensure perfection and obedience. The obedience was expected, sure, but he'd felt the love in that household. Living under Thren's roof he'd felt only paranoia, expectations, and disappointment. He'd loved Senke, loved Kayla, loved Delysia, even his older brother who had always been cruel to him in return. None of their fates had been kind because of it. At least Delysia had lived, though he'd lost her to the temple of Ashhur.

The pond was not far from the road, and he saw Matthew in the distance. Haern waved, and Matthew waved back. He promised himself he would return, not just to check on the fate of the boy, but also to have another night of sleep like he'd just had. So many nights and days he had slumbered on the side of the street, and he'd forgotten the comforts of a warm bed. Perhaps it was time to consider paying for lodgings at one of the inns, his various personae be damned.

The snow had stopped, and the coat did wonders to keep him warm. He nibbled on the meat Evelyn had given him, and despite its salt he found he enjoyed the flavor. He walked along the road and tried to determine how far he was from Veldaren. For much of his walk carrying the boy, he had been in a frozen delirium. He couldn't even guess how many miles he'd traveled, and like a fool he hadn't asked either Matthew or Evelyn how far to Felwood before he'd left. Oh well. She'd given him enough to reach the castle, and guessing by the food it should be four days, three if she assumed him a heavy eater. From there it'd be a week or so back to Veldaren.

Back to Veldaren. Which meant away from the mines, away from Tyneham, the reason for his trek north in the first place. Was he really willing to give up already?

Looking about the snow, and feeling the cold still nipping at his exposed skin, he decided he was. Whatever was going on with the Serpent Guild, he'd deal with it within Veldaren's walls. That was his home. That was the world he understood. Let the wild lands and dirt roads belong to the brigands and the rangers.

Near midday he heard the sound of hoofbeats. He felt his spirits brighten. If he could beg a ride he might reach the castle far sooner. But the woods had played tricks on his ears, and the riders came not from the north but the south. His pulse quickened at the sight of riders approaching from the distance. Clearly emblazoned upon their tunics was the symbol of the men who'd attacked the caravan. He hurried off the road, wishing he'd had time to hide his footprints. It'd be an easy trail to follow. Damn the snow!

They rode right on by. If they saw his tracks they didn't care about them in the slightest. Haern let out the breath he'd been holding and returned to the road. Tightening his coat, he hurried on, determined to gain as much distance as possible before nightfall. Only once did he look back, and he prayed the riders had passed by the farm as easily as they had his own tracks.

Evelyn had given him a small piece of flint and another of steel in his bag of food, which he found immeasurably kind. Off the road he built a fire and slept by it through the night, waking every few hours or so to toss a log upon it and poke the embers with a stick to reignite the flame. He ate lightly come morning, just in case it took him longer than expected to reach Felwood. He kept his eye out for more riders, but none came. He passed another caravan moving north, loaded with salt and farming equipment. The travelers offered him a ride, but he smiled and gestured south.

"Heading the wrong way," he said before continuing on.

Not long after he'd wolfed down the rest of his food, he reached the forest of Felwood. From there he continued until he reached the castle. He still had a few coins from the caravan, and he used them to pay for lodgings, food, and a warm room. He left come morning, feeling worlds better than he had before.

The days passed, and he continued his travel. Fires at night kept him comfortable, and steadily the weather warmed, a front of southern air coming along and mocking the snow. At last he reached the King's Forest. Heartened, Haern jogged at a steady pace. Once he curled around the woods he'd arrive in no time at Veldaren. He couldn't wait. Never before had he realized how much he considered the city home. It didn't matter that his trip had ended as a colossal failure, leaving him no wiser as to the Serpent Guild's mystery gold. Outside the city he was out of his element, and he'd remember that the next time he decided to pursue a lead that went beyond Veldaren's walls.

Twenty minutes later he saw smoke rising from farther ahead. Wary of the cause, he upped his pace while slipping closer to the forest so he might hide at a moment's notice. He rounded a bend and then stumbled upon a terribly familiar sight. A single wagon was under attack, but instead of horsemen, he recognized the attackers as members of the Wolf Guild. He counted eight of them circling the wagon, most holding bows or crossbows. From where he stood he couldn't see any of the defenders, but from the way the Wolves stayed low, refusing to approach, he knew they were still alive.

"I leave for a spell and you grow brave enough to assault travelers in daylight?" Haern whispered as he peered around a tree. Of all the guilds, the Wolves were the ones most likely to venture beyond the city, sometimes attacking merchant caravans, sometimes just attacking travelers for a bit of fun away from the danger of the city guard. But this, this almost felt like a slap in the face. The walls of Veldaren were in sight. The Wolves' lack of fear of the city guard didn't matter. But to be so unafraid of *him*? His pride was already wounded. This was more than enough to piss him off.

"No matter where you go, you won't be safe from me," Haern whispered, drawing his swords. "Perhaps it is time I delivered that message loud and clear."

He stayed close to the tree line, and once within fifty yards of the wagon he vanished into the woods completely. Three of the Wolves hid at the edge of the forest, using trees as cover while they fired their crossbows. Haern swung wide so he could approach them directly from behind. He heard them muttering as he neared, offering each other advice on where to shoot or where they thought the defenders were hiding.

Haern cursed the vegetation as he neared. He'd heard of men so accustomed to the wild that they could pass across dry leaves without making a sound, yet he crushed twigs and brushed at leaves no matter how stealthy he tried to be. What he'd give for a paved road and the shadows of a building. The three were too focused on the wagon, though, to notice what little noise he made. He thanked Ashhur for small favors.

"Watch for a hand," the rightmost Wolf said. He looked older than the others, and Haern wondered if he was their leader. "Don't let that yellow bastard have even a moment, or we're all dead."

Haern was less than five feet behind him. With his swords drawn he took another step, amused that they were so afraid of those in the wagon. Had they bitten off more than they could chew? And who might this "yellow bastard" be? It didn't matter. He was out of time. Already the Wolves on the other side were closing in, readying daggers and seemingly no longer afraid of the defenders inside. Deciding the one on the right was the most dangerous, he rushed in, his swords leading.

His first attack sliced through the Wolf's back and into his lung. Haern didn't bother muffling his scream or holding him steady, for the other two were too near. He slashed with his left arm, hoping for an easy cut, but the thief fell just out of reach. Twisting his blade free, Haern kicked away the dying man and turned his attention to the other two. The closest tossed his bow and drew a dagger, but the other...

Haern dropped to his belly, the crossbow bolt screaming over his head. The Wolf with the dagger dove after him and he rolled, deflecting the thrusts with his swords as he tried to gain distance. He rolled his knees underneath him and then kicked, leaping backward and to his feet. Instead of pressing the advantage his opponent remained back, a grin on his face.

"Idiot," said the thief as his comrade raised his reloaded crossbow.

Twisting his cloaks, Haern hoped to confuse him, but as a sharp pain bit deep into his shoulder he knew he'd only partially succeeded. He continued his spin, using his cloaks to obstruct their view. It'd only gain him a moment, an extra step closer, but if they were staying defensive, hoping to down him with arrows instead of blades...

He pulled out of the spin, putting every bit of his strength into his jump. He crashed into the closest, pure luck keeping the thief's dagger from impaling him. As they hit the ground Haern twisted so his elbow slammed against the man's throat. The Wolf spewed blood. Before the other could respond Haern lashed out, knocking the crossbow off its aim. The third bolt struck a tree, its dull thud music to Haern's ears. Without a melee weapon his opponent had no chance. Haern's assault was wild and brutal, with no hint of defense. Two slashes took out the man's throat, and a third across his hamstring brought him down to the dirt to die.

Finally given a chance to breathe, Haern cursed and grabbed the bolt in his shoulder. It was deep in his flesh, and a quick glance at the man's quiver showed barbed heads he wouldn't dare pull out. Gritting his teeth, he recited a mantra he'd been taught as a child, one to help him ignore pain. He clutched the shaft tighter. Another recital, followed by a deep exhalation. He pushed the bolt through and out the other side.

He screamed.

Tossing the bolt, he leaned against a tree and struggled to catch his breath. It didn't look as if the bolt was poisoned—another lucky break. Evidently the Wolves hadn't thought their upcoming ambush dangerous enough to spend the time and coin applying some. He looked to the wagon, trying to assess the situation. He couldn't see those on the other side, but he saw one Wolf lying dead upon the road, his body curiously aflame. That left four alive at the most. So far none appeared to have detected his intervention, for which he was thankful. He needed another moment to recover.

But then that moment vanished, for the wagon caught fire.

"Shit," he muttered. One of the Wolves must have tossed oil and a torch. Black smoke billowed to the air, blocking nearly all his view of events. Knowing the thieves would be rushing to cut down the survivors, he charged. Pain spiked up his entire left arm, and the sword hung limp in his hand as he ran. He'd block with it if necessary, but it seemed the killing would be restricted to his right.

A figure crawled out of the smoke toward him, a red-haired woman in white.

"Run to the trees!" he shouted to her, not stopping. He swerved about her and leaped straight into the smoke. The heat was tremendous, but so far the fire was restricted to the outer covering of the wagon. No survivors remained within. He saw a gap in the tarpaulin and jumped.

Just before he landed and rolled, he had a split second to survey the fight and react. Four Wolves formed a half-circle around the wagon, easily identifiable with their black cloaks striped with gray. Three men faced them, one in yellow robes wielding a staff, another in gray parrying with two maces, and the third a portly man hiding back with a single club to protect himself. There was something tremendously familiar about the way the man with the maces fought, but Haern had no time to consider it. He rolled closer to the fat man, no doubt the caravan's driver or owner. He seemed the least skilled, unable to fend off the single Wolf who weaved from side to side in front of him.

Haern kicked out of his roll, using his good arm to run the Wolf through. Their collision sent them both tumbling, and

Haern screamed as he felt something hard strike his wounded shoulder, screamed again as a sharp pain pierced his stomach. He rolled off the corpse and saw blood, his blood, covering the thief's dagger. This time his collision had not been so lucky. Struggling to stand, he turned to the others, his vision a blur of pain, smoke, and tears. One of the two fighting the man in gray had pulled off to address the new threat, and Haern put his swords in position and tried to feign confidence.

His opponent wielded two short swords, and he chopped with both, hoping to overpower Haern. Not a bad strategy, given his condition. Haern crossed his swords and blocked, the nerves in his wounded shoulder shrieking in protest at the collision. Twice, three times the man chopped, as if Haern were a wall to be broken down. The third time Haern's left arm gave out, and he twisted to avoid the deathblow. He feigned a retreat, but then kicked his right foot out, tripping the Wolf. He slashed with his good arm, but it wasn't lethal, just a cut across the thief's chest. It bought him time, and he retreated. Blood flowed across his shirt and down his pants. He felt its warmth along his left arm as well. He coughed, and hoped it was only the smoke, not something worse, that caused it.

His opponent, infuriated by the cut, charged like a mad animal. Haern braced his legs and met it head on, just barely slapping the thrusts aside. Again they collided, but this time he was better positioned. His knee slammed into his attacker's groin, and he let his wounded arm absorb most of the impact. When the Wolf collapsed to the ground, Haern practically fell upon him. The sword dropped from his left hand, but he stabbed with his right and leaned all his weight upon it. The blade pierced the thief's belly and bit into the dirt, pinning him there. He thrashed for a moment as he bled out, then went still.

Haern only felt marginally better than the man he'd killed.

The collision had torn the cut on his arm further open, as well as angering the arrow wound. His stomach still ached. He didn't know how deep the wound went, but it felt horrendous. He struggled to stand but couldn't. At last he yanked out his sword and fell to his back, his breath coming in hurried gasps. So much for leaving the guilds a message. So much for inspiring terror. He'd killed five, only five...

The sounds of fighting ended. His head swam. A man leaned over him, a face he recognized from his past. Another joined it, younger and female. He was delusional now, he realized. How else to explain why two people, one dead, one missing, spoke down to him, their voices muffled as if they were speaking through water? How else to explain why Senke was telling him to hold on? Or why Delysia was tearing at his clothes to see the wound in his stomach? He felt pressure there, and then his vision turned yellow, all shapes outlined in red. Sound faded, and then he saw nothing at all.

CHAPTER

9

She knew Garrick would want an explanation, but Veliana delayed him for several hours. The longer he wondered and worried the better. She wanted him to feel belittled, to realize her contempt for him. Anything else might make him think things were different. At last, when the day neared its end, one of their young guild rats found her at a tavern on the other side of the city and informed her of Garrick's request.

"Tell him I'm on my way," she said, flicking the boy a copper piece. "But I still plan on finishing my drink first."

She nursed it for another half hour. During that time several men arrived, all wearing the dark gray of the Ash Guild. They were recent recruits to the guild, men she knew very little about. Garrick's men, then. Again she cursed herself for being so blind to the man's ambition. Of course she'd vetted them, knew their names, but that was the limit of her influence upon them.

"Garrick's waiting," said one. He was named Gil, if she

remembered correctly. Why had she let him in? He looked like a dog had shit out a muscular version of itself that happened to walk on two legs.

"Surely he has more important problems," she said, draining the last of her drink.

"Than insubordination? No, Veliana, he doesn't."

She shot him a wink as she stood.

"Lead on, boys. Three to one to take me to the dance? I feel honored."

"Shut it."

It was an hour until sunset, and in the orange glow Veliana felt they were exposed wearing their cloaks as they traversed the city. They were deep in Spider territory, and instead of trying to travel through the less profitable outskirts, they marched together through its very center. She saw a few men in the paler-gray cloaks, but these men did not accost them, nor hail them to demand an explanation. Strange.

Deathmask was already waiting in the chamber when Veliana arrived. Garrick sat on his cushions, smoking as usual. He looked incredibly pleased, which threw her off. She had expected him to be ranting and raving. And why was Deathmask there? Was she about to witness another attempt on his life? Twelve other men were gathered about. All were armed. She felt her worry grow. What if this was it, the moment when Garrick tried to assert his control over the guild?

Her hands brushed the daggers at her hips. If it came to that, she'd take Garrick down with her, no matter the cost. Better the Ash Guild dissolve leaderless than continue in the hands of that paranoid bastard.

"You know how to keep a gentleman waiting," Garrick said as she arrived.

"I'm sure Deathmask will forgive me."

Garrick chuckled, not at all bothered by the slight.

"Well, we're all here now. Before we begin... Vel, would you care to hand over your daggers? I'd hate for someone to get hurt."

It took all her concentration to hide her panic. Should she do it? If she complied she'd be vulnerable, but if she refused it might be seen as a threat against Garrick. She glanced at Death-mask, and during the brief moment their eyes connected, she saw the corner of his mouth curl into a grin, followed by a wink.

Trusting him, she handed over her daggers and crossed her arms.

"Is it safe to say I won't like what I'm about to hear?" she asked.

"Perhaps, but I am not the one who shall be speaking." He turned to Deathmask. "Tell me, please, why is Veliana still alive?"

All about, men murmured, and she wondered how they were interpreting that statement.

"I do not understand," Deathmask said, feigning confusion. "Is there a reason she should not be?"

"Don't lie to me. I know she attacked you last night. One of my men watched your exchange. Tell me, why didn't you kill her? She did, after all, try to kill you."

"I assumed it just a training exercise," Deathmask said, the lie smooth on his tongue. "Veliana confirmed as much near the end of our fight. Was I wrong in my assumption? Was her response to me a lie?"

This was clearly not the answer Garrick had expected. He frowned and shifted on his cushion.

"Yes, you damn fool, you were wrong, and she a liar. You should be dead, yet are not."

Veliana held her tongue. What game was Garrick play-ing? She'd warned him about revealing attempts to murder an accepted member without reason or proof, yet here he was exposing his plans to the guild, and not just that, but showing how those plans had failed.

"For what reason would she attack me?" Deathmask asked.

"Isn't it obvious? She fears you. She knows with your skill you might quickly ascend to take her place. Isn't that right, Veliana?"

He grinned at her, his bloodshot eyes twinkling. Veliana's hands shook as she choked down her outrage. So that was it. He'd cast the shame of a failed intra-guild execution on her, and if she tried to deny it, it would be her word against his. Her word against the word of their guildmaster. One clearly outranked the other. The punishment for such a charge was limited to two options: banishment or death.

Staring at that grin, she knew which option Garrick had already chosen.

"You planned this from the start," she said, her voice nearly a whisper. Garrick stood and stepped closer as the rest of the guild tensed. They understood the accusation, and they too knew the possible punishments.

"I merely took advantage of an opportunity," he whispered so only she could hear. She glared at Deathmask, suddenly wondering how many of his promises had been lies. Perhaps all of them. He'd set her up, she realized. She'd wasted time debating and discussing with Zusa when she should have killed the masked bastard. All attempts on his life had been made in secret, with every man involved dying as a result. No one could prove Garrick's attempts. Once more, his word against hers. Damn it all!

"As you know," Garrick said, raising his voice to a theatrical level as he turned his back to her, "our laws are clear for such an attempt. We cannot have anarchy within our ranks, not in this crucial time while we fight for our very survival." He spun.

"You will be made an example, Veliana, one for the entire guild to see."

"Guildmaster, if I may make a request," said Deathmask. Garrick seemed worried, but gestured for him to continue. "Since it was my life she tried to take, I ask that I be the one to carry out her punishment."

"You fuck," she said, her hands clenched tight into fists. "You sick little fuck."

She feinted a lunge at Garrick and then hurled herself at Deathmask. She was unarmed, but Zusa had taught her a multitude of ways to kill with her bare hands. If she could strike him just right, crush his throat or snap his neck, then at least she'd die taking revenge. Her fist slammed into his mouth, just in case he attempted to cast a spell. With her other fist she doubled him over with a blow to the stomach. She heard men shouting, but she stepped closer and wrapped her arms around his neck. Just a single hard twist and then...

Something hard smacked the back of her head. Her stomach heaved, and her whole body went limp. Deathmask pulled free, and he shouted for the others to leave her be.

"She is mine," he said. "Guildmaster, I ask, is your punishment for this madwoman execution?"

"It is," said Garrick. He seemed amused by her display.

Her helpless rage grew. The men let her go, but it took all her strength to stand. Already a knot was growing on the back of her head. She felt ready to vomit. Deathmask closed the distance, and her wild punch missed. He grabbed her by the throat and flung her against a wall. A dagger flashed from his belt and pressed against her neck.

"Do you trust me?" he whispered into her ear. His grip tightened around her throat. Her eyes met his, and against all her instincts, something in those brown orbs gave her hope. She nodded, a barely perceptible movement because of how tightly he held her against the wall.

"Then stay perfectly still."

He muttered a few more words, soft whispers hidden by his grin. At last he pulled back his dagger and stabbed her chest, in and out with such speed her blood was flowing before she ever felt the pain. Black dots cluttered her vision as he held her still.

"Sleep in darkness," she heard him say as the Ash Guild hooted and hollered. No doubt Garrick was one of those cheering. She tried to curse his name as she died, but her whole body was turning rigid, refusing to cooperate, refusing to struggle, refusing to breathe...

And then the darkness came, and she could only obey Deathmask's request.

Oric waited until midafternoon before heading out. He traveled south along the main road, ignoring the peddlers and the beggars. He veered off when appropriate, making his way to the mercenary guild. While it had once been a weak entity, the years of battle and constant work had filled its coffers, drastically improving its recruitment and influence. Anyone wanting to be a sellsword had to go through it. There were some advantages to the system, such as guaranteed minimums in rates, and insurance should some of the higher-ranked members fail to fulfill their duties. Mostly Oric thought it a grand scheme to jack up the cost of hiring mercenaries, but what did he know?

The building itself was still small, little more than a large cube to house records and provide the wealthy with a place to visit that was close enough to the main road that they might not be afraid. Oric entered, crossing his fingers as he looked about the office hoping to see an old friend. Sure enough, there he was, white bushy unibrow and all.

"Oric?" asked the old man as he came from a back room to the front at the sound of a bell ringing above the door. "Come closer, my eyes aren't what they . . . so it is you! Good to see you, you ugly son of a bitch."

Oric grinned. "Was worried you'd died off, or been replaced by someone who can still remember what happened more than an hour ago."

The old man laughed. His name was Bill Trett, and in Oric's former sellsword life he had been a respected colleague. Bill had killed until his strength failed him, but by then he'd acquired such a wealth of knowledge of his various employers that the guild taught him his numbers and set him in charge of its transactions.

"You see this mess?" he asked, pointing to the various shelves stocked with expensive paper. "Only I know where everything's at. They'll keep me on until I die, and perhaps a little bit longer than that if they can figure out a way."

"Gods know they need you," Oric said. "The Trifect still filling your purses?"

Bill waved a dismissive hand. "The money's steadied, nearly every one of them just wanting the bare minimum. Not like when this mess first started, when I saw more gold change hands than I could count. Blood really filled the streets then, didn't it?"

Oric smiled, remembering the many thieves he'd cut down while in Leon Connington's pay. It'd been a very good year.

"I think Alyssa's going to give everyone some work later today, so be prepared," Oric said. Bill raised his eyebrows but didn't inquire further. "But for myself, I need a favor, Bill."

"What's that? Not that I should be doing *you* any favors. Last I remember, I saved your life up in Felwood, not the other way around."

"If not for favor, then for gold," he said, dropping a bulging coin purse atop the desk. "I need the best you have to hire, and I don't mean who the *guild* thinks is the best through their stupid rankings. You know every sellsword from here to Angelport, and I want your real opinion. I need someone who could find a mouse in a forest before an owl could; that damn good."

Bill rubbed his chin as his milky eyes stared off into nowhere.

"I suppose you don't mind if he's a bit unsavory?"

"He can be the ugliest, meanest bastard you know. Prefer it, even. We'd get along."

Bill laughed, but it was lacking in humor.

"I know of one, and he's good, Oric. He's all the way over from southern Ker, though some say he ain't even from Dezrel. Out of the nine jobs he's done for me, he's never once failed to catch his prey, and always done it with days to spare. Been tough getting work lately, though. Charges twice what anyone else does."

"What's his name?"

"He calls himself Ghost. I'm not brave enough to tell him to pick something more original. Besides, with this guy, it's fitting once you see his face."

Oric crossed his arms. "What's that mean?"

"No point in me telling you. You'll find out for yourself. He's costly, he's dangerous, but he's the best. You still want to meet him?"

Oric thought of the six men he and Arthur had lost when this lone Watcher had ambushed them along the northern road. He also thought of how Alyssa might execute him if she found out his and Arthur's role in her son's death.

"Yeah. I need the best. Where can I find this . . . Ghost?"

"Know where the Mug and Feather is? No? Lousy tavern built to the far south, just off the main road. Head there a few hours from now. The barkeep's a cheat, but he'll point Ghost out for you…though I'm thinking you won't need him to."

Bill opened the purse and dumped the coins across his desk. After he counted them up he nodded.

"You've got a few extra in here."

"Keep them," Oric said, heading for the exit. "Consider it a gift to an old friend for keeping things quiet."

"Understood. Safe travels, Oric."

Though Bill had told him to wait, Oric had no such plans. He wanted to be there when this Ghost showed up for a drink. Besides, if he had enough time he might glean some information from the regulars there. Just after midday anyone in there would certainly be a frequent drinker.

Finding the tavern was easy enough, given the sign hanging above the door: a poorly drawn mug and an even uglier feather. Owner had probably been cheap enough to draw it himself. Inside stank of vomit and alcohol, and the lighting was abysmal. In one corner was a fire pit, no doubt the only source of both heat and light at night. Among the various tables he saw a few stragglers, most eating. They glanced back at him as he entered and squinted to see in the dark. None stood out, at least not as dangerous assassins.

The barkeep was a thin man with a blond beard that reached to the bottom of his neck. He nodded at Oric and then waited for him to take a seat before coming over.

"Whatever's cheapest," Oric muttered, tossing him several coppers. When the barkeep came back with a third of his mug froth, Oric rolled his eyes. A cheat indeed. Deciding he needed information more than he needed to administer a good beatdown, he let it slide.

"Need anything to eat?" the barkeep asked.

"What's warm?"

"Haven't started the soup yet. Got a bit of bread, though, and butter if you're willing to pay."

"That'll do."

He kept his eyes to himself as he waited for his food. Just in case Ghost was already there, he didn't want to make it seem like he was looking. When they met, he wanted to have the upper hand, just in case this Ghost tried to haggle for more pay, which he might, given the target. When his bread arrived he smothered it with butter and ate. When he caught the barkeep watching, he pulled out a silver.

"Keep the rest," he said. "Care to answer me a question?"

The barkeep held the silver piece close to his eyes as he inspected it, frowned, and then put it away.

"Of course," he said. "Not so busy I can't stay away from the bar long enough to talk with a customer."

Oric chuckled, then lowered his voice.

"I'm looking for a man who calls himself Ghost."

The barkeep wiped his hands on his pants and laughed. "Not too many go looking for him. Usually he's got to go to those making offers no one else is dumb enough to accept. What business you have with that dark-skinned monster?"

An actual dark-skin from Ker? thought Oric. *Interesting.*

"No business of yours," he said. "Now fill the rest of my mug, and with ale, not foam, got it?"

The barkeep glared but obeyed. Oric washed the rest of the bread and butter down, then glanced around once more. No dark-skin in the tavern. Shit, he wasn't even sure if he'd seen a dark-skin in all of Veldaren. The people down south in Omn, particularly along the coast, were known for their darker skin, but it looked more like a deep tan. Those from Ker were claimed to have skin as black as obsidian. No wonder the guy had trouble getting work. Settling in for a wait, Oric moved from his table to the one farthest from the door. He leaned back against the wall and closed his eyes. He didn't actually sleep, but let it look like he did. If anyone was dumb enough to try to rob him, well, they'd get a nice surprise.

As the sun moved across the sky, with dusk steadily approaching, more men filtered into the tavern. Oric thought it might be one of the very few taverns left in southern Veldaren since King Vaelor's edict banned all caravans from entering the southern entrance, forcing them to enter through the east instead. All the merchants, and their wealth, had shifted farther and farther north. The men who entered looked tired and haggard, and he guessed many of them worked the nearby fields outside the city walls. The ale was terrible, same as the prices, but they were probably far closer to home and among friends.

"You're in our seat," he heard someone say. He opened his eyes to see three men, their tanned skin covered with soil. All three of them combined might still be skinnier than he was.

"That's a damn shame," Oric said, shifting so they could see the sword sheathed at his side.

"Ain't no swords allowed in here," said one of them.

"Like to see him stop me," Oric said, nodding toward the barkeep.

The men scowled, but armed with only their fists, they dared not challenge him and his blade. They backed down to another table, and as they moved out of his way he finally saw Ghost. He sat alone in the center of the tavern. His skin was indeed darker than Oric had ever seen on a man. His head was shaved, and he wore loose clothing more appropriate for a warmer climate. His enormous strength was obvious, his arms thick as tree trunks. Most shocking, though, was the brilliant white paint he wore across his face.

Oric stood, glared at the men who'd wanted his seat, as if daring them to try, and then approached Ghost.

"Mind if I join you?" he asked.

The man looked up, and he flashed a smile, revealing clean white teeth.

"I have a seat to spare, so take it if you wish." His voice was deep, intimidating. Oric sat and leaned back in his chair. If not for the white paint, this Ghost might have been handsome. Oric tried to decide why he wore it, yet could not. Was it because of his name? A pathetic attempt to fit in?

"Not much need to ask, but I assume you're the one called Ghost?"

The mercenary chuckled. "I am."

"They say you're good."

"Who is *they*? That blind fool running the guild's coffers? Or the rest of my colleagues? I'd be surprised if any bothered to speak of me except in disdain."

"It was Bill," Oric admitted. "And is it true? I'm starting to have my doubts."

"Is that an attempt to make me boast? No boast. There is none better. Now tell me your name, and your business, otherwise I might decide I prefer to drink alone."

"Sad man that'd prefer to drink alone."

Ghost grinned again, and there was something wolfish in his brown eyes.

"Come now, stranger, do you think I am unused to being alone?"

Oric felt put off guard, and he cursed his verbal clumsiness. Arthur would have been so much better at milking information from the man, figuring out who he was, what made him tick.

"Fair enough. My name's Oric. Who I work for is my own

business. I need you for a job, and I've already paid Bill for your services."

Ghost leaned back in his chair and crossed his arms. Oric saw two hilts just below his elbows. It seemed Ghost didn't care much for the barkeep's no-weapons policy either.

"I can refuse if I wish, so don't think I am already in your pocket, Oric. Do you wish someone found, killed, or both?"

"Both."

Again that wolfish smile.

"Excellent. Who?"

"They call him the Watcher."

Oric was surprised by the sudden burst of laughter. It seemed the rest of the tavern winced at the sound, as if they expected Ghost to explode any second.

"The Watcher?" asked Ghost. "Now that is interesting. I've heard a rumor of him here or there, but they make him sound as real as the Reaper. But now you come and ask me to kill him? Do you have anything for me other than a name?"

"I saw him with my own eyes," Oric said, annoyed. "He wore gray, and kept his face hidden with the hood of his cloak."

"You describe nearly every beggar in this city."

"He wielded two swords, one for each hand."

"I'd be more impressed if he wielded two swords in the same hand."

"Enough!" Oric slammed his hand against the table. "I won't be intimidated by a freak like you."

The entire tavern quieted at his words. Ghost leaned closer to Oric, not angry, just amused, but something lurked in his smile, something dangerous. His voice dropped to a whisper.

"A freak?" he asked. "Why is that? Is it my skin? There are thousands like me in Ker."

"Only a freak would paint his face to look like a dead whore," Oric said, still trying to rein in his temper.

"Ah, the paint." His voice dropped even lower, as if he was about to say something intimate for only Oric to hear. "It itches like ivy, and does not come cheap here. Do you know why I wear it?"

"Because you're trying to fit in?"

"Fit in?" He laughed loudly, a boisterous eruption that startled the nearest tables. Oric felt himself jump, though he didn't know why. He'd lost control of the conversation, he knew that much. If he wanted to be in charge of any further negotiations, he needed to get his act together, and fast.

"No, not to fit in," Ghost continued. "I wear it to stand out. When people see this paint, it only reminds them of why I must wear it. People cannot hide from me, Oric. That is why I am the best. Everyone I talk to feels fear, for they know nothing of who I am, only that I am different. Do you see that farmer over there? I could find out the name of his wife faster than you could introduce yourself. When *you* ask questions, they'll evade, they'll delay, they'll hope for bribes or favors. When *I* ask questions, they wish me gone, because I make them afraid without a single threatening word. Fear is stronger than gold. All the wealth in the world cannot make someone conquer their fear, not when it comes to death and blood. They will tell me everything so I'll let them go back to their safe little existence. Fit in? What an unimaginative man you are."

"Enough," Oric said. "Will you accept the job or not?"

Ghost took a drink of his ale and set down the glass.

"Triple what Bill told you," he said. "I won't accept a copper less."

"I could hire fifty men for that price!"

"And all fifty would stomp about unable to find their own assholes. Triple."

Oric stood, having had enough. "I won't, you damn mudborn. I refuse. Either accept your standard pay, or nothing at all."

Ghost drew a sword and slammed it onto the table. Oric jumped, but instead of reaching for his sword, he realized he had turned to run for the door. His cheeks flushed, and he knew Ghost had seen it as well.

"I expect the rest in Bill's hands by nightfall. Farewell, Oric. I will have the Watcher's head in two weeks. Should I fail, though I won't, all the coin will be returned to you."

He left, and it seemed the whole tavern breathed easier with him gone. To his shame, Oric realized he did too. He ordered another glass, drained it, and then hurried off. He still had another pressing matter to attend to, and he needed to handle it far better than he had the business with Ghost. Farther into southern Veldaren he approached a large wooden structure with two floors.

Inside, at least fifty boys and girls hurried about, cleaning, sweeping, and preparing their beds for nightfall. A man of forty hurried to the door to greet him.

"Hello, my friend," said the man. "My name is Laurence, and welcome to our orphanage. May I help you, perhaps with finding an apprentice or maidservant?"

"Show me the boys," Oric said.

Laurence whistled and sent the children running. They traveled farther in. The room looked like a giant warehouse, with rows of bunk beds on either side. He lined up twenty boys of various ages, parading them before Oric as if they were cattle. For the most part the children behaved, having certainly gone through this before.

"Anything particular you're looking for?" Laurence asked, licking his lips.

"That's my own business, not yours."

"Of course, sir, of course."

Oric kept Nathaniel in mind as he looked over the younger ones. One in particular looked close in size, maybe an inch taller. His hair was even the same color, which might help the illusion.

"Step forward," he said, nodding toward that boy. "He'll do. What's the cost?"

"Adoptions are not cheap, but he's still young, so it'll be nine silvers."

Oric reached into his pocket and pulled out twice the amount.

"No papers," he said. "I was never here."

Laurence's eyes bulged, and he glanced between the man and the boy.

"His name's Dirk," he said.

"That's fine. Come on, boy."

Laurence watched them leave but said nothing.

Oric traveled by foot, so he took Dirk by the hand and told him to hurry along.

"No questions," he said. "We're heading along the northern road. I've got a house for you there, where you can work off all that silver I just spent on you. You understand?"

Dirk nodded.

"Good."

He took the boy to the southern gate, not wishing to travel through the more populated areas of the city, regardless of how close to night it was getting. The guards gave them a cursory glance before letting them through. At a branch in the road they followed the loop back around the city and then to the north. Dirk looked maybe six, and his legs were nowhere near as long as Oric's. He tired rapidly, and by the way his skin clung to his bones, it'd probably been forever since he'd had a filling meal. Oric eventually picked him up and carried him until the city was behind them and the sun almost set.

"How long until we're there?" Dirk asked, the first time he'd spoken in an hour.

"No questions," Oric growled. He glanced about as the first of many stars appeared in the sky. He was nearing the King's Forest. Stretching out to the east were acres of hills. He turned toward one of them, still holding the boy.

"Almost there," he muttered. Once he put the closest hill between him and the road, he set Dirk down. "You see that forest over on the other side of the road? I want you to go fetch me some sticks, whatever you can carry."

"Yes, sir."

Oric pulled out his sword and a piece of flint. While the boy was gone, he gathered enough dry grass to create kindling. He carefully shielded it with his hands once he got it lit. When Dirk returned, holding about six sticks, Oric snapped them on his knee and carefully set them into the kindling. He sprinkled a tiny bit of lamp oil from his pack to get it going, then stood.

"We need far more wood than that," he said, still holding his sword. "But I've got time. First, Arthur's orders. Come here, Dirk."

While the boy's body bled out on the grass, Oric went to the forest and broke off several thick branches. He dragged them back to his camp, grunting as he did. He used his boot to break the branches into pieces, and one by one he tossed them upon the fire. Once it was roaring, he picked up the body. It felt stiff and cold. He hoped it'd burn. Without a bit of ceremony he tossed it into the fire. The ragged clothing caught first, then the hair, and finally flesh. The burning meat smelled sweet, but Oric always hated the scent of burning hair.

Deciding he could go without the warmth, he unpacked his bedroll and slept upwind so he wouldn't be bothered by the smell. Come morning, he gathered the bones in a sack and returned to Veldaren.

CHAPTER

 10

He had a soft bed underneath him, which confused Haern to no end. A bed? When was the last time he'd slept in a bed? Three years ago? Four? Wait, what about at that farm? No, that'd been on the floor, right? The inn, of course, he must be at the inn he'd stayed in afterward. Except he'd left there, traveling on toward home. He remembered an ambush, being stabbed fighting beside a wagon . . .

When he opened his eyes it didn't help much. He saw a low ceiling, poorly painted a dull cream color. A glance around took in the rest of his surroundings. The room was tiny, with barely any space to walk between his bed and the door. Opposite him was a single closet, stacked full of a strange assortment of clothing and weaponry. He recognized his own weapons in the pile, and he tried to go for them.

The pain in his stomach convinced him it wasn't a good idea. He lay back down and pressed a hand against his abdomen.

His fingers touched bandages sticky with blood. Larger fragments of the attack at the caravan came back to him. He'd killed several Wolves, been stabbed in the stomach, and then as he'd been passing out...

"What is going on?" he muttered as he inspected his arm. He remembered the cut there, and it'd been bad, if not to the bone. It was bandaged as well, but the pain was only a dull ache. He pried back some of the cloth and saw an angry scar, lacking any stitching to have helped it close. It didn't seem possible. For that much healing he'd have to have been out for weeks. The same went for the arrow wound in his shoulder. Either that, or a priest had come and healed him.

Or a priestess...

Haern remembered those last fleeting images, images no longer certain to be hallucinations. Could it be? After all these years, had Delysia exited the safety of Ashhur's temple? A part of him felt excited to meet her, but for the most part he felt terror. His hair was still a mess, his face unevenly shaven. His clothes fit the part of the beggar, the image that was like a second skin. But Delysia...she'd been his first glimpse of light in a world of darkness, something clean and pure. He felt like living dirt, scabbed over with his blood and the blood of those he'd killed. It seemed so wrong for her to find him like this, assuming she even remembered him, or recognized him through the filth.

He tried once more to sit up, and, now prepared for the pain, he managed a better job of it. Using his hand to support his weight against the wall, he limped into the closet and grabbed his swords. He knew it made no sense for anyone to try to kill him, not after bandaging him up and healing him, but he felt naked without their weight at his hips. Sweat dripped down his neck as he caught his breath. He offered a quick prayer to Ashhur for strength and then pulled the door open.

A very surprised Senke stood there, holding a slice of buttered bread, his free hand still reaching for the door handle that had swung away from him at the last moment.

"Going somewhere?" Senke asked.

It was too much. Haern staggered back and half sat, half fell onto his bed. He stared, his mouth hanging open.

"You look like you've seen a ghost," Senke said, seeming amused by the whole scenario.

"I think I have."

Senke laughed, and that familiar sound helped melt Haern's doubts. The man had shaved his head and grown out his beard, but underneath the disguise he had the same smile, same laugh, same guarded amusement in his eyes.

"Only a handful have recognized me, but I guess I shouldn't be surprised that you're one of them. Always were the observant one, weren't you, Aaron?"

Aaron...

A flood of memories tore through him, of days practicing with Senke, of walking at the side of his father, and of those few fleeting moments with Robert Haern before executing him at his father's command and then cleaning up the blood. Aaron...he hadn't gone by that name since that day. He'd adopted a new name, become a new person. A better person.

"Haern," he said. "Aaron died a long time ago."

Senke handed over the bread and leaned against the door, chuckling again.

"That you did, and I was one of many who thought so, though I forgot your little oddity about the name. Everyone heard how you died in the fire. I barely got out myself, though

I lost most of my hair in the process. Helped disguise me, though, and I'm kind of attached to the look now."

Haern looked at the bread as if he didn't know what it was for. At last he dropped it, stood, and flung his arms around Senke. He didn't say anything, didn't know what to say. He felt thirteen again, bewildered, torn, and suddenly given a link to a past that had had moments of good. It seemed Senke understood, for he patted Haern on the back and then gently pulled free.

"Don't get all sentimental," he said, winking. "Otherwise I might start thinking you aren't really Thren's son. Now have a seat. Del says you've got another day or two before you'll be in top shape, and I don't want you tearing those wounds open. You've grown up, gods damn, boy. Taller than me now. How about you tell me what you've been doing these past five years?"

Part of Haern wanted to, but mostly he felt an overwhelming sense of embarrassment. For the past five years he'd struck at the guilds out of vengeance. Whom else could he tell? Who else would understand the rage of seeing everything he'd loved broken and destroyed by that sick culture of the underworld? Still, strange-looking or not, there was Senke, the closest thing to a friend he'd ever had. The time melted away. He told it all, of his escape from the fire and living on the streets, always keeping his hair messed and unevenly cut, his skin a blanket of dirt and scabs. He stole food to live, and lived to kill those of the thief guilds. He felt keen shame admitting that, though he wasn't sure why. In his heart he felt justified.

"Why not just leave?" Senke asked. "Everyone thinks you're dead. You could move on, make a name for yourself as a mercenary or a thief in any other city but here. Why stay?"

Haern felt his neck flush.

"Because this is my home," he said. "This is all I know. I

wanted to punish the guilds, every one of them. I thought maybe, if I made them afraid of the Watcher, I could scare away the recruits. I could make them doubt their safety. I could...I don't know, Senke. I thought I could finally end it all."

Senke chuckled.

"Well, it seems the shy boy I once knew has grown up to be an ambitious young man. Shouldn't surprise me. Well, besides you being alive and all. How'd you end up at our caravan?"

"Investigating the Serpent Guild and their newfound gold. Was on my way back when I stumbled upon your attack."

"And good timing it was," Senke said, grinning. "We were hired on to protect some fat-ass merchant who'd done something to really piss off the Wolf Guild. I think he'd stiffed them on protection money or something, was trying to flee north before they noticed. Well...they noticed." He laughed. "I must admit, I first thought it was Thren who'd come to our aid. The way you just charged in, then danced and weaved, it all seemed so familiar, Aaron..."

"I said it's Haern now."

Senke lifted his hands to show he meant no offense.

"Forgive me, just habit. Why so strict?"

Haern felt a chill coming on, and he wrapped his blankets tight about him.

"Because that's not who I am anymore. I refuse everything of my father, including his name. I won't be what he wants me to be."

"Wanted you to be," Senke said. "He thinks you're dead now. And instead of being your father's pet killer, you instead spend every night killing. A neat trick, that."

"Don't you dare judge me!" Haern said, and he was surprised by his own anger.

"No judging, just stating the obvious. Well, guess it's my

turn. Not nearly as interesting. I fled the city for the first few years. Always wanted out, think I told you that, but Thren wasn't one to take such requests too well. Doesn't take too kindly to those who sell him out to the king either, but thankfully he never caught wind of my doing that. I used the fire that 'killed' you to die as well, make myself a new life. Spent some time down in Woodhaven, cutting lumber. After a while, got bored, took some odd jobs more favorable to a mace than an ax. All of a sudden I had a slow but steady stream of mercenary work. About a year ago I came back to Veldaren, going by the name of Stern and hoping for a bit more lucrative employment. Before you start thinking it, I wasn't exactly falling into that same old trap. I chose my contracts carefully, and while I wasn't always working for the nicest of people, I wasn't killing innocents or torching the homes of the poor either.

"Anyway, eventually met with my current employer. Even joined up with him as a permanent member of his mercenaries. Seems like he went through twenty guys, trying to find one who was . . . well, not scum. Lucky me, eh?"

Haern smiled but said nothing. He was still trying to wrap his head around everything. Here was someone he could talk to, could trust. After half a decade of silence and loneliness, it had all come crashing to an end because of a single poorly timed ambush. For all the many times he'd felt overlooked by Ashhur, he wondered just how unnoticed he really was. While he thought, he ate, figuring it a good excuse not to talk. All his confidence had flown out the window with Senke's arrival.

"I see your eyes drooping," Senke said when Haern finished his meal. "Let me send in Delysia to swap out some clean bandages and then you can rest, ponder over this craziness."

"Delysia?" he asked, thinking of the other images that had

flashed before his eyes as he lay bleeding after the fight. "Is she...is her last name Eschaton?"

Senke raised an eyebrow. "Well, yeah, but how would you... wait a minute. You did know a Delysia. Is she *her*, the one you killed Dustin to protect and...shit, that is her, isn't it?"

Haern nodded, and was totally unprepared for Senke's eruption of laughter.

"Looks like she returned the favor. She's the one that kept you from bleeding out like a stuck boar. Damn, this is too funny. You never told me she became a priestess. Always wondered how she hid from Thren so well."

"I never told anyone," Haern mumbled. "Kayla told me the night of the Kensgold."

Senke's face saddened at the mention of her name. "She was a pretty lass. What I heard, Thren killed her for aiding you. Such a shame. Didn't pay much to help you out, did it?"

The comment stung, and at Haern's pained look, Senke immediately started trying to take it back.

"I'm sorry, Haern, you know I don't mean that. It wasn't your fault, any of it. Your father's just a bastard, still is, though his influence is slowly dwindling, thank Ashhur."

"Senke, I...I'm not ready to see her yet."

"She's seen plenty of you."

He blushed a fierce red but remained adamant. "Please, just let me rest. Meeting you again is too much as it is. Let me think, all right?"

Senke shrugged. "I guess you'll survive. But if those cuts get infected, it's your own damn fault. Sleep tight, Haern."

"Thanks."

Even after Senke left, his words echoed in Haern's head.

Didn't pay much to help you out, did it?

How many had died because of him? Robert had died by his hand. His father had killed Kayla, again for helping him. Senke had nearly died in the fire. Delysia had been forced into hiding. And now, when every thief guild in the city would gladly string him up by his thumbs and let the entire underworld have a go at him, the two had brought him into their home and given him succor. Were they mad? He was a monster, a beacon of chaos and murder. The streets were where he belonged. Their gutters had room for the blood.

Besides, he couldn't face her. He just couldn't. The last image he had of Delysia was of her gasping in his arms after the bolt pierced her back. She'd looked so shocked, so betrayed, and then to see his own father approaching, crossbow in hand, he'd felt such guilt...

He tightened his belt and held back a grimace at the pain in his stomach. His cloaks were folded up beside his bed, as were his tattered clothes. Again he blushed a bright red as he remembered Senke's comment, and he prayed that it had been anyone but Delysia who had changed him into what he wore now, a plain white shirt and brown pants. Quietly he changed into his old clothes. In their dirt and dried blood he felt all the more wretched and eager to be gone. Everything about him was filthy, even the task he'd devoted his life to. Was he really any better than his father? At least Thren had developed an empire, however fleeting. All Haern did was destroy.

He shook his head, trying to banish such thoughts. He needed to concentrate. Drowsiness still tugged at his eyes, and that soft warm bed tempted him more than any woman ever had. Deciding it was now or never, he crept open the door and looked about.

Whatever building he was in was small in space but attempting to make up for it by being two stories tall. He saw a second door across from him, and a few feet away, stairs going down at sharp angles to the bottom floor. He heard muffled talking from the other door. Feeling like a trespasser, he hurried along as fast as his wounds allowed him to go. The bottom floor was blessedly empty. It was sparsely furnished: he saw a table, an oak desk in the corner, and a modest pile of books atop it. At the door he removed the bolt and stepped out into the street.

He looked around a moment, taking in his surroundings. The sun was rising, still low enough to hide behind the city's walls. There was an inn not far away, Prather's if he read the sign right, and that meant he was in... Crimson Alley, deep in southern Veldaren. He felt muted horror at the realization. Senke and Delysia lived in the Crimson, one of the most dangerous places in the city? No wonder he never saw either of them when he patrolled the night. They'd certainly keep their doors locked and windows bolted. How often had he passed right on by when scouring for isolated members of the guilds?

He worried about his injuries, but those desperate enough to rob in daylight he could certainly handle. Giving one last glance at the dilapidated building to memorize its location, Haern rushed north, eager to put some distance between himself and this sudden assault from the past.

Veliana floated in silence, and that alone convinced her she was dead. She didn't know if her eyes were open or closed. All she saw was darkness, though she didn't really see it so much as be swallowed by it. The numbness she likened to cold, so at least she felt something, however faint. Time drifted by as if it were bored of her. Then came a sudden, shocking pain to her chest, lighting up her darkness with streaks of red. Again she felt the pain, but this time there was a comfort to it, a strange familiarity. The third time it hit, she realized it was her heart-beat restarting.

Pins and needles came in waves, first to her chest, then her face, and last her extremities. The darkness gradually faded from black, to yellow, to red, and at last to an assortment of colors that congealed to create the unmasked face of Deathmask.

"Welcome back," he said with a smile.

She would have hit him if her limbs had bothered to listen to her commands.

He vanished. She lay on her back, and now she stared at a cobwebbed ceiling. Based on the cold she felt, she decided she was on a dirt floor. Her ears, about the only thing working properly, heard shuffling, followed by a laugh.

"I'm sure you're angry with me, but let me assure you, I hope I never have to do that again." Deathmask leaned over, and she felt him press his hands against her neck. "Pulse is getting stronger. Good. Never actually used that spell before, so consider yourself a lucky first try. Stopping someone's heart is never easy. Well, not if you want to start it again."

"What... happened?" she forced her dry throat and swollen tongue to ask.

"I faked killing you. The thrust to your chest wasn't deep, but I made sure no one bothered to investigate the matter. The spell I cast put your entire body in stasis. No breathing, no heartbeat. For all anyone would know, you were dead, and honestly I'm not quite sure how far from the truth that is. I took over the burial, and here we are. Simple enough explanation, and once you get your bearings I think you'll be pleased with the elegance of my solution."

The pins and needles returned throughout her body, and this time she felt herself regaining control. Her head pounded with the unholiest of headaches, but she forced herself to sit up, forced the memories to come back. She'd been in their head-quarters, Garrick had been there, accusing her of…

She reached for a dagger at her side but all she did was topple herself back to the floor.

"Don't rush things," she heard Deathmask say. "You'll be fine in a few more minutes. We have much to discuss, so try not to do anything stupid like killing me, all right?"

No promises, she thought amid her delirium.

As her body reawakened, so did her mind. She glanced about, taking in her surroundings. They appeared to be in a cellar of some sort, the only light coming from a single torch lit behind her head. She saw no door but assumed it was also behind her. Deathmask leaned against a stone wall to her right, his arms crossed, his face blanketed with a smug grin she'd have given everything to cut off. Feeling far better, she sat up, braced herself for the ensuing dizziness, and then sat on her knees.

"I'm fine now," she told him. "You say we have lots to talk about, so let's talk."

He nodded, as if perfectly willing to hurry through the bullshit.

"Garrick surprised me with his boldness. I'd feel more upset if he hadn't surprised you as well, and you've known him far longer than I. Even a rigged die will roll something new with enough throws, if you know what I mean. I tried to save us both, but clearly Garrick wasn't one to be persuaded. He wanted you dead, and I did my best to fool him regarding that. I succeeded, of that I'm sure. My position in the guild is tenu-ous right now, esteemed among most of the lower members that despised you, but Garrick wants me killed, that much is obvious. And now here we are. It's only been a day, and I man-aged to keep you wrapped and safe so no bugs or worms could get at you before I returned."

Veliana shuddered at the prospect.

"So here we are," she said. "What is it you want? Why keep me alive?"

"Because I made you an offer, and I won't let some idiot guildmaster interfere with my plans. That offer still stands, though I need your answer now. Will you aid me, or must I find another?"

"And if I say no?"

His eyes held no joy, no amusement, only grim truth.

"I'll put you as you were, though this time no spell will bring you back."

She thought of the cold, the darkness. An involuntary shudder coursed through her, too strong to hide. She couldn't go back to that, even if it hadn't been a true death. Garrick had turned against her, and now she would be an outsider, a ghost banished from her own guild.

"I'll help you," she said. "Even if I did have a choice, I'd still help you. I want that son of a bitch to die, slowly, painfully, and at my hand. That is all I ask. Can you promise me that?"

Deathmask handed her a small bottle of some red vintage. She tore out the cork and drank.

"That, my dear," he said, "is something I can assure you of. He'll be yours to kill, all yours."

The alcohol burned going down, but damn did it feel good.

"Then enough lies and games. I can hardly turn against you, now that I've been 'executed' by the Ash Guild. What is your plan? Why have you come to Veldaren?"

Deathmask smoothed his robe and then sat opposite her on the floor. He scratched at his chin, as if considering where to start.

"I was once a member of the Council of Mages," he said. "Less than six months ago, in fact. They preach noninvolvement in political matters, but it's nonsense. We had our eyes everywhere, especially on the kings and their capitals. When this war erupted between the guilds and the Trifect, I was assigned to watch. Through coin and magic I learned of every guildleader, their goals and the reaches of their power. As the years dragged on, and my boredom grew, I formulated various plans and contingencies. I was not a high-ranking member, Veliana; far from it. My strength was equal to many, but my years were few. Not enough gray hairs, if you will. I also had a reputation as a ... troublemaker."

"Shocking," Veliana muttered. He chuckled and continued.

"They told me nothing of why I was tracking Veldaren's underworld, nor did they keep a close eye on me, so I let my mind wander to far more interesting ideas. Profitable ideas. Recently I came up with a plan I was sure would work. It wasn't foolproof, and would involve risk to whoever tried carrying it out, but I was certain of its worth. This stupid grudge war wasn't going to end, not without killing off Thren Felhorn, and I knew a way to do it. When I tried to convince the Council of this, they gave me strict orders not to interfere. I saw a wealth of gold, but gold means nothing to those aging bastards. They want influence, power, and information. Gold helped with that, but was hardly their true ambition.

"I went on with my plan without their approval, and that is when I realized how dangerous they thought me. Several of my contacts were actually in the pockets of other higher-ranking members. My assassination attempt accomplished nothing but my banishment. They took my name from me, Veliana. They stole it with a spell, called my ambitions foolish, my desire for gold a young man's folly. *We call you nameless*, they said, *for you are death and folly.* They refused to see the power I might gain, the wealth the underworld of Veldaren smuggled every single night.

"I came here to prove them wrong. They want power, yet I will wield more power than they can imagine. They mock gold, so I will collect more than they would dream of. Your Ash Guild was perfect, Veliana. It was the smallest, the weakest, the one most easily breakable to my will. I have a plan, many in fact, and this is just one of them. We will take over the Ash Guild and turn it into a powerful force no one will dare act against. All I need is you at my side. We'll kill many accomplishing this, possibly hundreds. Does this bother you?"

She thought over everything he'd said. It did explain many of his strange powers. Of course he could be lying, but even if he was, it didn't change what Garrick had done to her. As for his question...

"No," she said. "Not if it lets me kill Garrick. The innocent aren't long for this world anyway."

Deathmask smiled.

"Good girl," he said. "Then you shouldn't mind what you must do next."

CHAPTER 11

Evelyn washed her hands in the bowl and wiped them on a nearby cloth. Feeling like a morbid butcher, she tossed her bloody apron aside. Matthew stood beside her, looking down at the boy.

"Will he live?" he asked.

"I believe so," she told her husband. "I sewed him up quick enough. Lost more blood tending to the Kenders' boy when he hit his head on their fence."

"He was also older," Matthew said. Evelyn nodded but said nothing. The silence stretched as they both looked upon the sleeping boy, his skin pale and slick with sweat. She hoped that meant his fever was finally breaking, but it easily could be because of the amputation. The human body did strange things when in pain, and Evelyn didn't want to imagine what the boy had felt when she took the saw to his shoulder. He'd been feverish and unable to talk, so maybe he hadn't felt much.

"Strange not knowing his name," Matthew said.

"We could give him one."

"Not much point. If he wakes he'll tell us it himself."

"*When* he wakes."

Her husband gave her a look, then nodded. It was the closest she ever got to an apology with him.

"Right. When he wakes. Give me a moment to take care of this."

The boy's arm lay wrapped in rags on the floor by the bed. Matthew scooped it up and carried it outside. Though he didn't tell her, she knew the hogs penned out back were about to get an interesting addition to their diet. They'd kept the children out of the house while she cut, though her oldest, Trevor, had tried to insist on watching. Just shy of fourteen, he might have been able to stomach it, but truth be told, she couldn't afford the distraction should he have cried out or lost control of his stomach.

"I've been thinking," she said when Matthew returned. "We might as well name him. Both him and that Haern were injured, and I have no doubt they're hiding from someone. I'd hate for one of us to let slip his real name before we can get him home."

"I reckon you're right. Any ideas?"

"Always wanted to have a boy named something fancy. How about Tristan?"

"Too fancy. No one would believe us when we say he's ours. How about John?"

She frowned. "He'll only have this name for a week or two at most, and you want something so plain as John?"

He blinked at her. "My father's name is John."

"Your father was a very plain man."

He took an angry step toward her, grabbed her wrists, and

then, laughing, pulled her against him. Her own laughter faded as he held her tight, and she wrapped her arms about him.

"You going to be all right?" he asked.

"Just blood and dead flesh," she said. "Not as if he was squealing like a hog."

"It's just you and me right now. You know that, right? We can open the stitches, say he bled out when we took the arm. Wouldn't be a lie..."

She pulled away.

"We gave our word," she said, as if that should explain everything. "I don't know what's going on, but what I do know is that anyone out to kill a boy that young ain't on the side of right. That stranger paid us a fortune for this. We can buy more land from the Potters, those acres they can't till worth a damn, but we could do it. We can hire help, extra salt and meat for next winter, lumber for the house...I won't better our life on the blood of a dead child, and I expect you to feel the same."

His cheeks flushed red. When he tried to speak, he shut his mouth again and waited another moment to get his composure back.

"True enough," he said. "Hard as it is to get the kids to avoid a lying tongue. Won't do no good to go lying ourselves. I'm scared, Evelyn. We're just farmers. I don't like going up to Tyneham to trade our wares to the miners, let alone all the way south to Veldaren where the real crooks are. Whoever's after this boy..."

"Tristan."

He laughed. "Fine. Whoever's after Tristan probably has money, soldiers...Who'll take care of Debbie, or Anna, or little Mark should something happen to us? Or, Ashhur forbid, what if something happened to *them*?"

She stood on her tiptoes and kissed his lips.

"Stop worrying. We'll deal with each problem as it comes, and Ashhur will keep us safe. Now let Tristan here sleep."

"Tristan," Matthew muttered as they passed through the curtain into the other room. "You really wanted to name one of our children Tristan?"

The newly named Tristan woke her a few hours later, well past midnight. Trying not to panic, Evelyn lit a candle and went to his side. The boy was moaning, and his legs and arm twitched every few moments. She touched his forehead. It was like touching fire.

"Get water in the tub," she told Trevor. "Mix in some snow too. If you can stand to keep your hand in it for long, it ain't cold enough."

"Yes ma'am," Trevor said, his eyes lingering on Tristan as he put on his coat and boots. They had a small tub inside their home ("A luxury if I ever saw one," Liza, her crone of a neighbor, had once told her). They had to bring the water in by buckets, and that would take time. Until then she tore off the boy's blankets and clothes, stripping him naked upon the bed.

"He going to be all right?" asked Anna as she poked her head through the curtain. She was twelve, old enough to help her mother when she acted the healer.

"Wake your father," Evelyn said, ignoring her question. "And make sure Mark and Julie stay in bed. Probably already scared, and I don't want them scared worse."

Anna nodded, and her head vanished behind the curtain. Evelyn lifted Tristan in her arms, and it was like picking up a burning log. When she brushed through the curtain into their living room, she found Matthew putting on layers.

"Trevor said you needed water in the tub. The fever gotten that bad?"

She nodded.

"I told you he hadn't had enough to drink," he said. "Can't sweat off a fever if you ain't got nothing to sweat."

"I know," she said. "Now's not the time."

She caught her younger children looking at her, and she turned her back to them and hurried to the tub. The door to the house slammed shut, whether from Matthew leaving or Trevor coming in she didn't know. In the tub she found a single bucketful of water, barely enough to wet the surface. She put him in anyway and held him down as his body flailed against the cold.

"Anna!" she cried. Her daughter hurried in after. "Help me hold him down. His shivers are going to get worse. Don't feel bad about the chill, either. He'll burn to death before he catches cold."

She shifted so that Anna might hold his arm, then pressed down on the boy's knees. Trevor came in with another bucket of water, and he looked lost about what to do with it.

"Just dump it on him," Evelyn said, trying to be patient. "It's only water!"

Trevor hesitated, but the look in his mother's eyes got him going. He upended the bucket, cold water from the well. Tristan's moan turned to a full-fledged wail. Rather than stay, Trevor hurried out. Evelyn leaned more of her weight on her arms as Tristan's struggling grew. Beside her, Anna quietly cried.

"Start praying," she whispered. "It'll help, but don't you dare let go of that arm."

Matthew came in with a larger bucket, and he poured it in by the boy's feet. The water was halfway up his body, and Evelyn told him one more should be enough.

"Still need the snow?" he asked.

"This water will be warm soon enough."

"All right."

When they came back she put the bucket of snow beside her, saving it for when the chill left the tub. Tristan was still shivering, and he cried when he had the energy, and moaned when he did not. After twenty minutes she dumped in the half-melted bucket of snow, sending Tristan's shivers back to full strength. Ten more minutes and she lifted him out, wrapped him in a towel, and brought him back to his bed. Matthew was there not long after, a small cup of milk in one hand, a slender funnel in the other. Evelyn recognized it surely enough. They used it to feed their animals various herbs and tonics should they become ill.

"Hogroot's in the milk," Matthew said. "He needs to drink. Hold open his jaw, and don't let him move. I have no intention of drowning him."

Once the milk was gone, they wrapped him tighter in blankets and waited.

"Go rest," she told her husband. "You have enough work in the morning, and it won't be no good for you to do it on a half night's sleep. Get the kids back to bed as well. I'll keep vigil on him."

Matthew squeezed her shoulder and then left. Once he was gone she gently stroked Tristan's forehead with her fingers. He looked like a drowned rat, but his fever had finally dropped. He'd fallen back asleep too, for which she was thankful. The hogroot in his milk would help break his fever, and she prayed it'd break completely while he slept. A quick inspection showed the stitches on his shoulder to be clean. No infection, thank Ashhur. There wasn't anywhere higher left to cut, other than his neck to end the suffering.

On her knees, her weight leaning against the bed, she waited out the night. Just before dawn his fever broke, and for the first time since Haern had brought him there he opened his eyes.

"I'm thirsty," he said, his voice a croak.

Evelyn smiled and clutched his hand.

"Fresh milk," she said, "coming right up."

A squad of twelve mercenaries escorted Alyssa's litter through the city. Anyone foolish enough to linger in their way received a quick slap with the flat edge of a blade. They stuck to the main streets, where thief guild presence was weakest, the town guards too numerous for the thieves to act rashly. The distance between her estate and Leon Connington's new mansion was enough to be a bother, but she felt it necessary to carry her message in person. She pulled her fox fur coat tighter about her and waited.

When they arrived she stepped out and surveyed the place. She'd been there once, just before its completion. After Leon's old mansion had burned down during the Bloody Kensgold, he'd rebuilt with security in mind. An enormous wall of stone surrounded his estate, perfectly smooth so there'd be no handholds. There were no trees in the yard either, nothing to hide behind. Four men stood at the gate, wearing ornate plate mail and wielding halberds. Beyond she could see the building, the walls stained a deep red, the roof sharply slanted. If Leon was nothing but roundness and fat, his new home looked the opposite, long and stretched thin.

"Greetings, Lady Gemcroft," said one of the gate guards. "Please wait while we summon an escort. Make sure you stay on the path, for an errant step might prove deadly."

Bertram wasn't there, but Alyssa could imagine the scowl he'd have given them. For her part she was willing to understand Leon's craving for safety. Perhaps he took it too far, but it had been his belongings destroyed in the fire, not hers. Ten armed men came from the front door, approaching in neat formation along the cobblestone path leading across the yard. When they reached the front they unlocked the gate from the inside and ushered Alyssa through.

"Your men must stay outside," said their leader when her mercenaries started to follow. Alyssa paused, gave him a glare to show she didn't appreciate being told just before entering, but then complied. If she felt safe anywhere other than her mansion, it was here. An assassin would have to be a lunatic to risk the guards, the wall, and the various traps hidden underneath the grass. The men's heavy boots clacked across the stone as they entered the mansion.

Leon waited just inside the door, a large smile on his face. Everything about Leon was big: his face, his eyes, his home, and most of all his belly. Hugging him was like hugging a giant sweet roll wrapped in silk. Only his mustache was thin.

"I'm so sorry about your loss," he said as he let go. "I'm sure he'd have been a fine man, very fine. If there's anything you need, please let me know."

"Thank you," she said, doing her best to smile and forget how he'd always glared at Nathaniel as if he were a cockroach whenever Nathaniel was in his presence. "Bertram is busy finishing the arrangements for the funeral, so I thought it best I stay out of his way."

"Of course, of course. It'd do you good to get out of that stuffy old mansion anyway. Always told your father he should fire whoever was in charge of his maidservants. Every breath in there was like licking the bottom of a dustbin."

Another smile. Her last head maid had died coughing and gagging on blindweed. She had a feeling Leon would have approved of such a fate for one who had let his sensitive allergies be affected.

"Have you any news from Laurie?" she asked as they walked toward—of course—the dining area.

"Ever since the Kensgold he's refused to come to Veldaren," Leon said as he took her hand. "I think your father's death spooked him more than a little. Such cowardice is inappropriate for a member of the Trifect, but what can you do?"

"Surely someone who lives with an army of mercenaries behind great stone walls has no reason to question another's bravery," she said, unable to hold back.

Far from upset, Leon only gave her a wink.

"It's one thing to be brave, and another to be stupid. I won't die from a garrote in my sleep. Neither would Laurie, if he took proper precautions."

"Maybe staying in Angelport is his precaution."

Leon laughed. "True, maybe it is. Still, he is going a little overboard, eh?"

They sat down at one end of a luxurious table easily able to seat more than eighty people. Alyssa watched the servants parade a variety of treats and pastries before her. She didn't feel like eating, but it seemed Leon would keep them coming forever until she picked. Deciding on a small flour cake topped with strawberries, she scooped a tiny bit with her spoon and ate. The flavor awakened a dormant part of her, a tiny voice reminding her of her own needs and not of others'. Her stomach grumbled, and she wondered how long it'd been since she ate. She was horribly tired, and in the fog that was her mind she couldn't remember.

The rest of the cake vanished as she wolfed it down. Leon smiled at her and tore into his own assortment of desserts, as if he'd known all along she'd been neglecting her appetite.

"You are more than welcome to stay the night," he said, sipping some wine from a silver goblet, but only after a servant tasted it first. "Just say the word, and I'll let your men at the gate know they can go home."

"Thank you, but I'd still prefer my own bed. Besides, the funeral is tomorrow, and I should make sure Bertram has everything in order."

"Where will it be held?"

She sipped her wine. The alcohol tasted strong, and she pushed it away, fearing how much it might affect her.

"My mansion. We'll bury Nathaniel in the garden out back."

"Beautiful."

She debated, then called over a servant and asked for another pastry. The woman bowed, and moments later returned with a cake topped with blueberries. Alyssa wondered how much Leon spent keeping such stock deep in winter. Did he have some secret to keeping it from spoiling? She made a note to ask him once she had some free time on her hands.

Halfway through her second cake, she decided she could delay no longer.

"There is another reason I'm here," she said, pushing her food away. "I will soon be putting something in motion, and I've come to ask for your cooperation."

"Oh?" he said, that one word pregnant with meaning. The way he lifted his eyebrow, the way he let his lips linger in an O shape...he knew he was about to be asked something he wouldn't like. He could read her too well. She had to improve. She felt like an imposter walking in her father's shoes. No wonder Bertram always harped at her to host more, visit more. Her social skills were lacking their proper finesse.

"We've crossed ten years of this nonsense with the thief guilds," she said. "I once thought my father inept, but I've come to see how difficult it is finding these rats and bringing them to their proper fate. Worse, I thought we could make peace, at least reach a level of understanding. There will always be those who steal from us, but neither of us should fear death in the night. They live off our trade, after all, and should that trade end, they will be like leeches sucking a corpse without blood. But this won't happen. Though it may sting, we must pull them off. My son died because we have gone soft, tried to pretend they would finally calm down and leave us be. No longer."

"Does this have something to do with what Potts has been telling me about you hiring every mercenary able to lift a sword?"

"It does."

Leon sighed and, shockingly enough, pushed his own plate away.

"Listen, you're just a silly girl trapped in your position, so I'll do my best to save you from this embarrassment. You can't find them all, Alyssa. You'll never win. You'd sooner drive out every flea from the southern district than bring the guilds down. Half those you're paying will just sit in taverns and claim they killed a rogue or three before dinner. How will you know? How will you keep track? Every damn beggar you passed on your way here might have been a Serpent, or a Spider, or a member of the Ash. Can you know for sure? Can you prove it? You're throwing your money in the damn gutter. I've killed more thieves trying to sneak onto my grounds than I have actually going out and looking for them."

She felt her neck reddening, but she pressed on anyway, his arrogance be damned.

"They want us to think that," she said. "But it isn't true. They act as if they'll endure, but their organizations can crumble, their loyalties break. They threaten us with poison and razor wire, and they've convinced the city that *they* are the ones to fear, *they* are the vicious ones. It is our fault for believing the lie."

A guarded look crossed Leon's face as if he realized how far off his first read of her had been.

"What exactly are you planning?" he asked.

"We break into every building. We search every crack of every wall. I have many men skilled in interrogation, and the men we've hired are even better at it. We'll find where they run, every time. These men have no pride, no honor. They'll point us the right way until they run out of places to hide. Every guildleader will fall, as will their replacements. If they wear a cloak, they die, regardless of the color."

Leon looked ready to explode.

"Are you out of your mind? We haven't had that level of conflict since this started, not even during the Bloody Kensgold. The guilds are growing complacent, Alyssa. You act as if you want an end to this war, but the war's already over. Sure, my guards die sometimes, but they take with them twice as many thieves. Veldaren is learning to accept this, to live with the precautions and the death. But what you want? What you'll do? You're throwing away an entire fortune to thrust fire into a hornet's nest. You'll get every single one of us killed, and all because you're grieving over the loss of some... of some... *bastard*?"

She stood and flung what was left of her cake into his face.

"Father was right," she said as he wiped icing from his cheek. "Your cowardice is as big as your gut. I will not fear them anymore, and neither should you. It was my fear that sent Nathaniel away, my fear that left him vulnerable. And his executioner, this... Watcher? He is no different from the rest of them. He lives among them, and from what Zusa tells me he is the best of them. And so I shall bring them down. *All* of them. The best to the last, the leaders to the dirt-crawling scum. Come Nathaniel's funeral, I will unleash my wrath upon the city that has sheltered the murderer of my son. Now if you would kindly request a servant to escort me to the door?"

Leon chewed on his lip a moment, his fat face blotched red. At last he clapped and did as she requested.

"Wait," he said, just before she exited the room. "Just how many men have you hired?"

"Close to two thousand," she said, and she felt a sense of victory at the way his jaw dropped. "As I said, Leon, I will destroy them. I will destroy *everyone* who dares try to stop me. Even the king. Even the Trifect itself."

He muttered something, but she did not hear it. Still furious, she turned and followed the servant woman out, more than ever wanting to be home to plan with her mercenary captains. Hiding was no longer an option. It was time to act. The time for putting up with the criminals was at an end, no matter the risk, no matter the bloodshed. Come the funeral, it was a lesson the whole city would learn.

CHAPTER

 12

Matthew was pouring grain for his cattle when he saw the men ride to his front door. There were two of them, their chain mail dirty from the road. Even far out in his field he could tell they were armed.

"Who are they?" Trevor asked beside him. He squinted against the light reflecting off the snow. "Do you know them?"

"No, I don't," Matthew said. "Remember, if anyone asks, Tristan's your brother, and he caught infection from a spider bite. You understand me?"

"Yes, sir."

"And just in case, get your knife, but don't you dare let them see you holding it. This is serious, Trevor."

The lad's eyes widened. He started to ask a question, thought better of it, and then just nodded.

Matthew led them back to the house. Evelyn had answered their knock, and after a moment invited them in. He trusted her to keep her wits about her, probably more than himself. His other children were in there, though, and once the strangers were outside the public eye, he wondered just what type of men they might be.

Should have made them wait outside until I got back, he thought. *Damn it, Evelyn. Sometimes you ought to act the proper wife.*

Just before reaching the house, he stopped at a small shed and ducked inside. He heard his son gasp as he yanked their pitchfork off the wall.

"Won't do much against their armor," he said, inspecting its four teeth. "But they ain't wearing helmets, so that's something."

He set it beside the door to the house, then opened the door and stepped inside. The two men sat beside the fire, their cloaks stretched out to dry at their feet. They both had swords, still sheathed, thank Ashhur. The rest of his children kept a safe distance away, again something to be thankful for. The strangers held small wooden bowls of a broth Evelyn had prepared for breakfast. His stomach grumbled involuntarily. He hadn't eaten yet himself. He wondered how much of his own portion sat in the strangers' bowls.

"Welcome, gentlemen," he said, taking off his gloves. "I see my wife has helped you feel right at home, which is proper. It's cold work riding in winter."

"She's a lovely host," one of them said. He was a plain-looking man, dark-haired, flat nose. Only the scar running from his eye to his ear made him seem dangerous. He wore no tabard, but his accent was distinctly of the north, most likely Tyneham or one of the smaller mining villages near it.

"That she is," he said. "On your way to Felwood, or beyond? I must say, I didn't catch which direction you came from while out in my field."

"Riding north," said the other. He was uglier, with brown hair in desperate need of a cut. "Our horses need a rest, and we must admit, the thought of a warm building was too much for us to resist when we saw your farm."

"A fire warms eight as well as six," he said. Evelyn gave him a glare, and he realized his mistake. He had seven in his family if he counted Tristan.

"Been times we had to cram twelve of us in here," he continued, hoping to make them forget the comment. "Neighbors had their house burn down, lost one of their sons too. Makes for a rough winter with no roof, so we brought 'em in until spring."

"It must have been tough," said the first, looking around the small home.

"Forgive me, I've yet to introduce myself. My name's Matthew Pensfield. You've met my wife, Evelyn. This here's my oldest, Trevor. Little Mark's over there, hiding in the corner. And these're my two daughters, Anna and Julie."

The girls smiled and tilted their heads in proper respect. The soldiers tipped their heads back, and each of them had a leer that sent fire up and down Matthew's spine. He hesitated, trying to decide what to do about Tristan. He didn't know what was the right course of action. The boy had been asleep when he last went outside. His wife took the decision away from him, and as much as it scared him, he trusted her.

"You must forgive us for not introducing you to Tristan. He's sick with a fever in bed. Just had to amputate an arm, the poor dear. Spider bite."

"That's a shame," said the dark-haired one. "My name's Gert, and this here's Ben. Like I said, we're riding the road, maybe to Felwood, maybe all the way to Tyneham."

"Only wanderers and thieves ride the road without knowing how far they wish to go," Matthew said. "I hope you're neither."

Gert laughed.

"Nah. We're looking for someone, actually. A lost boy, five years in age. Perhaps you've seen him?"

Matthew shook his head. He'd played cards only a few times when trading in the bigger towns. He'd never been good figuring the odds of things, but he'd always done all right because of one thing going for him: he had one of the best card faces of anyone he knew. Only Evelyn could read what was going on behind his eyes.

"I haven't, and I doubt I would, either. A boy that young running around in the snow? He'd be lucky to last a single night. How long's he been missing? I hope I cause no offense, but a coyote pack's probably gotten him, or at least what was left of him."

"There's the thing," said Ben. "He might not be alone. Had another man with him, wore gray and carried two swords. He's a kidnapper, and we're trying to capture him before he can think of asking for ransom."

"Kidnapped?" asked Evelyn. "From who?"

Gert sipped some of his broth. "That's something I'd rather we keep to ourselves. Either you seen the boy and that bastard, or you haven't. Don't matter none where either's come from."

As they talked, Trevor slipped into his room. When he came back Matthew saw the bulge in his pocket that was a knife. Matthew walked to the door and put his weight against it. His short sword leaned beside its hinges, sheathed. Whenever he'd needed it before, it'd always been at the door. If either of the two newcomers had seen it, they hadn't said anything.

"Well, I ain't seen a boy wandering around here, nor some man in gray. We've been shuttered inside for most of the past few days, the storm and all. If they went this way, they probably rode right on by."

"Not sure they're riding," said Gert. "Think they're walking, honestly. Not too many out right now, and we managed to find what might have been his tracks."

"That so?"

"Led this way, actually," said Ben. "You sure you ain't seen nothing?"

Matthew paused, trying to think of a lie. Again his wife beat him to it, bless her heart.

"We turned them away," she said. "They came wanting shelter, but they were bleeding, and he was armed. Looked like a thief, he did. We didn't want any trouble, and we don't want any now. He said he was on his way to Veldaren, if he's to be trusted."

The two men looked to one another, as if communicating silently.

"A hard woman that could refuse a wounded man asking for succor," Ben said.

Matthew watched his wife give them an iron glare, one he'd been on the receiving end of more times than he preferred.

"Life out here's cold and cruel, gentlemen. We do what we can for our family. Maybe things are different where you come from, but out here that's the way things are."

"I understand," Ben said. "We're just getting paid to ask these questions. Your broth's delicious, by the way. Feel it warming me all the way to my toes."

Matthew started to relax, but only a little. The men seemed too confident, too sure of themselves. They were no strangers to those swords at their hips, either. The sooner they left the better. When they finished they stood and flung their cloaks over their shoulders.

"Our horses are probably itching to continue," Gert said. "Or at least get out of the wind."

As they stepped toward the door they stopped, and Gert turned toward the curtain where Evelyn had said Tristan slept.

"You know, I've been fighting and killing for a long while. If there's anything I've seen before, it's a chopped limb. Mind if I take a look? I can make sure you stitched it up right, well as cut it proper. There's more art to keeping people alive than making 'em dead, after all."

Evelyn hesitated, and Matthew knew that if she was unsure, then he was in over his head.

"If you wish," he said, putting on his gloves. "I should get back outside. Only wanted to come visit with my guests, be polite. You two men have a good day."

"Want me to come with?" asked Trevor.

"No," Matthew said, harsher than he meant. "No, you ain't much use outside. Stay with your ma."

Trevor got the idea, and his hand brushed the knife hidden in his pants. Matthew winced and hoped neither of the soldiers saw. He pulled the door open and stepped outside. When he shut it he leaned his back against it, closed his eyes, and listened. Never one with an active imagination, he struggled to picture the most likely thing they'd do. They were searching for the boy, obviously. They'd step through the curtain, one inside to look, the other hanging back, watching them, waiting to see if anyone did anything stupid.

His hand closed around the pitchfork's handle.

Something stupid like this.

Matthew kicked the door inward. It seemed as if his entire vision narrowed down, just a thin window to see one of the soldiers staring back at him from the curtain, the one named Ben. His eyes widened for just a moment. His hand reached for his sword as if he were lagging in time. Matthew thrust the pitchfork for the soldier's exposed throat. Ben's sword couldn't clear his scabbard in time, so instead he ducked and turned away from the thrust, a purely instinctual move. It only made matters worse. When two of the teeth pressed against the side of his face, Matthew shoved with every hard-worked muscle in his body. The tips were thick, but with such force behind them they still punched through flesh and tore into bone.

Ben rolled his head downward, trying to pull free. When he did, blood spewed across the floor. He screamed. It might have been a word, a curse, but Matthew didn't know, didn't understand. Ben's jaw hung off-kilter, his right cheek shredded and the bone connecting it shattered. The look in his eyes reminded Matthew of the one time he'd encountered a rabid coyote attacking his animals. His sword free, Ben charged, not waiting for Gert. Matthew took a step back, braced his legs, and shoved the pitchfork in the way. The teeth hit his chain mail, and amid the screams of his family he heard the sound of metal scraping against metal. The teeth didn't punch through the armor, but they still bruised Ben's flesh and pushed inward hard enough to break more bones.

Matthew twisted the handle to the side, bringing Ben to his knees, still stuck on the pitchfork's teeth. Dimly he heard his wife cry out, the words not registering in his mind as having any meaning, only her tone. Gert rushed through the curtain, his sword swinging. Abandoning his clumsy weapon, Matthew lunged for the door. He landed on his knees, grabbed his short sword, and spun. Gert bore down on him, swinging with both hands. Their blades connected, and panic flooded him when saw a tiny chip break off at the contact. His sword was weaker, the metal cheaper. It wouldn't be long before it broke.

"Leave him alone!" he heard Evelyn shout, finally piercing through the haze. Gritting his teeth, he groaned as Gert pressed down with all his weight. He spared only a moment's glance to see Ben fling the pitchfork to the dirt and turn toward his wife. He had to help her, but he was pinned and badly positioned.

"Trevor!" he screamed. Where was his boy? Why wasn't he helping? Now wasn't the time for fear, damn it! He angled his sword to block another chop, realized it was a feint, and smacked aside the thrust aimed for his belly. "Don't you be a coward, boy, treat 'em like damn hogs!"

Evelyn hurried across the room, grabbing the poker from the fire. She held it clumsily, a pathetic weapon compared to the gleaming sword Ben wielded in his blood-soaked hand. Then he couldn't spare the glimpse, for Gert had dropped to one knee, knocking Matthew's sword out of position. Matthew struggled against it, but slowly his sword wavered, then hit the floor beside him. Gert's elbows pressed against his chest, his knee atop one of Matthew's legs.

"Don't worry about your wife," Gert said, his beady eyes inches away. "I'll take good care of her. Your daughters too."

It was the absolute worst thing Gert could have said.

Matthew let go of his sword, one hand grabbing Gert's wrist, the other ramming his eyes and mouth with his fingers. The soldier howled and tried to pull away, but Matthew dug his fingers in deeper and held on, feeling softness give way, then cartilage crunch in his grip. Gert tore his sword arm free, shrieking all the while. Blindly he stabbed. Matthew rolled, knocking his attack off balance. The sword struck the floor. With every bit of strength in his right arm, Matthew slammed Gert's head against the wall. He heard a wet crack, like the sound of a breaking pumpkin.

The abrupt end was startling. He heard his children crying, but saw no motion. He stood, shaking the gore from his hand. Evelyn huddled beside the fire, the poker at her feet, Trevor in her arms. The eldest son still held his blood-soaked knife.

Nearby lay Ben, bled out from the cuts on his face and the deep stab wound at the small of his back.

"Everyone all right?" he asked. Evelyn met his eyes, then nodded. "Thank Ashhur."

He gave his wife a hug, making sure he didn't stain her dress with his right hand. The rest of his children stayed sitting, and he could tell they were traumatized by the violence. He went to each of them, hugging them and whispering that all would be well. At last he grabbed the dead bodies and dragged them outside by their feet.

Once they were out of sight, he came back inside and plopped into a chair beside the fire. His upper body started shaking, and he closed his eyes to try to hold back a sudden bout of nausea.

"We'll bury the armor until we can sell it in the spring," he told Evelyn, talking in hopes of stopping the violence replaying over and over in his head. "Same with their swords. We'll unbridle the horses and send them on their way, hopefully far, far away. As for...you know...we'll give 'em to the hogs."

His wife made a soft cry. He shuddered but forced himself not to dwell on it. They'd do what they must, no different from ever before. Opening his eyes, he looked to the curtain, wondering if that blasted boy still slept, or if he was in there cowering in terror.

"Not worth the coin," he said, just before leaning to one side and vomiting.

CHAPTER

 13

Arthur Hadfield looked about the room in total disgust. He'd worked with mercenaries before, but to invite them into his home? So disgraceful. They gathered in the dining hall, over twelve of them. They were the captains, the ones with at least a hundred men at their disposal. They chatted with one another, killing time until Alyssa returned. They were a motley bunch, wearing various combinations of armor, ribbons, and tunics to distinguish themselves. Arthur dared not imagine how much coin was flowing into their pockets for simply picking their teeth and eating Alyssa's food.

"Not sure how much fun this'll be," said one, a bald man with a shaved head. "Proper fight is on a battlefield, not crashing into people's homes and searching for rats."

"Killing's killing," said another. "Since when you started getting picky?"

"I'll take the money, but don't mean I can't want a nice open place to swing my ax."

"Probably need that space too, otherwise you'll cut your own fucking head off."

"Fuck you, Jamie. You probably can't wait to start. Your men will feel right at home wading through open sewers."

Arthur turned to leave and found Bertram standing behind him at the door, looking just as miserable.

"The stains they leave on the carpet..." he said, shaking his head.

"Price of doing business, I suppose."

The old man nodded as he watched the captains bicker. Arthur went to his side, his arms crossed over his chest.

"Have you talked with Alyssa lately?" Bertram asked after a time.

"Just this morning. Her mood has soured as the funeral approaches. I'd hoped she might grieve like any other woman, but instead she's out for blood."

"She wants that boy's killer found."

"I'm working on it, but he's proven an elusive little fuck."

Bertram chuckled. "I am not surprised. There are a thousand criminals and murderers in this city. Finding one particular man must be difficult. Still, you might look at it a different way. Knowing one lowborn wretch from another is just as difficult."

Just like last time, Arthur wondered if he was being tested. This time the wording seemed too strong to be coincidence. He decided to go out on a limb.

"I'm sure that even if we do catch the Watcher, it'll be tough proving that's who he is," he said.

"No one seems to know," Bertram agreed. "Though I trust you in these matters, and would vouch for your opinion."

Arthur's eyes lit up.

"Is that so?" he said. "I don't think it will be long before I have a man to present to her. The city might be large, but there are too many eyes, too many mouths, for a man to hide forever. But I'm glad to know your trust in me is so great."

"I trust you more than I would any of them," Bertram said, waving a dismissive hand at the mercenaries. "The Hadfields have always been good friends of the Gemcrofts. I can only do so much. Alyssa needs help in matters such as these, a guiding voice amid her grief. If only you could talk to her, get her to *listen*..."

"I understand," Arthur said. "I have my own matters to attend to, but I should return before nightfall, or close to it. When I do, I'll see if Alyssa will open up to me."

"Thank you," Bertram said, bowing low. "Now, by your leave, I must try to convince those men that while the wine is a courtesy, it is certainly not free if you drink it by the barrel."

"Gods give you luck with that."

Arthur left the dining hall, retrieved his coat and sword, and exited the estate. Normally Oric would have gone with him, but he had headed north after bringing back Nathaniel's supposed remains. Arthur was skilled with a sword, though, and he knew his way. Besides, once inside the Serpents' territory, he'd be treated like a king.

Only minutes from Alyssa's mansion, he noticed the first of many escorting him from the shadows. Their cloaks were green, so he relaxed. No doubt William Ket, leader of the Serpent Guild, wanted to protect his investments. Arthur couldn't blame him. He took a few turns, vanishing deeper into the dark, dilapidated part of the city. Several more followed him, and for a moment he might have sworn he even saw someone along the rooftops. When he arrived at the guildhouse his escorts came into view of its torches, and they motioned for him to enter.

Amid the emerald cushions and gold-framed paintings, Arthur sat and waited for William. A pretty lady wearing thin veils, and nothing else, approached and asked him his preference of drink. Normally he refused, always fearing some sort of poison or drug, but tonight he needed the help.

"The strongest of whatever you have," he said. "Oh, but make sure it doesn't taste like piss."

"As you wish," she said, batting her beautiful green eyes at him. He watched her go, admiring her figure. With enough coin, he knew he could have her. Shame he had to spend the night at Alyssa's mansion. Tight figure like that, there was so much he could do to . . .

"Arthur! Welcome!"

Arthur stood and tore his attention away from the little tart.

"William," he said, offering his hand to his younger brother, who had been William Hadfield before he'd changed his name to Ket to protect his family from embarrassment. "My apologies for being gone so long."

"No need," said William. He was as tall as Arthur, and had the same eyes and hair. "I figure you have your hands full handling a grieving mother, am I right?"

"Hands aren't full just yet, but she'll give in to me in time."

The lady returned with his drink, and he accepted it gratefully. After a sip to test its flavor (somewhere between sewer water and burning oil) he took a large gulp. As it set his throat aflame, he chuckled at his brother.

"You've been late with your last shipment," he said, holding back a cough. Damn that stuff was strong. "I'm a little curious as to why."

William's smile drooped, but only for a moment before he fixed it. This time it was far more fake.

"I should have figured a leisurely chat with you was not in store for me this evening. The gold was stolen from us as we smuggled it into the city, and through no fault of our own."

"No fault? Is that so? A convenient excuse to not pay me my half, wouldn't you think?"

William sat down, and Arthur followed suit. The two stared at one another, a quick, silent exchange. Arthur knew William was trying to decide how much he should tell, and what Arthur's reaction might be. He hoped that for once his little brother told the truth, the whole damn truth.

"Have you heard of the Watcher, by any chance?"

Arthur was too surprised to hide his reaction.

"Should I take that as a yes?" William asked, raising an eyebrow.

"I have, but tell your tale first, and then perhaps I can better explain mine."

William waved over another servant girl, who brought him wine in a long slender glass.

"Well, whoever that bastard is got lucky," he said after taking a sip. "Stumbled upon us while we were lifting the crate over the wall. Killed my men, took the bags of gold, and then do you know what this motherfucker did? He scattered it across the street. Middle of the day, high market, and he just tears them open and flings them to the crowd. Not the first time he's done that to us, either, but usually with smaller amounts. Scary, really. If he'd throw away that much coin, then there isn't a chance we can bribe or deal with him. He's out to kill us, all of us, not just Serpents. Wish I knew what we'd done to piss him off."

"Normally I'd doubt the ability of one man to kill so many

of yours," said Arthur, "but I've seen it for myself. Lost six soldiers to the Watcher. Wrote his name with their blood as a message to me when I returned. He took some of the gold, but not all, thank the gods. Another day or two and I'll have the rest outside the walls and ready for you. Alyssa thinks all of it was stolen, which will help make up for what we lost."

"I can change most of it into royal crowns with my merchants, and, amusingly enough, by buying large quantities of food and wine from Laurie Keenan. Something quite appropriate about laundering the Trifect's gold using the Trifect themselves. Any large increase will take some time, though. When will you be ready to pick up your portion of what we've exchanged so far?"

"Keep it safe for now. Things are too chaotic. That's one of the other reasons I'm here. Tomorrow is Nathaniel's funeral, and come nightfall you need to make sure your men are prepared. Alyssa's hired at least a thousand mercenaries, perhaps far more. She's going to let them loose upon the city."

William's face darkened.

"Is she mad? What could we have done to spark such animosity . . ." He stopped, glared at him. "Unless you blamed her son's death on us?"

"I told her the Watcher was tied to the local thief guilds, thinking it would keep her from asking too many questions. I never could have expected this overblown reaction."

William flung his half-empty glass to the floor. "Of course not. You'll throw us to the wolves to make your life easier. Always have, always will. What do we do now? We can't face that many on our own."

"Then don't do it on your own. Spread word to the rest of the guilds. I want Alyssa humiliated by this course of action. She needs to doubt herself, her decisions, so she might trust me more. She is not in my pocket, not yet. In time she will be, I have no doubt, but until then I need your help."

The redness gradually left William's neck as he leaned back in his chair.

"I think I can convince the others, though I have little time. A single night to prepare a counter-ambush? Thank you for not telling me sooner. I like having to pull plans out of my ass."

A hardness entered Arthur's words.

"You chose this life, not me. I came here the moment Alyssa was away, now deal with it."

They glared at one another, but finally William relented.

"So be it. But what will you do about this Watcher? He's making life miserable for the both of us. If he left the city, then he's certainly caught wind of our scheme, or at least part of it. A wrong word whispered to Alyssa and you'll hang."

"We'll hang, you mean."

William smirked at him.

"I live my life in the shadows. She already wants me dead, and is about to spend a fortune trying to achieve that tomorrow night. But you? You live your life in the light. The only place you can hide would be with me. Are you prepared to crawl through the gutters and eat shit to save your own ass?"

"I think I might prefer the noose."

William stood, their conversation clearly over.

"Then you need to make sure the Watcher fucking dies."

CHAPTER

14

Zusa watched the ceremony from the rooftops, her long cloak wrapped tightly about her. With only a few days' notice, the crowd was smaller than it might have been. She recognized various merchants, wealthy nobles, and a few members of Connington's distant family, plus Leon himself. All were from within Veldaren or its surrounding estates. Tradition would have provided a long enough delay for Laurie Keenan to travel from Angelport, but Alyssa seemed to care less and less about tradition with each passing day. Zusa didn't blame her.

The bones, brought back to the city by Arthur's lackey Oric, had been placed within a small sealed coffin. As her house guards lowered it into the ground, Alyssa stepped forward to address the crowd. She wore a dress of black and dark blues, and she'd smeared ashes upon her face. Behind her the sun dipped below the walls of the city, and in the twilight she made her decree.

"It is despicable that such a thing could happen," she said, loud enough for Zusa to hear. "Worse that I might be expected to deny my son vengeance. So many of you here have made peace with the thieves. So many of you have come to accept the danger they pose. In doing so you have stripped away every shred of your pride and dignity. I will not! Those who prey on us, steal from us, kill and poison to claim their power, they die tonight. Go home if you must, or stay here if you fear the streets. But this night, only this night, must you fear them any longer. Veldaren aches for a purge, and I will be the one to deliver it. Cry out at me if you wish, but it will change nothing. The gold is spent, the orders are given. Let the blood flow."

She looked to the rooftop, directly at Zusa. Zusa nodded in return. That was the last command. There was no turning back. Spinning about, her cloak billowing silently behind her, Zusa raced to the front of the mansion and vaulted off the roof. When she landed, it was amid the gathered group of mercenary captains, who had been ordered to wait opposite the funeral.

"You have your orders," she told them all. "Bring the Abyss to Veldaren, and throw every cloak into it. Give vengeance to my lady."

The captains grinned and smacked one another on the shoulder.

"About damn time," said one. "Let's get to it!"

Zusa left to the south, still trying to decide on her course of action. The mercenaries were scattered throughout the city in taverns, camps, and houses of those loyal to the Trifect. They would spill out onto the streets, and no one would be there to stop them. Only King Vaelor could make a reasonable attempt with his soldiers, but he'd have to break a lifelong streak of cowardice, which Zusa knew would not happen. Ever since the Bloody Kensgold he'd given them all freedom to kill one another so long as their threats were never aimed at him. When the nightmare began, no doubt the city watch would turn the other way, if they even left the castle at all. She had an inkling they would not.

But the bloodshed would accomplish nothing if she couldn't find Nathaniel's killer. The Watcher. Where did he hide?

Those in the shadows were about to be flung into the light. She resolved to scour the city, keeping an eye open for anything unusual. If the Watcher was as skilled as Veliana made him sound, he would hold his own no matter how many mercenaries they flung at him.

Veliana...

Zusa might have offered a prayer for her, but she had turned her back on her former god, Karak. She had no one to pray to, so instead she just murmured the thoughts aloud, hoping that her friend might survive the night. So badly she'd wanted to warn Veliana of the coming slaughter, but to do so would have endangered Alyssa's efforts, especially if Vel informed the other guilds. That meant keeping her mouth shut and hoping for the best. If only the woman could have relinquished her desire for control of the Ash Guild, she might have made a new life at Zusa's side within the Gemcroft mansion.

"Stay safe, Vel," she said, crawling up the side of a small house with a flat roof. Once atop she leaped across, scanning her surroundings for a man in strange gray cloaks and wielding twin swords. A man skilled enough to defeat her.

Half an hour passed, painfully quiet. It seemed the entire city had drawn its collective breath. Then all at once came the exhalation. Two fires erupted in southern Veldaren, both at supposed headquarters of thief guilds. Deciding there was as good a place as any, she headed that way. She passed several patrols, and one even had the gall to fire a crossbow at her. She ducked lower and continued, realizing she would be far from the only one to travel by rooftop that night.

They were torturing a thief in the street when she arrived at the first fire. It was probably supposed to be an interrogation, but that would have involved a chance for answers from the victim. The thief had blood smeared across his face, and from the way his jaw hung, it looked like it'd been broken in multiple places. The best he could do was point. The light of the fire bathed him and the mercenaries in red, and in it the thief sobbed for mercy.

"This is your creation," Zusa whispered to the distant thief, hardening her heart against the violence. "This is the fate you have earned."

Still, it seemed a cruel fate. When a mercenary impaled the thief, she was thankful. She turned for the second fire when she caught movement from the corner of her eye. She backflipped into the air as a blade cut where she had been. Facing her attacker, she fell, grabbed the ledge of the building, and then flung herself at him. He was a giant man, his features shrouded in twilight. She slammed her knees against his chest. It was like trying to knock down an ancient oak. She rolled over his head, jumped away to give herself some distance, and then drew her daggers. As her opponent whirled, she used the half-second to examine him.

He was dark-skinned, darker than she'd ever seen, and wore light clothing with a long gray cloak. He carried two enormous swords, each a length most would need two hands to hold. His muscles looked more appropriate to a woodcutter or blacksmith than a thief. But most of all her eyes were drawn to the white paint across his face, making his shaved head look like a bleached skull.

"A woman?" he said. Zusa lunged, hoping to take advantage

of his surprise. She parried one of his swords to the side, then thrust her other dagger for the opening. The man seemed prepared for the maneuver. He twisted, slapped aside her thrust, and stepped closer. She tried leaping back to gain more distance, but he followed, trapping her at the edge of the roof. Falling to one knee, she tried to hamstring him, but again his swords were there, batting her far smaller weapons aside. Part of her wondered why, with such an advantage in reach, he forced them to remain in close combat.

Then one of his swords fell, and she felt a hand grab her hair, each finger as thick as a sausage. Her feet lifted off the roof. She held in a scream, all her focus narrowed to a razor's edge. Her daggers swung, both aiming for his neck. With only one weapon, he had no chance to block, or at least so she thought, but he used its flat edge to strike both her wrists as they thrust, pushing them over his head. Before she could bring her arms back down, the sword's edge pressed against her throat.

"Stop struggling," he said. "I'm not here to kill you."

His voice was deep, so deep it reminded her of the rare times she'd heard Karak whisper to her in the night. She forced herself to calm, to look into his brown eyes without flinching. The sword pressed tighter against her throat, as if he expected her to try to break free.

"What do you want?" she asked.

"Not you," said the man. "My target is not a woman. I might have said so if you hadn't jumped at me like a rabid dog."

"Who are you?"

He stared at her as if deciding something. Decision made, he unceremoniously dropped her. She landed on her feet and crouched before him, ready to leap at the slightest wrong move.

"I am Ghost. I've come to claim the Watcher's head, and other than the breasts, you fit the description rather nicely."

Zusa slowly straightened, though her muscles remained tense. Whoever this Ghost was, she had no intention of relaxing in his presence.

"Who has hired you?" she asked. "One of the thieves?"

He grinned at her. Something about it worsened her unease.

"I cannot tell you, as surely you can understand. You seem at home in the night, and you move as I expected the Watcher to move. Do you know of him? Tell me, and I might make it worth your while."

"Whatever I know, I cannot say, for I seek him as my own bounty. My mistress wishes to be the one to claim his life, and I would not dare risk cheating her of it."

"Mistress?" asked Ghost, raising an eyebrow.

Too much, stop speaking, you always say too much.

So she smiled, hoping to convince him that it wasn't a slip of a tongue, instead a ploy to make him wonder if she spoke truth or not. He probably didn't buy it, but it was still worth the attempt.

"So be it," Ghost said. One of his swords shifted and she moved to jump, but then he saluted her with the blade. "A game, then. I will let you search unimpeded, but I expect the same courtesy of you. If you somehow find him first...all I ask is that you come to me at the Mug and Feather tavern so I may know your name. Any lady more skilled in tracking than I is a lady I would sorely wish to meet with again. Consider it a repayment of my generosity."

"The generosity of a man who nearly stabbed my back before seeing my face to confirm a kill?"

Ghost laughed. "You are still alive, woman. That alone is proof of my generosity."

The way he said it, with no anger or pride, only amusement, chilled Zusa's blood. This was a man to whom death was a common companion, who believed he had nothing to prove. If such an agreement kept her safe from his blades...

"I accept," she said. "Now forgive me, but I have a man to find."

"Good luck," he said. "Oh, and stay safe. I hear there's a lot of mercenaries out searching for people like you."

She looked to the fire behind her, and the several corpses left there to rot in the street. When she looked back Ghost was gone. *No one that big should be able to move so silently*, she thought, but it seemed she was wrong. Cursing herself, she hurried north, following the distant cries of battle. If she was lucky, they might still scare out the Watcher, but now she wondered if she truly had any hope of finding him before Ghost. How great would Alyssa's anger be if she found out Ghost had captured him first?

Still, that would be better than their finding him at the same time. However that confrontation might end, she knew her blood would be spilled.

The city had gone to the Abyss. There was no other way to describe the horrors Haern watched as he hurried along the streets, keeping his head down and his swords hidden. It was too dangerous to remain on the rooftops. Every mercenary with a bow was firing at any shadow that moved. He'd counted four fires the last time he'd found a quiet enough spot to scale a wall and look over the city. Madness, total madness. Was this what it'd been like when his father first declared war against the Trifect so long ago?

The mercenaries traveled in squads, some as large as a hundred. They roamed the streets, smashing in doors, dragging out scared owners to ask questions, demand names, and sometimes execute them outright. He watched a group of three thieves, Spiders by their cloaks, chased by twenty men in armor. They died when a second group cut them off, another ten with naked blades and eager eyes. The mercenaries left only pieces of the three. Pieces.

Because he lacked guild colors and appeared the beggar, he'd managed to avoid much of their ire. He'd been questioned twice. The first time he'd feigned deafness. The second time he'd pointed the mercenaries toward the headquarters of the Serpent Guild. While following them he'd watched a couple dragged out of bed, the husband hollering, his wife holding blankets to her chest to hide her nakedness. While their children watched from the doorway, the mercenaries had cut the couple's throats and cheered the name of Alyssa Gemcroft as if she were a goddess of blood and murder.

All the while the city guards remained nowhere to be found.

Haern ducked through a side alley, not surprised to find two more there with him. They wore the brown cloaks and sleeves of the Hawks, and they drew daggers as he rushed by. He wished them luck, out of nothing more than professional courtesy. Part of him wondered how many would abandon their cloaks. Doing so was punishable by death. Still, it seemed the only way to survive. Of course he'd seen plenty without cloaks or colors dying in the street. Perhaps all it'd take was a single man whispering your name to find yourself in the arms of sellswords...

Deciding it worth the risk, he used a window ledge to vault atop a house that overlooked the headquarters of the Serpents. Thirty mercenaries surrounded the place, some wielding crossbows, some torches. There was no doubt as to their intentions. Those inside could die by blade or by fire. Hardly a choice he'd desire to make.

"By order of Lady Gemcroft, all those affiliated with the

thief guilds are to be executed," the mercenary captain shouted. "We know you're in there, so come out and die with honor!"

Haern flattened himself on the rooftop, making sure no one could see him. The last thing he wanted was some crossbowman with a twitchy finger putting a bolt through his eye.

"This city ain't hers!" challenged a hidden stranger. Haern's eyes narrowed as he realized the voice did not come from the surrounded headquarters. "Time you sellswords learned that!"

Five buildings had clear views of the headquarters, including the one Haern lay atop. From every one of their windows appeared green-cloaked men with bows and crossbows. With a loud cry they released. A third of the mercenaries died in the first wave. Some tried fleeing toward the main streets, while others stormed toward the buildings. The arrows gave chase. When the last fell, Haern saw William Ket step out from the headquarters, a gleaming sword in his hand. He found the mercenary captain, chopped off his head with three swings, and lifted it in the air. The rest of his guild cheered.

Haern's blood ran cold. The other guilds would certainly be preparing ambushes as well. While it'd be foolish not to expect losses on both sides, and he generally held no love for mercenaries, there were a few mercenaries he did care for.

"Damn it, Senke," he whispered, pulling back so he wouldn't have to see the executions of those who still cried out in pain. "Tell me you aren't part of this nonsense. You can't have been this stupid."

But of course he would have. It seemed every free man had been brought into Alyssa's fury. What had spurred this on? Why now? He so rarely heard news of her, or of the Trifect in general. They'd grown quiet, defensive. But this?

There was nothing quiet about the screams that seemed to come from everywhere as the stars vanished beneath great curtains of smoke. How much of the city would burn? Would any be desperate enough to form bucket brigades while the death squads marched? He didn't know, and didn't care. He had to find Senke and Delysia. Losing them once had been hard enough. He couldn't do it again. The city was large and swarming with men. Finding them would be near impossible, but at least he knew names to search for.

Haern dropped back to the street and began searching for a smaller group of men to ambush. He had to avoid several larger patrols, and at one point a crossbow bolt. At last he encountered a group of three, deep in combat with five members of the Ash Guild, a sixth bleeding out nearby. The mercenaries were cornered against the city wall, and it was only their superior armor and reach that kept them alive against the greater numbers. Haern descended upon them like a whirlwind, his swords cutting down two before the thieves even knew he was there. He cut the throat of a third, then watched the final two die at the hands of the mercenaries.

"Thanks," said one of them, a gruff man with a beard and a wicked cut across his nose that was still bleeding. "Fuckers led us here into a trap, jumped us from the rooftops."

The man pointed at Haern's cloaks.

"You one of them? If so, you might want to run while we're still feeling grateful..."

"I am no friend of the guilds," Haern said, making sure to keep his cloaks low so they only partially saw his face. "I'm searching for a small group of mercenaries. One is named Senke, sometimes using the name Stern. The other is Delysia Eschaton. They should be together."

"Not a clue," said the man with the bleeding nose.

"Don't know about no Delysia," said the second as he walked over and killed the sixth Ash member, who had been whimpering in pain. "But that name sounds familiar. I know a Tarlak Eschaton, and he runs his tiny group, nothing but small-timers. Guy's half off his rocker. Might be them you're looking for."

"Perhaps. Do you know where they might be?"

The man spit. "All them smaller groups got put together and sent to the far south. Alyssa figured it'd be easier to spread out and find the rats when they tried to hide in their slums."

Haern fought down his panic. They'd been sent into the very homes of the thieves, as if they would be the ambushers? When the guilds fled to safety there, they would be doing the killing, not the mercenaries. He had to get Senke and Delysia out of there, and fast. He bowed to the three men and then turned south.

"Hey, what's your name?" asked the man with the bleeding nose.

"I have none," he shouted. When he turned, he caught sight of something strange, like a white face peering down from the wall, round and hairless. A glance back revealed only darkness.

I'm jumping at shadows, he thought. *If you're alive, Senke, I'm going to murder you for accepting such a stupid assignment.*

He wondered where his father was in all this. He wouldn't hide, not from such blatant disrespect. The Spider Guild's headquarters were in the southeast. If these Eschaton mercenaries stumbled upon him and his best...

Haern ran faster.

Deciding speed was more important than stealth, he cut to one of the main roads and trusted himself to outrun any patrols. He raced south, all the while doing his best to ignore the pain in his stomach. The wound there hadn't quite healed, though it was hardly more than an angry red scar. Still, the movement was enough to stretch the skin and agitate it. What he'd have given for an extra day or two to heal before all this madness hit.

"You! Stop!"

Haern cursed as he saw a group of five mercenaries up ahead rush toward him, no doubt thinking him a fleeing member of the guilds. The houses were packed tight on either side, so it was either turn back in search of a route around, or go straight through.

"Move!" he screamed, hoping to startle them with his mad rush. He slide-kicked just before nearing, avoiding an arrow that whistled overhead. His kick took out the legs of one, and he rolled away. Smashed under that much armor, he'd be killed in seconds by the others. A sword swung for his head, but he twisted and fell to one knee. Two others lunged, their swords thrusting. Haern dove to his right, landing hard on his shoulder. He'd made it to the other side.

"We said stop!" one of them shouted. Haern laughed, wondering who exactly he thought would obey the command. He weaved from side to side, not surprised to see one last arrow plink into the dirt beside him. With their heavy armor they couldn't hope to match his speed. Last he looked, they'd abandoned the chase and instead smashed in the door of a nearby home. He offered a prayer for the inhabitants as he ran.

It seemed the very air grew thicker as he plunged deep into southern Veldaren. He counted five fires now, and one of them wasn't far off. The smoke whirled down the streets, its distortion good for the thieves, bad for the mercenaries. He heard sounds of combat from one home with a broken door, and he watched another group battle, four Hawks against two mercenaries. He let them be. There were too many fights for him to help them all. The gravemen would be busy tomorrow, he thought grimly. Whatever buildings didn't burn would soon have their walls painted with blood.

A plume of smoke erupted to his left, accompanied by a deep

explosion. His curiosity couldn't take it. He turned, climbed onto a rooftop, and hurried that way. Whatever he was expecting to see, it was not what he found.

The area opened up to a fountain carved in the likeness of two women bathing each other, the fountain long broken and out of water. At least twenty men lay dead, half mercenaries, half thieves, their blood mixing together to stain the surrounding cobblestones red. A large group of thieves remained, Wolves judging by their colors. They faced off against only four, a strange four at that. Senke guarded one half of the fountain, parrying and blocking with his two flanged maces. In the other half fought a short man in plate mail, a punch dagger in each hand. Delysia stood in the fountain behind Senke, her lovely red hair matted to her face by a cut across her forehead. She was taller than he remembered, and she wore the white robes of a priestess. His heart raced faster, and he forced himself to move. While Delysia cast spells that bathed them all in white light, the last of the four stood in the other side of the fountain with his hands surrounded by fire. He wore a yellow robe and a pointy yellow hat. The color reminded Haern of dandelions. He had red hair similar in color to Delysia's, and a well-trimmed goatee.

Guy's half off his rocker, the mercenary had said about Tarlak, their leader. Haern had a feeling that was him. Only the insane, or the extremely confident, would dare wear such an outfit.

This Tarlak swung his hands in a circle. Fire danced across his fingers, then streaked toward a group of three hiding behind an overturned wagon, trying to shoot crossbow bolts from cover. The wagon exploded into shrapnel and embers. The short man seemed hard-pressed fighting one thief, but the wizard kept zapping thin bolts of blue lightning, knocking the thief back and keeping him from scoring a kill. Senke fought three at once, yet seemed to be doing better at protecting the two in the fountain. Having been on the receiving end of so many smacks to the head and kicks to the chest while training with him, Haern wasn't surprised.

Decision made, he drew his swords and charged. It was Senke and Delysia he'd come to protect, so it was them he'd help. The wizard saw his approach and turned, magic shimmering on his hands.

"It's Haern!" Senke shouted just as the lightning arced out, having seen his approach as well. Haern rolled, wishing he'd had far more training in dealing with spellcasters. The roll seemed to work, for he heard the ground behind him crackle and break from the impact. He kicked back to his feet and jumped, having closed enough distance to reach the first Wolf. The man turned and tried to impale Haern with his sword. Having had enough of that nonsense only a few days before, Haern batted aside the thrust while still in the air and landed short. His opponent exposed, it was easy work looping his other sword around and cutting his throat.

"Sorry!" he heard the wizard shout.

Damn fool, Haern thought as he linked up with Senke, standing side by side with him as the Wolves closed in.

"Glad you could join us," Senke said between breaths. Despite the smoothness of his parries and kills, he was clearly winded.

"I shouldn't have to. What the Abyss are you doing out here?"

"Fight now, insult me later."

As one they went on the offensive. It felt like old times, carelessly training in Thren's safe house. But this time it wasn't dummies they fought, nor did they wield wooden swords. This time their opponents bled. Haern struck both high and low, forcing his thief to make desperate parries with his daggers. The shorter weapons made his arms move more than Haern's to keep up with the attacks, and Haern used that to put him more and more out of position. At last he feinted a wide slash, pulled his sword in, and stabbed. The edge sliced through cloth and flesh and into lung. As the thief fell, Senke gave him a good bash on the head with his mace, just to be sure. Two more rushed ahead, but a blinding flash from behind Haern dazed them. With such a handicap, they fell with ease to the skilled fighters.

"Help Brug!" Senke shouted as three more Wolves approached from the north, joining the others.

"Brug?"

"The short fat guy."

Haern felt a moment's hesitation. He'd fought alone for so long, he wasn't used to obeying orders. But then again, he felt himself slipping once more into the past, nothing but an awkward child learning from his masters. He turned and circled the fountain, joining Brug, who was bleeding from his shoulder and face. A dagger was lodged in the crease of Brug's armor. Haern yanked it out as he ran past, hurled it at Brug's opponent, and then followed it up with a flying kick. The dagger's hilt hit the thief's throat, and then Haern's foot cracked his chest. The Wolf dropped to one knee, lifting his dagger in a clumsy defense. Haern cut him down, a clean slice through his throat.

Brug looked ready to explode.

"I had him!"

Haern blinked. "Uh, sorry?"

A fireball sailed over both their heads, delaying the attack of several Wolves who had abandoned their attempts at shooting the wizard and instead chosen to close the distance. Haern felt the heat of it on his neck.

"Damn it, Brug, what am I paying you for?" shouted the wizard. "And you, Haern, right? Keep him alive, will you?"

Haern turned to the wizard's opponents, somewhat amused at how much redder Brug's face had grown. Brug blubbered, then rushed ahead, punching the air with his daggers. Haern's amusement left. The idiot was going to get himself killed because of his pride. He rushed after, the two of them barreling at the three Wolves as if they were madmen. At the time it was a fair assessment. The Wolves wavered, he saw the doubt in their eyes, and then they turned to flee. Haern killed two, for he was too fast and had far too much momentum to be outrun. He sliced the hamstring of the third as he ran on by, allowing Brug to catch up and eviscerate the thief with his punch daggers.

Sucking in air, Haern turned back to the fountain. The last of the Wolves were either dead or fleeing. Tarlak stepped out of the fountain, helped Delysia follow, and then waved.

"That wasn't so bad," he said.

Haern shook his head. Off his rocker, indeed.

CHAPTER 15

Ghost followed the Watcher south, though he did so with no hurry. He'd watched him fight, and learned two things: One, no puke-brained mercenary would do him in. Two, the Watcher had friends he cared deeply about. He might have thought his quiet voice concealed his emotions when he asked the mercenaries questions, but Ghost heard the hint of worry, particularly about the one named Delysia. With that, it was only a matter of time before he brought the Watcher down. You couldn't have attachments, not if you wanted to survive against someone like Ghost.

Tarlak Eschaton wasn't well known to him, but if he played the mercenary game he had contacts, friends, employers, maybe even a spot in the guild. There would be no hiding. So as he strolled down the street, always given a wide berth by the groups that rushed past with bloodied swords, Ghost paused and looked west. A strange commotion was brewing down there—he could tell by the torches and the way several of the recent patrols had all turned in that direction. Had the fighting coalesced into an actual battlefront? Surely not. The thieves weren't that organized, nor would that benefit them in any way. So what, then?

His hands on his hilts, he strode over to the mob. He estimated at least sixty men were gathered around what he realized was the temple of Ashhur. So far they remained at the steps, but that appeared ready to change at any moment. Fifteen priests stood in their way, their hands at their sides. They were proficient with many spells, he knew, but how effective those spells would be on armored men he was unsure. An elderly priest with a bald head stood in the center of the steps, and he faced the crowd without any semblance of worry. Sweat ran down the sides of his neck, though, and Ghost knew him just as scared as the rest.

"You cannot enter," the old man shouted, hardly heard over the din of the mercenaries.

"Let us in!" they shouted.

"Out of the way!"

"You harbor thieves!"

Ghost frowned. He needed a better look. Pillars lined the edges of the lengthy stairs. Hiding behind one, he climbed halfway up the steps, and from there he peered into the temple. Inside was chaos, hundreds of people crammed within for shelter. Given how many homes he'd seen ransacked, it made perfect sense. Where else might be safer? They sat on benches, huddled against walls, and lay in the aisles if need be. Sure enough, he caught sight of a few cloaks in there, but not many.

"I will not hand anyone over to be butchered in the streets," the head priest was saying. "Go on your way. Curse our city with your bloodshed if you must, but I will not allow it to happen on my doorstep!"

Another patrol joined the group, this one numbering twenty. They muttered among themselves, wanting to know the reason for the delay. Several more lit up torches. Ghost felt his blood boil. They would set fire to a temple to slake their bloodthirst? A thousand rogues must remain hiding elsewhere, but they would come here?

The head priest lifted a hand over his head. A bright light grew from his palm, and even from the side it was painful for Ghost to look upon. He didn't want to imagine staring into it from the front. This seemed to cause the mercenaries to draw back a little. A captain Ghost had met a couple of times, named Jamie Half-Ear, for obvious reasons, stepped forward.

"We don't want nothing bad to happen here," he said. "But we saw plenty run inside before we surrounded the place. No innocents need to be hurt. Just send them out."

"Those who came here for succor shall receive it," said the priest.

"I know, I know, you gots to say that," said Jamie. "Please, er..."

"Calan."

"Calan. I doubt you want us filthy men running through your fancy place, so how about I just send one or two to point 'em out to your little helpers? Only the guilty get taken out, and just a few. Everyone else stays safe, see what I'm saying? They ain't your flock. They ain't your children. They're damn thieves, and those with more power than you say it's time they die."

Calan shook his head. "In time, perhaps, but not tonight. Go on your way, all of you."

"They're dying tonight, you stupid ass, no matter what you do. I see a lot of stone, but this building's still got plenty that'll burn. You hearing me, Calan? It'll *burn!*"

That was enough for Ghost. Though he couldn't care less about their deity, the temple was a beautiful structure. Stubborn and blind, the whole lot of them. He reached into a side pocket and withdrew a handful of knives, weighted to fly true. Scanning the crowd, he waited, wanting his choices to be absolutely perfect. Jamie was too close, too public, but those near the front, most eager for blood...

Hidden behind his pillar, he flung his first knife into the crowd. It plunged deep into the throat of a man hollering at the top of his lungs, ceasing his cries for fire. The next three took down torch-bearers, as Ghost had decided fire was the greatest threat to the temple. Down they went, their torches clattering across the stone. By now the crowd had noticed the deaths, and while some wondered aloud, most roared for blood. They'd blame the priests, which was the goal. All the better to make the mercenaries appear fools when he stepped out.

"You'd murder us in the street while claiming to protect life?" Jamie cried, more to the mercenaries than the priests.

"We have done no such thing," Calan insisted. He might as well have shouted at a thunderstorm to cease its rumbling.

Ghost slipped to the other side of the pillar, then hopped lower, closer to Calan. He was directly behind him, with a clear view of Half-Ear. The captain was practically frothing at the mouth while screaming for blood, but he'd not yet drawn a blade. Not yet...but close...his hand twitching...now!

Ghost coiled his legs and pushed off, launching himself between them. He wielded a single sword in both hands, needing the power. Before Jamie could swing, Ghost's sword tore through him, slicing from collarbone to hip. When Ghost kicked, the upper half of him collapsed backward and rolled down the steps, spilling innards, while the legs crumpled and lay in place. A flood of gasps came from the crowd, those who were not stunned silent. Ghost held the bloody blade before his face, peering over it with his eyes.

"Be gone, damn cowards. You have no business here. Go elsewhere, and slay the cloaks in their homes, the streets, wherever but here."

"This is madness," Calan said behind him. "I can't allow…"

"Quiet, Priest. You may not want bloodshed, but it'll happen, and better here on these steps than inside your halls. Such disrespect, it's shameful. They deserve to die just as much as those thieves within."

"I'd rather neither die," Calan said, his voice dropping lower.

"Good luck with that."

Ghost had hoped the brutal display would cow the crowd, but he'd underestimated their desire. Too many seemed eager for a fight. They'd gone unchallenged, no doubt thought themselves already nearing the end of their task. If they went south they'd probably think differently. The fires were growing, the smoke blanketing the city. This fight wasn't over; not even close.

"Stun as many as you can," he said to the head priest. "Blind them, knock them back. Leave the killing to me. I'll be better at it than you anyway."

He drew his other weapon and lifted both high above his head, as if worshipping a god of the sky.

"Draw swords or flee!" he shouted to the crowd. It was time to end this stalling. It was time for blood or cowardice.

The mercenaries surged forward, not following any spoken command, only a collective realization that they had to attack now or be revealed as bluffers. The priests raised their hands, their palms facing down the steps. Light shone from them, the intensity blinding. Ghost heard the sound of a hundred claps of thunder, and it passed over him like a physical force. Those at the front staggered or fell back, forcing the rest behind to pull them out of the way. Ghost took advantage of the confusion, leaping forward to gut one mercenary and cut down another. He backed up the steps, parrying random thrusts that seemed wild, as if his opponents were still struggling to see.

"Fall back," he ordered. The priests exchanged a quick look, but then Calan nodded.

"As he says!" shouted the head priest.

The fifteen climbed the steps, prayers still on their lips. Walls of force slammed into the crowd, invisible but their effects not. He watched noses break, heads bruise, and fingers snap in painful directions. More stumbled upon the steps, crushed by those who rushed behind them. Ghost stayed before Calan, figuring him the most important to protect. He was the strongest, and as long as he stood, the other priests wouldn't break rank and flee.

"We must hide inside," Calan said. "We can't hold them back."

Ghost lunged from left to right, taking out those who pushed through the spells ahead of the pack. They fell, disadvantaged by their lower ground and disoriented beyond measure. If not for the sheer numbers, Ghost feared he might have gotten bored.

"We go inside and they'll burn us out," he insisted. "Stand and fight, old man. Stand and fight."

He kicked another body down the steps. They were gathering before the door, nearly out of space to retreat. Calan nodded, accepting Ghost's decision.

"So be it," he said, standing beside Ghost and lifting his arms. "Forgive me, Ashhur, but I need your retribution this night."

He lowered his hands. A sound of thunder rolled, and then the steps to the temple trembled and broke. Dust rippled outward in concentric circles, giving visibility to the shock wave. There had been about twenty men pressing upward, and they collapsed, crying out in pain. The number of broken limbs Ghost witnessed was staggering. It was like Ashhur had stepped down and crushed them with his heel. Calan trembled, then stepped back and accepted the support of two more priests. The rest of the mercenaries, not willing to even think of climbing those corpse-strewn steps, turned and fled. Ghost leaped among them, killing a few more for good measure. Coated with gore, he returned to the temple, where he heard songs and lamentations coming from within.

A couple of the priests thanked him, but most eyed him warily and scooted farther away when he neared.

"Why?" asked Calan, his arm still around one of the younger priests. "Why did you help us?"

Ghost shrugged. "Can't stand disrespect, and that's all that was. They should respect me, and respect you. They didn't, and now they're dead."

"Not all of them," Calan said, gesturing to the many wounded. He turned to his priests. "Go and tend to them."

"I doubt they'll bother you now," Ghost said. "But I'd consider getting rid of those with colors in your temple while it's still calm."

"If I did that," said the head priest with a smile, "I wouldn't be worthy of much respect, would I?"

Ghost laughed. "Maybe you're right. Then I hope your god watches over you. Before this night ends, you might still need him."

Deathmask watched the carnage from the window of a room currently absent of its original occupants. No doubt they'd fled to safer territory, assuming there was anywhere safe within the city walls. He'd gone out with the initial patrols, under orders from Garrick to help ambush some of the smaller mercenary groups. When the first fight began he'd slipped away, joining Veliana in the large apartments overlooking their headquarters. After a few initial confrontations that left many on both sides dead, the area had remained quiet for the past hour. Most recently a squad of fifty men had checked the headquarters for thieves, found none, and then moved on.

"I doubt there'll be much guild left for you to rule after tonight," Veliana said, relaxing on a moth-eaten chair. "Hope Garrick survives, though. Would be heartbroken if some lousy sellsword gets the honor of cutting off his head."

"He's too cowardly to die tonight," Deathmask said as he tied a gray cloth over his face and straightened it so the eyeholes lined up properly. Behind him Veliana did the same, using the knot of the cloth to also keep her dark hair in a tight ponytail. They both wore loose gray clothing, and cloaks of a darker shade. Veliana had killed a pair of Spiders in the initial chaos before joining Deathmask in the building, bringing with her their clothes and weapons.

"While unexpected, tonight certainly works in our favor," he said, once more looking to the window. "The fewer we have to thin out the better. Have you given thought as to who we should spare?"

"The only ones who come to mind are the twins," she said. "They have a head on their shoulders, though it seems like they share it. They think so alike it's creepy."

"Can they wield a blade?"

"They're better at throwing them than wielding them, but no average cutthroat could handle either of the twins in a fight."

"Good. Names?"

She tugged at her mask, trying to get it to fit comfortably. "Mier and Nien."

Deathmask rolled his eyes. "What wonderful parents. Gods forbid their names be even a little different."

He leaned away from the window as a man rushed down the road, a jittery fellow who kept glancing in every direction. Two more followed after. Veliana saw Deathmask's reaction and straightened in her chair.

"Someone there?" she asked.

"Looks like some scouts, no doubt making sure it's safe to come home. Get ready. We'll have little time between their leaving and Garrick's arrival."

The Ash scouts vanished into the building. Deathmask peered out the window, watching, waiting. When the scout emerged, Deathmask beckoned Veliana closer.

"Go!" he said when the scout turned a corner. They tossed a rope that was tied to the bed in their room, sliding down even as it uncoiled. They hit the street in seconds and sprinted for the headquarters. Deathmask led the way, Veliana at his heels. Once inside they slowed, walking through the hallway into the lavish rooms.

"Pick your spot," he said, his eyes darting about. "Keep close to the doors for when we make our escape."

"I'm no stranger to this sort of thing," Veliana said, glaring at him through her mask.

"Keep your hood raised. If they see your hair, they might figure out who you are, instead of just assuming you another Spider."

She lifted the hood of her cloak and let it fall across her face as Deathmask did the same. He entered one of the side sections curtained off to give privacy with the dancer women, leaving a gap so he could watch the entrance. Veliana adjusted a giant pile of pillows, hiding behind it with daggers drawn. Deathmask drew his weapons as well. There would be no magic for him, no spells of blood and shadows. Using such skills would reveal him to Garrick, which would ruin his current plan. No, it'd be just knifework. Veliana had trained him for a few hours, but it had only made clear how far from proficient he was. He'd spent an hour casting spells of speed and strength on himself to try to make up for the lack, but he wouldn't know for sure until the ambush if they'd worked. Not being much of a praying man, he crossed his fingers and swore to succeed whatever the cost.

The door slammed open. In rushed a collection of the Ash Guild: all men close to Garrick, Deathmask noticed. Their clothes were lacking in blood and gore. No ambushes for Garrick, which put a smile on Deathmask's face. That fact would work wonders for them later, should he and Veliana survive for the second part of their plan. The thieves went straight for the obvious: the bar filled with bottles of wine and ale. Deathmask was glad he couldn't see Veliana, who was no doubt smirking. She'd insisted that would be their first action, whereas he'd thought many would rest atop the pillows to relax after a brutal night of fighting.

"They'll drink it off before they sleep it off," she'd said while they waited through the night.

Need to listen to her more often, he thought. *She thinks more like a man than I. What I get for growing up among wizards, I guess.*

They both waited, Deathmask watching until he was sure… and there he was, standing amid his men, holding his glass the highest as they toasted a night of survival.

"To standing atop the dead!" he heard Garrick say.

Toasting your own cowardice? And to think I thought I was a bastard.

He pushed aside the curtain and charged, his dagger drawn and ready. As he pushed himself to the limit, he felt his feet move faster, the world almost imperceptibly slower. He buried his dagger in the back of the nearest thief, whose glass fell from his hand. Before it hit the ground, two daggers flew across the room, thudding into the back of another. Veliana scattered pillows as she lunged, much of her face thankfully hidden by her hood. She kicked the closest thief, the one she'd hit with her daggers, yanking out the blades as her foot slammed him into the others. Wine splashed to the floor as the rest dropped their drinks and drew their blades, crying out warnings of trap and ambush.

Garrick was in their center, and he fell back instead of drawing his dagger. Deathmask knew Garrick was Veliana's target, not his, but he had to clear a path for her. Sidestepping a thrust, he jammed his dagger into the chest of another, using the body to protect himself from several more. The Ash members were starting to spread out, the better to take advantage of their numbers. That thinned the wall toward Garrick, and Veliana wielded her daggers like a demoness, twisting and curling to avoid every thrust. Blood soon joined the wine that stained the floor. Deathmask felt pride in seeing her work. No one who survived could possibly doubt that the best of the Spider Guild had come to take the life of a rival.

Well, those who watched *her*, anyway. He, on the other hand, struggled to stay alive. His dagger flailed from side to side, sometimes faster than he expected thanks to the earlier enchantments. The impulse to cast a spell to blind his opponent filled him, and only at the last second did he refrain. The ruse was more important. He would gain nothing by giving himself away. The Ash needed to be his guild to rule. He couldn't do that if revealed in the clothing of a rival guild. His arms trembled as he felt steel cut into them. He fought three men at once, and they grinned at the sight of blood. He was outmatched, and now they knew it.

"Finish it!" he cried to Veliana, hurrying to the door.

Veliana was in the middle of disemboweling another man, and at his cry she shoved the man aside. The path between her and Garrick was clear. Instead of charging, she lifted a dagger and threw. Its aim was true. The point pierced his shoulder and lodged deep, burying itself up to the hilt. Garrick howled as his blood ran.

That was enough. Deathmask rushed for the exit, feeling like his legs didn't belong to him. Veliana hesitated for just a moment, and he saw her other dagger trembling in her hand. Trusting her to do the smart thing, he burst through the door and into the night. She appeared a moment later, looking none too pleased.

"Come on," he said. He took a zigzag course through the city, on a path he had memorized. They arrived at an inn with rooms they'd paid for several hours before. Deathmask climbed in through a window, which had no glass, only thick wood shutters that he had left unlocked. He was already changing back into his Ash Guild outfit when Veliana climbed inside.

"Did you kill him?" he asked.

"I wanted to."

"That a no?"

She yanked the mask off her face and flung back her hood. "What do you think?"

He grinned. Knowing his skill was nowhere near hers, he'd left the delicate task of harming, but not killing, Garrick up to Veliana. Up until the throw itself, he hadn't been sure if she would make it lethal or not.

"You did marvelously," he said, tossing the Spider cloak to

the bed and pulling off his tunic. "And now I can trust you all the more. If I were in your position, I might have accidentally hit Garrick's throat."

"That would have left me homeless and guildless," she said, grabbing her old Ash outfit from the bed. She reached for the door.

"Where you going?" he asked.

"To change."

The door shut behind her. Deathmask sighed. No fun at all.

She returned moments later, dressed in the colors of the Ash and looking to be in an even fouler mood.

"They're still stained with my blood," she said, referring to the red patch on her chest.

"I'll try to get you something newer when I can," he said. "Didn't want to attract any attention. They might wonder why I was requesting an outfit for someone half my weight."

"You're a thief now, remember? Steal it."

Deathmask shrugged. "Ready?"

She pushed him aside and climbed out the window.

"This better work," she muttered. "Otherwise we're in for a lengthy death."

"I'm in for one, perhaps, but you've already had your public execution, remember?"

She slammed the shutters in his face.

CHAPTER

16

In her grief, she had thought hearing the cries of pain and seeing the river of blood would give her closure, but instead Alyssa felt hollow as she watched the fires spread across the city. Standing at the second-story window of her private study, she touched the cold glass and wondered what it was she had done. Had she brought freedom to the city? Peace of mind? Or would every death just result in more death, every killed thief replaced by two more filled with thoughts of revenge? Bertram had told her the monetary cost of her single night, and it was staggering.

She knew there'd be no peace, not this night. But perhaps this was just like cauterizing a wound. There would be heat, pain, but then the bleeding would stop and healing could commence.

Someone knocked on the door, and she had a feeling who. Her help would be asleep, or perhaps lying awake in their rooms wondering about the safety of their friends and family beyond her mansion's walls. That left very few who would dare come to her room at night while the rest of the city was in chaos.

"Come in, Arthur," she said, surprised by how tired she sounded. She rubbed her face with her hand, discovering tears. Had she really reached such a low, crying without realizing it while she wasted the night away staring out a window?

The door opened, then softly shut. Moments later she felt Arthur's hands on her shoulders. When he started massaging she leaned back, pressing her head against his neck.

"People are too scared to form bucket lines," he said. "The fires will only spread."

She sighed. She should have known, of course. Probably had, even, but she'd let her hatred blind her. *Let the whole city burn*, she'd thought plenty of times, *so long as it burns the rats with it*. But this was her war now, and that meant dealing with all its ills, all its blame.

"Send someone to the castle. Tell the king I request the aid of his soldiers in putting out the fires. With the castle guard there, it should outweigh any fear."

"Self-preservation is strong," Arthur said, letting her go. "For so many to hide instead of fighting the fires shows how great a fear you have created."

"I meant to scare the thieves," she said. "Not the innocent. But are there any innocent anymore? How deep does Veldaren's sickness run? Maybe I should let it burn, all of it. My son is nothing but ash, so why not them, why not . . . ?"

He wrapped his arms around her and held her tight, and in them she let herself cry. She found herself crying often in his presence. There was a strength in him, and a desire to please. More than anything, she felt she could trust him. He'd been there for her when she needed him most.

"Was this wrong?" she asked. "Have I truly erred so badly?"

His response was long delayed, to the point that she thought he might not answer.

"You have done what you thought was right, and what was best for the Gemcroft family. I will not fault you for that, if you will do the same for me for what I am about to do now."

"And what is that, Arthur?"

He turned her about and kissed her. His hands were firm on her shoulders. She felt herself responding. She was so exhausted, so drained. His touch was like an awakening, a pull from a nightmare that threatened to consume her day in and day out.

"The messenger to the castle," she breathed while her mind remained able to think.

Arthur leaned close, his hot breath against her ear.

"Let the fires burn a little longer. If the cowards cannot save their own city, the blame lies with them."

The study lacked a bed, but the carpet was soft. They made love, her beneath him. She wrapped her arms around his chest and clutched him as if her life might end if she let go. She tried to forget the death and fire, her call for revenge. Even as the pleasure tore through her, she could not help but wonder if that wicked man responsible for the death of her son lay dead somewhere, his body nothing but ash in a distant fire. Atop her, Arthur continued to grunt and thrust.

The arrival of the sun was a blessed thing to Veldaren's citizens. The mercenaries retreated, having fought and searched long through the night. Those with cloaks and colors buried themselves inside whatever safe houses they had to recuperate and plan. Those who sided with neither filled the streets, forming bucket lines from the wells and digging ditches to combat the fires. Many others went to their families and friends, needing confirmation of their survival before beginning their daily tasks. The market's bustle was subdued, the streets awash with murmurs.

Haern watched it all through the window of the small apartment. The fire had gotten dangerously close to Senke and Delysia's home, reaching all the way to Prather's Inn and burning it to the ground. People were everywhere, half-buried in the smoke that billowed from the dying fire. The king's soldiers hurried about, but their presence in the streets did nothing to ease people's minds.

"Too little, too late," Haern whispered. He scratched at his face, which itched worse than it had in ages. Upon their returning to the apartment, Tarlak had insisted Haern bathe, shave, and wear something, as he put it, "not smelling like a rat just shit all over it." So he'd used their washtub, shaved himself with a slender knife, and then borrowed an outfit of Senke's, simple grays that he knew would blend well into the streets. The ordeal left him tired and feeling strangely outside himself, as if this clean, well-dressed individual were someone else.

"You look troubled," Delysia said, and he flinched as if poked with a stick. Blushing for no reason, he turned back to her and accepted the cup of warm milk she'd brought him.

"I mixed in some herbs," she said, sitting opposite him in a rickety chair. "You'll sleep well, and by the looks of it you could use the rest."

He thanked her and sipped the milk, wisely deciding not to comment on how terrible the drink tasted. His eyes lingered on her face, and he struggled not to make his staring obvious. She'd grown so much over the past five years. Her hair was longer, but still the same fiery red. Her cheekbones were more pronounced, and in her priestess robe she looked almost regal.

Her chest was also significantly larger. Out of everything, he tried to make sure his glances at that remained uncaught.

He continued to sip the drink, mostly to avoid conversation. He had no clue what to say to her. The last time they'd met, he'd come to her in desperate need of guidance. He'd needed to understand a life outside the cold retribution of his father. His tutor Robert Haern had spoken of the god Ashhur, and now here she was, a priestess of the same god. His thoughts had turned only to survival during the long years, yet now the name of Ashhur came back to him with a burning vengeance. What was it he'd told Delysia? He needed Ashhur, otherwise he'd end up like his father. He'd be a killer without mercy, a terrible creation the city feared.

Long live the Watcher, he thought. *What have I become?*

"I...I'm glad you're all right," Haern blurted, feeling stupid as he said it. He saw a shadow cross over Delysia's face, but she pushed it aside with a smile.

"I try not to think about that night," she said. "There's too much I don't understand, even now. Who you were. Who you are. What Ashhur's purpose might have been. I must confess, I almost hoped I'd die. I was so tired, so confused. But I feared I might never see my brother, and so I struggled for every breath..."

The room fell silent. The rest were asleep, exhausted from the long night, but Delysia had stayed awake, insisting she could manage for a few more hours. Haern, used to going long periods without sleep, had dully stared out the window and waited for a chance to talk. Now he had the chance, he didn't have a clue what to do with it.

I'm better at killing. Does that prove just how far I've fallen? You'd be proud, Thren.

"The man who shot you was my father," he said, figuring

to start with what he knew for certain. "He feared what your influence might do to me. He was right to fear it, too. They dragged me to Karak's temple and did their best to burn away everything good within me."

"Did they succeed?" she asked, sipping from her own cup. Her green eyes peered over its edge. He felt as if he were that same stupid kid she'd trapped in her pantry. He remembered watching her cry moments after Kayla executed her father. What could he ever be to her but a reminder of those painful times? He saw her watching him, and he remembered her question.

"No," he said.

The past five years, murdering men in the streets, seemed to have done a fine job of it, though.

"What have you been doing?" she asked. "How have you survived?"

He didn't want to answer. Why was he so afraid she'd judge him? So long ago, he'd come to her for advice. Now he feared every word she might say?

"I slept in the streets," he said. He was the Watcher of Veldaren, damn it. He would fear no one, nothing. "Ever since, I've been killing members of the thief guilds, hoping to destroy them. It's pointless, futile, but still I try. It's the only thing that gives me meaning."

He thought she'd berate him, or challenge his claim. Instead she looked at him with sad eyes, and that was worse.

"I'm so sorry," she said. "It's because of me, isn't it? Because you protected me?"

His mouth fell open.

"Of course not. Don't be...Delysia, I chose everything I did. I would have stayed with you, spoken with you forever if I could. That night...that single night, I've cherished that

memory. It was one of the few bright spots in my entire childhood. But then my father darkened it with blood. My precious
memories always lead to him, his murder, his guilt. It pushes
me on, consumes everything. I have become something I don't
think either that little girl or that little boy could ever have
understood or accepted."

He looked back to the window, not wanting to see her reaction. He was a damn fool, that's what he was. Hoping she'd
leave him be, he refused to react when she stood from her chair,
set her cup down, and came closer. Her hand touched his face,
and reluctantly he turned to her. Tears were in his eyes.

She kissed his cheek, then pressed her forehead against his.

"Go to sleep, and try to remember that while you are not
that little boy, I am no longer that little girl."

She trudged up the sharply curved stairs to the second floor.
Haern watched her go, and when she was gone he almost fled to
the streets. But he remembered that feeling in the Pensfields', of
having a home. He felt that same thing here, though the company was on the odder side. He downed the rest of his drink,
grimaced, and then set the cup aside. His chair was comfortable enough, far more so than the cold street he was used to, so
he crossed his arms and tried to sleep.

Footsteps coming back down the stairs caused him to open
his eyes. He didn't think he'd slept, but he wasn't sure. It wasn't
Delysia who had come down, though. Instead it was the wizard, her brother. He'd shed his pointy hat, though he still wore
those strange yellow robes. He rubbed his goatee as he plopped
down in a chair opposite Haern.

"Had some words with Senke," he said.

"That so?"

"Well, most involved variations of 'Get out of my room so I
can sleep, you idiot,' but there were some more intriguing bits

I dragged out of him. Most interesting was that of your father. Thren Felhorn, really? You look more like something two vagabonds might bump out on a cold, drunk night."

"Flattered."

Tarlak tapped his fingers together, and his mouth shifted about as if he were chewing on his words before saying them.

"Not much for talking. I get that. I like to talk, so perhaps I can make up for the both of us. Senke says you're good, really good. What I saw out there tonight certainly confirms it. Can't expect much less from Thren's son, of course. You've established quite a reputation, too. I've heard plenty talk of the Watcher, usually poor thieves grumbling into their cups about how much gold you cost them. A few even thought you were Ashhur's vengeance come down upon them for their lifestyle, though they usually had to be incredibly drunk to admit it."

"You have a point?"

"Several, one on my nose, one on my hat, and one where the ladies love me. But that's beside the, uh, point. It seems like, other than revenge, you don't have much going for you. Ashhur knows those streets out there aren't comfortable living. So how about you join my mercenaries instead? Pay isn't the best, but with half the city employed in killing thieves, I think we could make a few coins. Besides"—his eyes lit up—"can you imagine the rates I could charge if people knew the Watcher was in my employ?"

"I'm not for sale," Haern grumbled.

Tarlak frowned.

"Well, that's disappointing. You sure?"

"Very."

The wizard scratched at his chin. "This a pride thing?"

"I have no use for money."

Tarlak grinned. "I'm more thinking you feel you don't *need* money. Considering all the stories of you tossing gold coins in the middle of high market, I can believe that. But there are some things you can't buy with gold that you might be more interested in. Our introductions were a little haphazard, but you met Brug, right?"

"Short guy, cussed a lot, can't fight worth crap?"

"That's him. I didn't hire him because of his skill with those ludicrous whatever-they-are he fights with. Obviously. You want to know why I did?"

Haern stared at him with an expression showing he didn't think he had a choice in whether he found out or not. Tarlak blinked.

"Right. Anyway, he's a blacksmith, and with my help he can create items that many would sell their souls to own. Would you like to run faster? Jump higher? Or perhaps own a fancy sword or three…"

"I'm not much for bribery either."

"Don't see why you shouldn't be. You spend your nights crawling around the rooftops killing thieves. Might as well get paid for it, or at least better tools to do it with."

Haern turned his chair so his back was to Tarlak, and he stared out the window.

"Very well." Tarlak stood. "I'll leave you be. Take a nap, or vanish in the afternoon. You aren't held prisoner here. Think about my offer, though. We may not be much now, but I think we've got potential."

Haern snorted. Whether Tarlak heard or not, he didn't react, only went up the stairs. Staring at the men and women still fighting the fire, Haern wondered what in the world had gotten ahold of him. That wizard was no better than anyone else, not even his father. He killed for money, except he used fire and words instead of a blade. What could possibly have possessed Senke to join them?

He closed his eyes and felt the light of the sun warm his face. Come that afternoon he'd sneak his way out. Oh, he had no delusions of abandoning Delysia and Senke completely. He knew himself better than that. It'd be easy enough to keep watch on them, though, keep his eyes open for a wizard in yellow, accompanied by a beautiful girl with hair like fire...

When he opened his eyes, many hours had passed. He shook his head, fighting the grogginess. His back ached, and it popped several times as he shifted his upper body from side to side. Senke stood at a small counter, eating cold bread left over from that morning. His fingers drummed the counter, the sound no doubt what had awakened Haern.

"You chew like a cow," Haern said, pressing his thumb and forefinger against his eyes.

"And you look like one, only worse. When was the last time you had a bath?"

"This morning, you noisy bastard."

Senke shoved the rest into his mouth and wiped crumbs from his shirt.

"Here," he said, his mouth full. He pointed at Haern's swords. "Been a long time since we sparred. Thought it'd be a nice way to catch up."

"Where?" The room was cramped as it was. Senke nodded toward a back exit.

"There. Come on."

There was a small space of flat dirt out back, part of an alleyway that ran behind the group of apartments. The faint outline of a circle remained dug into it, and Senke refreshed it with his heel.

"Only person to train with has been Brug, and trust me, that's not much of a workout. You'll do me fine."

Haern stretched away the rest of his drowsiness. Senke had

been the better fighter when they last met, but the years had hardened Haern, granted him strength and height while his nightly excursions had honed his reflexes and skill. He touched the tips of his swords together and bowed. Senke had carried two short swords with him, and he wielded those instead of his maces.

"Maces will be too slow for you," he said. "So let's try the blade."

Eager to show how much he'd learned, Haern initiated their combat with a quick lunge. Expecting the ensuing parry, he followed up with a slash with his other weapon, using it as a distraction to allow his first blade to pull back and thrust again. Senke, however, hadn't been Thren's enforcer without good reason. He shoved both attacks high, stepped closer, and feinted an elbow to Haern's face. When Haern stepped back, trying to fall into position, Senke pressed the attack, keeping his swords out wide. The second elbow that came flying in was no feint, and it smacked into Haern's chest with a heavy thud. Again Haern stepped back, but instead of chasing, Senke pointed to where he'd stepped beyond the bounds of the circle.

"Out," he said.

Feeling his cheeks flush, Haern stepped back into the practice ring. He wasn't focused, wasn't analyzing Senke's reactions as he might other opponents'. Taking a deep breath, he forced himself to calm down. A nod, and they resumed.

This time he remained patient, and he swallowed down his pride to acknowledge Senke was just as fast as he. Most opponents he could overwhelm with simple brute speed, the massive gaps in their skill overriding any of his carelessness. Not now. Senke stepped closer, swinging both his blades in a downward arc. Haern parried them aside, then looped both swords around as he advanced. Senke blocked the barrage, then planted his back foot to halt his steady retreat to the circle's edge.

Seeing this, Haern pressed the attack, relying on his opponent's lack of mobility. But the planted foot had been a kind of a feint, for when Haern swung with all his might, ready for the clash of steel and challenge of strength, instead Senke twirled out of the way. Overextended, Haern could do nothing but accept the stings of Senke's short swords slapping against his arm.

"Come on now," Senke said, pausing to catch his breath. "I expected far better than that. King's sake, I saw you handle yourself better last night against those thieves."

Again he felt his neck flush. Was he holding back? He didn't mean to.

"Treat me like any other opponent," Senke said, clanging his swords together. "Fuck. Treat me like your father. Everything, Haern, show me everything you got."

Everything, he thought. *Everything*. It seemed like a red light bathed over him, flashing from a ring on Senke's finger. He forgot they only sparred, forgot they fought in a dirt circle instead of a real battlefield. He forgot his opponent's name was Senke, and imagined instead the glaring figure of Thren Felhorn, furious, deadly, a bow in his hands and Delysia dying at his feet. His father grinned, as if the corpse there didn't matter.

"Hello, Son," said Thren.

He gave that image everything. His swords wove in tight circles as he slipped from stance to stance, always shifting, always attacking. The sound of steel on steel became a song in his ears. Their blades looped and twisted, parrying away sure strikes and blocking cuts that should have hit before either could counter. Thren's grin faded; he was just a cold image that watched Haern without any sign of exertion or worry. Haern found himself wondering where he was, what was going on.

Around him the alley had become an old safe house they'd lived in for a year, the hardwood floor polished and prepared for practice.

"You've learned nothing!" Thren shouted, bearing down on him with his short swords. Haern's arms ached with each block, and that ache slowed his response when one of the attacks slipped to the side, curling back for a thrust. Haern twirled, his sword parrying moments too late. His chest burned, and blood ran down. As he grunted in pain, Thren rammed his heel into his stomach, knocking him back.

"What are you to me now? What could you hope for? Come at me, Son! Kill me! Your skill is nothing, *nothing*!"

Haern felt his mind change, becoming something whole, focused, and dangerous. The entire world ceased to exist, and even time struggled to keep him under its rule. He let out a cry and charged. This time his father's attacks were no longer so frightening. Despite Thren's feints, his parries, Haern saw through them all and refused to be controlled by them. Faster and faster he whirled, his body lost in a dance, their blades intertwined, their motions in constant reaction to each other's. He managed a snap-kick into Thren's face, dropped to the ground, and then swept his feet out from under him. As he fell, Haern lunged, one sword shoving his father's defenses out of the way, the other stabbing for his throat.

Instead of piercing flesh, he stabbed dirt. Thren scattered as if his body were made of dust, and then Haern was back in the alley. The wound on his chest vanished, his pain along with it. Senke leaned against the complex, his arms crossed. Haern felt naked before him, his heart exposed and bleeding.

"Your hatred for him is so great," Senke said softly. "It's all that keeps you alive, isn't it? You can't live like that, Haern. You have every reason to escape his shadow, yet you still let it lord over you. What have you become? How many have you murdered in his name?"

"They were all guilty," Haern shouted. "Thieves and murderers!"

"Were they always? I just saw what lurked behind your eyes, Haern, more frightening than anything your father might have done to me."

Haern thought of all the men and women he'd hunted in the night. They'd worn guild colors, yes, but how many had also been innkeepers, farmers, smiths, and butchers? How many had he killed for doing business with them, smuggling and trading and selling? Night after night, he felt the waves of his dead. For Ashhur's sake, he'd written his name with their blood!

"It's not hopeless," Senke continued. "I thought I'd lost you, but now finding you, I wonder what is left of that small boy who loved to read. The one who asked me about jewelry for a girl he liked. I'd always hoped that, if you'd survived, you'd have gone and experienced everything Thren denied you. Now I see you denying yourself... love, faith, friendship... and you do so out of *revenge*?"

Senke walked over and sat down beside him, putting a hand on his shoulder.

"Sorry about the illusion," he added. "Just a trick of this ring Tarlak gave me. I had to see. I had to know who you are, how good you can be."

"Now you do," Haern said, feeling his insides tighten and twist behind his ribs. "Is it truly so bad?"

Senke squeezed, then smacked his back.

"Doesn't matter," he said with a wink. "I'm still here for you, as is that pretty redhead Tarlak has for a sister. He's a good man, Tarlak. A bit strange, but he's a wizard, so that's to be expected. I've told them of my past, and they swore it didn't matter who I was then, but who I am now. Please, stay with us. Put this life behind you. If you're to have a legacy, it shouldn't be this. You've become the feared reaper of the guilds. Should Thren ever find out you still live, I cannot help but wonder if he'd be furious...or proud."

He stood and moved for the door.

"Go back to your streets," he said. "Think on everything I've said. There's so much good in you, I can see it still. It's never too late to change who you are, so long as you're willing to bear the consequences. You've carried heavy burdens your whole life, Haern. Maybe it's time you let some of them go."

Not waiting to see if he stayed or not, Senke stepped into the room and closed the door behind him. As it locked, Haern felt thrust back into the world he'd called his home for the past five years, but now the streets seemed foreign, their alleyways and rooftops offering no safety. His skin was clean, his clothes fresh, his face shaven.

For once he didn't feel like he belonged, but onward he ran all the same.

CHAPTER

17

Do you think he's telling the truth?" Matthew asked his wife as they cuddled in bed for the night.

"I don't see any reason for him to lie."

"I can think of plenty. He's hurt, sick, and in a stranger's home. Truth might be the furthest thing from his mind. What if he doesn't know Lady Gemcroft, only hopes she'll take him in if we show up at her doorstep?"

Evelyn put her arm across his chest and pressed her face against his neck.

"It would explain a lot though, wouldn't it?" she asked, her voice quiet. "Why those men were searching for him. We both knew he was no ordinary boy to be hunted like he is."

"But why would Arthur's men be after him? The whole bloody north knows he's been courting her." An unspoken question hovered in the air between them, until at last Matthew gave it voice. "What if the men we killed were actually trying to rescue him?"

Matthew waited for his wife to speak, trusting her to better understand these complicated matters. He could list the price of every vegetable that grew in Dezrel, what the color of the soil meant and what could grow in it, but these things were beyond him. He liked living outside the city, where so long as you paid the taxman when he came, you could live unbothered by your lord and trust in your neighbors. Hard luck comes in strangers' hands, his ma had always said.

"That man, Haern, might have kidnapped him," Evelyn said. "If he was wounded and low on food, he'd need someone like us to help out, but why leave the boy here? Why tell us to take him back to his parents whenever he could talk? Everything he paid us for, he could have taken by force. Still, I won't pretend to understand Arthur's reasons, and neither does Tristan."

"He says his name is Nathaniel."

Evelyn kissed his neck.

"I told him his new name, and we'll use it so long as he's with us. No need to risk undue attention should we go out and about."

Matthew grunted. Fair enough.

"It might be Arthur himself that came for him, though everything's just a jumble when Tristan tells what happened," he said. "But I think you're right. Those men were up to no good. Could see it in their eyes."

"So what do we do?"

Matthew sighed. He wished he knew. While he thought, he ran his rough fingers through her hair, enjoying its softness.

"We got to get him home, even if that means traveling all the way to Veldaren."

"What if you stop in Felwood and deliver him to Lord Gandrem? He's always been a close friend to the Gemcrofts."

"So was Arthur."

He was right, of course, and he could tell she knew it.

"Let us all go, then. I don't want to be left here, and it won't be safe for the kids, either."

"Our livestock'll die."

"With how much Haern gave us, we could buy our farm back twice over."

Matthew shook his head, thinking of all the work he'd put into raising his cattle and pigs.

"Still no good reason to let them die, waste all they're worth. Besides, me going to the city might be strange, but it ain't unheard of. All of us packing up to go? If there's more soldiers looking, and you know there are, then they'll hear about it in a heartbeat. I'll go alone, just me and the boy. He's light enough. We can ride together, make good time."

"We have no horses."

"I'll buy one from the Utters in the morning."

Evelyn pulled her arms tight across her chest as if she were cold. She recognized that tone in his voice. He'd made up his mind, and it'd take tears and a hysterical fit from her to change it. She didn't have it in her. They had to do something before more soldiers showed up looking for Tristan.

"Trevor's old enough to look after most things," Matthew continued, as if trying to reassure her. "And with the cold already breaking, we'll easily last until spring on what wood we have. I'll leave you half the coin too, in case something happens. You can afford salt or meat if need be."

"I know I can do it," she snapped. "Don't mean I want to, or will enjoy it. I'm scared, Matt, scared witless. What if men come looking while you're gone?"

He kissed her forehead.

"I trust you," he said. "And I'll pray you stay safe. I don't know what else to do, Evelyn. I just don't know."

Come morning he trudged east through the half-melted snow, across fields he knew by heart. The Utters were a large clan, and wealthier than most of the local farm folk. They had several horses, and while they might not be eager to part with one, Matthew knew the gold jingling in his pocket would be persuasive enough.

When he returned, it was atop a mare he'd paid for—far more than she was worth, but given how they were still waiting for winter to make its exit, and time wasn't on his side, he'd been forced to accept. He'd refused to be overcharged on the saddle, though.

"Without that mare you got no reason for it anyway," he'd argued, and after he threatened to buy a saddle from the Haerns or the Glenns, they'd relented. The mare was a beautiful horse named Strawberry by one of the Utter daughters. Matthew thought the name a little demeaning for such a majestic creature, but figured he'd leave it be considering the horse was already familiar with it. On his ride back he swung by Fieldfallow (the closest thing to a town for thirty miles) and bought trail rations and a thick riding coat.

"Little early to be heading up to Tyneham," the old store-keeper had said. Matthew only gritted his teeth and paid, again twice as much as he would have in spring. Back at the house Tristan was already bundled up and ready to go. His fever had come and gone, but never as badly as before the amputation. Matthew kissed his kids good-bye, hugged his wife, and then set Tristan on the saddle.

"You ever ridden a horse before?" he asked.

The boy nodded. "At the castle," he said. Matthew guessed

he meant Felwood, and again he felt tempted to stop there. Lord Gandrem was an honorable old man. Surely he wouldn't let something untoward happen to the boy. But Haern had told him to deliver the boy to his parents, and that meant Alyssa Gemcroft all the way south in Veldaren. There was also his nagging worry that Lord Gandrem might, however unlikely it seemed, also be involved in the attempt on the boy's life. Resolving to decide the issue later, he climbed into the saddle, shifted Tristan so they could both sit more comfortably, and then set off.

The first day came and went uneventfully. A caravan passed them heading north, dour men who didn't even wave in greeting. Just before nightfall he spotted a distant pond. Glad for once for the cold, since there'd be no mosquitoes flitting about, he set up camp beside it, Strawberry staked close enough to the water's edge to drink. Tristan had remained quiet through much of the ride, and Matthew didn't press him to talk. Come the fire, though, it seemed both their tongues loosened.

"How long until we get there?" Tristan asked.

Matthew poked the fire with a stick, shifting one of the thicker logs into a hotter section so it might burn better.

"It'll be several days to reach Felwood. From there, less than a week to ride into Veldaren. That's where your ma is, right?"

The boy shivered, as if the mere mention of her reminded him how far away she was.

"I think so," he said. "Do you...do you think she misses me?"

"Can't see why not. Evelyn would be sick with fits should one of our sons run off missing."

Tristan pulled his blanket tighter about him, and his eyes glazed as he stared into the fire.

"He died protecting me," he said.

"Who?"

"Mark. I liked him. He's nicer than Lord Hadfield."

The name Mark didn't ring any bells, but *Hadfield* sure did.

"Do you know why Arthur would want you dead, boy? You're young, sure, but you got ears and you probably know more than I when it comes to the upper crust."

"I don't. He always said I was like his son, and when he married Mom, he'd be my father."

Matthew felt a tingle in the back of his head at that. Perhaps it had something to do with marriage. Had Alyssa rejected Arthur, and he lashed out in spite? Did he want to remove any potential heirs? What foul plans might he have for Alyssa as well? Too many questions without answers.

"Safe to say he ain't planning to be much of a father to you," Matthew said. "Now eat up. Got a long ride tomorrow, and you'll need the energy for it. Riding's tiring work, though you wouldn't think it."

They slept under blankets. Halfway through the night Matthew awoke to distant howling. Coyotes, he figured. A tired glance to his side showed Tristan shivering, a shaking fist pressed to his lips. He was crying. Touched, Matthew reached out and put his arm around the boy, sliding him closer so he could wrap him in a hug. Tristan continued to cry, but his trembling stopped. Soon the crying turned to sniffles, which turned to steady breathing. Matthew fell asleep not long after.

Come morning, they both woke red-eyed. Tristan said little, and several times Matthew had to hold back an angry word. Evelyn always insisted he was a bear when he got up in the morning. No reason to take that out on the poor kid. They ate some rations, drank, and then rode south, stopping every few hours to stretch their legs and rest their backs. Matthew wasn't a stranger to a horse, but he hadn't ridden in over six months.

Muscles he hadn't known he had announced their angry presence to him.

"Starting to think walking would be a better idea," he grumbled.

Tristan said nothing.

By the second day the plains were spotted with trees, and with each hour they rode, the trees gathered more thickly, forming clusters that would soon be a forest. Felwood Castle was getting closer. It was one of those nearby clusters that saved both their lives. They'd stopped by one for a piss, and while dismounted they heard the thunder of hoofbeats approaching from the south. A warning instinct, like when he knew something was after his animals, told Matthew it was time to get off the road.

"This way," he said, grabbing the reins in one hand and Matthew's wrist with the other. He led them into the copse, far enough that they'd go unnoticed.

"Stay here and hold on tight," he said, handing Tristan the reins. Hurrying back toward the road, he peered from behind a tree as a group of five rode past at full gallop. They wore dark tabards that he easily recognized. Hadfield's men. Did they know of Gert and Ben's absence? More important, did they know where it'd happened?

Trying not to think about it, he returned to Tristan, who stood with wide eyes. "It's them again, isn't it?" Tristan asked.

"Yeah," Matthew said. "Looked like it."

"Will everyone be safe?"

Matthew's jaw clenched tight. He yanked the reins from the boy's hand and led them back to the road.

"Ashhur only knows," he said as the silence hung over them. "And if not, then may Karak curse every one of those bastards."

Including the one who brought you to me, he thought, not cruel enough to say it aloud.

Oric sped his men across the road between Felwood and Tyneham, the lightest touch of panic brushing his neck. It wanted to dig in, sink its claws deep, but he refused to let it. He hadn't failed his master yet, and so far he had no reason to think he would. Not a soul had seen or heard anything of Nathaniel. It seemed likely he'd frozen to death, that strange Watcher there for the gold and nothing else. The lack of information suggested the boy was a corpse in the melting snow somewhere, his body devoured by coyotes or vultures—except for one troublesome detail: they'd found Gert's horse unbridled, the soldier nowhere to be found. That meant he was dead somewhere, killed while searching for Nathaniel. So far Oric had no evidence, but he assumed the same had happened to Ben. For two of his men, armed and armored, to mysteriously vanish…

They'd found Nathaniel, and then paid the price. That's what Oric's gut said, and he trusted it over everything else in the miserable world. He needed to discover where they'd found the boy, and quick. If he'd even made it to Felwood, there'd be disaster. Lord Gandrem certainly knew of Alyssa's loss, and Oric had personally brought "the body" to be buried. All sorts of questions would need to be answered should Nathaniel appear alive and well, and none of the answers would endear Oric to anyone. It was either find the boy or hang from a noose.

The farms were few and far between as they rode north, and something clicked as he finally came upon where the ambush had first been.

"Let's say you're wounded and carrying a sick boy," he said

to his men. "Snow's falling, and you're low on food. What is it you'd do?"

"Ditch the boy," said one. "Either way he's dead. No reason to go with him."

"Assume yourself a better man than that. What then?"

"Carry him until I find the closest shelter."

Oric tapped his forehead. "Exactly. Patt, take Rat and go north. Stop at the first two homes off the road, and you search them thoroughly. The rest of you, come with me."

They split, two north, three south. Oric had a feeling this Watcher, when in danger, would have gone south instead of north, since by all appearances Veldaren was his home. They saw no dwellings for the rest of that first day, but come the second a farm appeared in the distance. Oric led the way, feeling his pulse quicken. This had to be it. The Watcher would have stopped here, maybe not for long, but at least for food and water.

When he knocked on the door, it was a long time before he heard a response.

"Who's there?" asked a woman's voice.

"Oric Silverweed, soldier of Lord Hadfield of the north. I demand entrance."

A lock rattled from inside. Oric leaned back toward his men and whispered, "Hands on your hilts at all times."

The door opened, revealing a mildly attractive woman in her early thirties. Beside her stood a teenage boy, a dagger tucked into his belt. From where Oric stood he saw several more children, all younger, huddled about a wood stove.

"Where's the man of the house?" he asked as they stepped inside.

"That's me," said the eldest boy. Oric raised an eyebrow as he glanced at the woman. Something already felt off.

"What's your name, boy?" he asked, glad to see him ruffle at being called *boy*. If he was angry he might say something stupid, something he'd rather have kept quiet about.

"Trevor."

"Where's your pa, Trevor?"

That brief hesitation, along with the woman's sudden flare of her eyes, was all Oric needed.

He had two men with him, one a young soldier named Uri, the other a skilled fighter named Ingle. Oric turned to them, purposefully putting his back to Trevor and his dagger.

"Ingle, search out back. Check the barn, the fields, anywhere they might keep him. Uri, search the house. Pull up the floors if you have to."

"You can't do this!" the woman shouted. Oric struck her with the back of his hand. Finally Trevor drew his dagger. Before he could do a thing, Oric crossed the distance, rammed his throat with one arm, and grabbed Trevor's wrist with the other. He held him pinned against a wall as the younger children screamed.

"You pulled a blade on me, boy," Oric said, feeling like a wolf among sheep. He let a wildness appear in his eyes, knowing it'd frighten them more. "That means I can do whatever I want, and I got half a mind to leave you a cripple. Think your ma here will keep feeding a worthless belly that can't help out in the fields? How you think she'll like watching me cut off your fingers one at a time?"

Trevor's eyes were wide, and he looked ready to cry. He couldn't speak, only cough, and Oric kept the pressure up to keep it that way. He wanted him light-headed, scared, convinced he was about to die.

"Stop it, please," the woman pleaded. She still stood near the door, a red mark swelling on her face. Meanwhile Uri flung open drawers and dressers as he searched the house, occasionally stamping hard with his heel to test for false floorboards.

"Stand over there with your children," Oric snapped at her. "You make a move toward me, anything at all, and you can watch as I pull your son's guts out one inch at a time."

She reluctantly obeyed, sitting between her two girls. A young boy was with them, and he moved to sit at her feet. Oric turned back to Trevor, who had dropped the dagger and started retching silently.

"Take a deep breath," he said, lessening the pressure. As he sucked air into his windpipe, Trevor coughed, every gasp he made strained. "Good. Now you listen to me, got it? I'm missing two of my men, and I'm thinking they were here. But let's not worry about that right now. Right now I want to know about a little boy, red hair, about five years old. Did someone bring him here? The truth, you worthless shit, tell me the truth."

Trevor's face contorted with pain. He had something to say, no doubt about it. But he didn't want to. Even threatened with death, he didn't want to say. He was protecting his parents, Oric realized. Nothing else could keep his tongue still when so blatantly faced with death. Well, there were ways around that.

"Uri," he shouted. The man appeared seconds later.

"Yeah, Oric?"

"Find anything?"

Uri shook his head. "He ain't in here. Nothing for Ben or Gert either."

Oric looked to the adjacent room, which was curtained off, decided there would work.

"Come take him," he told Uri. The other soldier grabbed Trevor by the wrists and shoved him through. Meanwhile Oric walked over to the woman.

"What's your name?" he asked her.

"Evelyn," she said through clenched teeth.

"Pretty name, that. You come with me now, or I'll drag you away by the hair while your little ones watch. Your choice."

She kissed her daughters and stood. Oric put a hand on her neck and guided her into the room where Uri pinned Trevor against a wall.

"You're trying to protect your ma, maybe your pa, or both," Oric said as he shoved Evelyn onto the small bed in the cramped room. "But you ain't protecting them, not anymore. Gonna show you what'll happen, Trevor, if you don't tell me what you know, got that? Hold him tight, Uri."

"Will do."

Oric struck the mother, spun her onto her stomach, and ripped at her skirt. When she started to sob, he took a wad of the blanket and shoved it into her mouth. Trevor struggled, but Uri stood a foot taller and easily outweighed him. Oric pulled off his belt, pushed aside the rest of Evelyn's skirt, and shoved himself inside. She screamed into the gag, tears streaming down her face. Oric beat her when her screams got too loud, or when Trevor's struggles lessened. He needed the horror to continue. He wanted that fucking brat scarred.

When he finished, Oric pulled back and refastened his belt. Evelyn pulled at her skirt, trying to hide her nakedness, but Oric yanked at it, denying her even that.

"Let him go," he said to Uri.

Trevor flung himself at Oric, who had expected the reaction. He ignored a single punch, caught Trevor by the throat, and flung him back against the wall.

"You want to know what will happen next?" he asked as Trevor clutched his wrist. "I'm thinking Uri wants a turn, but I'm not letting him. Know why? Because *you're* going next unless you tell me everything that happened here." He laughed. "How's that sound? Ever wanted to needle your ma, Trevor? Here's your chance. No one will blame you. You were just being a man, right, protecting your family? How about one of your sisters out there? Think they could use a good poke? Maybe I'll make you do all three, just one after another, until…"

"Just stop," he screamed with what little breath he had. "I'll tell, everything, I'll tell everything, please, just stop, just stop…"

Oric let go of Trevor, who collapsed at his feet. The boy huddled there trying to stop his crying. A grin on his face, Oric knelt so he and Trevor could stare eye to eye.

"You tell me every goddamn detail you know, or next time I might not be so nice."

Oric listened as Trevor told of Haern's arrival with a boy he knew only as Tristan. He listened as he detailed Tristan's amputation. Then came Ben and Gert's arrival, and Oric felt his blood boil as he heard of how their father had killed them. Both of them, Trevor insisted. He seemed determined to make that clear. Last came their father's departure for Veldaren only a few days prior, mounted and following the main road.

"Good boy," Oric said, slapping him across the face when he was finished.

"Mind if I have a go?" Uri said, nodding to where Evelyn remained upon the bed, her face wet with tears. Oric shrugged.

"Get on out, boy. No need for you to watch this."

The three soldiers gathered outside the house ten minutes later.

"No sign of anything strange," Ingle said. "Found where they maybe did some digging recently, but the ground's too hard and cold for me to check."

"Don't bother," said Oric. "We know what they did.

Nathaniel's with their father riding south. If we press hard we can overtake him."

Uri pointed a thumb back at the house.

"You leaving them alive? They helped kill two of us, tried lying as well. Don't set much of an example."

"Leave them all for now," Oric said. "When we find this Matthew, I want to drag him back to his home so he can watch as we kill every last member of his family. Let that story spread across the north. No one opposes Arthur, and no one dares kill his soldiers. Now ride. No matter what, they can't get to Felwood before we do."

CHAPTER

 18

Zusa had scoured the south and found nothing. The night had come and gone, bathed in blood and lit with fire, yet she had seen nothing of this elusive Watcher. Too much chaos, too much death. How do you pick one murderer out of a thousand? It was a question she had no answer for. Still, it seemed Alyssa's desires had been granted. Hundreds of thieves had died, though many mercenaries had fallen as well. She doubted her master would grieve their loss. Her grief was saved solely for herself.

Zusa's only strategy left was to hope the Watcher had lain low during the night, knowing he wasn't needed. Come morning, though, perhaps he'd try to escape, or survey the damage. As she ran along the rooftops, Zusa crisscrossed among the various thief guild headquarters, at least those that she knew. She saw various men pass below her, staying to the alleys and quiet streets, but they all wore the colors of various guilds. From what she'd gathered from those she'd interrogated the night before, the Watcher never appeared wearing any guild colors, only a multitude of gray cloaks and shirts. Still, gray was worn by both the Ash and the Spiders, so to those she went.

At the Ash Guild she leaned against a triangular rooftop, rested her arms on its tip, and overlooked the square. Nothing. The magnitude of her task set upon her then. She was trying to find a lone man in the entire city, one who appeared to have no friends, no allegiances, and no clear motive other than killing thieves. She had a vague description to go on based on his clothes, and a rumor that he had blond hair. Some said he had red eyes, but she dismissed that as easily as the stories claiming he had demon blood and blades for hands. But blond she could work with.

She dozed for a while, not meaning to. Sometime later she startled, ashamed of her weakness. It'd been a long twenty hours, sure, but she'd handled worse.

"Nava would be so disappointed," she whispered, feeling sad and tired. Nava had been one of the last three faceless women, killed at the hand of a dark paladin of Karak. They'd been deemed outcasts, traitors to their god. But it was their god who had abandoned them, and so Zusa had turned on his paladin, who had come for Alyssa and protected her. Zusa had given Karak no prayers for the last five years. She missed Nava and Eliora more than his presence.

Not far to her right, down in the alley, she heard someone cry out in pain. Curious, she rushed over and leaned down. Her eyes widened. Whirling below her was a mass of gray cloaks, spinning and sliding as if possessed. Three men fought against it, all wearing the colors of the Ash. A man lived inside those cloaks, and she saw his face, his blond hair... but that wasn't what convinced her. It was the sheer ferocity of the stranger, a shocking rage somehow still held in check. One by one the thieves fell, throats sliced and chests cut open. His skill was incredible.

"Watcher," she whispered, drawing her daggers. "I find you at last."

She felt a seed of worry planted in the back of her mind. Her master wanted the Watcher brought back alive, but the way he fought, the way he moved, it might be impossible. He'd die before surrendering, she knew that, just as she knew he'd be prepared for her attack from above despite all her silence.

His swords lifted high, colliding with her daggers. Her momentum continued, her feet kicking out mid-fall to slam into his chest. Still he held his ground. She pushed off, using a hand to cartwheel away before landing on her feet. The two stared at one another, a smile blooming across her face.

"Ethric was the last true challenge I fought," she said. "Can you be the next, Watcher?"

"I'm more than a challenge," said the Watcher. He pointed a blade at her cloak. "Who is it you work for? What fool have you sold your soul to?"

Zusa laughed, the amusement only half acted. The man was watching her, analyzing her. She felt naked before his eyes, as if in time he might know every movement. She was doing the same to him, true, but he was too guarded, too still.

"You seek my colors?" she asked. Slowly she lifted one arm, slashed it, and let the blood drip down onto the cloth of her cloak. She wondered if her spell would take hold. Her strength had come from Karak, or so she'd always thought. She'd once lived within shadows, danced with cold fire on her blades, but not since Ethric had she tapped Karak's power.

The color spread through the cloak in seconds, turning it a vibrant red. It coiled around her, as if suddenly alive. Zusa felt her blood pound in her ears, her head ached from the effort, but still she smiled. Perhaps Karak hadn't abandoned her after all.

"I serve willingly," she said, tensing for an attack. "I have sold nothing."

She lunged, one dagger looping upward to block, the other thrusting for his chest. Her cloak wrapped about her like a shield. When the Watcher countered, her dagger parried his blade away, but her thrust met his other sword, and her arm jarred at the strength of the block. Her cloak lashed out like a whip, its fine edges sharp as razors. It slashed across his face, blood splattered them both, and then he leaped back. His hood fell lopsided, and she saw how blue his eyes were, how dirty his face was. Who was hidden beneath the guise? Whom would Alyssa find when she dumped his body before her?

"Neat trick," the Watcher said before leaping into his own attack. Their weapons clashed again and again, his speed incredible. Twice Zusa had to spin and let her cloak snap inward, deflecting a killing thrust. This was no spar, no game. He wanted her dead. That seed of worry in her mind grew to a thorn. One of his swords slashed her thigh. The other pierced her chest, the wound shallow but painful. The worry bloomed like a deadly flower.

It was the narrowness of the alley they fought in that saved her. When he lunged for a killing blow she kicked off the wall, sailing over his head. Her feet hit the opposite side, the collision jarring, but she pushed off, higher. Her cloak trailed below her, twisting. It lashed at him, cutting deep grooves into his arms. He'd expected her to land, not continue back the way she'd come. The cloak kept him off balance, and when she landed she lunged in, daggers leading.

She underestimated his speed.

The sound of steel hitting steel rang in her ears, and her

carefully coordinated attack broke as his swords danced. She refused to relent, chasing every backward step he took. There was still no fear in his eyes, only death. Whether it was for her or himself she didn't know.

The ache in her head grew. She couldn't maintain the cloak's enchantment much longer. It'd never hurt like this before, never drained her so terribly. Maybe Karak truly had abandoned her, as she'd abandoned him. Or perhaps Karak wasn't with her at all? Intrigued, she suddenly somersaulted away from the Watcher, pulling out in mid-attack while he was unprepared to give chase. She'd once been able to treat the shadows as doorways. Could she still do so?

The sun was low enough that several deep stretches of darkness remained in the alley. Zusa focused on one behind the Watcher, then turned and leaped at the shadowed wall behind her. Part of her expected to hit stone, but she passed cleanly through. Again her mind ached, but when the distortion ended she was behind her opponent. Her cloak its normal color and shape, she flung herself at him, knowing her chance to surprise him like this again was nonexistent.

Any normal opponent would have died, but this Watcher was beyond normal. He looked a man possessed, and the moment she vanished he was already spinning, searching for her. He parried her leading thrust, and she was forced to use her other dagger to counter a slash aimed for her throat. Her momentum continued, and they slammed into one another. His head cracked against the wall. Her hands a blur, she cut once, twice, into the tendons at his elbow. The sound of his sword hitting the ground was music to her ears.

He screamed, but the pain did not slow down his other blade. She felt its edge dig into her skin, and she rolled with it to prevent too deep a cut. Blood ran down her face and neck, urging her on. She used both her daggers to pin his sword aside, then rammed her elbow into his throat. He gasped for air, his gag reflex leaning him closer. Pulling her daggers back, she hit his temple with the hilts. The Watcher dropped to his knees.

"I'll kill you if I must," she said as he leaned on his arms, as if bowing to her. "Come now, and face the woman you wronged."

"I've wronged no one," he said, his voice hoarse.

"Liar. Murderer of children. Surrender now."

He laughed. It was tired and broken.

"*I* am the murdered child, woman. Ask my father."

He flung one of his cloaks at her. As she batted it aside, his heel followed after, ramming into her forehead. Fearing an attack, she retreated, her daggers falling into defensive positions. Her blurred vision saw no one. He was gone, but where? Follow the blood, she thought. Follow the blood.

She caught a speck of it halfway up the building to her left. The rooftops. He was running away. Knowing her time was short, she jumped from one windowsill to another and grabbed hold of a ledge. Before she could pull herself up, a woman lurked above her, weapon drawn.

"I'm sorry, Zusa," Veliana said. "But this one is mine. Go back."

Zusa tensed, hating the awkward position she found herself in. The other woman's dagger was drawn, and in a flash of movement could easily sever her throat.

"Alyssa desires his blood for what he did to Nathaniel," Zusa said.

"And we need him for something more than petty revenge. Please, Zusa, I'm asking you."

Zusa frowned, finding her loyalties torn. Veliana was her apprentice, and had trained so much with her over the past five years. Yet Alyssa was even more than an apprentice, even more than a friend.

"Will you kill him?" she asked.

Veliana shook her head.

"No. Not unless he makes us. Just one meeting, that's all we need. Is my friendship at least worth that?"

Zusa met her eye, let Veliana know the seriousness of her words.

"It is, but consider it an end to our friendship. Do you still desire to take him?"

"I do."

"Then have him, Veliana. And pray we never meet again."

She released, and down she went, falling, refusing to look up as Veliana turned and raced after the bleeding body of the Watcher.

Deathmask strode into the Ash Guild's headquarters with a smile on his face and his head held high. His head pounded as if within his skull was a caged orc, and the wine he'd drunk with Veliana to toast their success had done little to take off the pain's edge, but that didn't matter. The sight before him, the horrible disarray of the room, was enough to lift his spirits. Pillows lay scattered and shards of glass covered the floor by the bar. Garrick stood trembling at the far end. About twelve Ash members were inside, and none seemed eager to be near their guildmaster.

"Greetings," Deathmask said, pretending nothing was amiss. "Good to see you survived last night intac—"

"Where were you?" Garrick shouted. Deathmask blinked, and he glanced at one of the other men as if to show how confused he was. In truth, after attacking his own guild, he and

Veliana had attacked the headquarters of the Spider Guild, slaughtering three and then leaving the symbol of the Ash scrawled into the dirt by the bodies. But he had no intention of telling Garrick that.

"Running for my life out in the streets, much like every other thief in Veldaren," Deathmask smoothly lied. "I stopped by here once, but found the place empty, so I hid until morning."

Garrick paced back and forth. His eyes were bloodshot. Deathmask wondered how much crimleaf the man had coursing through his veins. His speech was also slurred, perhaps from one, or several, of those broken bottles over at the counter. Drunk and stoned. Deathmask struggled to contain his amusement.

"Spiders!" Garrick shouted, as if none of them were there anymore. "Goddamn Spiders! What is Thren thinking? That I betrayed him? He think I'd be stupid enough to do that? We had a deal, you fucking Spider, you fucking...fucking... damn fucking Spider!"

Deathmask's eyes lit up at that. A deal? Could Garrick have been working for Thren? It would explain so much...

"Someone of Thren's showed up around half an hour ago," offered one of the nearest thieves, keeping his voice low so his guildmaster would not hear. "Claimed that two members of the Ash came and killed several of Thren's men, and he demanded an explanation."

Deathmask lifted his eyebrows in surprise.

"That obviously can't be correct," he said.

Garrick overheard and stormed closer. Deathmask saw how incredibly dilated his pupils were, and decided his guess was correct. If Garrick's strength and confidence were built upon Thren's protection, then having that suddenly taken away would probably scare the shit out of him. Deathmask couldn't wait to tell Veliana. She'd been ready to kill the man before. What might she do knowing he'd sold the entire guild out to the man who'd executed her former guildmaster?

"Serious accusations," Deathmask said, repeatedly telling himself not to smile, not to reveal how terribly amused he was. "What did you say?"

"That it's bullshit," Garrick said, waving an unsteady finger in his face. "And I'll convince him of that. But I want to know what's going on. Mercenaries by the hundreds running through the street, and for what? And tomorrow night, will they do the same? We need to plan. We need to prepare. Shit. What about the other guilds? Maybe they know what's going on. We should ask. Someone should go."

Behold your glorious leader, Deathmask mused, glancing at the rest of the Ash members who mingled about. *He was a puppet for Veliana, then a puppet for Thren. Now the strings are cut, and he can do nothing but collapse.*

"I will go," Deathmask said. "And to the Spider Guild, no less. We should show them we mean no ill will, and most of all that the survival of all the guilds is more important than our petty squabbles. How many of us died last night? This is a war now, a true war. Let me take that message to Thren."

Garrick bit his lip, no doubt trying to process the idea in his drug-addled mind. The rest of the thieves looked pleased. Deathmask wasn't surprised. He'd arrived in the chaos, remained calm, and then presented a plan. This was something they could latch onto, however simple. Let the guild see that he was in control, not Garrick.

"Fine," he said. "You may speak for me. Be careful, and don't press if Thren turns you away. Friends. That's what we must be. Good friends. We'll teach the Trifect to mess with us. Won't we? *Won't we?*"

A halfhearted cheer came from the rest of the thieves. As Deathmask left he caught the looks they gave him, and this time he did not hide his smile. He was a stranger, a newcomer to the guild, but he was still becoming more of a leader in their minds than Garrick. Come a crisis, men and women always searched for stability. Let them see that in him.

When he stepped out to the street, he looked to the rooftop for Veliana. At his request she'd remained hidden there when he went inside, just in case Garrick decided to do something stupid like try to kill him. Yet despite having been inside for only a few minutes, she was no longer waiting for him. Odd. Had someone else spotted her? He approached that same building, looped around to its back, and then climbed up. He expected Veliana to be lying there, perhaps bored or asleep. Instead no one.

"Vel?" he wondered aloud.

Then he saw it, a single streak of blood. He followed it to an alley, and when he peered down he saw Veliana kneeling over the body of a fallen man. His clothes were dark, well-worn, and lacking any local guild affiliation. His hair was short and blond, and across his chest was a smear of blood. At first Deathmask thought she'd attacked him, but when he climbed down he was surprised to see her bandaging the man's wounds.

"What the Abyss is going on?" he asked.

"It's him," she said, not at all surprised by his arrival. "It has to be. I fought him once, years ago, but who else might the Watcher be? It's Aaron...Thren Felhorn's long-dead son."

Deathmask's mouth dropped, and every plan whirling through his head rearranged itself to match this new set of circumstances. He could hardly contain his excitement. Every one of those plans was infinitely better than the last.

"Take him," he said. "Hurry. We have so much to discuss."

CHAPTER

19

Haern awoke with his head pounding and no clue where he was. The last thing he remembered was crawling across a rooftop, just before being struck from behind. Then he'd been thrown forward, off the building and to the ground below. Then nothing. His eyes slowly adjusted to the dim light. He saw stone walls. A dungeon perhaps? No, that didn't seem right. More of a cellar, windowless, lit by torches.

"You're awake."

He looked up. A man and a woman stood before him. The man wore a red robe, his dark hair pulled tight behind his head. As for the woman, she looked vaguely familiar, as if he'd seen her before a long time ago, in a dream. It had something to do with the long scar that ran down her face, bloodying her eye. He tried to stand, but he was tied to a chair. Whoever had tied the knots knew what they were doing. There wasn't the slightest give, and the moment he tested them, various cords across his chest and neck tightened, choking off his breath.

"Not sure I want to be awake," he said, doing his best to relax. He'd known this was the fate awaiting him. He couldn't make enemies of every guild and expect to live forever. Still, it seemed too soon. He'd accomplished so little. He'd die without mourners, without friends, without a legacy. A damn shame.

"Do you remember me?" the woman asked. "It was during the Bloody Kensgold. You were still a boy then, almost a man. We fought…"

And then he did remember. He'd seen her twice, once when his father had tried blackmailing her to turn against her guild-master, then later in the attic of Leon Connington's mansion. Her name was Veliana, and the last time they'd met she'd nearly killed him.

"You do remember," she said, seeing the recognition in his eyes.

"I could never forget," he said softly. "You showed me I would never escape. Aaron was dead, yet you never believed me. You refused."

She crossed her arms and leaned back against the stone wall. The man beside her remained quiet, seemingly content to let them talk.

"You could have let the smoke take me," she said. "Why didn't you?"

He shrugged the best he could, given the circumstances.

"It wasn't right to. I was there when my father left you to die at the hands of that disgusting…Worm. I couldn't do so again."

His words hung in the air. When she spoke, her tone didn't seem quite so hard.

"I spread word of Aaron Felhorn's death after that night. I told myself I did it to hurt your father, but I was lying. I did it for you, for sparing me. Aaron was dead, and it seemed true enough. What was the name you spoke to me that night? Something plain..."

"Haern."

"That's right. Is that who you are now? Haern the Watcher? I find it hard to believe you're that same boy who spared my life. Do you know how many friends of mine you've killed? How many associates? You're still Thren's son, aren't you? Perhaps you should adopt your old name, Aaron."

"Never call me that," he said, glaring.

In the corner the dark-haired man laughed.

"Such ferocity. Well, there's no doubt you're skilled, and Vel here was lucky enough to get the jump on you after you were injured. Seems to corroborate everything we've heard about you, other than the demon blood. I'd sense it if that were the case. Still, your father cavorting with a succubus *is* a rather amusing thought."

Haern shifted in his bonds.

"What do you want from me?" he asked.

"Before I tell you that, I want you to understand just how powerless you currently are. I could kill you right here, that's obvious enough. But I could also tell your father you're still alive. How beautiful a game that would be, watching him tear the city apart house by house until he found where you hid. My curiosity is almost strong enough to see what exactly he'd do. Would he greet you with open arms, or a dagger? Perhaps both?"

Haern glared. The man saw this and laughed again.

"Still, I'm in this for the coin and power, not the curiosity. I have a proposition for you, Aaron. Sorry, Watcher. Or would you prefer Haern? So many names, I find myself at a loss."

"Haern is fine."

"Very well then, Haern, my name is Deathmask, and I have a request of you. This is something I cannot do on my own, nor with just Veliana's help. But you...you have no loyalties, no weaknesses, no aspirations other than killing. So my request is simple, really: help me end this war between the guilds and the Trifect."

This time it was Haern's turn to laugh.

"I've slaughtered a hundred of you over the years, and even with my help the Trifect has sat on its hands and failed to do what needed to be done. Last night was a start, but it won't work, we both know that. It'll just anger them further. The retaliation will be terrible, if it hasn't happened already. What could I possibly do?"

"Your name carries weight, believe it or not," Deathmask continued. "Though really, I should say your reputation does. Every thief fears the night when the mark he goes to rob turns out to be you. Even the guildleaders are frightened of you, except for perhaps Thren. A rampage of dragons wouldn't make him soil his pants. But you have to understand something. All of these thieves, these underworld rogues, they've been trained since birth to survive. That's all they know. They'll claw and grab everything they can on their way up, but deep down they just want to live, and live well. If you threaten that, you can turn them to your side."

"No guildmaster would step down at my threat," Haern said. "You're a fool. They'd rather die than forfeit their wealth."

"And that's the other thing you must understand," Death-mask said, grinning. "They have no honor, no code. They want wealth, and they want to live, but they won't live with-out wealth, not when they've at last obtained it. So you must threaten their lives while at the same time offering them a chance to keep everything they've gathered. It can work. I know it."

Haern leaned back in his chair, still not convinced.

"What is your plan?" he asked.

"Do you know how much the Trifect pays to employ those mercenaries? How much money they lose year in and year out from Thren burning their goods, from Kadish slaughtering their help, from Garrick looting their wares? They're going bankrupt fighting this war, but they can't stop, they can't make peace, for Thren won't let them. No one wants this to continue. Before the guild wars, everyone made a tidy profit and hardly anyone died. We had a system. But Thren took offense, and the Trifect overstepped their bounds. A fair mistake by both, but now everyone's too stubborn to stop.

"Now, my plan is very simple; we gather every single guild-leader, all three members of the Trifect, and then stick them in a room. No one leaves until they agree to end all this."

Only the sheer audacity of it kept Haern from laughing.

"It'd never work, you have to know that. Who would dare agree to go? Someone would back out, and others would try to execute their enemies while they're in the same place. Too much greed, too much mistrust. Someone will turn on another. I expected something more clever from someone so . . . strange."

"You spent five years trying to single-handedly conquer the thief guilds," Deathmask said. "Yet you want to mock *my* imagination? But you're right: such a meeting would instantly fall apart . . . unless we had an enforcer during the deal. Someone they all fear, so they would know that stepping out of line would result in a quick, efficient death."

Haern remained quiet for a long time.

"Untie me," he said at last.

"Will you try to kill me?" Deathmask asked.

"So little trust for someone who wants me to work for him."

The man shrugged. "Fair enough. Cut him loose, Vel."

She did so, reluctantly. Haern stood and stretched his muscles, grimacing as his back popped. His arm also ached like mad, the muscles there definitely torn. He glanced about the dim cellar, then turned his attention to Deathmask.

"Tell me everything," he said.

Deathmask seemed all too willing to talk.

"We'll let every member of the Trifect, and every thief guild-master, know in no uncertain language that if they refuse to come to the meeting, they'll die. After that I'll work behind the scenes, grease a few wheels, and come up with terms that everyone can accept. Anyone who tries to make a fuss, or tries to refuse those terms, we send you after them. How does that sound?"

"Insane," Haern said. He looked for his swords, saw neither. "Were you not out last night? The blood clogs the gutters. They'll never agree, not to anything. You're delusional, Deathmask."

"If you don't accept," Veliana said, stepping in front of the stairs leading upward to daylight, "then we'll have no choice. You'll have no one to blame but yourself."

"For what?"

"We'll tell your father of your new name, and of who you really are," she said. "How long do you think your little crusade against us will last once he knows? Right now he sees you as a nuisance, a ghost to keep his men on their toes and to cull the weak from his guild. But for Aaron Felhorn to turn against his own flesh and blood..."

Haern stood before her, staring eye to eye. Even wounded and exhausted, he would not back down.

"Do it, then," he said. "But ask yourself who will find

who first...my father finding me, or me finding you? Move aside. Now."

She tilted her head so she could see Deathmask, who must have made some sort of approving gesture.

"Very well. It was good to see you, *Aaron*."

He stepped out into the street, winced at the daylight, and then hurried away. With nowhere else to go, he headed for Senke and the mercenaries, hoping he might reach there without any other strange women attacking him.

"Do you think he'll change his mind?" Veliana asked once he was gone. Deathmask shrugged.

"Depends on what you mean. About what I just offered? No. But I never expected him to."

Veliana raised an eyebrow. "Care to fill me in?"

"Of course. Haern will never put his heart behind a plan I created. It needs to be his own, one he feels will be his legacy. We need his pride involved, otherwise he'll be ineffective and dangerous. I've planted the idea, though. He knows many of us desire peace, and that he can be a key part of it all. The idea of an enforcer is what I think will appeal to him most. He'll return, I assure you, and it will be with a plan far more insane than mine."

She sat down on the pile of cushions that had been her bed since Deathmask took her away from the Ash Guild. "Even after we kill Garrick, it'll be tough getting the rest of the guild to accept any sort of plan involving the Watcher."

"I know," Deathmask said. "Which is why I turned the Spider Guild against them. Why should I have to do all the dirty work?"

Something about how casually he said it, how amused

he seemed, clicked everything into place. Veliana's mouth dropped.

"You hope to destroy the Ash Guild, tear it down to nothing but yourself."

"Not quite," Deathmask said. "You'll be there, as well as two or three others who have the skill to endure the bloodshed to come. I don't need a guild full of simpletons, children, and the like. I just need enough to put fear into the heart of the guilds, to ensure that all the coin I desire flows to my hands..."

"Then this was your plan all along? Tear down the Ash Guild and rebuild it with you at the top, and a few of us bowing around your feet?"

Veliana rubbed her temples, trying to think. Everything she and James Beren had created, it'd been dwindling since Thren killed James, but they'd still held on to shards of it. Might it all vanish? Could she let him do this, destroy the legacy of the Ash Guild forever?

"You'll ruin everything I've worked for," she said quietly.

"I'll give the Ash Guild a legacy all of Dezrel will one day fear. I don't expect it to be easy. We'll have to kill a lot, yes. But if we succeed, think of all that wealth, that respect. We'll fill every other guild with the fear of retaliation. We'll never need to guard, only attack. Those who turn against us will meet death, every single one. Once that reputation takes hold, we'll be gods in this city."

"You're a lunatic."

He smiled. "Perhaps. But oh what fun it'll be in the attempt. Are you getting scared on me, Vel? Aspire to greatness, and damn all others. Garrick took your guild. Help me take it back, and mold it into something never seen before in the history of Dezrel."

She still wasn't sure, but she'd not let Deathmask know.

"What of the Spider Guild?" she asked. "Weren't you to meet with Thren?"

Deathmask's eyes twinkled, and his grin pulled wider. Despite it, she thought she sensed fear hiding behind the guise.

"Come with me," he said. "Hopefully we haven't missed the show. I discovered something when in Garrick's audience, and I've rethought what Thren's reaction to our masquerade will be."

They removed their cloaks and dressed in drab colors that showed no affiliation. Veliana kept a hood low over her face to hide her scar. Given the cold wind of the morning, no one would think the hood odd. Deathmask led the way, taking a winding path back to the Ash guildhouse. Before they were even halfway there, Veliana could already see the smoke rising.

"What happened?" she asked.

"Careful," he said, hugging the wall and peering around every turn. "We might have a few more enemies now. Do you remember when the Hawks tried to ambush you, the attempt I broke up when I first met you? Garrick didn't do anything, did he?"

"No," she said. "But what does that—?"

"The Spider Guild attacked the Hawks barely a day later. Why do you think that, Veliana? Why do you think Garrick suddenly grew testicles and dared challenge your hidden control?"

The realization hit her like a battering ram.

"No. That cow-sucking shit-eating motherfucker. I'll kill him. It'll hopefully take days, but I'll kill him."

"Assuming he's still alive," Deathmask said as he led them into an apartment. They climbed the stairs, stopped at a door on the higher floor, and knocked. When no one answered, Veliana kicked it in. The room was disheveled, what little was left. The occupants appeared to have either fled or died. From the small window they could see the guildhouse. Deathmask looked first, then backed away so Veliana might see. The whole building was in flames. It had already collapsed on its supports, black smoke billowing. Surrounding it was a circle of thieves wearing the cloaks and colors of the Spider.

While she watched, a man crawled from the wreckage, and even from their distance he looked badly burned. One of the Spiders shot him with an arrow before he could rise to his feet.

"Unbelievable," Deathmask said as he took a second look. "An army of mercenaries descends upon us, and without hesitation he massacres a fellow guild, all for a single act of betrayal."

"Thren is not one to hesitate."

Deathmask muttered and flopped down onto the poorly stuffed bed.

"We need to establish control of the guild, and now," he said. "I'd hoped for a bit of backstabbing between the two, a thinning of members, but this... Thren's viciousness is astounding. We must take over before the guild disbands completely, and the rest of the city moves in on our territory. At least the mercenaries will keep them from doing so for a while. As for Thren... if there's to be any chance of peace, he'll need to be dealt with, one way or another. Tell me, where will the remainder of the guild flee now this place has burned?"

"The old house," she said. "Below the Split Pig Inn. We expanded their cellars and paid handsomely to do so. They should still be empty, and the owner was a crusty old dog that won't be intimidated by sellswords."

"Then that's where we'll go," he said, retying his mask over his face. "Let them see you alive, let them hear my demands of obedience. As of now, the Ash Guild is under my control."

"And if Garrick still lives?"

Deathmask flashed her a smile, all pretense of fear gone.

"Then you get your revenge, assuming you're strong enough to take it."

She patted her daggers. "I'll be fine. Follow me, and keep your eyes open. The last thing I want to do is die before my steel tastes Garrick's blood."

CHAPTER 20

Ghost woke when the sun shone bright on his face. He stirred, rubbed his eyes, and then forced them open. Midday, he guessed. His stomach rumbled, and his head pounded from the night before. He felt he could sleep another four hours or so, but his body would have to endure. Still, he wasn't in too much of a hurry. He had a name, after all, a place to search and question. Not much harm in grabbing a bite to eat.

Once he left his room at the shabby inn, he swung by the main market in the center of town, buying a thick slice of bread smothered with butter and honey. While he ate, he sat by a fountain in the center and listened to the idle talk as men and women passed by. The overwhelming sensation was not fear, as he'd expected. It was anger. More surprising was how it wasn't directed at the guilds, or even the Trifect. They directed it at the king.

Stupid dogs, he thought as he ate. *You've lived under this chaos for so long it's become normal to you. The Trifect and the guilds war, and you see this as acceptable, but only if the king protects you. Last night destroyed your apathy. Last night saw your blood joining the others'. So you rage, but only to your protector. Damn king. Should have put this nonsense to rest years ago.*

Still fairly new to Veldaren, Ghost knew only a little of the king, but what he'd gleaned wasn't flattering. As he listened to men swear against their liege's honor, and women insinuate he'd been born without his manhood, it seemed obvious that his cowardly indifference could no longer last. But whose side would he fall on, the guilds' or the Trifect's? Logic seemed to place him as a puppet of the Trifect, but Ghost was unsure. Which one would he fear more? If the man was a true coward, he'd fear the enemy he couldn't keep out with gates and walls, the enemy that'd fill his drink with poison and lay a dagger under his pillow while he slept.

Meal finished, he drank from the fountain and then headed to the mercenaries' headquarters. Not surprisingly, it was crowded with both the rich and the poor. They were pleading their cases, demanding compensation for damages done in the chaotic night. The old keeper, Bill Trett, shouted the same phrase over and over, as if by the fiftieth time it might finally sink in.

"Take all complaints to Alyssa Gemcroft's estate. She has promised to accept full responsibility. I'm sorry if your house burned down, or someone died, but please, take all complaints to Alyssa Gemcroft's estate. She has promised..."

Ghost slammed a massive fist against the door, the sound thunderous in the small room. The crowd, about twenty in all, jumped and turned.

"Enough!" he roared. "Get your asses out of here, and go to Lady Gemcroft's with your problems."

He kept his muscular arm pressed against the door, holding it open. The stance also revealed the weapons at his hips. He glared, letting them see he had no desire to argue. A few filed out, while the rest looked about as if trying to decide just how serious he was. Only a few carried weapons, and he doubted they were proficient with them.

"I'm letting go of the door," he said, his voice lowering in volume but not in depth. "When it shuts, I kill everyone in here not a member of the mercenary guild. That clear?"

He let go. A wiry man in silks lunged for it, sticking his hand in the way. The rest followed him, until only a thankful Bill remained.

"What the Abyss happened last night?" the older man asked. "I expected several of them to jump the counter and attack me."

"Frightened sheep," Ghost said. "Let Alyssa handle them. No reason for you to put up with their bleating."

"I doubt you've come here to be my savior," Bill said, sitting down and smoothing his hair. He pulled a bottle from a drawer and took a deep swig. "So what is it you need?"

"A small group of mercenaries, led by one named Tarlak. Do you know them?"

Bill raised an eyebrow. "I do, but only because they've caused me a bit of trouble. Tarlak Eschaton, leader of the Eschaton Mercenaries. Refused to join our guild or pay dues. The last representative I sent their way demanding they join came back as a toad."

Ghost blinked. "A toad?"

"A damn toad. Cost a fortune to send for a representative of the Council of Mages to come change him back. They weren't too happy with that Tarlak, either. Evidently he's a rogue apprentice or something, but since he's not an official member they don't consider him their problem, so long as he doesn't start blowing up houses or trying to become anything more than what he is now."

"Which is?"

Bill shrugged. "A small-time mercenary. Why do you ask?"

"I need to find him."

"Last I knew he was on Crimson Alley, thirteenth heading south from Ax Way. Should still be there."

"Do you know how many are with him?"

Bill took another long swig, paused to think, and then stood. After he'd locked the door, then put a wooden bar across, he sat back down.

"I'm thinking we're closed for the day," he said. "And I'm not sure I like where this is going, Ghost. Care to tell me why you want to know so much about this Tarlak fellow?"

"He knows something."

"From what I hear, people that know something you want to know have a funny way of turning up dead."

Ghost shrugged. "Depends on how loose their lips are."

"My, aren't you a piece of work?" Bill said, chuckling. "But considering they aren't part of the guild, and you are, I guess I can tell you what I know. He lives with his sister, young gal. Priestess, I think. Also got some guy named Brug, though why he's taken him in I don't have a clue. We turned down that guy's application twice. Too much temper without a shred of skill to back it up. Last is a guy named Stern, bald as you, but that's all I know. If he can fight, I haven't heard word of it. Like I said, small-time, with only his petty magic tricks to make him stand out in the slightest. Oh, and those gods-awful yellow robes of his. Their group's only been around for nine months or so, maybe a year. I don't expect 'em to last."

Ghost bowed, stealing Bill's bottle as he did. He took in several gulps, the burning in his throat doing much to awaken him.

"Enjoy your day in peace," Ghost said, handing it back. "And lock the door after I leave. There's still people gathering outside."

"Will do."

A glare from Ghost caused the few waiting outside to step back, and he didn't move away until he heard the thump of the wood barring the door.

"You've still got your lives," he told them. "If you've got that, you can move on. I suggest you do. Your pleading and curses won't do a damn thing to sway anyone, not in this city."

He trudged south, toward the Crimson, keeping an eye out for Ax Way so he could begin counting. Finding the thirteenth from there was easy. Eyeing the building's two floors, he crossed his arms and thought. Deciding his entry point, he continued. A block later he turned around, coming back by a side alley. The way was dark, and two men glared at him as he passed. Any other they might have tried to rob, but he'd flashed them a grin, and he saw the way they stared at his painted face. They'd have been more likely to try to rob a dragon.

The Eschatons' building itself was smooth wood on the outside, but not the one next to it. That was well-worn and cracked with many handholds. Climbing up to the roof, he turned and leaped the gap, rolling to absorb the impact of his landing. It wasn't that he feared injuring his legs; he knew they could endure the blow. He just didn't want to alert anyone inside to his presence. There was no direct entrance from the roof, but the second floor had a window, and that would be enough for him. Hanging upside down, he looked through it.

The glass was surprisingly clean, and he guessed it was because of the woman who slept beneath the window, red-haired and buried under blankets. The priestess, he figured. The muscles in his legs flexing to keep himself steady, he brushed his fingers against the glass, testing whether or not the window opened. It didn't.

He swung back onto the roof and debated. If he broke in through the front door, the surprise would be less, and he wouldn't have immediate access to the inhabitants. He could try coming back later, but if they slept through the day they'd probably be out with the other mercenaries come nightfall. Again, no good. It'd have to be now. He put his back to the ledge, then crouched down so he could clutch it with his hands. The window would be a tight fit, but if he stretched out enough he could squeeze through.

He kicked, shifting into a pivot. Feetfirst he smashed through the window, showering the woman's bed with glass. He let go of the ledge and held his arms high above his head. His momentum carried him through, and he landed on his back on top of her. Before she could scream he rolled over and clamped a hand over her mouth.

"Shush now," he said, ramming an open palm against the side of her head, knocking her out cold. Knowing time was short, he pushed off the bed and made for the door.

"Del?" he heard someone ask from the other side. His voice was nervous, but not yet worried. A broken window could be many things, most likely a stone, least likely a dangerous man built like a mountain. The door swung inward. Before it was a third of the way open, Ghost rammed it closed with his knee, then grabbed it with one hand and flung it wide. A man was falling on the other side, his balance broken by the sudden hit from the door. It was Tarlak, based on his outfit.

Bill was right. What is that, piss-yellow?

Ghost rammed a meaty fist into his mouth, just to make sure no spells got out. He had no intention of showing up at Bill's later as a toad. The punch split the wizard's lip, and blood flecked across Ghost's knuckles. Ghost followed it up with a punch to the stomach, doubling him over. He dropped the wizard with both his fists together, bashing the back of his head. Tarlak crumpled, easily unconscious. Neither he nor the girl would be out long, maybe a few minutes, but Ghost felt it enough time. When they came to they'd be bound, and the wizard gagged.

There was one other room up top, its door open. Deciding it was Tarlak's, he hurried to the stairs. If the other two were awake, they'd be rushing up them. Sure enough he heard hollering, and a short man with muscular arms and a beard met him halfway.

"What the bloody—?"

Ghost snapped a fist into his face, cutting the sentence off short. A knee to his groin sent the man rolling back down. Again Bill's information rang true. The guy wasn't much use, was he?

He followed Brug's roll down the stairs, kicking him at the bottom to convince him to stay down. One left, the one called Stern. His eyes swept the lower floor. Two doors were in the back, plus an exit to the outside. One was open, Brug's he assumed. The other...

The door blasted open as he reached for its handle. He spun immediately in the direction of the door, using it as a shield. A flanged mace cut through the air where he'd been. Ghost bounced off the wall, drawing both his swords. He shoved the mace aside, then slashed blindly around the door. The other sword hit something hard, and then they were both in view of each other. The man, Stern no doubt, glared back at him, a mace in each hand. Their weapons pressed against each other, testing strength. Stern, while stronger than he looked, was still no contest.

This didn't seem to surprise him, though, and when Ghost tried to push him back, Stern parried both swords to the side and tried to leap past. He wanted the open area, Ghost realized, hoping his speed might win out. Ghost couldn't stop him, but he could make life more difficult. He kicked as he rotated his body, taking out one of Stern's knees. Stern didn't even try to keep his balance, instead rolling forward, around an old wooden chair, and up to his feet before the front door. He lifted his maces and grinned.

"Clearly skilled," he said. "So what person with money did we piss off this time?"

"Don't matter," Ghost said. He feinted a charge, then kicked the chair at him. Stern blocked it with his heel, but it was enough of a stall. Double-slashing, Ghost gave him no choice but to block, and block he did. His arms jarred, though nothing broke as Ghost had hoped. Sometimes, if he swung just right, he could pop a collarbone or wreck the joints in an elbow.

Ghost looped his swords around for an attack from both sides. That left the only opening straight ahead, toward his chest. He wanted this Stern character to try it, to hold his own instead of bouncing about. Maddeningly, he didn't take it. Stern dropped to one knee, blocking the lower slash from his left and letting the right sail over his head. Immediately after blocking he rolled to the side. Ghost chased, but each slash smashed only floor. Time was no longer on his side. The others would be up soon, groggy and heads full of fog, but still up.

How much concentration did it take to turn someone into a toad, Ghost wondered.

Stern at last had nowhere to run. His back was to the wall. To his left were the stairs, and to his right the main door. His eyes flicked between both, deciding. Ghost gave him no time, rushing in while keeping his swords close. He would block a retreat with his own body and let his blades do the work. Stern had no chance of matching Ghost's strength, and without a retreat, dying would be his only option.

It seemed Stern knew this as well. His eyes widened, and he appeared pressed to the very edge of his control by adrenaline and fear. The look of a cornered animal. Ghost knew Stern would not roll onto his back and hope for mercy. He'd lunge, mad, vicious. And that's just what he did. Ghost feared those first few seconds as the maces came crashing in, slamming into his swords with shocking impact. He felt kicks strike his body, at one point an elbow, and still the maces looped and struck. But they were fighting Ghost's fight now, close up and animalistic. He blocked a swipe from the side, then savagely struck the mace's length with his other blade, knocking it from Stern's hand. Stern's other weapon came around, straight for his head. Instead of ducking Ghost stepped closer, chest to chest. The side of Stern's arm hit his face, but that was far better than the sharp edges of the mace.

One sword slashed Stern's arm, making him drop his weapon. The other thrust into his belly and twisted.

"Shit," Stern grunted, clutching Ghost's wrist with both hands. His whole body shook, and his face rapidly paled. Ghost pulled his weapon free, breaking Stern's grip as if it were that of a child. The man slid down the wall, blood pouring across his hands and down his legs. He held the wound with his palms, slowing the bleeding.

"You should have surrendered," Ghost said. "Though I respect your defense of your friends, this was all unnecessary."

He left him there, stepped over Brug, and climbed the stairs. The short fighter was moaning still, conscious but only just. He was no threat. Ghost found the wizard first, glad to see him still out. Unwrapping the rope he'd looped about his own waist, he cut a length of it and bound Tarlak's hands. Thinking for a moment, he cut a smaller length, wedged a piece of the wizard's own robe into his mouth, and then tied it there to form a gag. Hefting Tarlak onto his shoulder, he carried him back down the stairs and deposited him in a chair. Stern watched him with glazed eyes from where he lay.

Last was the girl. She opened her eyes when he stepped

inside, but she showed no recognition, nor any signs of fear. Concussion, he figured. She probably didn't know the difference between him and the King of Ker.

"To your feet," he said. "I'd hate to strike you again."

He grabbed her wrists and held them tight as he escorted her down the stairs. Once she was tied to another chair, he kicked Brug to see how he was faring.

"Damn it," Brug muttered, his eyes suddenly focusing. "What was that for?"

He saw Ghost standing over him, and then he tried to reach for his weapons. Laughing, Ghost slammed his heel onto his throat and pushed him back.

"I'd recommend you behave," he said, the tip of his sword dangling before an eye. "Otherwise I might just let go."

Brug ground his teeth, glanced about, then nodded. Ghost bound his hands and feet and then dumped him on the floor beside the others.

"Well, that was disappointingly easy," Ghost said, sheathing his swords. "I hope the Watcher proves more challenging than you four."

Stern said something, but his voice was too weak to hear. Ghost stepped closer and leaned down.

"You'll find out when he kills you," Stern said, then made a sound like a cross between a cough and a laugh. Ghost slapped the side of his face, the gesture almost playful.

"At least you put up a fight," he said. "So I'll forgive you for your frightened boasting. Stay still, and try not to let your grip slip. You might know something useful to me, and I'd hate to lose it because you can't keep your guts from squeezing through your fingers."

The priestess seemed to be getting her bearings, but Tarlak was still clearly out. Ghost reached into a pocket and pulled out some smelling salts. Shoving them under the wizard's nose, he held his head by his hair and waited. After a few sniffs Tarlak's eyelids began to flutter, and then he jolted as if splashed by a bucket of water.

"Whmmph," he said.

"Welcome back," Ghost said, smacking his shoulder. "Forgive the gag. I know how dangerous your kind is with a few silly words. I may take it out, but only for a moment, and only when my swords are at your throat. Understand?"

A soft gasp came from his right. It seemed like the priestess had finally come to her senses.

"Senke!" she gasped.

Senke?

He followed her gaze to the wounded man against the wall. A pet name, perhaps? Or maybe Bill had been wrong about the man's identity?

"He put up a better fight than the rest of you," Ghost said.

"Don't say nothing, Delysia," Brug muttered. "Just bite your tongue and say nothing."

"I don't think I'd listen to him," Ghost said, placing the name to her face. Many people he interrogated became much more compliant when he called them by their names.

"Please, I can help him!" She squirmed against her bonds. "He's dying!"

"If he's dying, he's doing a poor job of it." He watched her struggle to see if his ropes would hold. Satisfied, he took her chin in a giant hand and forced her gaze to his. "But if you want untied, you'll have to talk. That's all, little girl, just talk. No sin in that, right?"

"What do you want?" she asked.

"Don't!" Brug shouted. Ghost turned on him, and this time his kick was lower, and harder. Brug howled like an animal, and his face turned a beet red.

"Enough out of you," he said. "You're beaten, and at my mercy. Lies and silence get you pain, only pain. Not honor. Not sacrifice. Not nobility. Just pain."

Tarlak mumbled something into his gag. Ghost debated, but then left him alone. He'd go to the wizard only if the others proved uncooperative. So far this Delysia appeared the most compliant. He knelt before her, all teeth and smiles.

"Senke's bleeding over there," he said, dropping his voice lower. She tried to look, but his eyes held her. He knew he could do that, had so many times before. He felt like a snake charmer, controlling them by the sheer ferocity of his personality. "You can feel it, his pain washing over you like a heat. You're a priestess, so you could help him, tend his wounds. How badly you must wish to go to him. Such sweet compassion."

He shifted to behind her, pressing a painted cheek against hers as they both looked to where Senke lay.

"But is it just compassion? I don't think it is. I think it's fear. I smell the stink on you. It's rising in your chest, crawling upward like a beast. You don't want to watch him die, yet that's what you are doing. Life is draining away before you, and all you can do is sit here. Struggling against your ropes won't seal the hole in his gut, Delysia. Only one thing will, and that is talking to me. Tell me the truth, and only the truth. Can you do that, pretty girl? Can you do that for Senke?"

She bit her lower lip. Tears ran down her face.

"Yes," she said at last. Brug sighed. By the wall, Senke chuckled. Tarlak let out another *mrmph* into his gag.

"Good lass. It's a simple question, really. I have a contract to find the Watcher, and your group knows of him. Tell me, where can I find him?"

"I don't know," she said. She stared into his eyes, and he realized she wanted him to know she didn't lie. "He's only stayed here twice. Where he goes when he leaves...please, I don't know. None of us do."

Ghost frowned.

"Tell me his name, then. He must have a name."

Tears ran down her face. She looked to Senke, but Ghost grabbed her jaw and forced her back to him.

"Haern," she said. "He calls himself Haern."

"Last name? First?"

"Just Haern."

Possibilities ran through Ghost's head, and he didn't like any of them. A single, plain name would be marginal help at best in tracking him down. Still, it was better than nothing, which is what he'd been going on before. But mostly he didn't want a name. He wanted the man in person.

"Will he be coming back here?"

She hesitated, just for a second, but Ghost saw it and smiled.

"No lies," he said. "That just gives pain, remember?"

"I don't know," she said at last. "But I think he will. Please, can I help him now? He's almost gone."

"Of course, my dear."

He untied her wrists and then gestured for her to go. She ran to Senke's side and knelt. He whispered something to her, and he heard her begin to cry. Ideas raced through Ghost's head as he watched out of the corner of his eye. If this Haern was coming back, then he had to keep them all here until he did, otherwise they might find a way to warn him. Of course it could be days until he showed, or worse, Haern might spot the ambush through a window, or sense it from the lack of common activity. Troubling. He'd have to dump them in one of the rooms, preferably without a window. Once done, then he might...

And that was when the door opened, and in stepped the Watcher.

CHAPTER 21

Haern's elbow still ached like the Abyss, but at least it'd stopped bleeding. He felt naked without his swords, so he kept his head down and shambled along as if he were drunk. Given the horror of the previous night, he knew he was far from the only one who staggered along the road. Many had buried their grief in alcohol. His nerves rose as he hurried down the Crimson, but he reminded himself it was safer in the day than at night. Sure, some of the young cutpurses might try to swipe his coin, but he had nothing to steal.

When he reached the Eschatons' building he put his hand on the door and closed his eyes. Returning here meant many things, and he wasn't sure if he was prepared for the implications. Could this place become a home to him? Could he accept Senke's companionship, even knowing his presence would be a danger to his friend? Deep in his heart he knew he desired nothing else. It was his head that kept getting in the way. But sometimes you needed to think like that to protect others. To Haern, the self had never mattered more than those he cared for. He'd learned that lesson from watching his teacher, Robert, sacrifice his life to protect him.

He opened the door with his good arm. So lost in his thoughts, so focused on what he might say to them, and what they might say back, he was unprepared for the sight before him. Tarlak sat bound and gagged in a chair. Brug lay on the floor, also bound. Senke slumped against the wall, blood covering his clothes. Delysia knelt before him, her hands also covered with blood. And there amid them all was a giant stranger, skin like obsidian, face painted white as a skull. It seemed the stranger was as surprised as he was, and they both froze for a split second. Haern looked into this man's eyes and saw death.

"Watcher," said the painted man. Not a question, just a statement. His deep voice chilled Haern to the bone, telling him it was time to act. This was no game. Their lives hung in the balance.

"Run!" Delysia screamed.

But he couldn't leave them like this. Damn it, what he'd give to have his swords!

The stranger lunged, drawing two swords as he did. Haern dove farther into the house, tumbling to avoid the attack. His eyes searched for a weapon, any weapon. There, on the wall, he saw the short swords Senke had used during their brief spar. Scrambling to his feet, he ran for them, not even slowing when he slammed into the wall. His good arm snatched one free, and then he rolled aside, the stranger's sword cutting several inches into the thin wall.

"Who are you?" Haern asked as he held the blade before him and crouched into position.

"I am Ghost," said the man. His brown eyes shone amid

the paint. Sweat dripped down his neck and arms, every inch seemingly nothing but muscle. His swords lifted and dipped into a stance, perfectly smooth, perfectly calm. Haern felt terror at the sight. For all his reputation, all his killings, this man faced the Watcher unafraid. He even smiled.

Every instinct told Haern to retreat, but he wouldn't. He'd thought he'd lost Senke in a fire, and he'd never come back to look. He'd been dragged off by his father while Delysia bled. This time he'd stay until the end, whatever that might be. *Death or victory*, he thought. His father would be proud.

"Come then," Haern said. "Kill me if you can."

He kicked aside the table and in the limited space began spinning in place. His multitude of cloaks dipped and rose, hiding his presence. Ghost watched it, the concentration in his eyes frightening. When he moved to attack, out lashed Haern's short sword, nearly slicing off his nose. Again Ghost watched, waited. Haern had practiced the cloakdance over the years, trying to perfect it since it had first been used on him during the Bloody Kensgold. The constant motion kept his true movements unpredictable, kept the positioning of his swords hidden. Lesser foes he could defeat with ease, and it gave him an advantage against several attackers at once. But against someone so skilled? It was a stalling diversion, nothing more.

"Stop dancing and kick his ass!" Brug shouted, unable to do anything but watch from his spot on the floor.

A sword swung in. Haern dipped below it, his spine nearly parallel to the floor. Out went his blade, cutting into the thin flesh of Ghost's knee. It'd be painful, but not debilitating beyond a limp. He hadn't been able to apply enough force due to his awkward position. Worse was that the blade caught on the bone instead of slicing free. Ghost stepped in, unafraid of the cloaks and defiant of the weapon lodged in his flesh.

He swung downward with both swords. Haern's momentum had him rising to a stand, so he kicked out his own feet to fall instead. The swords missed, but only barely. Haern landed flat on his back, the impact knocking the breath from his lungs. His wounded elbow hit hard as well, and the pain of it filled his vision with black dots. Ghost twirled a sword in his right hand, pointing the blade downward, eager for a killing thrust.

But then Delysia was there, her hands raised, palms facing Ghost. Bright light flared, blinding even to Haern. Ghost roared, and he took a step back as if struck by a blow. Haern swung his legs wide, taking advantage of the distraction. His heel struck the wounded knee, hard enough to dislodge the sword stuck in the joint. Down Ghost went, the knee crumpling. Again Delysia let out a cry, shouting out the name of her deity. Her hand moved in a downward arc. A golden sword materialized in the air before her, mimicking the motion. It sliced into Ghost's chest. Blood sprayed across her, but she didn't appear to notice. Another prayer was already on her lips, demanding the strength of Ashhur.

"Begone!" she cried. Haern saw a faint outline, almost like an enormous hand, shimmer and vanish in the blink of an eye. Ghost flew back several feet, as if hit by a battering ram. When his body met the wall, it was the wall that gave, the cheap plaster breaking. Haern took to his feet, his wounded elbow held against his chest. It had started bleeding again, staining the gray of his clothes red. Ghost took a woozy step forward, then collapsed when he tried to stand on the other leg. Haern reached down and grabbed his sword while the giant man crawled toward the exit.

"Don't," Delysia said, grabbing his shirt. Her voice had authority now, and something in him was unwilling to challenge it. "Please, don't kill him."

"Are you mad?" Brug asked, still squirming against his ropes. Haern felt inclined to agree.

"He's beaten, and leaving," she insisted. "Don't. He let me save Senke. He deserves as much."

"He's also the one who did it in the first place," Senke said with a sleepy voice. "Just thought I'd point that out."

"Phggrrmpf," Tarlak chimed in.

Ghost looked at them as if they were all mad. He used a chair to brace himself as he stood, then limped toward the door, his teeth clenched against the pain.

"You were beaten," he said as he took a lumbering step outside.

"Sure thing," Haern said, Delysia still clutching his shirt. The moment the door closed he slumped backward, sitting atop the edge of the overturned table. Delysia checked his elbow.

"Senke needs my help more than you," she said. "It can wait. Untie Tarlak and Brug."

"As you wish."

Delysia returned to Senke and knelt before him. Haern heard her prayers, and white light shone around her hands. No wonder the wound on his chest had healed so quickly those few days ago.

"Friend of yours?" Tarlak asked once the gag was removed.

"You aren't funny," Haern said.

He cut the ropes around his hands and feet, and while the wizard stretched, he did the same for Brug.

"Son of a whore ambushed me coming up the stairs," Brug said, grabbing his punch daggers. "Otherwise I'd have torn him a new hole."

"You mean like this one?" Senke asked.

Brug flushed and looked away. Haern tossed his short sword

to the floor. He felt sick, and he still hadn't recovered from the blow to his head earlier in the day. His elbow throbbed, feeling even worse than when he'd first received the cut. He saw Brug and Tarlak glaring at him, and he felt he deserved their ire. He tried to stumble for the door, but Tarlak blocked the way, holding it shut with his arm.

"Not yet," he said. "And not anytime soon. It's time we talked, Watcher."

CHAPTER

22

Matthew's relief upon seeing Felwood Castle lasted only as long as it took him to see one of Hadfield's men standing watch far from the other guards. It was as he'd feared. Less than ten minutes ago he'd had to drag himself and Tristan off the road, and when the horsemen rode on by, his gut had told him who it was they served. And now the sentry was there, keeping a close eye on everyone entering and leaving Lord Gandrem's castle.

"What do we do?" Tristan asked. Matthew had abruptly turned them both around and back north on the road, hoping the soldier hadn't seen their approach. Given the distance, it seemed probable.

"I don't know," he said. He could imagine what would happen if they tried to pass by. The soldier would cut them down before letting them reach John Gandrem. Whatever punishment the soldier received would be bearable so long as no one identified the one-armed boy as the son of Lady Gemcroft.

Given his disfigurement, the dirt on his face and the plain clothes he now wore, it seemed doubtful that anyone would.

"Will we continue on to Veldaren?" Tristan asked.

"Quiet, boy, I don't know!"

He waited until his temper calmed, then resumed.

"And I'm not sure we can. Don't have the food, and water might end up scarce too. I need inside to resupply, but that might mean leaving you behind for a while. They won't know me from shit, since you're the one they want. That, and I don't know who John's sided with in all this."

"John was always nice to me," Tristan said. "I stayed with him for a year. What if... what if I get us inside? Will he keep us safe?"

Matthew shot him a look.

"How could you get us inside?"

"I don't know. I could run real fast. I'm a fast runner, even Arthur said it!"

Matthew bit his lip. It was just one man, a professional soldier perhaps, but still just one. He touched the old sword at his hip. If he could last for a little while, just a little...

His eyes fell upon the near-empty sack that had carried their food.

"I have an idea," he said. "But you better run like the wind, you hear me? Like it, and even faster. My life is depending on those legs of yours."

Ingle mumbled curses as he shifted his weight from foot to foot, trying to generate some heat to counter the cold. After another minute he pulled a blanket from a saddlebag and wrapped it around his shoulders. Beside him his horse clomped the ground.

"Blanket ain't big enough for two of us," he said. "We'll get you somewhere warm once we find that brat, though, I promise."

Ingle and his horse waited a hundred yards outside the castle's entrance, near the fork where the main road turned toward him. The woods had been thinned out toward the front, though they were still thick enough to make him worry. Nathaniel and the farmer might try to sneak along the walls, using the woods as cover. Doing that was a good way to earn an arrow in your back from a guard, though. They would come traveling down the road, he felt certain of it. According to his bitch of a wife, Matthew had left immediately after killing Gert and Ben. Dimwit farmer couldn't know how many were actually looking, or that they might have beaten him here. Ingle expected him to come riding full gallop, the boy behind him on his horse, thinking he'd finally reached safety. Already Ingle had practiced his excuses for when the castle guards came running.

"Guy looked mad as a dog," he'd say. "Started hollering for me to hand over my money, then sent the boy to do his dirty work."

No one would question him for killing two hungry thieves too stupid to know better. Even if they did, what would it matter? John Gandrem wouldn't challenge Arthur, not over something so petty as a dead farmer and his boy.

While he held the rough blanket and looked about, he saw a man approaching. He walked on foot, leading his horse. A large sack lay slung across the saddle. Ingle raised an eyebrow at the sight. No boy, but what could someone be bringing to trade this late in winter?

"Slow down there," Ingle said, tossing his blanket back toward his horse and putting a hand on his hilt. "Strange time for travel, don't you think?"

"Pigs die when they die," said the man. "Come to see if his lordship would like a fine meal tonight."

The cogs and wheels in Ingle's brain were never the most tightly fitted, but still they turned the words over, again and again, unable to get rid of a deep feeling of someone putting something over on him.

"Let me see it," he said. The man continued leading the horse right on by, forcing Ingle to jump in his way. Still the man didn't slow, and Ingle took several steps backward to keep from getting knocked over. At last he drew his sword and stood his ground.

"I said let me see," he said. "I don't think that's no pig."

"If you say so," said the man. He pulled the sack off the horse with a grunt and plopped it to the ground. "Just a small one, maybe good for John and some of his closest..."

While he talked, his hands messed with a tie at the end. The moment the knot came undone the sack was flung open, and out ran a boy who even Ingle knew had to be Nathaniel. The boy darted underneath his horse's legs and then shot straight for the castle.

"Fuck!" Ingle shouted, turning to give chase. Matthew flung himself in the way. He wielded an old sword, recently polished but still timeworn and unreliable. Didn't seem to matter, though, for he wielded it as if it were Ashhur's blade itself and Ingle the dark-spawn of Karak.

"Outta the way!" Ingle shouted, slashing with his sword in the hope of overpowering the unskilled farmer. He blocked, clumsily perhaps, but Matthew still banged his sword away. Instead of pressing the advantage he retreated, fully defensive. Behind him the little brat hollered like his lungs were on fire.

"He's gonna kill my pa, he's gonna kill my pa, he's gonna *kill* him!"

Damn right, thought Ingle.

Ingle feinted, smirked at how easily the farmer fell for it, and then cut from the other direction. The edge of his sword slashed into Matthew's arm, eliciting a cry of pain. Ingle swung again, lower, hoping to split his belly open. The man put his blade in the way just in time. The sound of metal on metal rang out, though there was something funny to it, as if one of their weapons wasn't flexing as it should. Ingle doubted it was his. Blood spilled down Matthew's arm, and Ingle saw the elbow below it shaking.

"Should have turned him over," Ingle said. Their eyes met, and for that brief moment he could tell Matthew thought the same. Behind him the guards approached, alerted by the boy. Fear bubbled up in Ingle's throat. Even if he lived, what might Oric do for such a screw-up? The least he could do was kill the stupid man who had given them so much trouble. He thrust, the tip nicking ribs before Matthew managed to parry it aside. Stepping closer, Ingle pulled his sword around, smacking it against Matthew's, which had pulled back to defend, and then he slashed once more at exposed flesh. Matthew fell back, but he was too slow, too unprepared for the maneuver. He was a farmer, not a trained fighter.

The sword cleaved through his shoulder and shattered his collarbone. In the distance Ingle heard Nathaniel scream. Matthew coughed once, his sword falling from limp fingers. His eyes grew wide. His lips quivered, his skin turning white. Ingle put a boot on his chest and kicked him back, freeing his crimson blade. The body clumped to the ground and lay still.

"Stubborn little shit," Ingle muttered as he wiped his sword clean on Matthew's leg.

"Drop your blade!" ordered the two gate guards as they arrived. They had their swords drawn, and Ingle promptly obeyed. He gave a smile to Nathaniel, who cowered behind the two guards, tears on his face.

"What is the meaning of this?" asked one as he picked up Ingle's blade. The other circled around and pressed the tip of his sword against his back to ensure he did nothing stupid. A hand reached in, yanking his dagger from his belt and tossing it to the dirt.

"I can explain, though Oric can do it better," he said. He pointed to the body. "That man there's a kidnapper. I know it 'cause we been searching high and low for him. And that boy there, well…"

He turned to Nathaniel, whose eyes looked like white saucers. He grinned, for he felt his lie building, the slow gears in his head turning.

"That's Nathaniel Gemcroft, back from the dead, as we always hoped."

The guards looked to the boy, whose skin had gone pale.

"I wasn't kidnapped," he insisted to the guards. "I wasn't. He was helping me, and you let him kill him. Why didn't you run? I told you to run!"

He was crying now, snot dripping from his nose. The first guard took him by the hand while the other grabbed Ingle by the arm and led him toward the castle.

"This is something Lord Gandrem will settle," said the guard. "Stay quiet, and answer only when you've been asked directly, understand?"

"Sure do," said Ingle. "But don't squeeze so rough. You'll be treating me like a hero soon enough."

The four entered through the castle gates, then followed the emerald carpet into the main chamber. Uri and Oric were already there, in mid-conversation with John Gandrem on his throne. He sat up straighter at their arrival, clearly recognizing the boy.

"Nathaniel?" he said, his mouth hanging open.

Ingle saw Oric glaring at him, his eyes ready to bulge out of his head. Not knowing what his captain might have been saying, he knew he should set things in motion, let his captain know what lie he'd created.

"I just saved him from his kidnapper," he said, loud and boastful. A mailed fist struck the back of his head, and for a moment his vision turned to yellow stars over a purple sky.

"You weren't addressed," said the guard behind him.

"My apologies," Ingle muttered.

Nathaniel rushed into the lord's arms, and in their comfort he sobbed uncontrollably. John patted his back and whispered comforting words, but his eyes remained drawn to where his missing arm should have been.

"Milord," said one of the guards, "we found him attacking another who had traveled with the boy, killing him before we could arrive. We've brought both here for you."

"You told me you were searching for a man," John said, looking to Oric. "Though you said he was merely a thief."

"And indeed he was," Oric said. Ingle beamed as his captain took his lie and ran with it. "We suspected him of taking Nathaniel from one of Lord Hadfield's caravans. Never could we have hoped we'd find him here, of course. Perhaps he had come to issue ransom?"

Nathaniel had begun shaking his head, and Ingle watched him carefully. A child's story against that of several men shouldn't matter, but one never knew. If only he'd keep his mouth shut, keep crying.

"I was told Nathaniel had died," John said. "Learned too late of the funeral, sadly. I was told they'd been given a body, by you in fact, Oric."

Oric licked his lips.

"We suspected too late it was another child. The body was badly burned, you see. When I thought it might be a trick to throw us off the kidnapper's trail, we went looking. We learned nothing worthwhile, not yet, so we've been keeping our reasons a secret. Don't want harmful rumors flying about, nor giving Alyssa false hope."

"He's lying," Nathaniel said. "Don't listen to them, he's lying! He was my friend, he killed my friend. He helped me!"

Oric's voice dropped lower.

"Men do strange things to boys in their capture. Given time, he might twist their head around, make them friendly. He needs rest. This all's clearly been too much for the lad."

"He called the stranger his pa when running to us," offered one of the guards.

John nodded, as this bit seemed to support what Oric was saying. He kept Nathaniel close, as if afraid he might lose him should he let go.

"What happened to your arm?" he asked.

"They said my arm got sick and had to be cut off."

"Who is they?"

Ingle's eyes widened. This might be tougher to explain. Maybe they could spin some blame onto that wife of his…

"She's just a filthy liar, that's all," Ingle said, ignoring Oric's glare. "Probably cut the arm off to torture him."

John's face darkened at this.

"She?" he asked.

Ingle opened his mouth, then closed it. He didn't know how to respond to that.

"Meant *he*," he said lamely.

"We discovered a lady who claimed her husband had Nathaniel," Oric said, trying his best to mend the situation but clearly fighting a losing battle. John's eyes had narrowed, and he had a look like a snake ready to strike. "That's how we knew to come here is all."

John patted the boy on the head and leaned closer to him. He whispered something, too quietly for Ingle to hear. Nathaniel whispered something back. When finished, John sank deeper in his chair.

"Take them into custody," he said to his guards.

"Wait," Ingle shouted. "You got things wrong!"

Men grabbed his arms and wrenched them painfully behind his back. It seemed like the very curtains had spawned armored guards. Oric reached for his sword, but the sheer number made him decide not to. One of the guards smashed his face with his fists, as if insulted Oric had even considered it.

"I wasn't there," Ingle shouted as he was yanked backward, but it only seemed to infuriate the lord more. "Oric was, he saw it all, I was just doing what I was told!"

"Bring him to me!" John roared, standing from his throne.

Two guards dragged Ingle across the carpet, then shoved him to his knees. A fist grabbed his hair and forced his head to bow reverently.

"I want you to watch this," Lord Gandrem said to Nathaniel. "You deserve it. With your arm as it is, you'll be living a hard road, and this is something you should always remember. This is how we treat the scum who dare strike against us."

"No," Ingle moaned as he felt his head pulled back. John held a beautiful sword, and he pressed its edge against his throat.

"Pull back the carpet," he said to his servants. "I don't want to stain it."

Ingle felt hollow fear building and building.

"Please," he begged. "I didn't do nothing, I didn't, I was just..."

They lifted him up, and when they set him back down, his feet touched smooth stone.

"You killed a good man," John said.

"Says who?"

"Says Nathaniel, and I trust his word over yours."

The sword moved. He felt pain, but when he gasped to scream, it was as if he'd been dunked underwater. His exhalation was a pitiful garble. His head swam, and he thought to faint, but still the guards held him upright. Until the darkness came, he watched John and Nathaniel watching him die. There was no mercy in either of their eyes.

Guardsman Mick trudged up the road away from the castle, having drawn the shortest straw of the lot. One of the men's horses remained standing on the path. The other had wandered off, and he grumbled and hoped it wouldn't be far. He'd have to stable them both, work out ownership, probably even send one or both back to whoever had originally owned them. Bunch of hassles. Of course there was also the body, which needed to be stripped of any valuables and then disposed of.

Deciding the horses could wait, Mick knelt beside the body, and he glanced around to see if anyone was watching. No one was, so he put a hand into the dead man's pockets, searching for loose coin. Of course, not all valuables needed to be handed over...

When the dead body let out a groan, Mick startled, fell back on his rump, and nearly soiled his armor. He closed his slack jaw, put a hand on the man's chest, and leaned close. Both were weak, but he felt the tremors of a heartbeat and heard the soft hiss of breath.

"Goddamn, you're a stubborn one," he said, unable to believe it. He took to his feet and ran toward the castle, crying out for a healer to make his way to the gate.

CHAPTER

23

Haern sat atop the roof of the Eschatons' home and watched the sun dip below the wall. His elbow rested upon his knee, his chin on his hand. Tarlak's words haunted him, and no matter how hard he tried he could not shake them from his head.

I don't care who you think you are, or how good you might be, he'd said. *You're a danger to me, and a danger to my sister. I made you an offer, and I won't go back on it now, but you better put some serious thought into it, because otherwise you're just a renegade killer with a vendetta. There's no reason to house you then, no point. How many more will come storming through my windows, come kicking down my doors? I'm terrified the secret's out, Haern, or it will be soon. What do you expect me to do? Fight for you? Protect you? Give me a reason. Any.*

Haern had none to offer. His neck had flushed, and he'd shook his head. What could he say? *I'm sorry a mercenary broke into your home, hurt you, your sister, and your friends, all while trying to find me?* He'd always thought he was so careful, but he'd slipped up as usual. What had Senke said? It didn't pay to be his friend. Yet again that remained painfully true.

He'd left, but lacked the heart to go far, so up to their rooftop he went. Part of it was because he didn't want to leave them, to say good-bye to Delysia and Senke forever. Part of him also feared that the giant man with the painted face might return, and if he did, Haern wanted to be there, waiting.

"Haern?"

He looked down from the roof to see Delysia peering up at him.

"Will you come down?" she asked. He shook his head. "Then can you help me up?"

Sighing, he grabbed the side of the roof with one hand and hung. He offered her his other hand and she took it, still trusting him for reasons he'd never understand. Using him as a guide she stepped on a window ledge, then with his aid jumped up to catch the roof. Once she had climbed all the way up, he swung himself up to join her.

"I think a set of stairs might be easier," she said, brushing off her priestess robes.

"And defeat the whole point of me coming up here," Haern said, immediately regretting it. Why should he snap at her? Her silence showed the comment stung, and he tried to think of something to say.

"Is Senke all right?" he asked.

"I stopped his internal bleeding, and I sealed the wound best I could. He'll be sore for days, but yes, he'll be fine."

He walked back to the center of the roof and sat down. She sat beside him, and immediately he felt himself pulled back to the past. Would Thren arrive once more, a crossbow in his hand?

"I'm sorry about my brother," she said. "He can be a bit of a hothead."

"No kidding. Why'd you join up with him, anyway? Mercenary work doesn't seem suited to you."

"Because he asked," she said, as if it should have been obvious. "When I left the priesthood they gave me back my father's wealth from their safekeeping. It wasn't much, not after it'd been used to settle my father's estates and debts. We used it to buy this place. Was all we could afford."

"But here?" Haern asked, gesturing about. "On the Crimson? You deserve someplace better. Someplace safer."

She shrugged. "My brother had a place he wanted, but the king refused to even hear his offer. It's no matter. I spent two years in the temple unable to leave for fear of Thren's anger. I'm used to keeping inside."

"It's not right," Haern said. She smiled at him.

"You living on the street is what isn't right. At least I have a warm bed, and a family to share my meals with. What do you have, Haern? What have you done over the years?"

He thought of his deals, his rumors, his ambushes in the night and days spent sleeping with the homeless and destitute.

"I tried to stop my father's war. I tried to kill until there'd be no one left to fight in his name. I failed."

She took his hand and held it.

"Don't be so hard on yourself. We all make mistakes. You once wanted something more, to understand a life beyond what your father taught you. I think you still do. But you won't find a new life in vengeance, Haern, only sadness and loneliness. You grew up alone, I could tell that immediately. You change nothing by remaining so."

Silence fell over them. He let it linger, trying to find the courage to ask what he needed to know.

"Do you hate me for killing?"

"No. I am not so naïve. I would like to live in a world where no killing was needed, but I fear I may never see it. I won't judge you for what you do, Haern. I can only try to be a light, and to shine as long as I can in a world that seems obsessed with darkness. If you need forgiveness, then know you have it from me, and from Ashhur. If you need guidance, ask, and I will do my best to answer. I'll heal your wounds, and pray for you before I lay my head down to sleep. I won't hate you. How could you ever think so?"

He felt like a child, and he clutched her hand tight. She shifted so she might sit next to him, and her head rested against his shoulder.

"All those years," she said softly. "Where did you sleep? Where did you live?"

"On the streets," Haern said, feeling uncomfortable speaking of it with her, but forcing himself to anyway.

"Even in winter? How did you survive the cold?"

"Thousands do so in this city every year. In that, I was nothing special."

"I doubt many of those thousands did so by choice. You *are* special, Haern. Pretending otherwise is pointless. Why would you endure that? Why not flee, why not become anything else?"

"Because I…" Haern paused. He wanted to answer her truthfully, but that also meant knowing what he himself believed. "Because I couldn't let my father win. And not just my father. The whole damn underworld that rose up to swallow you, me, and everything else good in this city. I learned the true face of this city, who operates it, who controls what. And then I did everything I could to slowly tear it all down."

Delysia shifted closer to him, and he felt her arms wrap around his.

"I'm sorry," she whispered. "You must have been so alone."

Again that discomfort, that shame for all he'd done. He didn't like it. He'd endured the years with a single-minded purpose, a desire for revenge that felt pure enough to justify his squalid conditions, his brutality, his entire purpose for existing. The last thing he wanted was to have light shine upon that darkness.

"Will you go out tonight?" Haern asked her, wishing to change the subject. "You and your mercenaries, I mean."

"No," Delysia said, shaking her head. "Tarlak didn't understand the magnitude of what was going on when he first agreed. Our fault for not being part of the mercenary guild, I guess. We gave one night, and that is all Alyssa will get from us." She paused. "Will you?"

Haern let out a sigh.

"I think I will. I have some part to play in all of this, whether I want it or not."

She pulled back and gently took his injured elbow into her hands. For the first time he truly looked at her, and he saw how tired she was, the whites of her eyes rimmed with angry veins. Still she closed her eyes, took a deep breath, and began praying. Soft light shone from her fingers, and he felt their healing magic pour into his elbow. Several minutes later she stopped. The pain had become a vague ache, like a sore muscle, but little else. He flexed the elbow twice, and it felt strong enough for combat.

"I should go," she said. "It's not safe for me out here after dark."

"Please," he said, taking her hand. "Just...sit with me a while longer. You're safe at my side. I promise."

He saw the look on her face, and he wished he could understand what it was she thought. Her hesitation was brief, and then she sat back down. Her arms wrapped around him, and he allowed his own eyes to close. It was only with her that he relaxed, all other times a coiled spring. But there, with her, he felt able to let it go. He had nothing to hide, and no reason to. Together they watched the sun sink farther, until it was nothing but a glow peeking over the wall.

"Help me down," she said at last. "Senke wants you to see him. He seemed certain you wouldn't be staying tonight, yet would still be close. I think he knows you better than I."

"He understands the world I came from. Tonight will be worse, for everyone. I think he knows that."

The rest were eating when the two came in. Brug and Tarlak seemed to act as if he weren't there, but Senke greeted him warmly enough.

"Follow me," he said, leading Haern to a closet built into a space underneath the stairs. He pulled out a wooden crate, wincing at the effort. Feeling guilty, Haern ordered him aside and pried open the crate himself. Inside were an assortment of weapons, from knives to two-handed swords.

"I saw your fight with that mercenary," Senke explained. "That cloakdance thing you did was something special, puts Norris Vel to shame, I'll tell you that. But your swords weren't right for it at all. Here, take these."

He lifted a pair of weapons out and handed them over. They were long and slender, with the ends gently curved.

"These sabers are designed for slashing, and should do well with how you're always moving. The points are sharp, but you'll still have a hard time thrusting through heavier armor. Same with heavy chops, but I have a feeling brute force isn't your usual method, given your speed."

Haern swung the swords about, getting a feel for their weight. They were lighter than his previous swords, with a slightly longer reach. Their grips were comfortable, making them feel natural, like an extension of his body when he wielded them. He could tell they were expertly made.

"Thank you," he said.

"Don't thank me. Thank Brug over there. He made them."

"Just don't break 'em," Brug muttered from the table.

"Both sides will be out for blood tonight," Senke said, leaning against a wall and holding a hand against his stomach. "You sure you have to go out? People will kill each other just fine without your help."

He realized they were all looking at him, either blatantly or from the corners of their eyes. In his heart he felt something harden, as if he wanted to prove them wrong, to show he didn't care what they thought. But what did it matter? Why *did* he go out? What might he accomplish? Deathmask's biting words returned to him, mocking him in his mind.

You spent five years trying to single-handedly conquer the thief guilds. Yet you want to mock my *imagination?*

Something clicked in his head, several pieces tumbling together as the idea took form. He looked to them, then out the window. No, there was nothing out there for him, not this night. Come the day, he'd find Deathmask, assuming he still lived. Perhaps there was a chance to have a legacy that was the opposite of his father's.

"You know," he said, feeling a great weight lift off his shoulders. "I think I will stay here tonight, if you'll have me."

"Pull a seat up at the table," Senke said with a smile. "You bet your ass we will."

"Are you prepared to do what must be done?" Deathmask asked her.

"I am," said Veliana.

"You'll have to kill many of them. They were once your friends, your guildmates. Maybe you even considered them family. They won't understand, and their loyalties are anyone's guess. This is Garrick's guild, and you're nothing but a feeble woman who got in his way. Last time I ask. Can you stick a knife in them, every one of those familiar faces?"

"Not so familiar anymore," she said. She tapped her sickly, bloodied eye. "Too many hate me for this. I've heard their whispers, their insults of my ugly mark. They never loved me, not like they loved James Beren. This guild may or may not be mine, but more than ever I know it should not be Garrick's. If he sold his soul to Thren, then he betrayed every shred of James's memory. Anyone who stays at his side is no friend of mine."

Deathmask smiled at her.

"I want to do something for you," he said. "This will take just a moment, but I hope you'll appreciate it."

He put a finger to his eye, the same as Veliana's injured one, and then whispered the words of a spell. They seemed simple enough, and then came the change. His iris bloomed from a dark brown to a bloody red.

"This is what I think of your ugly mark," he said. "I'll proudly bear it so long as you stay with me. I will never cast aside your loyalty, for I've been cast aside enough in my own life."

Veliana felt strangely touched by the gesture.

"One day," she said, "I hope to believe you."

They turned their attention to the unassuming building before them. The rooms appeared dark, but both knew of the expansion belowground, no doubt housing the last remnants of the Ash Guild. A few men and women wandered past them on the streets, several with dead eyes and drunken gaits. To Veliana it seemed the entire city was suffering a massive hangover, a crude comparison given how many of her kind had been mercilessly butchered. So far Deathmask hadn't explained how he planned on dealing with all the mercenaries, but she had no choice but to trust him. Patting her daggers, she told him to lead the way.

"Keep your hood low," he told her as they approached the door. "Surprise is everything. Theatrics can turn even the most ordinary of foes into something fearsome, and you are no ordinary foe."

A single thief leaned against the door, looking like he'd been up for two days straight. Through bleary eyes he watched their arrival, recognizing Deathmask when they were almost within striking distance.

"Hey, we thought Thren—"

Veliana cut his throat before he finished the sentence. As his body fell, she glanced to Deathmask, and her meaning was clear. *Look what I can do. Do not fear my loyalty. They are no longer friends of mine.*

"Atta girl," he said, his mismatched eyes sparkling behind his mask.

When she tried the door, it was both locked and barred. Deathmask gently moved her aside, put his hands upon the wood, and closed his eyes.

"Theatrics," he whispered.

His hands shimmered between red and black, and then the door exploded inward in a great shower of splinters, accompanied by a shock wave that thumped against Veliana's chest with enough force to make her catch her breath. Deathmask stepped through the dust and debris into a small entry room. Two men sat in chairs on either side of the doorway, their hands over their faces. Specks of blood dotted their clothes: damage from the shrapnel. Veliana rushed the one on the right, thrusting a dagger into his chest before he could react. Deathmask waved a hand at the other, who suddenly dropped to his knees, gagging. Before she could see the total effects of the spell, Veliana stabbed his heart.

"Sometimes quick is better," she said.

So far it seemed their arrival had gone unnoticed by those farther in, hidden behind a second door. Deathmask pushed it open, and they stepped into the last remnants of the Ash Guild, all gathered from the various corners of Veldaren. There were twenty of them, sitting on chairs and pillows and looking miserable. Veliana felt both anguish and elation at seeing Garrick among them. Part of her had hoped he'd died in the fire, for he deserved nothing better, but at least his survival meant that he would be hers, all hers.

"Members of the Ash," Deathmask said, screening Veliana with his body. He wanted to maximize the impact of revealing her, she knew. A smirk crossed her lips. They all thought her dead, Garrick included. How his mouth would drop, how his eyes would go wide...All around, the thieves stood and drew their weapons, for though Deathmask was one of them, there was something dangerous about his arrival, in the way he walked, the way he addressed them.

"You," Garrick said, pointing a shaking finger. "You turned the Spiders against us, didn't you? Why else would they let you live?"

"I am not the one who went into bed with the spider thinking I might not get bitten," Deathmask said. "This destruction is your doing, all your doing. Listen to me, guildmembers! He sold your souls to Thren Felhorn, all so he might sleep well at night."

"You lie!"

About a third of the men around them were exchanging glances, and their daggers and clubs lowered. Veliana watched and waited. She had to be fast. The first attacker needed to die immediately if she was to discourage the rest. When it came to a battle of personalities between Deathmask and Garrick, there would be no contest. At some point Garrick would call an end to it before he lost completely.

"How else would you have maintained leadership?" Deathmask asked. "Why else would the guilds have made peace with you, even though your position was weak? Weeks ago you made your pact, and one by one the other guilds realized and left you alone. Only the Hawks attacked, and only once. Thren punished them severely for that, didn't he?"

More mumblings about them. A couple glared at Garrick. These were the rumblings of treason, Veliana knew. Normally such accusations would be whispered from ear to ear, allowed to fester and grow. But the Trifect had pressed too hard. If they were to survive, they needed new leadership, and now.

"I don't know what you're talking about," Garrick said. He had drawn his dagger, but it remained at his side, as if he was afraid to even point it at Deathmask.

"Come now. We all know whose guild this truly was, before it was Thren's. It was Veliana's, not yours, never yours. That is why you wanted her dead."

Louder grumblings, though many were disparaging her. She felt anger simmer in her heart. Even now they would deny her work, her sweat, her toil. The gods damn them all.

"She died because she tried to kill you, that's all," Garrick said.

Veliana stepped to Deathmask's side and pulled her hood

back. She smiled, and the look on Garrick's face was everything she'd hoped it'd be.

"I never died," she said. Her voice was soft, but even a whisper could have been heard in that suddenly quiet room. "But you will, you traitor. You sold your soul to Thren. I can never forgive you."

She flung herself at him, not caring for her safety, nor the guild's greater numbers. She would have his head, and this time no one would stop her. Garrick cried out for aid, and several thieves jumped in her way. Spinning away from a club, she gutted one on her left, rolled along the ground, and hamstrung another as she stood. The one with the club tried to smash her back, but she twirled again, her spine bending at an unnatural angle so the swing passed above her breasts. And then she was up again, stabbing him repeatedly, kicking away his corpse with seven bleeding holes in his chest.

"Make your choice!" Deathmask cried out. It seemed many had. They turned on the others, striking at those who moved toward him. The room was now in chaos, and within it Veliana thrived. She kicked out the legs of one rushing for Deathmask, burying a dagger in his ribs as his body hit the ground. Pulling it free, she flicked blood off it toward Garrick, who stood with his back to the wall, his dagger held before him.

"Where's Thren to protect you now?" she asked as she stalked him, her daggers hungry in her hands. "Where's the men who would rather rape me than serve under my leadership? Where's your *guild*, Garrick?"

A blinding flash burst from behind her, a spell of some sort from Deathmask. In its light she rushed Garrick, her knee leading. It slammed into his crotch while she swatted away his dagger. Her other dagger's hilt struck his forehead. She rammed an elbow into his mouth, then slashed across his face when she pulled back. Blood spurted from a gash across the bridge of his nose. His cry of pain was a garbled, weak thing.

"Now you're the example," she whispered to him. She stabbed her dagger into his throat, twisted it left, then right, and finally yanked it free. Blood splashed across her chest, but she didn't mind. At his death much of the chaos slowed, for it seemed there was little point left in fighting. She glanced around and saw all eyes upon either her or Deathmask. Only ten remained of the initial twenty.

"Those who would betray their loyalties deserve nothing less," Deathmask said, kneeling beside Garrick's body. He put a hand on the head, which burst into flame. The body blackened and smoked, and in seconds it was nothing but a pile of ash. Taking a handful, Deathmask stood and flung it into the air. It revolved around his head, hiding his visage, making him look like some strange monster instead of a man.

"I am the Ash now. None of you are worthy of my leadership. You killed for me, and for that I spare your lives. Begone. Throw down your colors, or prepare to have them stained with your own blood."

It seemed none there had the will to challenge the blood-soaked Veliana and her master. Her heart felt a pang at their exit, feeling like the last remnants of the guild she and James had built were gone, but Deathmask had promised her something greater, and she had to trust him. She scanned those exiting, looking for a set of faces, men who had remained out of the fight like the sensible opportunists they were.

"Nien, Mier," she said as they left. "You two, stay."

The twins looked back. They had pale skin, dark hair, and brown eyes that seemed to twinkle with subdued amusement.

"Yes?" they said.

Deathmask approached them, and he offered his hand.

"Veliana has vouched for your skills. Would you remain with me, and fight not for the Ash Guild that was, but for what it might yet be?"

The two glanced about the room, as if to point out the obvious to them.

"What guild?" Mier asked.

"There are only us four," said Nien.

"And as long as the four of us live, there will always be an Ash Guild," Deathmask said. "You have seen what we can do. Join us. We need your strength tonight. The mercenaries must be shown that we will not roll over and die for them."

The twins shared a look, and Veliana swore some sort of mental conversation was going on between them that she was not privy to. Then they accepted Deathmask's offered hand and shook it.

"Why not?"

"Could be fun."

"Indeed," Deathmask said, grinning behind his mask of cloth and ash. Veliana shook her head, wiped the blood clean from her daggers. She spit on what little was left of Garrick's remains.

CHAPTER 24

In the dark of Felwood's dungeon Oric shivered. He sat on a wood cot and listened to the water drip. Where it dripped he didn't know. To pass the time he'd tried to guess, but the echo always seemed to change on him. His cell was completely dark, without a single shred of light. He'd scoured the floor with his palms, but everywhere he touched was wet, and a drop never landed upon him. Still, the search did better to pass the time than thinking about his fate. Anytime he thought of that, or of how long he might be in total darkness, his head swam and his heart lurched into his throat.

He'd tried talking to anyone else, a guard or fellow prisoner, but his voice only echoed through the emptiness, never answered. For some reason that always made it worse. Without light, company, or a single meal, time was meaningless. At least two times he slept, and in his dreams he saw color, women, friends. He wished he could sleep more often.

A loud creak startled him from a doze. Heavy footsteps echoed down the hall. Orange and yellow flickered along the walls, at first a wonderful sight but soon painful in their brightness. Holding a hand before his eyes to block the pain, he felt a wretched sight as John Gandrem stepped in, soldiers at his side.

"Stay seated," he said, "otherwise my guards will open you up in many places."

"But a man should always rise at the arrival of a lord," Oric said. He held back a cough. His voice felt scratchy, dry. He remained sitting despite his protest. Given how light his head felt, he thought he'd pass out if he stood too quickly.

John crossed his arms and looked down at him. In the yellow light John's skin seemed like stone, old and unmalleable. His eyes looked even worse. For all the stories Oric had heard of Lord Gandrem's kindness, he'd yet to hear a story describe those eyes. Mercy didn't belong in them, not now, maybe not ever. Perhaps this was the lord of the dungeon, a different man from the lord of Felwood.

"Before we start, there's a few things you should know," Gandrem began. "First, I have talked extensively with the boy, Nathaniel. His story is consistent, and most damning. Second, the man Ingle thought he killed, the farmer Matthew, is not dead. Third, my men have already worked over Uri, and how he *sang*, Oric. I know what you did to that farmer's wife. The idea that you could claim they assaulted a caravan and held Nathaniel hostage is laughable."

"I never claimed it. That was Ingle's stupid idea."

The faintest hint of a smile stretched at Lord Gandrem's lips, but then vanished.

"Perhaps. A shame I cut his throat before I could tell him the farmer lived. I plan on ensuring Matthew is well rewarded, as is his wife. But the question remains now, what do I do with you?"

"Well, between the rope and the ax, I think I'd prefer the ax."

"In time, Oric. In time. See, my biggest problem is not with you, but with your master, Arthur Hadfield. Mark Tullen visited me before meeting with you and Nathaniel in Tyneham. I know he was escorting the boy back, and I'm not a damn fool. Everyone knows he was a potential suitor of Alyssa, and Arthur wanted him gone. Proving that, however, is another matter."

His soldiers rushed in and grabbed Oric by either arm. Up went his hands, back and above his head. Chains rattled, and then he felt clamps tighten about his wrists. With him safely shackled, John sat on the small cot and pulled his heavy coat tighter about him.

"Now I don't mean proving it to just Alyssa," he continued. "She's a bright gal, and there's too much here for her to ignore. However, Arthur's long held those mines at the edge of my lands, always refusing to pay taxes. I want those lands. It is my knights that have protected them. It is my lands his traders travel across to Veldaren. It is on my roads he ships his gold and sends for his supplies. By all rights they should be mine, and would have been if not for the Gemcrofts."

"What could I possibly have to do with that?" Oric asked. His shoulders were starting to cramp, and he had a creeping feeling it was about to get a whole lot worse...especially if they left him like this for several hours, if not days.

"King Vaelor has rejected every claim of mine for taxes, no doubt because he fears the Trifect more than he fears me. That, and their bribes. But Arthur has no heir, and he's never written a will in case he does have a son. If he dies as such, his lands will be joined with the closest lord's."

"You," Oric said, starting to understand. If Arthur died before marrying Alyssa, then the land would become John's. "But you aren't the one holding Arthur. Alyssa is. And if she finds out..."

"If she finds out, then she'll force him to return the lands to her," said John. "But she'll only do that if she discovers what happened. Now do you understand? I hold all the control here. Arthur won't dare challenge me about your deaths, for the truth gets him killed. He can only keep his mouth shut and pray for the best. I, however..."

Oric tried to flex his back, but he was held too closely to the wall. He rolled his neck back and forth, and it popped loudly. Minutes. It'd only been minutes, but he already wanted out. Far better to shiver freely on the floor than sit unable to move half his body. He didn't want to think about hours. Or days. Or, gods forbid, years.

"I hold Arthur's life in my hands, and yours as well," said John. "I might have used Uri for this, but he didn't take well to my low servants' questionings. We had to ensure he spoke the truth, of course. So it is down to you. Where do your loyalties lie, Oric? You deserve death, we both know this. What might you do to be spared that fate? Help me, or otherwise...you said it yourself: rope or ax."

Oric couldn't believe his luck. He'd thought that he'd have nothing of value to offer, but if he could roll on his former master and somehow escape with his own head...

"What is it you want from me?" he asked.

"I need you to kill Arthur before he can discover things have gone awry, and before Alyssa might realize his involvement. Before you do, I want you to sign a statement I might use in the king's court detailing every bit of your, and Arthur's, involvement."

"What do I do once I kill Arthur?" Oric asked. "What happens then?"

This time the lord did smile.

"A man of your talents? Surely you could disappear into a crowd afterward, and then, well...Ker's a long way away, and Mordan even farther. I also hear the sailors in Angelport often need a good sellsword aboard their ships."

"What about the farmer?"

"He's injured, and my healers say it will take several days for him to recover. We should have this concluded before he can be of any concern. Besides, these matters are far above his station, and his word in any court would be suspect at best, being just a low-birth simpleton."

It couldn't get any better. Oric was hardly afraid of a little travel, and killing Arthur would be no skin off his nose. Given the nature of his mission, it'd only be natural they go somewhere quiet to talk, and after a bit of knifework he'd have his freedom.

"I'll do it," Oric said.

"Excellent. We'll claim you escaped the dungeon after we extracted your confession. When you went to Arthur, he tried to cut ties and claim everything was your plan. You killed him and fled, and to where, I don't want to know. Is this understood?"

"It is."

"I'll have a servant down here with candles and parchment. Tell him everything you know, every possible detail. Farewell, Oric."

He stood and left, and to Oric's great relief John had his guards remove the clamps at his wrists before he went. True to John's word, an elderly man with a crooked nose arrived.

"The beginning, please," he said, dipping his quill into an inkwell.

So Oric told him, starting with Arthur's thieving from the Gemcroft mines and smuggling the coin to the Serpent Guild for laundering.

"Will you truly let him go?" asked one of the soldiers walking alongside John, a veteran and trusted knight named Cecil.

"Of course not," the lord snapped. "The Gemcrofts have had

those mines tied up in legal protection for over a century. I could wipe out half their family, their extended family, Arthur included, and they'd still find someone besides myself to be legal heir. To be truthful, I don't even want them. Giant hassle, all of it."

"Then why the ruse?"

"I need his confession, quick, truthful, and most importantly damning to Arthur. I'll be sending you to Veldaren with that confession in your hands, along with a letter of my own."

Cecil bowed to show he was honored.

"Will we not be bringing Nathaniel back to his mother?" he asked as they exited the dungeon, doused their torch, and headed toward the mess hall.

"Nathaniel was already abducted once on the road, and when he should have been in my care, no less. My own damn foolishness for trusting that snake, Arthur. I will keep him here, and in safety, until Alyssa comes for him. But you... you can let Alyssa know of his survival. She's a bright lady, but Arthur has a way with words, and who knows what lies he has spun about her to protect himself? That confession should burn them all away, and if she is who I think she is, she'll deal with him accordingly. Let me get some food into these old bones, and then I'll pen my letter. When you have mine and Oric's, ride hard to Veldaren. If Arthur suspects something's amiss, I fear he will make a move against her."

"Of course, milord," Cecil said, bowing again. "What of Oric?"

John grinned.

"He said he preferred the ax, so prepare the gallows. He deserves nothing, not even the choice of his own death. Let him hang from my walls, the honorless bastard."

CHAPTER

25

For a second night Alyssa watched the city burn from her window. There were more fires now, at least seven she could see. She wondered what it meant. Were her mercenaries finding more of the thieves' ratholes? She held an empty glass in her hand, and she toasted the stars, which were hidden behind a blanket of smoke.

"You deserve better, Nathaniel," she whispered.

"I too can think of better homages for your son," Zusa said, having slipped inside without making a noise. Alyssa had trained herself not to jump at Zusa's voice, but still she quivered, her nerves frayed.

"Perhaps," she said as the woman came to her side. "But this is the best I can do."

"You lie to yourself. This is for you, your hurt. Do what you must, but do it in truth, and bear the burden proudly."

"Enough," Alyssa said, hurling her glass against the window. It shattered, small flecks of red wine dripping down to the floor. "I don't need speeches. I don't need your wisdom. I need my son back, my little boy..."

She pressed her head against the glass and refused to break. As the tears ran down her face she stared at the distant fires and tried to revel in the bloodshed they represented. But she only felt hollow.

"As you wish," she heard Zusa say.

"Stay," she whispered, knowing the faceless woman would leave her.

"As you wish."

"Tell me, how goes it out there?"

Zusa gestured to the city. "The thieves are ready, more than they were last night. They started those fires, and they've killed many innocents. I think they're hoping to turn the people against the king, and it might work. If Veldaren is an altar, you've covered it in blood as a sacrifice to your son. I don't know which god will honor it, though. Perhaps they've both washed their hands of this miserable city."

Alyssa nodded. It sounded right. She had opened up her coffers and replaced their stores of gold with bodies of the dead. Was it a fair trade? Could it ever be?

"What about the one who killed my son?" she asked.

Zusa thought of her fight with him, and how she'd been stopped at the last minute by Veliana's insistence. What the other woman wanted with him she didn't know, nor did she care. Veliana had sacrificed their friendship to take him from her and Alyssa. If that was all she was worth, then so be it. But she didn't want to let Alyssa know how close she'd come to taking the Watcher back to her, as much as she hated to lie. So she stretched the truth as far as it would go.

"I fought him," she admitted. "But he escaped before I reached victory. Where he is now, I do not know."

"Did you hurt him?"

"Yes. I drew blood."

"Good. At least that's a start. Will you go out again before the night is over?"

Zusa put a wrapped hand upon the glass and stared out. Slowly she shook her head.

"No. There's nothing out there, just men killing one another. I think even the Watcher has stepped back to let it run its course. May I leave?"

Alyssa nodded. When Zusa was halfway to the door she stopped and glanced back. She looked as tired as Alyssa felt.

"If I may be so bold, I have a request. Make this the last night, Alyssa. Killing doesn't cover the pain of loss. It'll only drain you, leave you empty. I do not pretend that these men deserve mercy, not all of them... but this path you've chosen will only lead to ruin. Even if it does, I will follow you into it, even unto death."

"I don't know if I can stop this," Alyssa said.

"You're strong enough, Lady Gemcroft. I know it."

And with that she left, the door closing with a soft click of wood. Alyssa watched the fires, but it seemed she could no longer keep her mind upon them. She felt tired, and she often thought of returning to her bed. She hadn't slept well lately, maybe a few hours at most. All throughout the day men and women had come to her, claiming damages for what her mercenaries had done. Near the end she had paid every claim, whether its validity could be proven or not. She hadn't had the energy left to care. At last she'd delegated the responsibility to Bertram.

As if thinking his name had summoned him, the old man opened the door, then knocked on it after the fact.

"Yes, Bertram?" she said, keeping her face to the window so

he couldn't see her tears. "If this is about the cost of damages and repairs, spare me. I am in no mood, and you should be asleep in any case."

"As should you as well," Bertram said, quietly approaching. "But it seems sleep is a difficult thing for most of us in these troubled times. I've come to discuss a different matter."

"And what is that?"

She could see his reflection in the glass, and she watched him chew his lower lip while he clasped his hands behind his back.

"I've gone over the mercenaries' pay, along with our promised payments to the citizens, and the total is..."

"I told you I had no interest," she snapped.

"It's more than that," Bertram said, doing his best to keep his tone soothing and controlled. "I did as you requested, and treated cost as no object, but I feared the folly, and as I feared, it has come to pass. The cost has been unbelievable, especially with how many have died. The guild requires extra compensation for men who fall in the line of duty, for wives, children, mistresses, and the like. Plus the fires were more than we expected, and you have accepted blame for nearly all cases."

"Your point?" she asked.

He stood up straighter as he spoke.

"We have nothing left, Lady Gemcroft. Your fortune is spent. Unless we delay payments for several years, we will default on at least a third of the mercenaries, and aid with only half of the repairs."

Her mouth dropped open.

"Are you certain?"

He nodded. "I have checked multiple times."

She saw the fires burning before her, and suddenly they took on a different meaning.

"Is that counting tonight?"

"For the mercenaries, yes, but not necessarily any extra for the dead, since I cannot know for certain until tomorrow. But not the fires, no. I can only assume the worst."

She felt her whole world spiraling away from her. How could all her wealth have vanished so quickly? It didn't seem possible. Of course the mines in the north had lessened in their production over the past year, but still, what of their contracts, their trade? Had the thief guilds truly destroyed so much?

"All is not lost," he said, sliding closer and wrapping a comforting arm around her shoulders. "I have thought of a way to help ease this burden. We still may delay some payments, especially for those who died without families or still have means to survive."

"What is it?" she asked.

"Lord Hadfield has an extensive amount of wealth saved up, an amount he hoped to bequeath to an eventual heir. If you were to marry, he would assume your debts. I have already discussed the matter, and he is willing to do his part to help you move on from your son's death, including this debacle you have unleashed upon our city."

She crossed her arms and held them against her as if she were cold. Could she marry Arthur? True, he'd been kind since he arrived, and he seemed to have no intention of leaving. They'd shared a bed, even, and with him she did feel some measure of comfort. Her heart ached for Mark, but he was gone, as was her son. Should she continue to let that haunt her? Maybe Zusa was right. Maybe it was time to end all of it.

"When?" she finally asked.

"It will need to be soon, especially given how deep our debt is. If we make significant payments we can hold our debtors at bay, as well as convince them we have every intention of making good on our promises. Leon Connington will help if you ask. No member of the Trifect would let another fall so far as to bring shame upon them as well. Perhaps in a few days I can have the ceremonies prepared, and all the proper documents written and presented before the king's council for approval."

There was something chipper about his tone that scraped against her spine like metal on glass.

"Enough," she said. "Start on whatever you must, but don't tell Arthur anything other than that I am open to the idea. He should at least be the one to propose, not my father's old advisor."

Bertram smiled. "Quite right, quite right. Good night, milady. Perhaps soon you will finally have pleasant dreams."

"Good night, Bertram."

Once he was gone she blew out her candles, returned to her bed, and tried to sleep. She couldn't.

"Arthur Gemcroft," she whispered, moving the name about her tongue as if trying to taste it. He would adopt her last name, as all men and women did when entering into a family of the Trifect.

"Arthur Gemcroft. Arthur…Gemcroft."

It had a ring to it, she had to admit. She'd put off marriage for long enough. It was time for her to be practical. Still, as much sense as it made, it gave no comfort, and she tossed and turned until the morning light shone through her curtains, falling upon her haggard face and bloodshot eyes.

The wound in Ghost's leg was worse than he'd originally feared. Without much reason to join the night's slaughter, he'd instead languished in his favorite tavern, drowning himself in alcohol to dull his pain. He'd passed out, and no one had had the nerve to wake him. Finally he'd returned to his squalid inn, carefully put his weapons aside, and then collapsed onto his bed. The windows had no shutters or curtains, and the light streamed in upon his face. The dressings on his leg, haphazard at best, had soaked through, and he feared it was now infected.

As he lay there he felt the pain crawling its way up his thigh, as if it were a spider scurrying through his veins. If he didn't do something soon he'd lose use of the knee, if not the entire leg. He wouldn't be the best anymore. He wouldn't even be a threat. A man of his strength, his skill, was not meant to be a cripple. Surely the gods did not intend such a fate for him.

The gods...

Ghost rolled off the bed, putting all his weight on his good leg. Damn that priestess. The Watcher had been his, thoroughly beaten. He didn't give a shit that he'd appeared wounded and weaponless. Assassinations, by their very nature, were unfair. But he'd been a fool to let her tend to the wounded Senke. He'd thought her too young to be a threat, but how wrong he'd been.

"It's not the big snakes you need to fear," he remembered a friend telling him once as they crossed the grasslands toward Veldaren. "It's the tiny ones who carry the real venom. Put that on your darts if you want a sure kill."

The priestess was the tiny snake, the insignificant one among the wizard and warriors. Stupid. Stupid!

He took a hobbled step toward a large dresser full of clothes and outfits. Leaning against it for support, he yanked out the top drawer, letting it crash to the floor. Reaching into the hole where it had been, he pulled out a small bag of coin. It'd have to do. Retrieving his swords, he opened the door and stepped out into the painful morning light.

Twice on the way to the temple he collapsed, his knee unable to bear his weight. A black bruise swelled across it, and the pus where the Watcher's sword had cut him was turning green. No one paid him any attention, the crowd flowing to either side as if he were an overturned cart, or a dead body.

Reaching the temple offered Ghost little comfort. He still had to climb the many steps, a fact made no easier given their ruined state after the spell their high priest had cast the previous night. After the first few Ghost gave up any pretense of pride. He sat down upon them, put his back to the temple, and pushed himself up one at a time. At the top he braced himself on a pillar and used it to keep his balance while he stood. Men and women gathered about the wooden doors, crying out for aid. No doubt the temple was swarming with people inside as well. He'd seen the fires, heard the sounds of combat flowing up and down the streets. The thieves had put up a fight this time, firing arrows from the rooftops and preparing a hundred ambushes.

He pushed his way through them, the wound in his leg meaning nothing to his enormous arms. Most turned to glare at him, then decided otherwise seeing his size and painted face. Once inside the temple he leaned against a wall and surveyed the madness. Priests and priestesses of all ages were running about. They looked like white bees zipping from flower to flower. They'd kneel, exchange a word, maybe say a prayer, and then move on. The older ones lingered, and he saw many put their hands on wounds and whisper words of prayer to Ashhur. White light would cover their hands, sometimes weak, sometimes strong, and then sink into the wound. That was what he needed. Faithful or not, he wouldn't deny that the priests had their uses. But he wouldn't risk some juvenile treating him. He wanted a master, someone who knew what he was doing.

"Where is Calan?" he asked as he grabbed an elderly priestess, her face a circular web of wrinkles.

"Busy," she said, giving him a reproachful glare. She didn't seem the slightest bit unnerved by his size or skin.

"Bring him," he said, refusing to let go despite her tugging to.break free. "He owes me one. Tell him Ghost is here, and that I'm the one who saved this damn temple from the mob two nights ago."

She looked him up and down, and though it seemed impossible her frown grew deeper.

"I'll see if I can find him," she said, then hurried on her way. He leaned back against the wall and closed his eyes. If he could ignore every noise, every visual distraction, he could focus on the pain, and doing so made him feel better. His temples throbbed with each pulse, but he kept it under control. He felt the pain's limits, how far it stretched throughout his leg. Time passed, and he was dimly aware of it.

"I see you've returned," a man's voice said. Ghost stirred to see Calan standing before him. He looked tired, with dark circles under his eyes and his smile forced. "May I ask why you've given us the pleasure?"

In answer, Ghost pulled up his pant leg to reveal the wound. He winced when he saw it himself. The purple bruise had spread, and the green pus was filling up his bandage. Calan's smile immediately vanished, and he grabbed Ghost's arm.

"This way," he said. "You need a bed, now."

Ghost wanted to protest but didn't. He'd hoped for a bit of healing magic, and then off he'd be. Instead he obeyed without argument, for his head ached, his stomach was doing loops, and he felt intensely drained. It was as if the pain were a fire burning away his energy. Calan led him through the maze of people and pews. His head swiveled, but he saw no opening, no space available. Muttering, he turned Ghost toward the back, then through a door to a modest room. It had a small desk, a bookshelf, and a bed, and it was that bed Calan set him upon.

"My quarters will have to do," the priest said. "Though I fear the bed might be small for you."

"A bed's a bed," Ghost mumbled.

"I suppose you're right."

"Here." He tossed the small bag of coins to pay for his treatment. "Save my leg, will you?"

Calan rolled up the pant leg, carefully folding it over and over until it was up to his thigh. Ghost closed his eyes. For some strange reason he didn't want to watch. He didn't want to understand what the priest would do, or what its implications were. Gods were for other people, not him. Gold and killing, that was god enough for him. He heard whispers, undoubtedly prayers, so he leaned his head back and tried to relax. The pain continued to throb, its reach growing. He felt it down to his shin, as if instead of giving him a single cut, the Watcher had beaten and smashed his whole leg with a club.

A strange sound met his ears. It was like a soft breeze blowing past the entrance of a cave, yet deeper, fuller. Even through his closed eyelids he saw the light flare. When it plunged into his leg it was like fire. He clutched the sides of the bed and clenched his teeth. His nostrils flared as he breathed in and out.

"The infection is deep," he heard Calan say. "Bear with me, Ghost. I know you're strong. You will endure."

More prayers, and another burst of light. This time when it plunged into him there was no feeling of fire, only a cold numbness that spread with alarming speed. He worried that if it reached his lungs he'd never breathe again. It stopped at his thigh, though, and then seemed to shrink back in on itself. With its retreat he realized he felt no pain, even when the coldness left his leg entirely.

"What did you do?" he asked, daring to open his eyes.

"What you wanted me to do," Calan said, looking down at him. "What else?"

The priest resumed his prayers, and as his hands hovered over Ghost's knee, the flesh began to knit itself together, forming a pale scar on his dark skin. When finished, Calan took a step back and more collapsed than sat with his weight pressed against the door. His head thumped against the wood, and it seemed those dark circles had worsened.

"A long two days," he said, as if to himself.

"Blame the Trifect," Ghost said.

"I blame no one. Have no reason. Some days are long, and some painfully short. Must say, I do prefer the calmer ones to this, however."

Ghost chuckled, but he didn't have the strength to continue. Drowsiness was stealing over him. He'd only slept a few hours in the tavern, and it'd hardly been deep or comforting. The pain had found him even in his dreams.

"I think I'll sleep now," he said.

And then he did. His sleep was deep, dark, and strangely without dreams. When he awoke he felt as if an immense amount of time had passed. His leg felt worlds better, though he was still hesitant to bend it. What if it was all an illusion, and the pain would return tenfold when he finally tested it? Rubbing his eyes with his hand, he shook his head to speed up his waking. He found himself alone in the room.

When he put his weight on his knee, it buckled and gave completely. He caught himself on the bed and collapsed back atop it.

"What the fuck?" he asked, then felt guilty for cursing in the middle of a temple. It was a silly feeling, but still his neck flushed. He stretched his arms and back, then settled in. What should he do now? It wasn't like he was in any real danger, and he'd already paid for the bed and healing. The only thing nagging at his mind was the Watcher. He needed another confrontation, one without those annoying mercenaries getting in the way. How could he manage it? And would the Watcher be foolish enough to return to that building, return to where he knew others might find him? What he knew about the Watcher could be written on a pebble. The man might still be with the Eschatons, or he might be halfway to Ker.

Ten minutes later the door opened, and in stepped Calan. He looked a little better, but not much.

"Was your rest pleasant?" he asked. He sounded distracted, the question more obligatory than anything.

"Best in years. How long was I out?"

"My guess is five hours," Calan said. He pulled the chair out from the desk and plopped into it. Massaging his forehead with his fingers, he stared down at the wood and appeared to soak in the calm. Ghost had seen people look like that before, after they'd endured a long stretch on a battlefield. Once the blood and bodies were gone, the men looked as if solitude were something physical they could soak in like a sponge, silence a concoction they could massage into their temples and necks.

"It bad out there?" he asked, disliking the lack of noise.

"It was," Calan said, his eyes staring through his desk. "Better now. A lot of dead, and even more anger and hopelessness. Too many expect miracles, as if I had any to give."

Ghost felt another awkward silence descend over them. Deciding he was out of his league, he pulled things back to something more grounded, more real to him.

"What's wrong with my knee?" he asked. "I can't stand on it."

Calan looked up. "I cleansed the infection and knit the flesh, but it is still tender. The spell I used to numb your pain will take time to fade, and until it does, most of your muscles will ignore any request you make of them. Don't fight it; there isn't much point. In another hour or so you'll be walking, albeit with a limp. A few more and you'll be back to doing whatever it is you do. Killing, I assume, sending me even more men and women to care for."

"I came and paid good coin for healing, not insults."

"My apologies," Calan said. "That was uncalled for."

"It was."

He tilted his head toward the wall, not even wanting to look at the old man. The only ones he'd killed recently were those he'd been contracted to kill, and those who had been attacking the priests' temple. That was the thanks he got? Vague accusations of making the priest's life harder, and a claim that he was nothing but a killer?

"You know what it's like to live in a place where everyone who sees you either hates you or is afraid?" Ghost asked.

"There are many who are unsettled by my presence, and more who are angered by what I speak."

"But it isn't the whole city. Even those who fear you do so because you've got something they don't understand. They don't understand me either, but you, they could choose to be like you if they wanted. They can't be like me, no matter what they do. The best they could do is smear themselves with coal, and that'd vanish with a good scrub."

Calan leaned back in his chair, and he seemed to truly look at Ghost for the first time.

"Is that why you paint your face? To show them how different you are?"

Ghost chuckled. "You want to know why? Truly why? It should show them how the difference between us, between me and you, is something as stupid as a strip of paint, something so thin and artificial we think nothing of it if done to a wall or a piece of armor. But that never happens. Instead they look at me with even greater fear. When I first started, those I hunted called me Ghost, and so I took the name and abandoned my old one. At least if they hated the Ghost, feared it, it was my own creation they feared. It wasn't me; it wasn't who I really was. Let them focus their hatred on something I can shed as easily as I shed this paint upon my face."

"Are you a killer?" the priest asked.

"No. But I think Ghost is."

"And who are you when you are not this Ghost?"

Ghost looked at him, trying to understand the true desire behind the question. Calan seemed interested, almost invested, in what he might say and do. There was no deceit in him, and of that quality Ghost considered himself an excellent judge. Who was he when not the man with the white face? Who was he when not hunting, when not contracted to capture or kill another?

"I'm not sure I remember anymore," he said.

"Do you still remember your name?"

He should have, but suddenly it didn't seem so clear. It'd been over ten years since he adopted the Ghost moniker. Before that he'd gone by a dozen names, changing them as he traveled east, for each city a new name. He tried to pull up childhood memories, of hearing his mother say his name, but each one was different in the timeworn haze. Suddenly he felt ashamed, and he wanted to be anywhere other than beneath the priest's unrelenting gaze.

"No," he said at last. "And I may never. Why does it matter to you, old man?"

"If you have to ask, I fear your mistrust has sunk in far deeper than any infection."

Ghost used the wall to shove himself onto his good leg.

"Enough," he said. "My thanks for your help. Good luck with your wounded."

"And you with your wounds as well."

An hour later Ghost limped from the temple, more than ever certain that Haern needed to die, if only to put his suddenly troubled mind at rest.

CHAPTER

 26

Veliana pulled her dagger free of the man's neck and kicked his body away. All around her rose the stench of blood and dead bodies. They'd thoroughly trashed the home, broken chairs and shattered tables. Deathmask stood at the door, scanning for more trespassers on their territory, while the twins entered from the house's other room.

"I'm bleeding," said Mier.

"He's bleeding," said Nien.

"Badly?" Deathmask asked, not bothering to glance inside.

"No."

"No."

That seemed good enough for Deathmask. Veliana cleaned her dagger and jammed it into her belt. She felt ready to pass out. Between mercenaries and other members of the guilds, they'd killed over thirty men since the night started, and now it was halfway through morning and still they continued, the most recent dead being from the Wolf Guild. It seemed Deathmask's desire for blood knew no bounds. She felt ready to collapse at the slightest breeze, yet he was still searching, still bouncing as if he were an excited maiden.

The worst was that the territory they'd chosen to make their stand on was a single street aptly named Shortway, poorly traveled and worth a meager handful of coins in theft and protection money.

"This is hopeless," she said, approaching her guildmaster. Some guild, she thought. Four of them slaughtering trespassers on a single street. Surely the other guildmasters were quaking in their boots. "We've accomplished nothing other than a few bodies."

"Rumors," Deathmask said, still scanning the sparsely populated street. "Whispers. Exaggerations. Given time they will work for us. We start with a single road, and let the rest of the city know that it is ours. Then we take a second, and a third. With each passing day we spread until we can take no more, and by then they will fear us more than any other guild, for we will be few, we will be skilled, and we will have shown they cannot stop us, cannot even slow us down."

Veliana rolled her eyes but decided not to press the point. She felt too tired to argue.

"Sleep would be nice," said Mier, or perhaps it was Nien.

"Very nice," said the other.

"Very well," Deathmask said. "Let's return. Tomorrow will be just as long, and longer should the mercenaries finally slack off. We have more to fear from the guilds than from them. To the mercenaries we are a small nuisance, a paltry four worth no bounty. It's the other guilds they want. But Thren, Kadish, William...they'll understand. One of them will descend upon us with all their fury, and that is the battle we must win, that our entire fate will rest upon."

"Rest," said Veliana. It was really the only word from his spiel that her mind could latch onto. "I think that's the smartest thing you've said."

His eyes narrowed behind his mask, but then he laughed.

"We have longer days ahead of us than this, you three. I hope you understand that. Still, no reason to press ourselves without reason. We've accomplished what we must. Let's get back to our little hideout."

Deathmask led the way. No one accosted them on their travels, and it seemed none were tracking them either. Shortway was hardly the center of much guild activity, and those few who had stumbled upon it had died. Most of their kills had been thieves fleeing from other territories, where the mercenaries had been at their thickest. When they reached their safe house, a cellar rented from a well-bribed tavernkeeper, Deathmask flung the doors open, lit a waiting torch with a touch of his finger, and led them down.

The cellar was not empty.

"It took you long enough," said the Watcher, leaning against the far wall.

The twins drew their daggers, and Veliana felt her hands reach for her own. Deathmask put an arm before them all, then took off his mask and grinned.

"Forgive us. We didn't know we had company waiting. Have you come to accept my offer?"

Haern nodded toward the twins.

"Have you made new friends?"

"For now," the twins said in unison.

The Watcher chuckled. "Very well then. I take it you can read?"

A pouch hung from his waist, and he pulled one of many scrolls from it and tossed it to Deathmask, who caught it and began reading. His eyes widened, so Veliana glanced over, but he was moving it too much for her to decipher anything useful.

"The whole city?" Deathmask asked. He looked ready to both laugh and lash out in rage. "Have you lost your mind?"

"Perhaps. Have you lost your courage?"

"Don't turn this on me. You want to present every guild-leader and member of the Trifect with the same demand, and then force them to accept within the span of a *single night*?"

Veliana yanked the document from his hand and read further. In a tight, careful script the letter warned the reader to either accept the following terms or die: A yearly sum, to be determined by the king or his advisors to be equal to one-third the gold lost to theft or spent on mercenaries in an equal amount of time, would be equally distributed among the remaining five major thief guilds. In return the guilds would protect everything within the city walls from theft by any of their members. Following these terms was the date on which the Watcher expected an answer: the winter solstice...two nights away.

She rolled the document up and tossed it back to Haern, who deftly caught it.

"You've lost your mind," she said.

"If I remember correctly, it was your idea, not mine. So the insanity should at least be shared."

Deathmask laughed, but he looked ready to explode. "I wanted them to meet to decide terms. I wanted delays, chances to manipulate various parties, and to thin out the guilds who might resist. You want to force the guilds and Trifect to become bedfellows, and even worse, you want to do it all in a single night. How? What madness in you makes you think this could work?"

"You know several will agree," Haern insisted. "Those

mercenaries are devastating everyone, and will continue to do so as long as the Trifect can afford them. This war has lasted ten years, far longer than even Thren wanted. The Trifect itself is hemorrhaging money, but they currently have no way to end this while saving face. And that's assuming Thren would even let them end it."

Veliana shook her head. "You of all people should understand, too many would resent this. You'd turn us from honest thieves to low-rent bodyguards. The very nature of the guilds would shift."

"They shifted before," Haern said. "When my father took rule, the guilds were full of simple thieves, nothing more. They stole from who they could, rarely even having the courage to go after the Trifect. The drugs, the trafficking, the protection money, it all came from his mind. His vision. He changed the game."

Haern's voice softened.

"My father turned poor men with deft hands into an empire of organized theft and murder, and every guild followed. Give me my chance to replace his legacy with another. I've killed, and killed, and now I will make it have meaning. Every guild-master or -leader who refuses will die by my hand. Those who assume control will be given the same demands, and suffer the same fate if they refuse. My father began this chaos, and I will end it."

Veliana looked to her guildleader, who was deep in thought. It was almost as if she could watch the idea growing in his mind, taking shape, every potential reaction sifting through a spider web of end results.

"You have the Ash Guild's approval," he said suddenly, as if snapping from a daze. "Will you deliver the letters tonight?"

"I will."

"Then go do it. I only have one request: leave your father to me."

Haern paused, and his eyes glanced away.

"Very well," he said when he looked back. "You stand to make a fortune, Deathmask. That is why I trust you. But remember, the same deal applies to you as well."

If her guildmaster was upset by the threat, he didn't show it.

"Save your energy for those who will give you the most trouble."

When the Watcher was gone, Veliana spun on Deathmask, shoving a finger into his face.

"I can understand *him* wanting to perform this madness, but you?"

Deathmask winked at her with his red eye.

"If he succeeds, he succeeds. If he fails, we lose nothing. Besides, Veliana, what else does this plan need but some theatrics? The Watcher's plan is insane, and most likely he'll get himself killed...but I won't stop him. He already frightens the lower members of the thief guilds. If he lives he'll become a terror to them, the only real chance of keeping this agreement in order long enough for us to benefit."

"Why Thren?" asked Mier.

"Why us?" asked Nien.

"Because," Deathmask said, turning to the twins with his smile nearly ear-to-ear, "if Thren accepts, or dies horribly, the rest of the guilds will fall like dominoes. You wouldn't think I'd leave the most important part of the entire plan to someone *else*, would you?"

Not since the hunger riots preceding the Bloody Kensgold had Gerand Crold seen the people of the city so furious. As advisor to the king he had listened to the many complaints about guards, fires, and theft, and the overall demands for compensation. He'd sat in his uncomfortable chair, a ledger before him, and denied every single one. The line of petitioners seemed endless, and that was with the castle guards filtering out some of the more unkempt individuals.

Once the sun had finally set, Gerand spoke to the king, whispering lies in his ears about how the people still respected him. Finally free to retreat to his chambers, where a full bottle of wine awaited him as per his orders to his servants, Gerand let out a sigh as he passed through the stone hallway.

"Fucking thieves," he muttered as he shut the door. The past five years had filled his head with gray hair, and his marriage had plummeted into occasional nights with his wife, but mostly him sleeping in the castle, her in their home. Removing the cork, he poured a glass and toasted the empty room.

"To you, Alyssa," he said. "For destroying in two days everything I built in five years."

"To Alyssa," someone whispered, their breath upon his neck.

Gerand nearly choked on his wine. He spun, torn between diving for a weapon and falling to his knees to beg for his life. The last time a thief had sneaked into his room, it'd been Thren Felhorn and a female companion. They'd threatened his wife to make him fulfill certain desires of theirs. The first thought that ran through his mind as he saw a man cloaked in gray was that they'd have to kidnap someone better if they wanted him to obey this time.

"Thren?" he said, startled by the sight. It looked like Thren, only much younger. Gerand had a sudden fear that the man was immortal, immune to time, and determined to haunt him for all his life. As a wolfish grin spread across the intruder's face, he choked down such irrational thoughts. This wasn't Thren. The hair was the wrong color.

"No," said the man. "Close, though. I am the Watcher. Perhaps you have heard of me?"

"I have, though I've wondered if you were actually real." Gerand chuckled. "I guess this should count as proof?"

The Watcher snatched the glass from his hand and drank the remaining half. As he smacked his lips he tossed Gerand a scroll.

"Read it," he commanded.

Gerand did, his eyes growing wider with each sentence.

"You want the credit for the idea to go to the king?" he asked when finished. "But why?"

"The more involved the better," said the Watcher. He leaned against the wall, just beside the door. Even if Gerand managed to call the guards, and not die doing so, the man would still get the jump on them. "Besides, I need someone neutral in all this, someone both sides view as on their side. You've accepted bribes from both the thieves and the Trifect. Both will think you'll be in their pocket once the smoke clears."

"But Edwin will never agree. He's terrified someone will poison his tea or put shards of metal into his bread. By the gods, he thinks every shadow in his bedroom is a man poised with razor wire."

"He has something more real to fear, and we both know it. Veldaren is furious. You've failed to protect its people, and this time it's gone too far. Fires have burned down a quarter of the city. Innocent men and women died at the hands of mercenaries, and they come here finding no justice, no empathy. They have no one to turn to, no one to trust. Do you remember the riots five years ago? They will make those look downright orderly."

Gerand nodded. He'd seen the anger simmering in the many waiting in his line. They'd certainly not left in a better mood after talking to him, either. Getting King Vaelor to agree would involve marginal effort at best. Once Gerand played on his fears, then offered him the deal as a way to come out a hero, he'd agree in a heartbeat. Gerand glanced down at the parchment in his hand, still trying to determine the loophole, the underhanded secret hidden beneath the words.

"What do you gain from this?" he dared ask.

"We all want a legacy," the Watcher said. "This will be mine. The arrangement will rely on you, once everything is in order. Can you enforce it?"

Those words, of a stranger demanding enforcement, sparked a memory, and coupled with seeing such a familiar face, Gerand couldn't keep his tongue still, keep the question unasked. Years ago Gerand had tried to capture Thren's son, Aaron, and had even used the king's old advisor, Robert Haern, to aid him in the task. Time had dulled his memory, and no doubt the child had grown, but still...

"You have to be Thren's kin," he said. "His long-lost son, Aaron, perhaps?"

The Watcher pulled his hood lower over his face, and his mood seemed to sour.

"I would keep such thoughts to yourself, friend. They are dangerous."

Gerand felt his blood chill.

"Of course, of course. I guess it is no matter. But can you pull this off? A bluff won't work with either side."

"I have lived on the streets, hunting them like dogs. Every single guild has initiated me into their order without knowing it. I know where they live, where they hide. Few can challenge my skill, and none my determination. I will kill them, all of them, if I must. Make the king listen to you."

He stood and put a hand on the door.

"I've already delivered the rest of the messages. They'll bring their answers to you. Come tomorrow I'll check here first, to see who is safe and who must be dealt with."

"I understand."

As the door opened, Gerand couldn't hold in a chuckle. The Watcher stopped, as if he suspected a trap.

"No, it's not that," he said as the man closed the door. "I just found it humorous, is all. A long time ago your father came to me, threatening my wife to help him escalate his conflict. Yet now you come here seeking to end it. This time the apple fell far from the tree, didn't it?"

This seemed to put a smile on the Watcher's face.

"Good night, advisor. Do your part, and trust me to do mine."

He vanished out the door. Gerand plopped down onto his bed, and now that he was alone he felt his hands start to shake, his nerves finally getting the better of him. It seemed, despite the guards and walls, those with enough skill could still reach him. Perhaps the king's jumping at shadows wasn't so irrational after all...

"Where's that damn wine?" he asked. Seeing the bottle, he held it by the neck and drank straight from it. Given what he was about to go through the following day and night, he'd need all the courage he could get.

CHAPTER

 27

Delysia stumbled upon him getting ready as night fast approached.

"Where are you going?" she asked.

He'd shared Senke's room, but the other rogue had gone out to spend a night relaxing in the taverns.

"I've got some business to take care of," Haern said. Brug's trunk of weapons lay open before him, and he slid several daggers into his belt, plus another into a pocket of his boot.

"My brother did some digging," Delysia said, crossing her arms underneath her breasts. "And he says the mercenaries won't be going out again tonight. So what is it you're planning? For once the night might be peaceful."

Haern felt a half-smile tug at the corner of his mouth.

"The nights are never peaceful here. Quiet, perhaps, but killing can be silent work when done right. Never mind that, though. Promise me you'll stay inside. Things are about to get very dangerous."

She put a hand on his arm. "For you as well?"

He shrugged. "Can't help it. I have a chance to do something great, Delysia, something real."

"Will you kill?"

He rolled his eyes. "This isn't the same."

"Then what is it?"

"Safety," he said. "For all of us. My father wants a legacy, and I'll deny him it. What he started I'll end, or I'll die trying."

"You don't have to do this alone," she said. "Let us help. Let *me* help."

"You lost enough because of me. I won't risk the life you've rebuilt here."

"Who said you had a choice?"

He winked at her.

"Where I'm going tonight, I don't think a priest or priestess has ever been. Good night, Del."

He took her hand, kissed it, and then left.

The trip to the castle wasn't long, though scaling the outer wall, sneaking past the guards, climbing up to one of the higher windows, and then stealthily descending to Gerand's room took more time than he would have preferred. Probably should have made the advisor meet him at the front gates, he thought. Would have saved him the hassle.

When he slipped inside, Gerand looked ready for him. He smiled at Haern's entrance, but Haern saw the way his eyes darted about, and how the edges of his smile quivered. The man was nervous, but Haern didn't think it was because he'd set a trap. No doubt he felt the eyes of every guild upon him, plus the anger of the Trifect.

"What were their responses?" Haern asked, having no time to waste.

"I've received an answer from everyone but the Ash Guild and Laurie Keenan. With him down in Angelport, there's no way he might give an answer, and no keeper of his estate here would dare agree to something like this without confirmation."

"Don't worry about the Ash Guild. I have their answer. Laurie will fall in line when the other two Trifect leaders agree. Tell me, have any said yes?"

"The Wolf Guild will, but only if Thren agrees as well. If the Spider Guild doesn't fall in line, though, they'll deny ever saying so."

"Is that it?"

Gerand licked his lips. "The Serpent Guild's man said they'd rather kiss the asses of a thousand corpses than the Trifect's. The Hawks fired an arrow over our wall, a cloth tied to the shaft with the word *Never* written in blood upon it. Leon Connington's advisor sent a letter saying they were open to negotiations, but not under such conditions. Lady Gemcroft's response was cryptic. I received a letter from her saying you'd have to kill her, while her advisor came by later insisting she might change her mind given time. As for the Spider Guild..."

He gestured to a package waiting beside his bed. Haern opened it to find a severed head, eyes and mouth sewn shut.

"Who is it?" he asked, frowning.

"Look closer."

He did, saw the gray hair, thin nose, and most noticeably the fresh cut running from the head's left eye to its ear. Haern glanced back at the advisor and saw a similar, albeit faded, scar on his face. He felt a pang of guilt, and he wondered who the poor guy had been.

"Intimidation," Haern said. "Don't fall for it. I won't let them get to you."

"How?" asked Gerand, exasperated. "There are five guilds, and three leaders of the Trifect. Three of the guilds, and two of the Trifect, have denied you. Can you kill them all? I might be better off having you killed instead, and letting them fight amongst themselves."

Haern narrowed his eyes, and the advisor immediately retracted his comment.

"Forgive me, I'm stressed, and have had more to drink than I probably should. How will I know if you succeed?"

"They'll come tell you," Haern said, turning to leave. "Oh, and escort me out, will you? I don't have time to mess around with your guards."

"Sure," said Gerand. "Why not? A king's advisor and an assassin, side-by-side as friends. I've suffered through stranger."

They walked through the halls toward the castle's exit, and several times Gerand had to calm soldiers who saw Haern's cloaks and sabers and immediately assumed the worst. At the giant doors Gerand grabbed his arm and pulled him close.

"Be careful whom you kill first," he said. "If you fail, but still strike down the leaders of either side, you will unbalance everything. You must succeed in this, Watcher."

"If I unbalance things, at least you'll finally have a winner," Haern said, grinning. "And I don't plan on dying. I'll visit you come the morning. I promise."

He flew down the streets, his legs pumping. His eyes darted every which way, knowing that the guilds would be prepared for his arrival. For the longest time he'd only been a phantom to them, but now they'd heard his promise. This was their chance. Deathmask had asked him if he was insane. Perhaps he was. But at least Deathmask had also seemed to understand. If he was going to try, why not try for the impossible?

He decided the first ones to visit would be the Hawks. They were no friends of the Spider Guild, and their recent conflict with both them and the mercenaries had surely devastated their numbers. Their leader, Kadish Vel, was a sensible enough man, a bit of a gambler. If Haern could convince him to give the treaty a chance, especially as a way to diminish Thren's danger, then he should be able to win over the guild's cooperation without having to kill its leader.

The Hawk Guild's headquarters had shifted several times, but even after Thren's attack they'd refused to move from their current tavern. No doubt Kadish was tired of running. They'd emptied out during the mercenaries' rampage, but with the night turning quiet he felt certain they'd return. With the strange threat of the Watcher hanging over them all, they'd want to be where they felt safe, where they recognized every face, knew every shadow, every entrance. If he was lucky they had thought his offer a bluff, or even an opportunistic lie of the king, an attempt to save face before his furious populace. Still, their eyes would be open even if they doubted. Nothing that night would be easy. If he had to open up with a stealthy kill, he would, conversation be damned. Dead bodies spoke clearer than anything else in the world of thieves. He'd given them their warning.

Two men stood at the entrance, obviously on the lookout. The one on the left looked bored, as if he'd drawn the short straw that night. The other was older and more aware. Haern drifted along on the left, hunched over, limping, and muttering to himself as if he'd had too much to drink. Neither Hawk gave him a second glance. Once out of their sight Haern walked closer, a hand leaning against the tavern as if he needed it for balance. Upon reaching the back he saw a door, most certainly locked and barred. He tested it just to make sure. No lock, but it was barred. A veritable army of feral cats lurked about, and one hissed at his presence as it hunkered down over a scrap of fat.

"You're right," Haern whispered to the feline. "I should wait my turn, shouldn't I?"

The alley was thin, dark, and full of places to hide. Ten minutes later he heard a thud from the other side of the door, and then it creaked open.

"Enjoy," said a burly man, chucking a bucket of what seemed to be a mixture of vomit and woodchips. The mess splattered onto the stone, and in leaped the cats, there to hiss and growl while they searched for something edible. When the man's back was turned, Haern stepped from his hiding spot, jumped into the opening, and flung his arms around his neck. A quick jerk and he fell, his scream muffled by Haern's palm.

"Sleep well," he whispered, slipping inside.

Haern stepped inside a storeroom, cramped and occupied almost entirely by the two shelves on either side. The man he'd knocked out wasn't the barkeep, one of the few things that might allow him to remain hidden. Already he heard the raucous drinkers at the front, and they would not have tolerated any sort of absence from the one supplying their liquor. Judging from the man's size and duty Haern had taken out a heavyhand, someone to deal with those who got out of line. Haern chuckled. Now that was someone who would *not* be missed by the crowd.

He ducked underneath the lowest shelf, peered out the inner door, and was rewarded with the sight of a pair of hairy legs as the barkeep scratched at a scab near his ankle. Rows of bottles stretched before him. He was behind the bar. From his time inside before, Haern knew there'd be a locked door to the right of the bar, blocking off a staircase that led into the lower quarters that the Hawks had enlarged and adopted as their own. Question was, how did he get inside?

As he pressed his back against the wall, an idea came to him. He waited a moment to see if the barkeep noticed the movement, then pressed his elbows against the wall. There was no plaster or paint, just a thin piece of wood. Bracing with his feet, he pressed inward, hoping the laughter and singing might drown out the noise. He pressed harder, every muscle in his legs taut, and then the board gave. Wincing at the noise, he pushed it all the way in until it snapped in half. He worked an arm through, then his head, and finally the rest of his body. When he fell out the other side, he was behind the locked door and inside the small staircase leading to a second door.

Haern drew his sabers, thrilled by the way they handled. Senke had given him a fine gift. Hopefully he'd put them to good use. The time for stealth was over. He tested the door at the bottom of the stairs, found it unlocked, and then kicked it in. As the loud crack echoed in the room, he leaped inside, already searching for his first victim. There were four men inside, sitting at a table with cards and wooden chips stacked before them. They shouted and reached for their weapons, but they were too slow. Haern whirled through them, rolling across the table and to the other side. Chips clattered along the floor, mixing with the blood.

"Shit," he said as he stared at the bodies. None was Kadish Vel. He glanced about, seeing only one other room. Within were some ledgers, a shelf stocked with tiny bottles, and a bed. Haern couldn't believe it. The first of his many places to attack, and he hadn't even bothered to check inside the tavern first. Kadish was probably with his men, drinking. So much for being the feared Watcher of Veldaren. So much for his plans.

He rushed back to the stairs, trying to decide on a course of action. No one would know he'd come down there yet. Kadish was in a public place, with lots of people, but that could work in Haern's favor. Halfway up the stairs he turned back and hurried to the small side room. Scouring the shelf, he looked to see if his idea was possible. The tiny bottles weren't alcohol as he'd first assumed. They were tonics, tinctures, and most important, poisons. Only half were labeled, as he'd expected. Haern recalled his lessons when training under his father. For three months he'd had a tutor who knew more about poisons than Haern could ever have learned in a lifetime. Many of his lessons during those long days had involved discovering the nature of unlabeled poisons.

He shook several, checking their color, their consistency, and their weight. He pulled four aside, cleared a space on the shelf, and put the bottles atop it. One of the bottles was clearly an extract of shadeleaf, but that was only part of what he needed. He took two others, shook them, and then poured drops of each together. When they turned green, he frowned. Trying another bottle, he mixed it with the nightshade. When the drops turned clear, he grinned.

Dumping out half the bottle of shadeleaf extract, he poured another bottle, a common mixture of kingsblood and dandy-blooms, in with the rest and shook it. The resulting mixture turned clear. It had a strong taste to it, which meant it only worked with certain alcohols. That was if you planned on putting it in someone's drink, of course. Haern had other ideas. Among the marked bottles was a useful paste that bonded with most poisons, thickening them into something akin to glue. Haern applied the poison to the blade of one of his daggers, being careful not to rush. The last thing he wanted was to prick a finger and die in the Hawks' basement dwelling. That hardly seemed like the noble end he felt he deserved. Last, he found one more particular bottle and smashed it.

Haern climbed back through the hole in the wall, slipped out the rear of the tavern, and then circled around to the front. The two thieves remained on guard, and they sneered at his approach.

"Hey, you got to have money first," said the one on the right, blocking his way with his arm. Haern glared, then pointed through the door, slurring his words and making sure his hand bobbed up and down in the air.

"That...that guy there's my brother. He'll cover for me, really. Ask him, he's a great guy, married a whore who makes more money on her back than I...I could...that could make in a *month*."

Haern made sure he pointed between two tables, and the movement of his arm made it no clearer whom he was referring to as his brother. The guard on the left looked inside, as if he could somehow pinpoint the man anyway. The one on the right grabbed Haern's arm.

"I said get out," he said, but Haern moved too fast. He spun out of his grip, slashed open his throat, and then turned to the other. Before he could let out a cry, Haern stabbed his chest with an unpoisoned dagger, ramming his arm over his mouth to hold in the scream. It came out muffled, not loud enough to attract any attention within. It seemed the men and women were eager to celebrate their first moment of peace in two days. No doubt they thought they'd beaten the mercenaries, or at least they wanted to think so.

Knowing time was far from an ally, Haern lumbered into the tavern, resuming his drunken gait. With his head low he scanned the bar, looking for Kadish Vel. He found him in the far corner, sitting with his back to a wall. Six men sat with him at the giant round table, along with a pretty lady at his side. She seemed bored with the proceedings, and Haern wondered if she stayed with him for coin or for safety. The rest were joking or boasting, their voices loud and slurred. All but Kadish. He seemed mildly amused at best. Haern drifted toward him. He had one chance at this, just one.

"Hey, hey, hey!" shouted one of the men as Haern slid between them, directly opposite Kadish. Haern put his hands on the table, and he leaned forward as if keeping balance were a struggle.

"Kadisshh?" Haern asked, looking lazily at the guildmaster.

"I'm sorry, friend, the bar might be mine, but the drinks still don't come free," said Kadish.

Haern never responded. His hands, leaning there on the table, were also within inches of the sabers at his hips. As his cloaks folded away, Kadish saw them, and that was when Haern moved. He drew them both, and in one smooth motion sliced through the necks of the men to either side of him. As they collapsed, their blood splattering across the table, Kadish flung himself out of his chair, pressing his back into a corner. The pretty girl looked dazed, as if she didn't believe what she saw. Two of the men moved closer to defend Kadish, the others drawing daggers and lunging. Haern batted one aside, killed another with a riposte, and then spun, a whirling machine of death. Cries of alarm spread across the tavern as the rest realized what was going on.

Falling to one knee, Haern let go of a saber and yanked the poisoned dagger from his boot. From underneath the table he saw the lower half of Kadish's body. No armor. No realization of the danger. He flung the dagger, trusting his aim. It plunged into the meat of Kadish's thigh, and Haern allowed himself a smile.

And then he was moving again, his sabers reveling in the blood of his opponents. The whole tavern was in chaos, half the customers fleeing, wanting no part of whatever might happen. Many others cried out in warning, expecting an ambush. One shouted Thren's name, as if he must be the one responsible. Haern weaved through them all, deflecting sword strikes and slicing into the arms of those who thrust their daggers. A heavyset man tried to block his way at the door, but Haern rammed into him with his left shoulder. His right hand stabbed repeatedly. The two collapsed through the door, landing beside the bodies of the guards.

Out in the open Haern took to his feet and ran. Curses followed after him, but he was too fast, the city so familiar that he could weave and turn without pause through the maze of alleys and streets. He wished he could have talked to Kadish, convinced him to change his mind, but there'd been no way. The poison would work its way up his leg and to his lungs, locking them in place. There was a cure, but that had been in the bottle Haern smashed before leaving. By the time they found another, Kadish would be dead.

A list of targets passed through his head. He'd taken out one of the guilds, so it was time to move on to a member of the Trifect. From what he'd learned, the recent wave of mercenary attacks had been the doing of only one. If there was to be any peace in the city, Alyssa Gemcroft would need to die next.

CHAPTER

 28

Alyssa was hiding in her room from her relatives when Zusa arrived, a letter in hand.

"He's coming," she said as she handed over the parchment. "The man who killed your son. He wants you to agree to his terms, or he'll kill you."

"This man, the Watcher..." Alyssa crumpled the letter without reading it, needing only the signature at the bottom to know her answer. "He kills Nathaniel, then dares make demands?"

"He'll come tonight," Zusa said. "And he's skilled, milady. He might carry out his promise."

"Let him come," Alyssa said. "You will protect me. He cannot hide from you, not here in my mansion. This is our home, and he the stranger. I trust you with my life, Zusa. Don't let me down."

"The terms aren't so unfair," Zusa insisted. "Bertram would have you agree."

"I don't care. Let the Watcher try. He dies tonight."

And so the day droned on, Alyssa with less and less patience with the relatives who had remained after the funeral, preferring the safety of her mansion to their own homes. Bertram came to discuss the wedding, but she ordered him away. She was even curt with Arthur, who brought her a plate of food and a glass of wine.

"You have eaten nothing all day," he said. "Please, take something. You will feel better. We have things we must discuss."

Fearing he might bring up the subject of marriage, or, gods forbid, propose right there holding a plate of bread, boiled potatoes, and cabbage, she told him to get out. His caring demeanor faltered a bit, and he stormed away.

"You have no time left to be a little child," he told her before slamming the door shut. "Already your immaturity overstays its welcome."

"And you yours!" she screamed, hurling the glass of wine he'd left behind.

She wished Zusa were there, but she'd vanished, although promising to never be far.

"If you know, then you might reveal my presence," the faceless woman had argued. "If you trust me, then trust me. Trust the shadows to hold only me."

The night dragged on. This time there were no fires to watch, no men rushing up and down the streets. Just quiet. It seemed eerie, as if the city was suddenly waiting for something. Bertram had told her he feared terrible retribution from the guilds for her actions, but so far it seemed none were coming. Or maybe one was, coming in the form of the Watcher.

Alyssa checked the lock to her room for the fourth time.

With nothing to read and nothing to do she sat down on her bed, closed her eyes, and wished she could sleep. It'd be so much better for her to die that way, unable to feel the pain. Part of her expected just that to happen, though another part was revolted by the sheer weakness involved in considering it. She should be stronger, better, but she was so tired. The Gemcroft estate felt like chains attached to every inch of her body, dragging her down, pulling her into an exhausted pit where she could feel no emotion, cry no tears, and express no love. It was in that pit that Arthur waited.

The sound of cracking glass startled her to a sitting position, her heart leaping all the way up to her throat. Any calm she might have felt in accepting this fate vanished with the threat finally there. A man was outside her window, hanging from a rope. The glass had cracked in a circle of veins where his heel rammed into it. She saw him kick off, his momentum bringing him back into the glass. This time it shattered, and in rolled the Watcher, all cloaks and blades and broken shards.

Alyssa rolled off the bed in the direction opposite him. Hitting the ground with a thud, she scampered toward the door. A dagger flew, and she felt a tug as it passed through strands of her hair before thudding into her locked door. Panic struck her, and she spun to face her attacker.

"Lady Gemcroft," said the man, and he bowed low as if in respect. It seemed so comical coming from him that her mouth dropped open. "I've come for an answer to my offer, and for your sake I hope it differs from the one I last received."

She thought to lie, or bargain, or maybe just turn, fling open the lock, and hope she was faster than him even though she knew she wasn't. She'd die with a dagger in her back, or maybe a saber in her neck. With each step he took, she took one back, until she realized he was carefully guiding her away from the door. If she was to flee, she had to do it now, either that or give in. Before she could choose either option, the shadows above her shifted, and from the corner Zusa leaped, her cloak uncurling from about her body as if she were an insect emerging from a cocoon.

The Watcher, instead of retreating at the ambush, rushed toward her. Alyssa dove out of the way, and only when she landed did she realize she'd done as the man hoped. He'd cut her off from the door. From her knees she watched Zusa and the Watcher clash. His sabers were longer than Zusa's daggers, and he had the greater reach, but it seemed not to matter. Alyssa had seen Zusa leap naked into a river to fight a dark paladin of Karak, seen her wield her blades with shocking speed and skill.

But Alyssa had never seen her fight like this.

Sword and dagger clashed in a constant echo of noise, sharp and painful in the closed room. The Watcher whirled, his weapons a blur, yet Zusa met every move. Her body arched and weaved as if her bones were liquid and her balance relied on will alone. Alyssa tried to follow them with her eyes, but could not. Over and over a saber would pass so close to Zusa's flesh she'd wince, expecting a shower of red, but it never happened.

"Alyssa!" someone shouted from the other side of the door. Something heavy thudded against it, most likely a fist striking in a panic.

"Send my guards!" she screamed back, returning to her wits. Another thud, this heavier, but the lock on her door was sturdy, designed to hold out far more than a single man. She desperately wished she'd left it unlocked.

The Watcher leaped from side to side, avoiding Zusa's thrusts, and then spun about, hiding his body with a sudden flourish of his cloaks. From within its folds she saw the glint of his sabers, darting out with a quick slash from the chaos. Zusa retreated from them, careful to keep herself between him and

Alyssa. For a moment Alyssa thought it might work. If Zusa could hold on until help arrived, the man would have to retreat.

But then Zusa cried out, and blood splashed across the carpet. Alyssa felt her heart stop. Zusa continued fighting, even as the wraps on her left arm were soaked crimson. Could she fight through it? For a few long moments she did. Zusa went on the offensive, her whole body twisting into her thrusts, giving her a reach beyond even the sabers. This time the Watcher fell back, batting each thrust aside, the contact ringing in Alyssa's ears. Their speed . . . it was unreal. At one point their weapons entangled, looping and parrying in what could only be described as a lethal dance. Faster and faster they moved, each refusing to give the other an inch of room. The sound of their battle escalated, and Alyssa found herself clutching the carpet, her whole body tense. The second she saw another splatter of blood, she would run for the door, risks be damned.

But it was all bluster. She saw the pain on Zusa's face, and her heart broke. The Watcher's foot struck her protector's chin, and as she staggered back, in sliced a saber, cutting into her arm. Zusa dropped one of her daggers and, suddenly at a disadvantage, she could not hold him back. His assault came, vicious and quick. Another thin cut opened on her leg, the slash so quick Alyssa never even saw it. Fists and knees slammed into Zusa, and she rolled with them, rolling . . . away from the door.

She was granting Alyssa a way out, sacrificing her body, her life, to do it.

The Watcher kicked her again, hard in the throat. As she fell back he descended upon her, a saber tip pressing against her chest, just above her heart. His elbow trapped the arm still wielding a dagger, the rest of his weight pressing against her waist to keep her from moving.

"Why do you hunt me?" she heard him ask Zusa. It seemed

so strange to her, to hear him wonder, but she dared not think of it. She wouldn't allow Zusa to die for nothing. With her fall, Alyssa knew there was no way for her to escape. Men shouted from the other side of the door, but they were yet to begin breaking it in. At least she could accomplish something with her death. At least she could reward such a loyal servant for all she had done.

"Wait!" Alyssa screamed before she might lose her courage. "Take me, but let her live!"

The Watcher looked over to her, a quick glance before returning his gaze to Zusa, who even in such a state remained dangerous.

"Why?" he asked. "Why would you kill yourself? I offered you a chance to end all this! Are you so vain that you would rather die than work with men such as me? All of Veldaren suffers, and I offer you a chance to save it!"

"Damn your offer," said Alyssa. "I could never agree, not after what you've done. Now take my life, and spare hers."

"What *I've* done?" he asked, and he sounded genuinely perplexed.

"Her son," Zusa said, her voice hoarse from the kick. "You killed her son, then scrawled your name in the dirt with his blood."

The Watcher looked taken aback. His eyes glanced between them. When something heavy thudded against the door, his body tensed.

"When?" he asked, his voice soft.

"Weeks ago, on the road north to Tyneham."

Using one of his sabers, he pushed the final dagger free from Zusa's hand, then stood.

"Murderer of children," he whispered, as if finally understanding something. "I know what child you speak of. Five years old, perhaps six, red hair? He *lives*, Lady Gemcroft. I saved him, though he was wounded and with fever. I left him in the care of a family, and paid them well to protect him."

Alyssa shook her head. He had to be lying. It didn't make any sense.

"Why?" she asked. "How? The caravan was attacked..."

"I came upon an ambush of a caravan, but not by thieves. They were men wearing the same insignia, a sickle held before a mountain. Your boy was the target, though at the time I never learned his name. That caravan contained crates of gold bearing your family's crest. They were smuggling it in to the Serpent Guild, though why I do not know."

It was too much. That crest, that was the Hadfield family crest. Could Arthur have attacked Mark, attacked Nathaniel? But why would the Watcher lie? He could easily kill her and Zusa. And besides, she'd seen her son's body...his burned...

"Arthur claimed to have found the body," Zusa said, as if she were following Alyssa's thinking. "His men brought it back, burned beyond recognition. His men found the caravan. Mark, his competition. Nathaniel, your heir."

As the door to her room cracked, the hinges wincing in protest, she saw the Watcher tighten the muscles in his body. He was preparing an action. Time was nearing its end. She couldn't stall. She had to make a decision, the one that felt right.

"If you did save my son, you have my most sincere gratitude," she said. "I'll agree to your terms. Zusa told me they were fair, and I trust her. But if find this to be a lie, I will bring the wrath of the entire Trifect down upon you."

The Watcher grinned at the threat.

"I have a date with the Serpents, so I must be going. I'll keep your threat in mind."

He turned to the window and ran, leaping out as if a

madman. Then she saw him catch the rope still hanging, and like a spider he zipped back up toward the roof and out of sight. Zusa gingerly rose to her feet, holding her bleeding arm with her hand.

"You know what you must do," she said, and Alyssa nodded.

"Enough!" she shouted to the men trying to break down her door. "Stand back; he's gone."

Zusa went over and unlocked the door. Guards spilled in, their weapons drawn as if they refused to believe her. One checked underneath her bed, while several others looked out the window and swore.

"Are you all right?" asked Bertram, pushing through them and hugging her.

"I'm fine," she said. "It's Zusa who was hurt, that's all."

Bertram didn't even glance the faceless woman's way.

"Thank the gods. I wish you would spend the night with the rest of the guards. It was folly to remain in here alone in the first place."

"I said I'll be fine. I'm safe here, save for a bit of a draft." She tried to smile, but her hands were shaking, and her smile trembled on her lips. And the night wasn't done just yet.

"Leave me," she told her guards. "Trust me, I will be safe."

The men grumbled, and they looked none too happy, but she was their employer, and grumble was all they could do. Bertram waited until the rest were gone before bowing.

"Is there anything else you need from me?" he asked.

"Send for Arthur. I need his comfort."

"Of course, most understandable."

When he was gone, she looked to Zusa.

"How bad are your wounds?"

"I have suffered worse."

"You're bleeding all over my expensive carpet."

Zusa smiled, then suddenly let out a rare laugh.

"I guess I am."

Alyssa walked to the door, stopped, and outstretched her hand. Zusa put a dagger into it and folded her fingers closed.

"Tell Arthur to meet me in the gardens," Alyssa said. "I'll be waiting at Nathaniel's grave."

She hurried out of her room and down the hallways. Every twist and turn was second nature to her, and she managed her way out to the darkness without alerting any of her guards or, more important, Arthur's mercenaries. In her garden behind the mansion, she felt the cold air bite into her skin, felt the moonlight shine down upon her. A few minutes later Arthur arrived, his arms crossed over his chest to keep in his warmth. She turned and kept her hands folded behind her back, the hilt like ice in her fingers.

"Are you safe, my dear?" Arthur asked, immediately wrapping her in his arms. "I only heard the commotion at its end, and Bertram found me before I could dress."

Alyssa smiled at him, but when he made to kiss her she tilted her head away, her eyes falling upon the grave marked by a stone angel, the lettering at its feet reading "Nathaniel Gemcroft."

"I just want to ask you something first," she said, her hands still behind her as if she were shy.

"Anything."

She looked into his eyes, watching his every reaction.

"Whose body is truly in this grave?"

The hour was late, and Arthur had not the slightest reason to expect the question. He paused, and for one second she saw the guilt in his eyes, and the fear. What replaced them was cold cruelty. Without a word he lunged for her throat with his bare hands. Before they could close around her, she stabbed him with Zusa's dagger. As his blood spilled across her arms, he looked at her with wide-eyed shock. She could almost read his thoughts as they flashed over him. *This can't be happening, not to me, not when I played this so perfectly.*

She twisted the dagger, taking pleasure in the pain that crossed his face.

"I wish I could make it hurt worse," she whispered into his ear, as if they were still lovers. And then his body collapsed, and she stepped out of the way, letting go of the dagger. She stood there, breathing heavily, and watched the blood mix with the soil. When Zusa arrived moments later, Alyssa did her best to smile.

"At least I didn't stain the carpet," she said, but her smile was forced. Zusa put her arms on Alyssa's shoulders and kissed her forehead.

"Thank you," Zusa said.

"For what?"

"For being willing to sacrifice yourself for me." She gestured to the body. "What do you want me to do with him?"

"Hide him for now, until we know how Arthur's mercenaries will react. But first...the Watcher's plan...will it work?"

Zusa shrugged. "It's possible. He'll have difficulty doing it alone."

"I can't do this anymore, Zusa. If Nathaniel's still alive, I want him here with me. I want him safe. Go with the Watcher. Help him against the Serpents, but the Serpents only. I won't help him harm a member of the Trifect, but for one more night I can bring revenge on the guilds that have harmed us so. They stole from me, them and Arthur. Bring ruin upon them as they deserve."

"As you wish, milady," Zusa said. Despite the wounds on her body, she offered no protest. Dragging Arthur's body by the arm, she hid him behind a row of rosebushes, currently nothing but thorns and brown stems.

"I'll inform Bertram," the faceless woman said, cleaning her dagger. "He'll need to replace Arthur, and perhaps much of the Hadfield family, in their rule over our mines. If he acts quickly, we might find that which was stolen."

"Thank you. I could use a moment's peace until then."

Zusa returned to the house, and Alyssa followed. Their paths branched, she to her room, Zusa to Bertram's. Once back, Alyssa collapsed on her bed, eager for the night to be over. Doubt gnawed at her, and she hoped she'd done the right thing. At least in time she'd know for sure. If Nathaniel lived, then everything would be justified. Everything would be made better. She thought of the carnage and chaos she'd unleashed upon the city, all in a desire for vengeance, only for it to be Arthur's doing, not the thieves'. Not directly, anyway, though it seemed the Serpent Guild had had a hand in it. Hopefully the gods might forgive her.

The door opened, and in stepped Bertram. Not surprisingly, he looked rather upset.

"I can scarcely believe what Zusa told me," he said. "Is it true? Did you kill Arthur?"

"I did, and I was right in doing so."

The old man locked the door, then placed his head against the wood as if he needed its support to remain standing.

"He was our last hope," he said. "We've squandered our wealth on mercenaries, destroyed the Gemcroft family's reputation, and now you ruin the only chance of bringing back any respectability to our name? Why?"

He turned to her, and the look in his eyes sent a chill running through her spine.

"Bertram?" she asked, sliding her legs underneath her. "Why did you lock the door?"

The old advisor pulled a dagger from his bed robes. For a

moment his cold rage turned to pity, and she wasn't sure which infuriated her more.

"You had such potential," he said, stepping toward her. "Instead you've denied your duties. You've led us to ruin, destroying everything I've worked my entire life for. If there's any hope for us now, it is someone, anyone, taking over."

"Including you?"

He looked insulted by the notion.

"I do this for the legacy of your entire family, generations before and generations yet to come. Not myself. Never for myself. I hope you understand."

He lunged for her, and she rolled to the side. Compared to Zusa or the Watcher he was slow, but she had no weapon, no dagger or club. She grabbed the sheets as she hit the ground beside her bed and flung them at Bertram.

"*Help!*" she screamed as she circled around, putting the broken window to her back. Bertram shoved the sheets aside, his dagger catching momentarily on them. He was between her and the door, and she thought to run past while he was entangled, but it wasn't a long enough distraction. He stepped over the sheets, his eyes locked onto her, watching, waiting for the slightest twitch so he might react. For an old man he seemed reenergized, his movements carrying purpose.

"It won't matter," he said. "You will be gone by the time they arrive, and even if they execute me, I'll have removed the sickness within our house."

She thought of Nathaniel, of Arthur, and of Bertram's insistence on marriage. Deep inside she wondered just how involved he'd been with those events, and the anger that burned within gave her the courage to do what she might never have done otherwise. When he stabbed for her chest, she didn't dodge. Instead she flung herself at him, twisting to one side in hopes of avoiding the blow. The dagger's edge slashed her flesh, the pain almost unbearable, but her mind was full of fury and the rush of battle. Her left hand grabbed his arm so he couldn't stab again, the other clutching the front of his robes. She might have lacked the strength of a man, but Bertram was old and thin.

With a mindless cry she flung him face-first toward the shattered window, where many shards still remained. He cried out once, a surprised yelp that ended in a painful shriek. Still trembling with rage, she watched as blood poured across the glass. He'd been impaled by one of the thick shards, the pointed edge digging deep into the flesh below his throat. Bertram tried to suck in another breath, but it came in gargling and wet. His arms flailed uselessly at his sides, and he sliced his hands as he grabbed more shards trying to push himself off the window.

Behind her the door broke as her guards smashed it open. They poured in once more, and this time they did not allow her to resist as they took her by the hand and led her out. She looked back only once, to make sure Bertram was still there, still bleeding.

The sickness within her house, she thought. Bertram was right. At last it had been removed. And then she broke down and cried.

CHAPTER

 29

The main quarters for the Serpents were unsurprisingly empty when Haern searched them. Given what he knew of William Ket, their leader, they would not dismiss him as lightly as the others. William took every threat seriously, and he dealt with them all as harshly as possible. Kadish was a gambler, a drinker, and a man too proud to stop celebrating when he should have been in hiding. William was easily the opposite, and would therefore be far more difficult.

Of course Haern knew where they'd go. They'd retreated there several times, usually after one of the other guilds had engaged them in a skirmish over territory. This one was smaller than their main guildhouse, with only a single door and no windows. It had once been the armory for the city guards stationed deep in the south of Veldaren, before the king repositioned them farther north and sold the building.

On his way there Haern checked the cut on his side. He'd

hidden it from Alyssa and her frightening female guard, though the guard might have noticed given her incredible skill. It was shallow, a flesh wound along his ribs. It was bleeding, though, as such cuts liked to do. Pausing to catch his breath, he leaned against the wall of a smithy and drew one of his sabers.

"Something tells me you'll get reopened a dozen times tonight," he said as he cut the edge of a cloak to make a bandage. It reminded him of trying to bandage that boy's arm while out in the snow. At least he knew who the boy was now: Nathaniel Gemcroft. No wonder he'd been a target. Of course, who had attacked him and why were no real concern. The Serpents were all that mattered right now. Assuming Deathmask handled the Spider Guild as he'd said he would, the Serpents were the only guild left to be dealt with one way or another.

A shadow shifted in the corner of his eye, elongated in a way that was unnatural to the moonlight. His mind cried out in alarm, and he dropped to one knee just in time. A crossbow bolt smacked into the wood behind him and then ricocheted off. Haern drew both his sabers as he rushed toward the main street, where the buildings would be farther apart and he'd have more room to dodge.

Some finely honed instinct in him lifted the hairs on his neck. He slid as he heard the twang of two more crossbows. Bolts flew above him, striking the ground harmlessly. At least three attackers, he realized, given how closely together they'd fired, with all three firing from the rooftops. Not good. Back on his feet in a heartbeat, he continued running, relying on the slow reloading of a crossbow to give him time.

His way was blocked, however. A man in the cloak of a Serpent landed before him, his dagger already drawn.

"Damn fool," the Serpent said.

"Same to you."

He crashed right into the man, positioning his sabers so they pushed the tip of his opponent's dagger to the side. Haern's forehead rammed the man's nose. Blood splattered across them both, blinding one of Haern's eyes. Trying to ignore the pain, Haern rolled atop him and into the wide street beyond. When he spun he saw bolts flying in. The first missed. A second passed an inch from his leg as he dodged. The third thudded into his side, and he gasped at the impact. *Is it poisoned?* he wondered, but he dismissed the thought. Poison wouldn't matter if several more buried their tips in something vital.

The man he'd rammed struggled to his feet, and Haern reacted on instinct. He knew he needed to get away from the men with the crossbows, but he also couldn't leave an opponent free to chase. He lunged, slashed away the Serpent's pitiful defense, and then cut his throat. As he bled out, Haern dove around a corner. A single bolt was fired after him, missing by a foot. And then he was running. He sheathed one of his sabers so he could wipe at the blood in his eye, then glanced back. Three Serpents leaped after him, two men and a woman, their green cloaks trailing, the color an eerie haze in the moonlight.

He crossed to the other side of the street, giving them no choice but to climb down. Again he made a decision, this one more from pride than rational thinking. They'd hurt him, maybe even poisoned him. They had to pay. His reputation was all that would hold this arrangement with the guilds and Trifect together. If they felt they could wound him, make him run, then all would be for naught.

"Come on!" he shouted, slamming his sabers together before charging. The three had abandoned their crossbows on the rooftop so they could climb down, and all of them drew short swords. As he charged they formed a triangle, trapping him in the center. He grinned at the maneuver. Clever, but it was too late to change his mind. His tactics, however, he could change. Instead of lunging at the first, as they thought he would, he spun in place, beginning his cloakdance. His feet twisted and spun, pushed to the very limits of his speed. He relied fully on instinct, for what his eyes saw through his cloaks were but snippets of his opponents. Thrust after thrust he smacked away, until one overextended, his attacker confused as to where he actually was within the cloaks. Haern broke out from the spin, double-slashing the man's arm. Down went the weapon as blood spilled and the Serpent screamed.

Back into the dance, but just for a moment, just long enough to confuse the remaining two. No time left to mess around. The pain in his side was escalating, and his fingers tingled. Assaulting the nearest, he unleashed a furious display, his swords weaving around the woman's short sword as if it were motionless. He spun as he cut her, whirling toward the last Serpent in a single smooth motion. The thief blocked only one of the two sabers, the other taking his life.

"Damn it," Haern said, pausing to catch his breath. He gingerly touched the bolt in his side, wincing as his fingers made it move the slightest bit. Too deep: he'd have to push it through and pray there'd been no poison. Before he could, he heard movement above. Too late he brought up his sabers, but instead of the expected bolt a single Serpent fell bleeding to the ground, crumpling in a heap. From the rooftop Zusa waved at him.

"The one you don't see is the one that kills you," she called down to him.

Despite his exhaustion he gave her a smile.

"Why are you here?" he asked as she climbed down to the street.

"My lady wishes the Serpents punished, and so I've come to help you. Clearly you need it."

He gestured to the bolt in his side.

"Clearly."

Without giving him warning she stepped forward, grabbed the shaft, and pushed. He clenched his jaw and ground his teeth together to hold in his scream. Warm blood dripped down the small of his back. Zusa pushed aside his cloak, retrieved the bolt, and then held it close to her eyes so she might see in the moonlight.

"Not poisoned," she said. "Either one of the gods favors you, or they were too stupid and lazy to prepare for you properly."

"Perhaps both?" He grinned at her, but the grin faltered. "Sorry about your arm."

"Sorry about your chest."

So she had noticed. He chuckled.

"If I stumble from the blood loss, make sure you kill me. I'm not sure who would be happiest to torture me, but I'd rather not find out."

"They'd probably auction the right. More money."

"Aren't you a cheery soul?" He pointed farther down the street. "Come on. The armory isn't far."

He led the way, Zusa trailing behind him, like a feminine version of his own shadow. Silent as ghosts they crisscrossed their way toward their goal. Haern checked the alleys and Zusa the rooftops for any more potential ambushes. At the armory they stopped and peered around the corner of a nearby home.

"No guards on the outside," Zusa whispered.

"That would give them away. They think this place is safe, otherwise they wouldn't come here."

"Nowhere is safe in this city."

"Well," Haern said, drawing his sabers, "let's go reinforce that lesson for them."

"How many entrances?"

He thought for a moment, then held up a single finger.

"They boarded up their windows. Together, through the door. No mercy, Zusa. Can you handle that?"

She gave him a look that showed how insulted she was.

"I was raised in the heart of Karak's temple," she said. "Mercy is not my bedfellow."

As if to prove the point she rushed ahead, and silently cursing her he followed. The door was locked, but when Haern went to draw his lock-picker's kit, she only shook her head. She mouthed something to him, but he only caught half the words. She wanted to try something, though, that much he understood. Putting her hands on the lock, she closed her eyes, and to him it looked like she was praying. Shadows slipped off her fingertips like water dripping from a melting wedge of ice. A moment later they both heard an audible click from within the lock.

Her balance wavered, but when she regained it she shot him a wink. Haern rolled his eyes.

"Ladies first," he said, spurring her into action. She flung open the door and in he followed, two deadly phantoms in the night. A single thief waited on guard, looking half-awake. They cut his throat as they rushed past. He never even had a chance to cry out an alarm. They bashed through a door and into an elaborate room, one that instantly felt familiar to Haern. It was like so many others of the posh headquarters the guilds created, all curtains and pillows, alcohol and sex.

Their first warning something was wrong came when the door behind them slammed shut. The second was when William Ket greeted them with a warm smile from his chair on the far side of the room.

"Well, well, well, at last I meet the Watcher," he said, sounding far too pleased with himself. "And you've brought a friend.

Excellent. Did you think I'd be foolish enough to think you couldn't find me here, not with your...storied reputation?"

"The curtains," Zusa whispered, her body tensed like a cat's before a pounce.

"I know."

William's grin spread.

"Alyssa called off her mercenaries, the silly girl. She had us on the run, but then suddenly she flooded Veldaren with bored, unemployed men with a penchant for violence. How could I not take advantage of such a gift?"

The curtains pushed aside, revealing armored men standing in every little alcove. Haern estimated at least thirty. He felt his blood run cold. So this would be how it ended. His side ached, every breath hurt his chest, his head pounded from exhaustion, and standing before him, William Ket laughed.

"Don't you give in," Zusa whispered, her voice almost a hiss. "They are children to you, you understand? We are the lions. We are the hunters."

Haern thought of his moment in Karak's temple, when he'd been in the very presence of the Lion of Karak. It had roared, and he'd gazed into an emptiness that seemed to go on forever. He remembered the terror, and he realized that he'd been far more afraid then than he was now. Focusing upon that fear, he knew he could be that lion to these men. He looked at them as they waited for the order to attack, let them see in his eyes that same emptiness, that same certainty of their death. Pulling his hood low, he let the shadows of the torchlight scatter his features. Beside him Zusa wrapped her cloak tight about her body and then hunched low.

"Kill them," William said.

Haern went left, Zusa right. He felt every nerve in his body firing, and he gave in to his instincts completely. This was the beast Thren had created over the years, day in and day out with training, practice, lectures, and tutors. This was the monster whose teeth had been sharpened by half a decade skulking in the shadows, slaughtering the thieves of the night. His sabers were a blur as he cut down the first, the mercenary's ax too slow to block. The two closest rushed in, wielding long swords. He parried their thrusts, which felt slow, as if his opponents fought in molasses. Blood soaked his sabers as the rest came rushing in, swinging with their clubs, maces, and swords.

Cutting, twisting, never staying in the same place. As his feet shifted and turned he thought of the hours he'd been forced to stand in strange stances to pacify a tutor. As he curled his body around thrusts, he remembered the complicated stretches another tutor had taught him to do every morning. As he slashed and dodged, he thought of the words of his father.

They can't kill you until you let them. That is why you must be better. That is why you must be perfect. Never, ever let them think they can win.

Said to a thirteen-year-old boy. More than anything, he wished his father could be there to see what he had created. One after another the mercenaries fell. They knew how to bully. They knew how to put the strength of their arms into their blows, and they could handle the rudimentary thrusts and parries of the battlefield. But Haern felt himself beyond them, beyond anything. They scored cuts on him, to be sure, but he felt the pain in a distant place locked in the back of his mind. They would not kill him. He would not let them. His wrist might bleed from a lucky stab of a sword. His chest might ache where a club struck him before he could dodge. His eyes might sting from blood running into them from where a blade had slashed his forehead. But they would not kill him.

Zusa's cry pulled him back from the animal, from the

mindless killer. Despite the many dead she was overwhelmed. Refusing to give the thieves anything, Haern descended upon them. Their backs were turned to him, and he thrust and stabbed and kicked, shoving them aside so he might link up with Zusa. She was bleeding, and so was he, but they grinned.

We were made for this, he thought.

Back to back they turned to their foes. Of the original thirty, only ten remained. Blood and gore soaked the floor where it wasn't covered by a body. The psychological damage was just as bad. None looked ready to attack. Whatever they had been paid, it wasn't enough. The first turned to flee, and as if a dam had broken, the rest rushed for the door. Ignoring them, Haern looked for William, not finding him.

"Where is he?" he asked.

Zusa rushed to the chair he'd been sitting in and flung it aside. Hidden behind it she found a ring, and she pulled, revealing a trapdoor. Haern followed her as the mercenaries broke down the door behind them and poured out into the night. The trapdoor led to a tunnel, tight enough that Haern had to crawl along on his elbows, worming his way through. It wasn't a long tunnel, and Zusa pushed open another trapdoor and then helped him out.

They emerged behind the armory, the trapdoor hidden by a compacted layer of dirt. Haern felt his muscles aching, the familiar feeling of receding energy after a fight coming over him. He'd expected to search for William, to have to hunt for wherever he'd run off to, but instead saw him lying dead in the street, two men standing over him.

"You look like shit," Senke said, still cleaning William's blood off his mace.

Haern tried to think of a response, but only stared dumbly

at him and Tarlak, who looked vaguely amused by the whole ordeal.

"Delysia spent the better part of tonight begging us to help you," the wizard said, his arms crossed. "And as usual, I finally gave in."

"How?" Haern asked. He'd meant to ask how they had found him, but breathing suddenly seemed difficult. His body was finally taking account of all the blows and cuts he'd received, and it wasn't happy.

"What, find you?" Tarlak asked. "I'm a wizard. That's just what I do."

Haern saw Zusa down on one knee, bracing herself with one of her arms. Her normally dark skin was disturbingly pale.

"Are you hurt?" he asked, stepping to her side.

"Of course I am," she said. "Farewell, Watcher. I have done as my mistress asked. Let your friends help you from now on."

She rose to her feet, took an uneasy step, then another, and by the time she was running her balance looked like it had returned. Haern watched her go, hoping she'd be all right.

"So," Tarlak said, smacking him on the back. "What's next on the agenda?"

Haern looked back at the body of William Ket, and he mentally checked another off the list in his head. One left, just one.

"Leon Connington."

Senke whistled. "Going after the big dogs, are we? Who else after that?"

Haern shook his head. "He's the last. Everyone else has agreed, or..."

He gestured toward the body.

"The last?" Tarlak laughed. "Aren't you a freak? Well, let's go. Leon's not exactly close to here."

They walked down the street, and for a moment Haern let himself relax. With the three of them, one a wizard, any thieves would have to be incredibly brave or reckless to consider an ambush. He used his shirt to wipe the blood from his forehead, then pressed it against his eyes. They watered, but when he pulled the shirt away he could see better. Senke twirled his two maces in his hands, and Haern wished he could feel as energetic as Senke looked. He might have just been the lion, but now he felt like a lamb, ready to give up everything just to lie down and sleep. Every single part of his body ached.

"How long until dawn?" Haern asked.

"About two hours," said Tarlak. "You been at this the whole night?"

"Just before sunset, yes."

"We of the magical profession call that biting off more than you can chew."

"And we of the stabby profession call that getting yourself killed," said Senke.

Haern winced as an awkward step flared pain along his chest and to his back.

"You two are such wonderful help," he muttered.

Leon Connington's estate was one of the best-guarded places in the city, and all three of them knew it. The warning letter Haern had sent certainly hadn't given them reason to slack off, either. Tall stone walls surrounded the mansion, the single opening a thick iron gate with two guards. They stood at attention, no slacking there either. From far down the road Haern and the others observed the gate and planned.

"There will be mercenaries stationed throughout the mansion," Haern said as they stared. "And traps along the ground, other than the path leading directly to the door. If we're to get to Leon, I think we'll need to be stealthy about this."

"Stealthy?" asked Tarlak. He gestured to his bright yellow robes. "Stealthy?"

Haern gave him a dumb look, then shrugged.

"Any other ideas?"

The wizard lifted his arms high, and a steady stream of magical incantations slipped from his lips. Fire burst about his hands, growing, growing, and then soaring toward the gate as an enormous ball. It hit the iron and detonated, blasting the gates aside and tearing off chunks of stone. Haern didn't see what happened to the guards, and he didn't want to think about it either.

"Stealthy," said Tarlak, hurling a smaller ball of fire that rolled across the ground. It detonated the various traps along the grass leading toward the mansion, filling the night with the sound of their explosions. Haern didn't know whether he should laugh or cry.

"Stealthy?" he asked Senke, who only shrugged.

Tarlak sent one more blast, this one aimed at the front door. He frowned as the spell evaporated into smoke just before contact. He sent another at a window, this a thick shard of ice. Again it broke, this time into water that showered the ground harmlessly.

"Strong wards," the wizard said. "Looks like the rest is up to you. Have fun!"

Senke led the way, Haern following.

"Out of his damn mind," Haern muttered.

Tarlak watched them go, offering a prayer for luck. He wished he could help, but the few spells he'd cast had put a deep ache in his head, and he knew he had but a few more before he'd be worthless. Unable to help it, though, he neared the gates to observe his handiwork.

"Getting better," he said, estimating the size of the explosion. "Tarlak Eschaton?"

He turned, and with mild surprise saw the giant man with the painted face approaching from down the street.

"I'm thrilled we could meet again," he said. "Especially with my mouth un-gagged."

Ghost pointed toward the mansion. "Is the Watcher inside?"

"He is," Tarlak said, standing in the center of the gate. "He's a bit busy right now, so you'll have to wait until tomorrow to resume whatever grudge you have against him."

"No grudge," Ghost said, still approaching. "Just money."

Tarlak snapped his fingers, summoning a spark of flame at his fingertips.

"No closer," he warned. Ghost only laughed. "Well, don't say I didn't warn you."

He slammed his hands together, and a ring of fire rolled out from his waist, burning the air with a heavy roar. His opponent fell back, and he landed on his shoulder so the fire could pass harmlessly above him. Tarlak gave him no reprieve, another spell already on his lips. This time it was ice, thick shards that flew like arrows. Ghost rolled, the shards shattering upon the ground behind him. Only one drew blood, a thin gash along his side. On a man so giant, it looked like a cat scratch.

"How long?" Ghost roared, back on his feet again and lunging. Tarlak tried to ignore him, kept focused on his spellcraft, but he knew what Ghost was asking. How long might he last casting his spells? How long until the well of energy within him ran empty, and the best he could summon was a little puff of smoke from his fingertips?

Given the pounding of his head, he didn't think it'd be long.

His hands clapped together, and the space before him filled with a swirling wall of smoke and fire. Ghost's swords passed through it, but his feet dug into the ground, halting his momentum and preventing him from continuing into the inferno. Tarlak muttered. He'd hoped for a charred corpse to leap through. How the Abyss did this guy react so fast?

Leaving the wall of fire intact, Tarlak guessed a direction and pointed. This time luck was with him, for of the two directions in which Ghost might have leaped, he'd chosen correctly. A bolt of lightning shot from his finger, striking the giant man square in the chest. He fired a second one, this one hitting his leg. Ghost screamed, but more in anger than pain. Tarlak felt the hairs on his neck stand on end. Short of taking the man's head off, it didn't look like there'd be any way to stop him.

"You hurt my friend," Tarlak said, summoning small meteors of lava and flinging them. Ghost hunched on his knees, blocking with his swords. The meteors plinked off the steel, coupled with an impressive but harmless shower of sparks.

"You hurt my sister," he said, pressing his wrists together and hurling shards of stone from his palms. Ghost jumped and leaped like an enormous spider. Only two shards hit, and again the wounds were superficial.

"You even hurt Brug."

His bolt of lightning shot out, but his aim was off. Ghost didn't dodge this time, instead lunging straight for the kill. A sword slammed into Tarlak, piercing his flesh. He gasped as the white-hot pain spread throughout his body.

"And I hurt you," Ghost whispered, his cheek pressed against the wizard's.

Out came the blade, and Tarlak collapsed. Unable to stop him, he could only watch as Ghost passed through the gates, continuing the hunt for his real prey. The blood flowed, staining his yellow robes red. His mind throbbing from pain and exhaustion, he crawled across the ground, bleeding upon the street as he headed for safety.

Damn you, Haern, he thought as he collapsed after hardly crossing any distance. *You better kill him for me, or I'll... I'll...*

And then he felt his thoughts slipping away like leaves in a storm, and unconsciousness came and took him.

CHAPTER 30

Deathmask knew he might be walking into an early grave, but he didn't let worry show on his face, not with the rest of his guild watching him.

"Keep an eye out for anything suspicious," he said to the others. "I don't expect him to do anything stupid, but it is Thren Felhorn, after all. Stupid to us is step five of a plan for him."

They approached the headquarters of the Spider Guild. It was more a mansion than anything else, though careful examination would have shown how the windows were reinforced so no one could break through, and all doors but the front were boarded over. Two men in gray waited at the front, and they drew their swords and daggers at his approach. Veliana glared at them, but she remained quiet.

"I am Deathmask, leader of the Ash Guild. I've come to speak with Thren."

"Only if Thren says," one said. The other banged on the

door. A small window opened, and the guard relayed the message to someone inside. A few minutes later the door opened.

"Just him," said one of the Spiders from inside, pointing to Deathmask.

"It's all right," he told Veliana, who looked ready to object. "I can handle myself."

He stepped inside.

The interior of the mansion might have once been well decorated, but nearly all its original treasures had been plundered by the Spider Guild and sold off. Bright squares on the walls showed where paintings had once been, and in many places the floor was scraped and dull, as if the carpet had been ripped up, or a long-present rug removed. Deathmask tracked the turns and doors to ensure he could find his way back, all the while going over every bit of information he knew about the near-legendary leader of the Spider Guild. At last they reached a door, and the thief gestured. Deathmask opened it, stepped inside, and closed it behind him, finding himself alone in a small den with Thren Felhorn.

Thren looked old. That was the first thing that struck Deathmask. He knew the man's age, still in the late forties, but his hair was fully gray. His skin had a tight, stretched look about it, but his eyes still shone with intensity. He stood beside a fireplace, a drink in hand. His two short swords hung at his sides, their hilts gleaming in the light. He smiled at Deathmask, but the smile hid a strong sense of impatience and contempt. Thren surely knew the reason for his coming, and was not pleased.

"Welcome," Thren said. His voice was deep, and the power in it impressed Deathmask to no end. He wished he had such a commanding voice as that. The man could probably describe himself taking a shit and still make it sound authoritative. "I've heard rumors of your assuming control from Garrick Lowe, not that there is much to assume."

"What is it we say to the ladies, it's not the size of the sword, but the skill in the wielding?"

Thren chuckled. This was good. If he could get the man to feel a sense of kinship, things might go more smoothly.

"Maybe so, but even I wouldn't assault a man with a spear wielding only a butter knife."

"You know you would, Thren, if the price was right. You'd cut the man three times before he knew where you were, too."

The flattery didn't get him what he'd hoped. Thren waved a dismissive hand and set down his drink.

"Enough. The night is late, and you didn't come here to banter, nor to make introductions. This is about that Watcher madman, isn't it?"

"I must admit, I am curious as to your thoughts on the deal."

"Deal? *Deal?* This is no deal. This is enslavement. This is the king severing our testicles and selling them to the Trifect. Do you know how this world works, Deathmask? The strong take what the weak cannot hold, and that is the proper order of things. The foolish and the naïve try to prop up the weak, to protect them with strength that is not their own. Babes, all of them, nothing but babes forever suckling their mother's milk."

"We would still make plenty of coin," Deathmask said. "And we have accepted protection money before. Is that not a way of the weak voluntarily giving up what they have to the strong?"

"Never on this scale before," Thren insisted. "They don't just protect their own, but the entire city. What insanity led to this? I have watched them bleed before me. Entire nations could live and die on the wealth I have taken from the Trifect's safes. Yet now they throw gold at me in a pitiful attempt to barter safety and peace of mind. At least Alyssa was willing to fight back, though even that moment of pride lasted only two nights before coward-ice returned, no doubt replaced by this deal from the king."

Deathmask saw an open bottle on a small stand, and he walked over and poured himself a drink. He sniffed it once, and was pleased by the scent of strawberries. Thren didn't object, so he took a drink and set it aside.

"This is how I see it," he said. "It's been what, ten years? A man can only fight for so long, even the greatest of us. We need a break. We need a return to some shred of normality."

"Says the man wearing a mask."

Deathmask laughed. "Relative normality, then."

He watched Thren carefully, though he knew it was pointless. The man could guard his emotions better than anyone, probably better than even him with his mask on. Thren was watching him as well, gauging his reactions, staring into his eyes as if he could divine the true purpose of his visit.

"This Watcher..." Deathmask said. "He claims he'll kill everyone who refuses. Do you think he'll succeed?"

"You and I are alive," said Thren. "It seems to me he is doing a poor job. And it doesn't matter. He could kill everyone, but he won't kill me, and as long as I survive, the Trifect will never have a moment of peace."

Deathmask tapped his forehead with a finger.

"As long as you are alive...that's the clincher right there, Thren. Don't tense up, I'm not here to kill you. That wasn't a threat, just a statement. This war is yours, solely yours, and it is yours to end as you see fit. But you won't have the ending you're hoping for. The Trifect is too big. Yes, you've hurt it, killed many, and taken away their coin. But has it mattered? If an opponent is not allowed to surrender, they'll keep fighting and fighting. Give them the option of defeat. That's what this deal is, if you look at it from their perspective. They admit they cannot defeat you, cannot protect themselves from you. So they make it worth your while to instead do the protecting for them.

It's a bribe, nothing more, nothing less, and in a city where this is hardly an unusual circumstance."

Thren looked tired of the debate, and Deathmask knew he was treading on thin ice. He'd lied, at least partially, when he said he hadn't come there to kill Thren. Could Thren have read him correctly, despite his best attempts at subterfuge? More than anything he wanted a victory here without bloodshed. Other thief leaders could come and go, but if Thren died the Trifect might decide it didn't need protection after all. Thren's power had shrunk considerably over the past few years, but his reputation had not.

"Aren't you tired of this?" he asked, letting his voice soften. "Every man and woman in this city has lost someone these past ten years. Despite the rumors, I know you are human, and lost as much as any."

For a moment, so quick Deathmask thought he might have imagined it, Thren allowed himself to look exhausted, look torn with despair.

"It's for that loss I continue," he said. "Why else would I go on? To accept anything less than total victory would be an insult, not just to myself, but my wife, my..."

He seemed to return to his senses, and he glared at Deathmask as if he were the reason for the sudden weakness.

"I will not agree," he said. "And if that is your sole purpose here, get out now."

Deathmask chuckled. The slightest misstep might cost him his life. But this was it. This was the heart of everything.

"That Watcher, I hear he is good, almost impossibly good. I also hear he fights like you. Did you know that? As if he might be your own son, but we both know that couldn't be. He died in a fire, of course. I'm sure you saw his body..."

He looked to Thren, letting the guildmaster know there was far more he wasn't telling. No lie. No bluff. Thren opened his mouth, then closed it. Those blue eyes barely moved. *What firestorm of thought rages behind them?* Deathmask wondered. Taking a deep breath, he tried his wildest gambit.

"If he succeeds, the Watcher will be a legend. He'll have beaten both the Trifect and the thief guilds, all in a single night. He'll have ended ten years of conflict with a stroke of his swords. The entire city will fear him, for he will be the King's Watcher, enforcer of the truce. The night won't belong to us anymore. It'll belong to him."

He swallowed. Now or never. Take the risk.

"He'll have surpassed even you, Thren. How amazing must that man be?"

Thren looked like a heavy burden had settled upon him. His muscular frame wasn't quite so strong anymore. The terrible will that had ruled him weakened, and a million questions died unspoken on his lips. For perhaps the first time ever, Thren Felhorn looked uncertain.

"Did he send you here?" he finally asked. Deathmask nodded. "So be it. Give him his chance. My guild will accept the terms, so long as the Watcher lives. This city is a cruel one, and even now it might have claimed him."

"I doubt it," Deathmask said, his heart pounding in his chest. "Given who he is and who made him. Come the morning we'll count the bodies, and we'll see what remains of those in power. I have a feeling, though, that tonight is when it all ends."

"Leave my home," Thren said. "And never speak a word of this to anyone, or I will kill you."

Deathmask bowed low.

"As you wish," he said, glad the mask could hide his enormous smile. More relieved than he'd ever been in his life, he exited the room, wove unguided through the halls, and emerged from the mansion, alive and victorious.

CHAPTER

31

Because of the breastplates the guards wore, Senke led the way, his flanged maces able to punch through if swung hard enough. Haern followed, watching behind them as much as ahead. The entire mansion was in chaos. Servants fled every which way, and several times he heard them cry out the names of thief guilds. His lips curled into a vile grin every time. No thief guild, not this time. They were worse than any guild. They'd come, live or die, to complete their mission, though so far it was only the guards who were doing the dying.

"Where might Leon be hiding?" Haern asked as he yanked his saber free from the armpit of a dead mercenary.

"Holed up in his bedroom?" Senke suggested. "He's not the most mobile of men."

"And where would that be?"

Senke gestured ahead, and then behind them.

"Your guess is as good as mine."

The cries of "Intruder" followed them as they rushed along. They shoved servants aside if they got in the way, but most were smart enough to cower or turn and run.

"Bottom floor," Haern said as they passed a set of stairs. "I can't imagine him climbing those every night."

Senke opened another door, then slammed it immediately shut, and on the other side arrows sank into the wood with heavy thunks.

"I think we're getting somewhere," Senke said, and he grinned.

They backtracked, weaving through the corridors so they might curl around their ambushers. Sure enough, they found them at the intersection of another hallway, kneeling behind small overturned tables that had once housed vases of immeasurable wealth. All three held crossbows and wore boiled leather armor. Senke crashed into two, Haern the third. Making quick work of them, they turned left and continued along.

"It should be harder than this," insisted Senke, needing to shout to be heard over the commotion.

"Don't say it, or it might come true."

In the next hallway they met six mercenaries, all wielding short swords and small circular shields of wood latched together with iron. Senke laughed and rushed the six with wild glee, as if he could see Haern's glare behind him. Despite his exhaustion, Haern couldn't help but feel energized, and he raced to Senke's side so they might crash into the mercenaries in a single brutal collision. Every turn might house more men ready to kill them. Every door might hide archers ready to shoot barbs into their throats. And neither could care less.

The shields proved difficult, mostly because Haern had little experience dealing with them. A shield was hardly standard issue for the men who stalked the night. He kicked and stabbed as he and Senke slammed into the mercenaries, cutting the tendons of one guard's arm and tripping another. Before Haern could finish this one off, another was there, and his saber slapped harmlessly against the wood of his shield, not even drawing a splinter from the finely polished surface. The soldier thrust for his midsection, but Haern parried it aside with his left hand, leaped closer to the wall, and then kicked off it to give his maneuver speed. His saber crashed into the guard's neck, punching through the leather armor and into flesh.

Swords stabbed for where he should have been, but he dropped to the ground and rolled. Senke, as if in some mental link with him, saw and jumped over him, blocking blow after blow with his maces. Haern leaped to his feet, slamming his left shoulder against the wall to painfully kill the rest of his momentum. Only one guard remained within reach, and Haern desperately shoved one of his sabers in the way. The guard's short sword deflected the saber and stabbed the wall, close enough that Haern could see his reflection in the blade. And then his sabers were thrusting in, and the shield could not block all his attacks.

Senke took down the last mercenary, hammering his shield with his maces until the guard made a mistake, not surprising given how the rest of his fellows had fallen and panic was surely crawling through his veins. His sword slashed, but he overextended, and Senke broke his elbow with an upward swipe of his mace. A kick to his neck blasted him against the wall, and he slid to the ground unconscious.

"You hurt?" Senke asked. Haern shook his head. "Good. One of those sons of bitches cut my leg. Delysia's going to be pissed at me."

Deeper and deeper in they went, until at last they found Leon's bedroom. It was empty.

"Slap me silly," said Senke, looking around. "Where could that giant tub of lard have gone off to?"

He took a step forward, not seeing the thin string laced across the door. Haern did, and he pulled Senke back by his cloak just before the entire room erupted in flame. The fire swirled about in a momentary funnel before fading away, leaving nothing but ashes inside, the rest of the house safely intact.

"A trap?" Senke asked, his eyes wide. "A fucking *magical* trap?"

"You're welcome," Haern said. He leaned against the wall and closed his eyes, wishing he could just order away the headache pounding in his forehead.

"Damn traps. Where to now? He might have left, Haern, and then what the fuck do we do?"

"Stay calm," Haern said, eyes still closed. "He slept here until an alarm sounded because of your wizard friend, and so he gets up, activates the trap. He's in a hurry, but not moving fast. The rest of his guards are ushering him along. Where do you go? Where is safe, close, and defensible?"

"You take him where no one could have gotten to yet, where there couldn't possibly be an ambush waiting. You take him to the mercenaries' quarters."

Haern opened his eyes and shot his mentor a wink.

"Good a guess as any. In the back, and away from the other quarters. He wouldn't want their low-class manners upsetting any of his privileged guests."

"You going to make it, Haern?"

"Worry about yourself."

They rushed along, and this time Haern pushed himself to the front. Despite the help, this was still his task, his responsibility. If anyone should be walking into traps, it should be him. But there was only one trap left, and they sprung it together.

Finding a long corridor leading to a thick set of double doors, they rushed into it only to have doors behind them fly open. Out rushed mercenaries, five in all.

"Leave them to me," Senke cried. "Go after Leon, now!"

Haern accepted the order without delay. He rushed toward those double doors, and when he reached them he leaped feet-first, wanting to go crashing in with a frightening display of skill and strength.

His foot slammed into the door, followed by the rest of him, and then he dropped to the ground. His whole body aching, he realized the doors opened outward only. Feeling far more humble, he grabbed a handle and pulled. Instead of making a vicious display of skill and strength, he walked inside a hurt, calm, exhausted man.

"You," said Leon from the far side of the room. Rows of bunks were built into either side. Four personal guards stood before him, forming a human wall of protection.

"Me," Haern said, bowing low.

"Who is paying you for this?" Leon asked. Sweat dripped down his thick neck, and blotches covered his face. To Haern he looked like a pig that had been overfed and then stuffed into fine clothing. "Thren? Alyssa? Maybe the king? Tell me, what did they offer you?"

Haern laughed. He couldn't help it. Would Leon even believe the truth? Could a man in his position understand there were things beyond wealth and influence? Could he understand a desire for atonement, for a single moment of rest and relief from a life devoted to slaughter and revenge? Or would he just see a madman? Would he hear only nonsense and lies?

"I do it because I want to," he said, figuring that if there was anything Leon might understand, it would be that. "And you have the ability to make me not want to. Last chance, Leon. Accept the terms, or accept my blades."

"Neither. You're just a rabid dog, and my men will put you down."

Two of the guards pulled out crossbows. In a single smooth motion Haern unclasped the cloaks from his neck and spun them into the air, just before the guards pressed the triggers. Twisting behind the cover, he made himself as small a target as possible. The arrows punched holes through the cloaks and sailed on, neither hitting flesh. As the cloaks fell, Haern rushed the mercenaries, his sabers feeling light as air in his hands, just extensions of his body, keen edges of his will. This was it. This was the last. His night was done. The men would die, Leon would die, and he would have his truce.

The two abandoned their crossbows and drew swords, falling behind the others, who pushed ahead. There was only enough space for two to stand side by side, and that only barely. Haern used his greater mobility to his advantage, weaving like a snake preparing to strike. He smacked down every thrust and then struck with the other saber, cutting thin slashes across their faces and necks. Each hit made them angrier, until at last they tried rushing as one.

Haern wrapped an arm around the post of a bunk, whirling across the mattress and to the other side. A whirlwind of steel, he cut down two mercenaries from behind, then turned on the other two, who were unprepared for the sudden assault. A third fell before lifting his sword into position, and one versus one, the last stood no chance. He was only a sellsword, and had maybe killed a handful of men in his lifetime. Haern had killed twenty just breaking into Leon's mansion.

When Leon realized he was alone, he fell to his knees and pleaded in his high-pitched voice.

"Please, you're a reasonable man. You can listen, yes? I'll pay you, double, triple whatever you were offered. That deal of yours, that's it, right? I'll accept, of course, anything you want!"

Haern approached him, his sabers dripping blood.

"You're lying," he said. "I see it in your eyes, your lips, your trembling hands. Besides, I'm just a rabid dog."

He cut Leon's throat, and he watched the life leave the fat man's eyes as the door behind him opened.

"He dead?" he heard Senke ask.

Haern turned. He wanted to smile, but he felt exhausted, and he knew getting out of the mansion might not be any easier than entering. Senke stood in the doorway, and he seemed happy enough, but something was wrong. Something was moving…

And then the sword pierced the front of Senke's chest. The man arched back, his eyes wide. His limbs trembled, and blood dribbled from his lips. As his body collapsed, slipping free of the blade, Haern was too stunned to even scream. Behind him, now occupying the doorway, stood Ghost, the white paint on his face speckled with red. His grin was as wide as Senke's had been.

"I found you," he said, his deep voice rumbling in the confined room.

"Why?" Haern asked. It was the only question he seemed able to think. "Why? Why now?"

"Because I have a reputation to keep, Watcher. I've been paid to kill you, and so you'll have to die. It's the way things work."

He lifted his swords into position, and slowly, as if in a dream, Haern did the same. In the back of his mind he felt anger building and building, like it belonged to someone else yet would soon be given to him whether he wanted it or not.

"You monster," he said, crouching into position.

"Monster? I see one body at my feet, Watcher, and five at yours. How am I the monster?"

What could he say to that? That his kills had a pure motive? That he wasn't motivated by greed? The arguments felt hollow, petty. They were two killers, and they eyed one another with an understanding so few could know.

"Then I'm the monster this city needs," Haern said. "But we don't need you."

Ghost lunged, no doubt hoping to catch him off guard while he talked. Haern was better than that, though still his heart leaped in his chest. How could the man be so huge and yet so fast? With little ground behind him, he refused to retreat. His sabers met the swords, and they rang with deafening volume. Haern's tired arms jolted with pain.

"Need?" Ghost asked, and his voice washed over Haern like a physical wave. With every word he struck again, hammering away at Haern as if Haern were a door barring his way. "This city needs its eyes opened. It needs its cowardly heart ripped from its chest and held up to the light. What it does *not* need is some damn fool vigilante."

So fast were his movements, and so strong, Haern could only twist and parry without hope of retaliation. The few times he blocked, he felt the impact travel all the way up his arm. Even at the peak of his skill he might have struggled to win. Now, after a full night without rest, his nerves frayed, his energy spent, he had only one last desperate gasp to hold on to, fueled by the corpse of Senke slumped beside the door.

"No," he whispered, a denial of everything before him. Of failing so close to his goal. Of letting Senke's murderer go unpunished. Of succumbing to the anger in those brown eyes surrounded by paint and blood. Of dying.

"No."

At the end of the room was a single large window, and Haern turned toward it, running with a speed Ghost could not hope to match. He crossed his arms, ducked his head, and leaped through. Glass shattered, and he felt its edges cut into his flesh. It didn't matter. Hitting the ground, he rolled, then dug his heels into the earth. He glared back at the window, suppressed anger bursting free with a fire he felt sear his veins. Not caring about the blood, not caring about the jagged edges still lodged in his arms and forehead, he took two steps and leaped back through.

He caught Ghost pulling up before the broken glass, and his sabers slashed an X across his muscular chest. Their bodies collided. Haern's knee rammed into Ghost's groin. His forehead slammed the man's neck. The glass lodged in his head tore skin, blood ran freely, but several shards ripped into Ghost's throat. Despite Haern's momentum and surprise, Ghost refused to go down. He held his ground, matching Haern fury for fury. With no room to cut or thrust, he punched Haern in the chest with a hilt, then caught his chin with a roundhouse. Feeling a tooth fly loose, Haern dropped to his knees and rolled forward. His sabers slashed out, cutting the tender flesh above Ghost's heels. The giant man's shriek rewarded his efforts.

But Haern wasn't done. Tears filled his eyes, born of pain both physical and from the torment of Senke's corpse refusing to fade from his sight. He kicked back into Ghost then stabbed his sabers. Warm blood poured across his hands. Steel pierced flesh again and again. Ghost crumpled to his knees, then fell upon a gore-filled smear atop the bare floor. Haern hovered over him, one eye swollen shut, the cut on his chest reopened, his face rivulets of blood from shards of glass, his clothes equally soaked. And then he screamed, the saddened, burdened, victorious monster.

Slowly the sane part of him returned. He thought to carry Senke's body, to make sure they could bury him properly, but he knew he lacked the energy. Limping over, he knelt and kissed the man's forehead.

"I'm sorry," he whispered. Thinking of a distant memory, he reached underneath Senke's bloody shirt and retrieved a pendant—that of the Golden Mountain.

"I hope you're with him now, Senke," Haern said, slipping the pendant around his own neck. "Think well on me. Might not be long before I need you to plead my case to enter within."

Beside him Ghost let out a moan, somehow alive despite his many wounds. Blood dripped from his lips as he pushed his head up. Haern slowly stood, and he pointed a blade toward the man's neck. He felt his rage ebbing, leaving behind something hollow deep within his chest.

"Do you want mercy?" Haern asked him.

"Not..." Ghost coughed, the sound wet and certainly fatal. "Not from you."

Haern sheathed his sabers, went to the broken window. Ghost's head settled back on the bloodied floor, and he let out a long, shuddering breath.

"Suffer as you wish," Haern said before stepping out. "But it's your choice."

He stayed close to the house, wary of any more traps. At the front he followed the path. The gateway was empty, and dimly he wondered where Tarlak had gone off to. He stood there dumbly, looking, and then saw him two blocks down the street, his yellow robes rather hard to miss. As he approached, he saw that Tarlak was slumped against a building.

"Had to get away," the wizard said, sounding drowsy. "Just in case he... just in case he came back."

All across the front of his robes was an ominous circle of blood.

"How bad?" Haern asked, kneeling beside him so he could check the wound.

"Not bad," Tarlak said, his eyelids drooping. "Better than you, from what I see. Where's Senke?"

The name nearly made Haern choke. Every last bit of his self-control kept him speaking, kept him moving.

"He won't be coming back," he said.

Tarlak heard this, started to ask something else, then remained quiet. Tears fell from his eyes.

"He'll be with Ashhur now," he whispered.

"Come on," Haern said, putting an arm around him to help support his weight. "We'll be joining him if we don't hurry. I think there's about to be a lot of angry people on the street."

"I think I agree."

They limped down the street, and whether through luck or the grace of Ashhur, they made it to the Crimson and Delysia's healing hands without any further trouble.

CHAPTER

 32

Come the morning, Alyssa awoke feeling like her temples were ready to explode. The dim light hurt her eyes, and she covered them with an arm.

"Milady?" she heard someone say.

"What is it?" she asked. "Can it not wait?"

"Forgive me, milady. My name is Cecil Glenhollow, and I come with a message from Lord John Gandrem of Felwood."

Alyssa removed her arm and glared. The knight stood over her, looking a mixture of awkwardness and impatience. She wondered what fool of her guard had let the man come to her, especially with her so indecent. She pulled her blankets tight about her and sat up.

"Whatever business you have, it can wait," she said. "Have my servants prepare you some food, and my guards will—"

"My lady," said Cecil, "it is about your son."

Her mouth dropped open, and then she saw the parchment

in the knight's hand. She took it from him and unrolled it. Her eyes scanned, not reading, only looking for the one sentence that meant everything. She missed it the first time, but there it was, just the second line of the entire thing.

I believe you will be pleased to know that, contrary to what you have been told, your son Nathaniel is in my company, and alive and well.

Alive...

She flung her arms around the knight and hugged him as tears wetted her face.

"Thank you," she whispered. The knight stood shocked-still, as if unsure what he might or might not do to avoid insult. Pulling back, she kissed the man's scruffy cheek, then rushed for her bedroom, not caring that she wore only loose bed robes.

"You'll take me to him?" she asked even as she exited the room.

"But, yes...of course," said Cecil, having to hurry to keep up.

Alyssa couldn't believe how giddy she felt. The Watcher had not lied. Nathaniel was alive, and now she could go to him, could hold him, could keep him close for the rest of his life as he grew into the man to lead her fortune.

Nathaniel was alive. No matter how many times she told it to herself, it never lost its impact. Nathaniel was alive, alive, praise the gods, alive!

When she arrived at her room, Cecil respectfully remained outside. Hurrying about, Alyssa opened a closet and ran out-fit combinations through her head. Someone else knocked on the door, and she told whoever it was to enter without a thought. In stepped a younger man, a distant cousin of hers named Terrance. His features were soft, his reddish-blond hair carefully trimmed. He walked into her room trying to put on a somber face, but he was clearly giddy with news. When he saw the joy on her face, his own lit up. He must have thought she'd be grieving Arthur's loss, she realized. Foolish man.

"Forgive me for the intrusion," Terrance said. "When I heard about Bertram's...betrayal, I went through his things. I'm learning my father's trade, you see, and he works with accounts and..."

"Hurry it up," Alyssa said, yanking off her robes and pulling a loose dress over her head. The man flushed a deep red, and he stammered a bit, but he continued.

"Anyway, rumors have it that you wouldn't be able to pay the mercenaries, or to help with repairs. Bertram told my father that, anyway, and several of the servants." He saw the look she gave and so he skipped to the point. "Thing is, Bertram was lying. I found his ledger for the mercenaries' payments, and it only comes to a third of your current wealth. Expensive, to be sure, but not near what he..."

She kissed the man, laughed, and then tied a sash about her waist before flinging open another closet and searching for a thick-enough coat for the ride north.

"I need a replacement for Bertram," she said. "And I have no time to search for one, so you'll have to do, Terrance."

His jaw nearly hit the floor.

"Me? But I'm still an apprentice, and my father says I can't own my own store until I reach my twentieth year. To try and manage all this...?"

"Well, you start today."

"But why? Where are you going?"

Alyssa laughed again.

"I'm going to get my son."

*   *   *

Matthew Pensfield felt the first twinges of consciousness pulling at him, and he resisted. Dull aches felt like the only welcome awaiting him. His gradual awareness thawed from whatever cold sleep it'd fallen into, and he remembered fighting, protecting the boy, Tristan. Or was it Nathaniel? And how was he alive? He *was* alive, right?

His eyes fluttered open, and there in front of him sat the boy with two names, his head in his hands as he stared at the floor.

"Tristan?" Matthew asked, his voice coming out like a strained croak. The boy startled, but his surprise didn't last long. A smile spread across his young face, and it lit up his eyes.

"You're awake!" he said.

"I reckon so."

Tristan hugged him, eliciting a cough. It felt like half his body was full of fluid, the other half aches. He tried rolling over in bed, was denied by a terrible spike of pain from his shoulder. He glanced at it and saw an impressive amount of stitchwork in his flesh. A bruise spread from the wound all the way across his chest. Cut, that was right, he'd been cut down through the collarbone by that bastard at the castle gate.

"What happened to him?" he asked.

"Who?"

Matthew grunted. "Never mind. You're alive, and so am I, so it must have worked out fine."

"Lord Gandrem's said you should be treated as a hero."

"That so?"

Tristan bobbed his head up and down. Matthew chuckled.

"If this is how heroes feel, count me out. The plow fits me better than the sword." He frowned. Tristan kept looking to the door, and his smile never seemed to last long.

"Something the matter, Tristan? Well, guess I should call you by your real name, shouldn't I? Not much point in hiding who you are now."

The boy obviously looked embarrassed, as if he wasn't sure how to respond.

"You can call me Tristan still, if you want, sir."

"I guess I'll let the habit linger, least until I can get out of this damn bed. What is the matter? You look like you're expecting the executioner."

Something about the way Tristan's face paled made him wonder what he'd said wrong.

"It's nothing," Tristan said. "I just, it's…nothing. I'm glad you're awake. Really glad."

Matthew's head felt groggy and stuffed with cotton, but he pushed through to see his surroundings better and to make sense of them. He was in a small room with stone walls, a single red carpet, and a large bed with sheets stained with what must have been his blood. Tristan wore fine clothing, far beyond anything Matthew could have afforded at his farmhouse (before that Haern guy dumped a pile of gold in their hands, anyway). It didn't look like everyday attire, but then again he was hardly knowledgeable about the ways of courts and castles.

"They treating you well?" he asked.

"Yes," said Tristan.

"Something bothering you?"

He looked once more to the door.

"Is it…is it all right if we just talk for a while?"

Matthew smiled. "Sure, son. You care about what?"

When he shook his head, Matthew began discussing his plans for the farm. He prattled on about cattle, where he bought his pigs, and how if Nathaniel ever should get into the business in the north, to never ever buy from the Utters in the middle of winter unless he wanted to bend over and let them have their way with him. Tristan remained silent, but it seemed as if the tension drained out of him, until at last his eyes sparkled and he laughed at what few lame stories Matthew had to tell.

Every bit of that tension returned, though, when John Gandrem stepped into the room.

"Milord," Matthew said, tilting his head to show his respect. Getting up and bowing was obviously out of the question.

"I'm pleased to see you well," the lord said, though his voice hardly carried much pleasure. "You'll be rewarded handsomely for protecting young Nathaniel here. Once I found someone who recognized you, I sent a rider to inform your loved ones of your stay in my care."

"Thank you, milord," said Matthew. "My wife will much appreciate knowing."

"Rest, Matthew, and when you're better, we can discuss giving you and your family appropriate compensation. For now, I must borrow Nathaniel. We have matters to attend to."

"I'll talk to you tonight," Matthew told Nathaniel. "Right now, I feel like eating a little, and then sleeping for a while, so don't worry about me."

They left, and servants arrived immediately after, carrying bowls of soup, and bread, and changes of clothing. While they buzzed about, Matthew thought of Nathaniel, and offered a prayer for whatever trial seemed to await him.

Nathaniel followed after Lord Gandrem, feeling like an obedient dog. The thought was unfair, for he had been treated absurdly well. But already he heard the murmuring of the crowd as they climbed the stairs toward the front wall of the castle. The sunlight was glaring when they emerged, and the crowd of hundreds below cheered at their arrival. Four guards flanked them upon the ramparts. Directly ahead, atop a retractable plank of wood hanging over the wall and with a long rope tied about his neck, was the man named Oric.

Lord Gandrem waved his greetings to the crowd gathered to watch the execution.

"This man was a coward and a traitor," he cried out to them. "He dared lie to the lord of the lands, to mock the honor of Felwood! My allies he struck against. This fiend, this foul murderer, even sought to coat his blade with the blood of children. What fate does he deserve?"

Those gathered below howled for his hanging. Nathaniel heard their cries and shivered. Lord Gandrem turned to him and beckoned him forth. His feet feeling made of lead, he approached. Oric's face was covered with a black cloth, and his hands were tied behind him, but still he appeared dangerous.

"He's bound and gagged," John said, seeing his hesitation. "And even if he weren't, you should not show fear. The eyes of the people are upon you, and more than anything, they want certainty from those who rule their lives."

Nathaniel nodded.

"Yes, sir," he said.

The older man guided him to where a lever waited, connected to various gears and wheels that would drop the platform Oric stood upon. It was as tall as him, and when he put his hand upon it, he worried he might be too weak to move it.

"This way," said a nearby knight, gesturing the direction for him to push. Hurling his weight upon it, Nathaniel felt the lever budge, then lurch forward. The crowd gasped, and before he could look away, Lord Gandrem took hold of his shoulder and forced him to watch. Oric fell, the rope snapped taut, but as he swung, his feet still kicked. A sickening groan floated up to them, barely audible over the cheer of the crowd.

"Bastard's neck didn't break," said one of the knights, leaning forward so he could see him.

"Just following orders," said the man beside him. "John wanted to send a message."

The words flowed over him, but Nathaniel refused to give them any meaning. Instead he just watched as below him Oric kicked, gagged, and swung from the castle wall, John's hand holding him with a strength frightening for his age.

"Remember this always," John said to him. "This is the fate that should meet all who challenge you. If you deny them this, then you become as cowardly as they. Besides, listen to that roar, Nathaniel. Listen to them cheer. Our people want blood, crave it. Every dead man hanging is a man worse than them. They'll spit on his corpse when we cut him down, and they'll unite in a hatred of something they hardly even understand. We are their lords. We are their gods. Never deny them the spectacle they deserve. So long as your acts are just, they will follow."

Nathaniel swallowed.

"Is it just?" he asked.

"Doesn't matter, boy," Lord Gandrem said. "All that matters is you believe it is just. And do you believe it?"

Nathaniel opened his mouth to answer, opened his mouth to say he did, but instead he vomited, his stomach shifting from side to side within him, perfectly in time to the convulsing body of the dying Oric.

EPILOGUE

Haern found Deathmask and his Ash Guild back in their hiding hole, and they greeted him like a long-lost friend.

"Behold the legend," Deathmask said, but his laughter cut with dark humor.

"Gerand told me of the Spider Guild's acceptance," Haern said, not wishing to waste any time. "As for the Conningtons, a man named Potts has assumed control while his relatives bicker and position themselves. I wouldn't be surprised if it takes a year or two for them to settle things. For now, though, the old advisor's in charge, and he has agreed to the terms. Only two guilds have refused, but they're both currently leaderless."

"Already we move in on their territory," Veliana said. "The Spiders and Wolves join us in the feeding frenzy. Whoever finally takes control of the remaining guilds will readily agree, just to save themselves from certain annihilation."

"So this is it then," Haern said. He looked to Deathmask. "Gerand will arrange a set of terms to distribute payments to be divided equally among the five guilds. I imagine that much wealth will divide much better among you four than, say, the hundred or so of the other guilds."

"That thought had come to mind," Deathmask said, grinning. "It's going to be rough these next few days. Everyone will be testing limits, seeing what they can get away with, and if you are capable of holding things in line. I'd say you normally could pull it off, but right now you look like an animal after a carriage has rolled over it a few times."

"I'll be fine," Haern said. "And I'll be watching you as closely as any other guild. Don't forget that."

Deathmask laughed.

"We aren't allies, Watcher, and I never intended to be. Keep your eye upon me all you want. You won't find anything, and your blades will never touch my skin. Go worry about those who truly present a danger to this truce. We'll be here reaping the rewards. For now, I've accomplished everything I desired, albeit in a more...chaotic fashion than I imagined. My former colleagues assumed the chaos in Veldaren could never be ended, and never be made profitable to us. I dare say I've proven them wrong. Or I will have once the Trifect's gold starts being delivered my way, without me having to lift a finger."

"At least someone profited from all this," Haern muttered.

"Given your position, I doubt you'll be living as a pauper either," Veliana said. "Yet you whine like a mule."

"I don't want gold," Haern said. "I want peace. Let me have that, and the Ash Guild will have nothing to fear from me."

He left without giving them any more chances to mock or gloat about their own cleverness. With much of his business done until nightfall, Haern debated on where to go. In the end he went back to the closest thing he had to a home. On the Crimson he found a wagon sitting in front of the Eschatons' place, half-loaded with trivial things. That none of it had been stolen yet seemed a miracle to him, until he remembered the very truce he'd just set up. Well, that was a start. He went to knock on the door, but it flew open. A very tired and surprised Tarlak stood before him, a stack of books in hand.

"Oh, you," he said.

"I've come to..."

"Save it, Haern. I'm sure you did your absolute best, and I doubt Senke would have changed a thing. Well, other than him dying. He might have...look, the offer still stands. No speeches, no apologies, no nonsense requirements. I bought a tower on the outskirts of the King's Forest, and I plan on making it a far better home than this dung hole. I told you I thought we had potential to be something special, and I still mean it. You want to come, be useful and grab a box."

Haern stepped aside, and Tarlak set his things on the wagon. Glancing inside the building, Haern saw Brug packing up various smithy tools. Delysia helped him, the two joking with each other in hushed tones. He could see the redness in their eyes, but they were moving on the best they knew how. The priestess saw him, and despite the loss of a friend, Delysia smiled and beckoned him inside.

"Why not," Haern said as Tarlak came back to the door. He stepped inside, grabbed a box, and hoped that just perhaps the newly titled King's Watcher might finally have a home.

A NOTE FROM THE AUTHOR

I think, looking back at all these books so far, *A Dance of Blades* is currently my favorite. *Cloaks* was written by some strange, clearly deranged madman. This book? I opened my original Note from the Author with this line: "I think I'm getting the hang of this." And I think it is still very much appropriate. In preparing everything for re-release under Orbit's guiding hands, this was the one needing the least work. Not to say it didn't need work...Devi will slap me if I claim that. Plus it'd be a total lie. But this was the point I was writing toward even when I started *Cloaks*. This was the big moment.

But it also helped immensely that I got to bring in all these other characters I'd spent so much time with in my Half-Orc books. Haern without the Eschatons just wasn't the same. But Tarlak? God, he's so much fun to write. Mocking Brug never gets old. Even having Veliana finally meet up with Deathmask was immensely satisfying, building up everything that would come later. Bringing in new characters to interact with the old kept *Blades* in a perfect balance for yours truly, something I always strive to reach in any book I write.

Speaking of new characters, I should probably confess my absolute terror at writing the character Ghost. A quick glance at my author photo should probably explain why. I'm about as white as it gets, and living here in the dead center of the US heartland, what the heck do *I* know about walking in someone like Ghost's shoes? But I had to try. His concept, his character in my head, it was just too awesome, too striking, too memorable. Going back over *Blades*, I fell in love with him all over again. I'm glad I didn't wimp out, I'm glad I stuck to my guns. Did I succeed? Heck if I know. But I think I did.

Some of you might be wondering at Thren's diminished role in this book. That was very much on purpose. The final confrontation between Haern and Thren comes (much) later, which meant I couldn't keep him as a central villain, especially not in this book, where Haern needed to develop fully into his own character. So I found it better to have Thren lurking in the background, always referenced, always affecting decisions and outcomes even when he's not there. That one scene between him and Deathmask? Hardest one to write in the entire book.

Speak of hard scenes...yeah, Senke dying? I know it may sound odd for an author to have regrets. I mean, we're gods of our little universes. I could have Senke come riding back to life on a pink pony with rainbows shooting out his fingers. But it wouldn't work, and it wouldn't be right. And I wish I could have found a way to have Senke survive. He was fun, he was useful, and most important, he had a connection with Haern that even now I struggle to replicate with other characters. The closest I come, as you'll see in *A Dance of Mirrors*, is with Zusa. May seem odd now, but if you look at what both of them endured, the restricted upbringing, plus the sheer skill each of them wields and can appreciate in the other, it won't seem quite so strange.

They're such a cute couple, really.

Well, I've rambled enough, so probably time to wrap this up. Thanks again to Michael for the agent stuff, Devi for pushing each draft to be that much better than the previous, my wife for putting up with my lengthy phone calls and inability to talk about really anything else at the dinner table, and you fans who have been with me since the very beginning.

And you of course, dear reader. I'd be foolish, if not professionally suicidal, if I did not accept that it is your time, your patience, your entertainment that keeps me writing my silly little stories. I hope, as the years pass and I crank out more and more stories of Haern, Tarlak, and the rest of the world of Dezrel, that you never once get bored. Mad at me? That's all right. Sad at times? Perfect.

But never bored. I do that, and I'll call it good.

David Dalglish
April 9, 2013

extras

meet the author

Mike Scott Photography

DAVID DALGLISH currently lives in rural Missouri with his wife, Samantha, and daughters Morgan and Katherine. He graduated from Missouri Southern State University in 2006 with a degree in mathematics and currently spends his free time playing not near enough Warhammer 40K.

introducing

If you enjoyed
A DANCE OF BLADES,
look out for

A DANCE OF MIRRORS

Shadowdance Book 3

by David Dalglish

Haern pulled his hood low over his head and tied his sabers to his belt as the leader of the Eschaton mercenaries, the wizard Tarlak, sat at his desk and watched.

"Do you want our help?" Tarlak asked, picking a bit of dirt off his yellow robe.

"No," Haern said, shaking his head. "This one needs to be a message for the underworld of the city. Brann crossed a line that I need to make sure no one else ever crosses. I'll do this on my own."

Tarlak nodded, as if not surprised.

"What about Alyssa?"

Haern tightened the clasp of his cloak. They'd heard word that Alyssa planned some sort of retaliation against the thief guilds, though the reason was unclear. Their source was fairly respected in the Gemcroft household, so much so they had no choice but to take it seriously. At some unknown point in the night, there was to be a meeting at her mansion to discuss the circumstances.

"After," Haern said. "I'm sure you understand."

"I do," said Tarlak. "Good luck. And remember, I can't pay you if you die on me."

"I won't be the one dying tonight," Haern said, feeling the cold persona of the King's Watcher coming over him.

He left the room, descended the staircase to the tower's exit, and then ran the short distance toward the city. A dozen secret passageways, ropes, and handholds were available to him as a way to cross the wall, and he drifted to the southern end before climbing over. Alyssa's potential conflict with the thief guilds was a greater threat in the long run, but Haern could not bring himself to focus on it just yet. His target was a piece of scum named Brann Goodfinger. He operated in the far south of the city, and it was there Haern went.

Normally he felt pride as he traversed the rooftops, carefully observing the doings of the various guilds. Ever since the thief war ended two years ago, the factions had settled into an uncomfortable truce. The first few months had been the worst, but Haern's sabers had spilled torrents of blood. Through sheer brutality, he had brought both sides to their knees. He was the silent threat watching all, and tolerating nothing. But tonight his accomplishment felt bitter. For the first time, his plan had been turned against him in a most cruel, personal way.

Thieves who stole from the Trifect died. They all knew this, knew that every night Haern patrolled the city as the King's Watcher to ensure the agreed-upon peace. And so Brann had recruited children, a bold dare against the Watcher's threat.

"Where is it you hide?" Haern whispered as he lay flat atop a roof. For two days Brann had eluded him, and his children had gone unchecked. No longer. He spotted one of their youngest, a boy surely no older than seven. He was exiting the broken window of a shop, a handful of copper coins clutched to his chest. He ran, and Haern followed.

The boy tried to vary his pattern, as he'd no doubt been trained to do, but against someone like Haern the tactic was a minor inconvenience, nothing more. Haern kept far out of sight, not wanting to alert him to his presence. Twice he'd tracked Brann's child-thieves, but one had spotted him, abandoned his ill-gotten coin, and fled. The other had been killed by a different thief guild before he could question him. Children bled out on the streets of Veldaren. The Watcher's wrath would be terrible.

Haern turned a corner and watched the child hurry inside a warehouse. Approaching the door, Haern slipped into the shadows and looked through the crack near the hinges. A faint lantern burned inside, and from what he could make out, two other children were within. Hoping it was Brann's hideout, and not a simple gang of orphans, he drew his sabers. There would be no stealthy entrance. This wasn't a time for quiet deaths in the night.

He slammed the door open with his shoulder at full charge. Without slowing, he took in the surroundings, his finely honed instincts guiding him. The storehouse was full of crates and bags of grains, limiting his maneuverability. At least twenty children were gathered in a circle, and before them, his dirty face covered with a beard, was Brann. The man looked up. His jaw dropped, and then he turned to run.

"Stop him!" Brann shouted to the children.

Haern swore as they drew small knives and daggers. He leaped between them, twirling his cloak as a distraction. A sweeping kick took out three, and then he pushed through the opening. The storehouse was divided in two by a high wall, and Brann vanished through the doorway in the center. Haern raced after him, again slamming aside the door with his shoulder. To his surprise, Brann was not the coward he'd believed. His sword lashed out from behind the door. Haern's speed was too great, though, and he fled beyond Brann's reach, pivoted on his heels, and jumped again.

Brann was only a gutter snake, a clever bully who relied on size or surprise to defeat a foe. Haern had fought his kind, knew their tactics. With three strikes, Brann's sword fell from a bleeding wrist. Two kicks shattered a kneecap, and then he fell. Haern clutched his hair and yanked his head back, his saber pressing against Brann's throat.

"How dare you," Haern whispered. His hood hung low over his face, and he shook his head to knock it back. He wanted Brann to see the fury in his eyes.

"You hold this city prisoner yet ask me that?" said Brann.

Haern struck him in the mouth with the hilt of a saber. As Brann spit out a tooth, the children rushed through the door, surrounding them both.

"Stay back," Brann said to them, and he grinned at Haern, his yellow teeth stained red with blood. There was a wild look in his eyes that made Haern uncomfortable. This wasn't a man who cared about life—not his own, nor that of others.

"What game is this?" Haern asked, his voice a cold whisper. "Did you think I wouldn't find out? Using children, here, in my city?"

"Your city?" Brann said, laughing. "Damn fool. All the rest are scared, but I know what you are. They think you're as bad as us, but you're not... not yet. Once the thief guilds find out, they'll have your head on a spike."

He gestured to the children, all prepared to attack. Haern

didn't want to imagine what Brann had put them through to achieve such a level of control.

"Kill me," Brann said. "Do it, and they'll swarm you. You won't die—you're too good for them—but you won't escape without killing at least one. So what'll it be, Watcher? Can you take my life if it means taking the life of a child?"

Haern looked at the twenty children. Some were as young as seven, but others were maybe eleven or twelve. All it'd take was one lucky stab by any of them and he might go down.

His saber pressed harder against Brann's skin. He leaned closer to whisper into his ear.

"Nothing, Brann. You know nothing about me. You die, they go free."

"I die, then innocents will as well. You don't have the stomach for it. You aren't the beast the others think you are. Now let me go!"

Haern glanced at the children, all poised to act. He tried to decide what to do, but he knew what life someone like Brann would lead them to. No matter what, no matter the risk, he couldn't allow it.

"This was never a choice," Haern whispered.

He slashed, spilling blood across his clothes. Hoping to move before the children reacted, he turned and leaped, vaulting over their circle. They gave chase, not at all bothered by the death of their master. Haern rolled to his feet, his sabers crossed to block their weak stabs. A quick glance showed no exits except the door he'd come through. Doing everything he could to fight down his combat instincts, he shoved through the group's center. His cloak whirled and twisted, pushing aside feeble attacks.

Pulling out of the spin, he lunged for the door. One of the older boys was there, and Haern felt panic rise in his chest as he saw the deadly angle of the boy's thrust. He reacted on instinct, blocking hard enough to knock the dagger free, then following it up with a kick to send the boy flying. Breaking back into a run, he kicked off a pile of crates to vault into the air, catching a rafter with one hand. Swinging himself up onto a perch, he stared down at the children, several of whom gathered around the body of the one he'd kicked.

"Listen to me," Haern said to them, trying to forgive the children's attack. They didn't know any better. The rage he felt was misguided, born of frustration. "Your master is dead. You have no hope of winning this fight."

"Fuck you," said one of the kids.

Haern swallowed down his anger at such disrespect. They were frightened and living in a world Haern knew all too well. If reason would not work, he knew what would.

"Say that again, and I'll cut out your tongue."

The boy stepped back, as if stunned by the coldness in his voice. The rest looked up at him, some ready to cry, some angry, but most were heartbreakingly indifferent. Haern pointed to Brann Goodfinger's corpse.

"Take his coin," he said. "Go, and make better lives than this. Remain thieves, and you'll fall to the guilds, or to me. I don't want to kill you, but I will. There is no future for you, not in this."

"None for you, either," said another, but Haern could not tell who. With practiced efficiency the children took everything of value from Brann's corpse and vanished into the streets. Haern didn't know where they went, nor did he care. He only felt fury. Brann had died quickly, hardly the example Haern desired to set. As for the boy he'd kicked...

He dropped from the rafter, landing lightly on his feet. Gently he rolled him over, put a hand on his neck. No pulse.

"Damn you, Brann," Haern whispered. "I hope you burn forever."

Leaving the body there was not an option. Haern considered himself better than that. Lifting him onto his shoulder, he rushed out to the streets, praying no gutsy member of a thief guild spotted him and tried something incredibly heroic and stupid. There were several gravekeepers in Veldaren, plus another who burned bodies instead of burying them. Haern went to the burner, picked the lock of his door, and went inside. The owner was asleep on a cot in a small room, and Haern woke him with a firm prod of his saber.

"What? Who are... Oh, you."

The elderly man, Willard, rubbed his eyes, then opened them when Haern dropped a handful of coins onto his lap.

"Spare no expense, and bury his ashes."

"Who was he?" asked Willard, looking over the boy's body as Haern set him down on the floor.

"An accident."

"Then what shall I engrave on his urn?"

"Pick something," Haern said as he left.

In a foul mood, he raced off for the Gemcroft estate, wishing he could put the prior events out of his mind and knowing there'd be no such luck. Brann's death would still be a warning to the others against using children to break the arrangement between the guilds and the Trifect. He'd accomplished that, though not how he'd hoped. But it was that nameless boy who haunted him, made his insides sick. Brann had been convinced Haern would not have the stomach for what might happen. Turned out he might have been right.

Scaling the fence around the Gemcroft estate was easy enough, though avoiding the guards was another matter. There was a secondary building in the back, where he'd been told the meeting would take place. Most of the patrols kept close to the mansion, which helped tremendously. Haern lurked beside the gate, running along it when outside the patrols' vision and lying flat amid the shadows when they passed. At last he reached the small building. Timing the patrols, he knew he had about thirty seconds to slip in and out without being seen. Faint light burned within. He pressed his ear against the door and heard no discussion.

Too late, or too early? The door was unlocked, so he opened it and slipped inside. The room was surprisingly bare, containing only a single bed atop a padded floor. Hardly the servants' quarters he'd expected. The lone lantern kept the place dimly lit, with plenty of shadows in the far corners. So far, it appeared empty.

"Damn," he whispered.

He headed for the far corner, figuring to wait a few hours just in case the meeting was yet to transpire. In the center of the room, though, he stopped. Something in the corner wasn't right, the shadows not smooth . . .

Haern lunged for the door, his instincts screaming *trap*. Before he could get there, something latched on to his cloak and tugged, hard. He spun to the ground, torn between attacking and tearing his cloak free to flee. Already furious because of Brann, he kicked to his feet and attacked. To his surprise, his sabers clashed against long blades, his thrusts perfectly blocked. He was already preparing a second strike when he saw his opponent's outfit. Long dark wrappings covering her body—all but her shadowed face.

"Enough, Watcher," said Zusa, her slender body contorted into a bizarre defensive formation. "I am not here to kill you."

Haern pulled away, and he put his back to a wall, the door at his side.

"Then why are you here?" he asked.

"Because I desired it," said a voice at the door.

Haern turned, then dipped his head in a mock bow. "Lady Gemcroft," he said. "It is good to see you, Alyssa."

The ruler of the Gemcroft fortune smiled at him, not at all bothered by his tone. Zusa sheathed her daggers, though her hands remained on their hilts. She joined Alyssa's side, her dark eyes never leaving him. Alyssa seemed relaxed, far more so than when Haern had last seen her. Of course, he'd been trying to kill her at the time, back when Alyssa was flooding the streets with mercenaries. She wore a slender dress underneath her robe, her red hair let down loose about her shoulders. Haern almost felt flattered she'd dressed up for him, as if he were some noble or diplomat.

"I was told of a meeting concerning the thieves," Haern said. "Was there any truth to this?"

"I assure you, Terrance is loyal to me, and me alone," she said.

The side of Haern's face twitched. Terrance had been his informant, of course. He felt at a disadvantage, with no clue as to the reason for their meeting. He didn't like that. The two also blocked the only exit. He really didn't like that.

"Then I was told a lie, just to bring me here," he said. "Why is that, Alyssa?"

"Because I want to hire you."

Haern paused, then laughed at the absurd notion. "I am no pawn for you to force your will upon. And if what you say is true, why this secrecy and deception?"

"Because I don't want anyone—not the guilds nor the Trifect—to know. I leave for Angelport, and I wish for you to accompany me and Zusa."

Haern's hands fidgeted as they held his sabers. Answering

such a request with someone as dangerous as Zusa blocking his way out was not his idea of a fair bargaining position.

"What reason could you possibly have?" he asked. "I assure you, Zusa is quite capable of keeping you alive."

A bit of impatience finally pierced Alyssa's calm demeanor.

"Someone broke into Laurie Keenan's home, slaughtered his son and daughter-in-law, along with a dozen guards. I'm going for their funeral services, as is appropriate. I want you and Zusa to hunt down this killer and bring him to justice while I'm there."

Haern shook his head. "I can't leave Veldaren," he said. "The peace I've managed to create—"

"Is no peace at all," Alyssa said. "The thief guilds prey on each other, killing themselves in an endless squabble over the gold we pay them. The few that steal are more often caught by their own kind, not you. No one will know you've left, not for weeks. It's been two years, and you've spilled enough blood to wash the city red. Those who remain have settled into their comfortable lives of bribes and easy money, and you know it. You've become a figurehead, a watcher against only the most reckless of the underworld. The city's changed. It won't miss you while you're gone."

Haern did know that, but that didn't mean he liked it.

"This is your problem," he said. "I've had enough dealings with the Trifect to last a lifetime. Find your killer on your own. Now let me through."

Alyssa glanced at Zusa, then nodded. They stepped aside. As Haern walked out into the night, Alyssa called after him.

"They found a marking," she said. "Drawn in their blood."

Haern stopped. "What of?" he asked.

"A single eye."

Haern turned, and he felt his anger rise. "You would accuse me of this crime?"

"No accusation," Alyssa said, stepping out. "I have already looked into the matter and know you were in Veldaren both the night it happened, plus the nights before and after. Laurie's kept word of it a secret and told only those closest to him of its presence at the murder. He knows you didn't perform the deed, though he still fears your involvement somehow…"

Grinding his teeth, Haern tried to think through what any of it meant, but it left him baffled.

"This makes no sense, Alyssa," he said. "Why would someone frame me so far away? I've never been to Angelport, nor used that symbol for years. Not since the war between the Trifect and the thief guilds ended."

"It's not a frame," Zusa said, as if it were so simple. "It is a calling. You're being summoned, Watcher."

Haern tried to think it over, but he felt so tired, so unprepared. The boy's dead face kept flashing before his eyes.

"How do I know this isn't a trap?" he finally asked.

Alyssa looked away, as if embarrassed by what she had to say. "Because of you, my son lives," she said. "And because of you, I was able to bring vengeance to the one who tried to kill him. I will never betray you. Someone murdered powerful citizens of Angelport, my friends and colleagues, and is using their blood to send you a message. Help me find him. Help me stop him."

Haern sighed. "So be it," he said. "When do we leave?"